Jane, Actually
or Jane Austen's Book Tour

Jennifer Petkus

Mallard Sci-Fi
Denver, Colorado

Jane, Actually
or Jane Austen's Book Tour

Published by Mallard Sci-Fi,
an imprint of Mallard Press, Denver, Colorado
ISBN-13: 978-0615796710
ISBN-10: 0615796710

visit www.janeactually.com

"It seems a great pity that they allowed her to die a natural death"

Mark Twain

Jane lies in Winchester—blessed be her shade!
Praise the Lord for making her, and her for all she made!
And while the stones of Winchester, or Milsom Street, remain,
Glory, love, and honour unto England's Jane!

From Rudyard Kipling's "The Janeite"

Thanks

I would like to thank my advance readers and proofreaders, especially my sensei, Susan Chandler; fellow JASNA member Maryann O'Brien; my husband James Bates; UK Janeite Christopher Sandrawich; and fellow Sherlockian Michael J. Newman. Their kind assistance is not meant to be endorsements of this story. Any mistakes are my fault.

Apologies

The real-life characters mentioned in this book have no association with or knowledge of this book. Garrison Keillor didn't write an introduction to *Pride and Prejudice*; Brian Cox and Stephen Fry have never been on a radio program with Jane Austen; Amanda Vickery has never interviewed her; Jane has never been on the Graham Norton Show; and Colin Firth and Jane have never met. The Austen scholars/authors Joan Klingel Ray, Deirdre Le Faye, Elisabeth Lenckos, Janet Todd, Paula Byrne and Jon Spence mentioned in this book have my deepest respect but I cannot claim their imprimatur. This book also draws on the work of Claire Harman (*Jane's Fame*) and Claire Tomalin (*Jane Austen: A Life*). I must also credit Vic Sanborn, Laurel Ann Nattress and Julie Wakefield, authors of the influential blogs *Jane Austen's World*, *AustenProse* and *AustenOnly*. None of these persons should be blamed for this book.

For reasons understandable only to myself, I decided to employ a trans-Atlantic narrator, but who generally follows UK spelling and grammar.

As to Jane's voice, please realize I've imagined a Jane Austen who's been observing the world for two centuries, who's been online for a decade and who now has a close friend, almost a sister, in her mid twenties. She's read and enjoyed Hemingway, Dickens, Chandler and Christie. She may not be the Jane you were expecting.

Chronology

I borrow from a device employed by Stella Gibbons, author of *Cold Comfort Farm*, who prefaced her book: "The action of the story takes place in the near future." The world of the AfterNet takes place in the recent past, but a past that diverged from our reality in 1997. I choose to parallel and depart from our timeline at my pleasure. This story takes place in 2011.

The Real Jane Austen

J ane Austen died in 1817.* In her forty-one years alive, she published four novels, *Sense and Sensibility, Pride and Prejudice, Mansfield Park* and *Emma,* and two were published posthumously, *Persuasion* and *Northanger Abbey.* She left *Sanditon* unfinished, and it promised to be quite different from her previous works, which have been described and criticized as both romantic, dull, witty, plotless, brilliant, complex, insightful, second only to Shakespeare and boring.

To millions of Janeites, however, the best way to describe her novels is only—only six novels, plus two unfinished novels, and her Juvenilia (early works).

Her novels are third person, chiefly from the viewpoint of the heroine; they always end happily with a marriage; they're devoid of explicit sex but filled with rakes, cads and bounders; and the plots are simply driven by two people clearly meant for one another who still manage to deny their love for an entire book. The reader is rewarded, usually

---

* Jane lived during the reign of King George III and his son, George IV. The Regency period, during which Jane's novels were published, began in 1811, when George III was incapacitated (just watch the movie *The Madness of King George*) and his son became Regent, and ended in 1820 with the death of George III, whence his son was crowned king.

after considerably more than 100,000 words, with a single kiss (but only in the movie versions) and a wedding.

Jane was born to George and Cassandra Austen. Her father was a rector (Church of England priest) of the parish of Steventon in Hampshire, a southern English county. Jane had six brothers (James, George, Edward, Henry, Francis and Charles) and a sister, who was also named Cassandra.

Jane never married, although shortly before her twenty-seventh birthday, she famously agreed to Harris Bigg-Wither's proposal and returned it the next day. The only sure romance in her life was with Tom Lefroy, who at the time was studying law under the sponsorship of a great uncle. The romance fell apart and Jane shows no great sorrow in her letter to her sister: "At length the day is come on which I am to flirt my last with Tom Lefroy, and when you receive this it will be over. My tears flow as I write at the melancholy idea."

Most detect a sarcastic tone, although perhaps her arch words disguise a true disappointment. Lefroy never proposed; it would have been an unsuitable match for him and had they married, who can say whether Jane would have pursued her career.

That career began early, encouraged by her father, his library and her perusal of it. She began early versions of *Sense and Sensibility*, *Pride and Prejudice* and *Northanger Abbey* while the family lived in Steventon, but in 1801 her father decided to retire and the Reverend Austen and his wife and two daughters moved to Bath in Somerset. The hot mineral baths of the resort town attracted the fashionable and the infirm and the city was also a marketplace where parents could hope to find their children suitable marriage partners.

For Jane, however, the move was a wrench from the home and the country she loved and to a city that she grew to dislike. With his death, Mrs Austen and her two daughters were in dire financial difficulties. Jane's sister had income from the bequest of a fiancé who died before they could marry, and Mrs Austen had income from her family, but Jane had little to call her own. Fortunately her brothers contributed to the upkeep of the Austen women, but they remained largely homeless after George Austen's death, constantly visiting friends and relatives, including the homes of Edward Austen Knight. It was this same Edward, the third child of George and Cassandra, who offered Chawton Cottage as a home to the Austen women in 1809.

If you're wondering about Edward's last name, it came about after he was adopted by wealthy relatives who saw in him the child they never had. Austen's novels also had several examples of children raised *in absentia* by wealthy relatives (or relatively wealthier friends in the case of Jane Fairfax in *Emma*). Whatever grief or disruption or relief this caused Jane's parents, Edward's adoption provided an important safety net. Even before the death of Jane's father, they often visited Godmersham Park, the home of the Knight family, and later Chawton House, Edward's estate very near the cottage.

The offer of Chawton Cottage meant a return to Hampshire for the Austen women and for Jane it meant a return to writing. She revised *Sense and Sensibility* and *Pride and Prejudice* and gave them their final titles. With the financial help of her brother Henry, *S&S* was published in 1811. *P&P* followed in 1813.

In her lifetime, all her novels were published anonymously, first attributed to "By a Lady" and later as the author of the previous books. It wasn't until *Persuasion* and *Northanger Abbey* that her identity was acknowledged.

The choice of keeping her identity secret was largely her own. She did see some financial success and critical acclaim in her lifetime, but her works lapsed out of print after her death, until they were revived in 1832. Since then, they have never been out of print and her fame has risen steadily. The Jane Austen Society of the United Kingdom, started in 1947, and the Jane Austen Society of North America in 1987, have contributed to her fame. Her novels have been made into movies, television serials and even computer games. Many authors have written continuations of her stories and have recast her characters as vampires, zombie slayers and detectives.

The afterlife explained

I n 1997, a researcher inadvertently confirmed the existence of the afterlife. Her research and her invention confirmed both the existence of souls and the terrible knowledge that each soul remains alone after death, unable to communicate with the other dead and with the living.

Then in 2001, the technology she invented gave rise to the AfterNet, a worldwide network that allowed the dead—or disembodied as most preferred to be called—to interact with the living via the Internet. The device or terminal she had invented projects an electromagnetic field that the disembodied can recognize and manipulate.

Unfortunately there is no easy way for a disembodied person to prove who they were in life. The energy of a disembodied person is unique, however, and could be used for later identification, but gave no clue if that person was male or female, of what race or ethnicity or when they had died. People could record their individual energy signatures before they died (for later identification), but that didn't help those who'd died before the discovery of the afterlife.

One could petition the AfterNet to verify one's identity, but obviously the more famous a person one claimed to be, the harder it was to prove. And consequently the more famous an identity, the more claimants there were to it.

The majority of the disembodied, however, were just happy to be able to communicate again. Sadly, an eternal existence trapped with no ability to interact with the world had left many disembodied psychologically damaged.

⁓

Even if a disembodied person has not succumbed to despair, the reality of the afterlife is still daunting:

The disembodied cannot be seen and cannot hear, although the dead can see the entire electromagnetic spectrum. They also have a 360-degree field of view. The disembodied cannot smell, touch or taste. They do not sleep.

The disembodied are so insubstantial they cannot affect the physical world, but their energy can be contained. They can't walk through walls, open doors or clank chains. They are easily trapped in rooms until someone opens the door. The living are constantly colliding with them. To the living, the collision is unnoticeable; to the disembodied, it is very annoying.

The disembodied vastly outnumber the living, but still have little economic and political power because of the difficulty in laying claim to their legacy, unless they made provisions before death. Thus many disembodied still work after death, to help provide for family members left behind or to pay for those amusements that help make eternity bearable. After all, reading books and watching movies and television (with subtitles) require the wherewithal to pay Amazon and Netflix.

The disembodied are unaware of each other and can only communicate via an AfterNet terminal and the Internet. The AfterNet is a multinational, non-profit organization that provides free public terminals and maintains the AfterNet portal, which offers free email to the disembodied.

The AfterNet also maintains the free terminals that most disembodied use to communicate. These nondescript black boxes can be found in shopping centres, libraries and post offices.

Using a terminal is not easy; a disembodied person has to form his or her thoughts clearly enough for the terminal to translate those thoughts into text or speech for the living to understand.

A living person who wishes to speak directly to the disembodied cans simply use the Internet, or use a portable terminal, a device similar in size and appearance to a smart phone. One speaks aloud and the terminal translates the words and projects them into the AfterNet field for the disembodied to read. The thoughts of the disembodied are similarly turned into speech for the living to hear, usually through an earbud.

A person who can project his or her thoughts directly into an AfterNet field—a difficult task for the living—could find employment as an avatar, representing a disembodied person who had managed to claim their identity and their legacy.

Dramatis personae
Principals

Jane Austen, disembodied Regency novelist
Mary Crawford, Jane's avatar
Melody Kramer, Jane's agent: Her life partner is Tamara Johnson
Albert Ridings, Jane's friend, who died in the Great War. His wife was **Catherine**
Dr Alice Davis, Austen scholar at the University of Chicago.
Stephen Abrams, Dr. Davis' graduate student
Courtney Blake, freelance journalist/writer, author of *The Real Jane Austen*

Supporting

Alan Pembroke, Random House editor
Ajala Johnsson, JASNA President
Cindy Wallace, JASNA North Texas Regional Coordinator. Her fellow coordinators are BethAnn and Megan.
Mrs Westerby, the inheritor of several Austen documents

Fictional

Many characters from Jane Austen's novels are mentioned in this book, including:

Elizabeth Bennet and **Fitzwilliam Darcy**, from *Pride and Prejudice*

Fanny Price and **Edmund Bertram** from *Mansfield Park* (also, of course, Henry and Mary Crawford)

Emma Woodhouse and **George Knightley** from *Emma*

Catherine Morland and **Henry Tilney** from *Northanger Abbey*

Anne Elliot and **Frederick Wentworth** from *Persuasion*

Elinor and **Marianne Dashwood** and **Edward Ferrars** from *Sense and Sensibility*

And from *Sanditon*, **Charlotte Heywood** and **Sidney Parker**

Table of Contents

Table of Contents

VOLUME III

VOLUME I

Titbits

DENVER (AFN)—Today the AfterNet announced another celebrity whose identity has been verified, but this time it's no actor, politician or sports figure reclaiming their name. Instead it's the grande dame of English letters, Jane Austen.

The author of "Pride and Prejudice," "Emma" and "Sense and Sensibility" is the third oldest person—based on the date of their death date and not their age—to be recognized by the AfterNet. Austen died in 1817 at age 41 in Winchester, England, and was the author of six published novels, two of which were published after her death. She was writing a seventh novel, "Sanditon," at the time of her death.

Her novels have been made into films numerous times, with "Pride and Prejudice" being most frequently adapted, most fa-mously in a 1995 BBC miniseries starring Colin Firth and Jennifer Ehle as Fitzwilliam Darcy and Elizabeth Bennet, and again in a 2006 film starring Natalie Portman as Elizabeth and Rupert Penry-Jones as Darcy.

Austen is quoted as saying, as related through her agent Melody Kramer, "I am delighted to reclaim my name and thankful to the AfterNet committee that researched my claim and decided I spoke the truth. I confess to being overwhelmed by the many congratulations I have already received. I know, of course, of the popularity of my novels and the many ways they have been interpreted, from musicals to movies and even interactive games. I hope that I can contribute again to the world I created but that many others have kept alive."

Austen's agent predicted there

SEE AUSTEN on 13A

RANDOM HOUSE

Sanditon: Two Hundred Years in the Making

FOR IMMEDIATE RELEASE
ARC Inquiries contact: Jeremy Rohrbach

Fans of Jane Austen, the author of PRIDE AND PREJUDICE,
SENSE AND SENSIBILITY and EMMA, will rejoice to learn that
SANDITON, her first new novel in nearly two hundred years,
will be released this September.

Of course, SANDITON was also Austen's last novel,
uncompleted at the time of her death in 1817, but now we
know Austen did complete it. Thanks to the discovery of
the afterlife, the birth of the AfterNet and the recent
certification of her identity, the completed SANDITON will be
available in hard cover, as an audio book and as an e-book
for the Amazon Kindle, the Barnes and Noble Nook and many
other platforms such as Apple's iOS and Android devices.

SANDITON follows the efforts of Mr. Parker and Lady Denham
to reinvent their sleepy seaside town into a resort that
will attract the young, the old, the fashionable, the
desperate and the infirm — or in other words the perfect
cast of an Austen novel.

Finally Janeites (a name suggested by a Rudyard Kipling
story) and other more casual fans will learn if romance
is awaiting Miss Charlotte Heywood, Austen's astute,
young observer of the comings and goings in SANDITON. All
the characters from the original fragment are here: the
handsome Mr. Sidney Parker; the West Indian heiress so
desired by Lady Denham; Mrs. Griffith's boarding school; the
hypochondriacal Parker sisters and their equally afflicted
brother; the impoverished Sir Edward Denham; and Lady
Denham's poor relation, the beautiful Miss Clara Brereton,
the target of Sir Edward's advances.

And the arrival of SANDITON in September couldn't be
better timed as Janeites celebrate the 200th anniversary of
Austen's first published book, Sense and Sensibility, making
it likely Austen will be the first author to have two best

-- MORE --

ᐅ New York City ᐊ
An offer from her publisher

A woman writer, especially one long dead, should think seriously before turning down any offer from a publisher, even if it be for completing a book that one had long ago abandoned. After all, the passage of time, circumstances and not least the loss of one's body, affords a new perspective.

These thoughts compelled Jane to look again at her agent's email conveying the offer from her publisher regarding *The Watsons*. They appeared quite interested that she complete her fragment of not quite 18,000 words, but in all honesty she had given it little thought over the years. She had re-read it since the advent of the AfterNet, of course, and she knew the general opinion of it, that she had abandoned it because it was "too close to home."

She pondered the phrase. It was true that the death of her father and the decline of her family's fortunes uncomfortably paralleled the plot, but her memory was that the book simply wasn't going where she wanted. With herself, her mother and sister moving so frequently, the book simply was passed over, especially after she returned her attention to *Elinor and Marianne*.[1]

Of course, there were still parts of *The Watsons* to recommend. Most readers seemed to enjoy Emma's dance with—*oh, what was the little*

---

1 The original title of *Sense and Sensibility,* Austen's first published novel

boy's name? Jane was forced to Google her own book and found the answer—*Charles Blake!*—at the *Republic of Pemberley*.

She was a little embarrassed at not being able to recall his name. *No one will credit me if I can't remember the names of my characters.*

Jane was also leery of finishing the book because others had already attempted it, including her niece Catherine, taking rather more liberties than she ought.

I should say no, but if a year from now I am still unable to think of some new project, perhaps I might be desperate enough to attempt it.

She sighed, inaudibly of course, which was never really as satisfying. The cold fear that she still might be unable to write a year from now was too awful to comprehend.

Best to leave some options open, she thought, and composed a reply to her agent:

Dear Melody,
I thank you for conveying this offer from our publisher, but after careful consideration

She stopped and looked at what she'd written, deleted it and instead wrote:

Melody,
Thanks for the heads up about the offer, but I don't think I want to revisit The Watsons right now. I keep saying I should write something that's relevant today. However, I don't want to say no, as I am sure you'd advise. Could you say that Sanditon has all my attention for the moment?
Jane

She hit send and hoped Melody would not be jarred by the tone of her reply, but now was as good a time as any to leave the Regency behind. Having spent nearly a decade online, her casual "speech" had evolved, but into what she could not say. Even before the AfterNet made it easy for her to read, she had absorbed what she could of the current idiom by looking over the shoulders of people reading books, magazines and newspapers. Not until the discovery of the afterlife, however, was it possible for her to employ any of what she had learned. And thus it was that her speech was a mixture of the here and now and the past and forgotten.

When she was appearing before the identity committee, she decided, and had been advised, not to retreat to the speech patterns of her corporeal existence—"It will just sound too precious," Melody told her—but to adopt a more modern tone.

She had to avoid sounding too modern, however. Those anticipating conversation with Jane Austen would be confused if she employed the phrase "friends with benefits" or remarked on a "cringeworthy" performance on *Strictly Come Dancing*. So she must adopt a style that allowed her to speak with her natural—well, she must own up to it and call it sarcasm—but neither sound too modern nor too quaint. But with her very few close friends, such as Melody, she might relax her caution, although Jane already regretted the "heads up."

For the moment, however, she did not regret rejecting the proposal. *I must write something new, damn it! I don't want to be the grande dame of English letters forever.*

She looked around guiltily, both embarrassed and amused by her outburst, but of course no one in the Starbucks at 63rd and Broadway in Manhattan had heard her. After all, she had no body, no voice, no physical presence. She was just one of the—she looked at the counter on the AfterNet terminal—14 disembodied people online in the store. None of them knew the novelist Jane Austen shared the terminal with them and naturally none of the living customers were aware of her presence.

Nevertheless, she decided to leave, having spent the better part of two hours surfing the net. She also hoped to avoid Melody's displeasure, but her agent knew her too well, having replied immediately.

From: MelodyKramer@JanetApplebaumLiterary.com
To: JaneAusten3@theAfterNet.net
Date: Jan. 6, 2011 09:31:11
Subject: RE: The Watsons
"Heads up?" Really? At least consider the offer. Now is not the time to rest on your laurels just because you're the hot dead author of the month. After all, what if Hemingway proves his identity? Or a Bronte? Admittedly you're one of the bigger fish out there, but still, what happens when God forbid Mark Twain pops up?

She laughed at Melody's favourite bogeyman. She invoked Twain whenever she wanted to goad Jane into action. She could picture Melody shaping her hands into bear claws, her shorthand for Twain coming back from the grave to continue his character assassination of her.

As amusing as the image was, Jane had to take Melody's advice seriously. The small, plump woman was undoubtedly her best friend and her champion. She had helped organize the search of Chawton House that had resulted in the proof of her identity. Jane knew she owed Melody far more than the 15 per cent an author owes an agent.

So it was that Jane composed another email:

Very well, Melody, you may amend our reply to say that I shall consider it, if you think that a better response. You do have my best interests in mind, as you constantly remind me.
Speaking of reminders, when do we meet with Mr Pembroke again? I had thought him determined to arrange our next meeting for today or tomorrow. Or have they decided not to publish Sanditon after all?
Jane

Her last sentence was a bit cruel and would worry Melody unnecessarily, but Jane decided that it would at the very least occupy her for a time. She hit send and quickly logged out, determined to leave before seeing another reply. She waited until she saw a customer leaving the store and then darted out behind.

She remained on the sidewalk, undecided what to do. She was at 63rd and Broadway through a concatenation of events involving a subway car she could not exit in time and then being distracted by the sight of a naked beggar, which consequently caused her to be struck by a lorry. That experience naturally confused her and then she entered a bus going north instead of south. Once she escaped the bus, she entered the Starbucks to compose herself, look at a map and, of course, surf the web.

Before receiving the email from her agent she had already determined that she should visit Central Park, the southern end of that vast, urban green space being only a short distance away. Standing outside the Starbucks, she decided to pursue that goal, thinking that a stroll in the park might restore her equanimity.

She crossed Broadway, this time giving close attention to the traffic, and proceeded along 63rd toward Central Park West. The human traffic on the sidewalk was also heavy at 10 o'clock on a Monday morning. She found herself dodging hurried New Yorkers intent on their business, talking on their phones and paying little attention to their fellow man. She did, however, see several young men loitering outside a store, paying close attention to their fellow women.

She paused to pay particular attention to a young woman, who despite the cold January weather wore only a cropped jeans jacket—she might almost call it a Spencer[2] with its frog buttons—over a thin form-fitting knit top and low-slung jeans. As the young woman approached, the men offered their compliments. At least Jane assumed the young men were saying something complimentary; as she had lost her hearing upon her death, she had to presume upon her knowledge of the behaviour of young men in the 21st century. Unfortunately, despite her facility at reading lips, she could not discern their words, owing perhaps to the men being non-English speakers. The young woman tried to give the appearance of ignoring their comments, but the slight smile on her face betrayed her ready understanding.

O tempora, o mores, Jane thought. *Or perhaps more aptly and less pretentiously, the more things change, the more they stay the same.* Women displaying their bodies was nothing new to her. Even in the Regency, some women revealed far more than was modest, ostensibly concealed under a veil of muslin[3] that, in fact, concealed little. And the compliments the men were uttering would undoubtedly have been familiar to the men of her time, although she hoped not to men of her acquaintance.

She continued on her journey and not for the first time she tried to imagine what her behaviour and appearance would be were she young and alive today—today, of course, being a constantly moving target. She would have hated the strictures of the Victorian age—*what purpose does a bustle serve?*—and would have delighted in the 1920s. But when she thought how she might have dressed during the 1960s ... well, her first wish was to giggle and share the thought with her sister, which triggered the usual ache of no longer being able to share with Cassandra.

That ache brought her to a halt and she became aware that she had entered the park and was already strolling on one of the paths.

---

2 A short jacket with long sleeves, probably modelled after the military dress of the second Earl Spencer. Some fashions cut it ridiculously short.

3 A loosely woven cotton fabric that was very popular for women's dresses during Austen's lifetime. Some *risqué* women would wet their muslin dresses.

I really must limit my daydreaming, she told herself. *I must exist in the now or I shall forever be trapped dreaming of the past.*

She well knew the danger of losing herself, as she had the first few years of her afterlife. She tried to put nostalgia about Cassandra from her mind, but to no avail. She often worried whether her sister could endure the loneliness of the afterlife.

If she has lost herself, perhaps the news of my identity or the publication of Sanditon will help her find her way back to sanity, but it does me no good to morbidly dwell on the past.

She thought this as she watched a nanny pushing a pram, followed by a middle-aged man with paunch, receding hairline and sweat-stained running gear, who barely managed to pass the young woman. He managed a smile at the attractive nanny nevertheless, who brilliantly returned his smile, which occasioned him to stumble. He only barely recovered his equilibrium and increased his speed to put some distance between himself and his embarrassment.

Especially as the here and now continues to prove worthy of amusement.

She continued on her path and reflected upon her last visit to Central Park shortly after the end of the Second World War. It was her only other trip to America, when she took advantage of the many military aircraft crossing the Atlantic. She recalled that where she now walked were planted numerous Victory Gardens: plots of lettuce and tomatoes and spinach in place of the beds of roses she saw today. It was a world away and a time away, when the jubilation of a world free from war swept through the city.

So much for my decision to think of the here and now. She thought perhaps she should address the idea of completing *The Watsons*—it was at least a pressing concern—and how she might make it differ from Catherine's version, although *The Younger Sister* had not stood the test of time and was largely forgotten save for Austen scholars.

I could, however, follow Catherine's lead and not feel beholden to my original text, as I was with Sanditon. There's no reason I couldn't add to the opening or even rewrite it. I really should re-read it.

That thought made her desirous of finding an AfterNet terminal and perhaps an e-book copy by which she might refresh her memory. And she could check her email again to see if they were meeting with their publisher today. She pondered for a moment, trying to recall the map she had earlier studied and decided as she was already travelling north, she might find a terminal, comfortable chairs and pleasant surroundings at the New York Historical Society Library and it was to this location she propelled herself, in no particular hurry.[4]

---

4   The disembodied do not walk. Like PG Wodehouse's Jeeves, they shimmer from place to place. In a *Washington Post* story, comedian Stephen Fry, who played Jeeves opposite Hugh Laurie's Bertie Wooster, said of Wooster's valet: "... his feet don't touch the floor, he shimmers into rooms, he oozes out of rooms. He seems to flicker and then he isn't there. He coughs and it's like a sheep clearing its throat of a blade of grass on a distant hillside or something."

    To move, the disembodied imagine where they want to be, and will themselves there. They are as affected by gravity as the living, and would fall to the ground unless they will themselves to maintain the same vantage point as a living person.

· 15 Per cent ·
"I am Jane Austen's Agent"

Melody tapped her front teeth with a pen, a habit that gave her girlfriend fits. "How can you do that? Doesn't it hurt? Stop it!" Tamara would say. Which, of course, forced Melody to tap her teeth even harder.

It was a nervous habit that Tamara, for all her cleverness, would never understand. Melody would resort to the habit whenever she had a difficult or unpleasant task at hand or when she felt out of her depth, as now. It was a way to distract her from a larger problem by giving her a more immediate unpleasantness.

I'm Jane Austen's agent! she thought, not for the first, second or third time that day. It was her last thought before going to sleep and her first thought upon waking. While she brushed her teeth or made the coffee the thought uppermost in her mind was, *I am Jane Austen's agent!*

Especially now while on hold with Random House, the thought sent a steady drumbeat in her head, a drumbeat echoed in the tapping of the pen against her upper incisors.

She thought of the first time she had read Jane Austen, in high school. She still dreamed of her Darcy then, even though she was fast coming to the conclusion that it was not a man she desired as a lover. But Darcy represented someone bigger than just a man. He represented that ideal mate who knew your thoughts, who knew what you were thinking because he took the time to understand—*even if he had that stick up his butt upon his first meeting with Elizabeth Bennett.*

"I'm very sorry to keep you, Ms Kramer," Mr Pembroke's assistant at Random House said. She started from surprise, the pen dropping to the desk and then to the floor.

"That's all right … Jeremy," she said, hoping his name was, in fact, Jeremy.

"Alan's just making sure all the paperwork's ready for you and Miss Austen. It is Miss Austen, isn't it? She doesn't use Ms Austen?"

Melody smiled as she bent down to retrieve the pen from the floor and then straightened. Her headphones kept her connected to the phone and she hoped she didn't make too much of a groan while she was bending. *I really need to exercise more.*

"No, it's Miss Austen, most assuredly." *Most assuredly, where did that come from?*

"Good, will 3:30 work?"

"Um …" How embarrassing it was to admit she'd lost track of her client, but Jane had insisted on her walkabout. Melody put the pen back in the desk drawer while she thought how to answer Jeremy's question.

"We can of course schedule it whenever convenient, but …"

Melody knew that though Jane might play at avoiding her, she was a slave to her email and would not long be out of touch.

"I think our schedule will allow for a meeting at 3:30. Let me just confirm with Jane."

"Good, I hope to hear back from you shortly then."

She said her goodbye to Jeremy and then sat back in her chair, amazed at how composed she thought she sounded. *Our schedule will allow.* There was nothing on her schedule more important today than to secure her client one of the biggest publishing deals in history.

OK, something of an exaggeration, but still pretty historic.

She opened a new email, quickly typed the information about the meeting and sent the message to Jane. With any luck, she was still in that Starbucks by the park.

Fifteen minutes of waiting for a reply did not produce one, however. Jane was either ignoring her emails or had left the coffee shop.

I don't think she would intentionally ignore me, not when we're just about to sign the deal.

But she knew her client had a prickly nature. Most of the analyses of the author over the years had identified her as a brilliant mind with a brilliant and oft times caustic wit, and she could be very kind and very unforgiving. Her association with her client had taught her the assessment was largely correct, although brilliant wit came nowhere near sufficient praise.

But Melody recalled the advice her mentor, and the woman whose agency she had inherited, gave her.

"Authors are barely human, Melody. Remember that and never trust them. They'll stab you in the back or abandon you when you least expect it. Show them no mercy."

Which she knew was sage advice she could safely ignore. She still maintained many of the clients that Janet Applebaum had suffered through thick and mostly thin, including the brilliant but reclusive writer who only wrote during leap years, and the one who continued to write ghost stories. Ghost stories were marketable when he first came to be represented by the Janet Applebaum Agency, but understandably out of fashion after the discovery of the afterlife.

She had yet another of his proposals on her desk where he argued that the time was right for people to read ghost stories again. *Maybe he's right in a nostalgia market sort of way,* she thought.

She was already deep into the first chapter he had included when her email pinged to let her know she had new mail.

Jane was spending the day at the New York Historical Society Library at 76th and Central Park West, she learned, and could easily meet her at Random House at 3:30. Melody thanked her profusely and quickly put in a call to Jeremy to confirm.

After she hung up, she thought again, *I am Jane Austen's agent!* She pulled the pen out of her desk and began tapping her teeth again, even faster this time.

~

Melody stood outside the Random House building, nervously looking at her watch although it was only 3:05. She also checked the portable terminal she wore on her right arm and saw yet again, "No user connected." It was set to only recognize Jane and ignore the many hundreds or thousands of disembodied roaming the streets of Manhattan at that spot.

She walked back and forth in front of the building, stupidly worried that Jane could not see her in her bright yellow, Dick Tracy trench coat.

"Hello, Melody," Jane said. Melody spun around as she often did after hearing Jane's digitized voice in her earbud, and as always was not rewarded by seeing anyone resembling a dead Regency author.

"Hi, Jane. You're early."

"I suspected you might be nervous and would wish to confer before the meeting."

"Nervous, why should I be nervous?" she tried to laugh lightly but she knew she failed. Luckily she knew the terminal couldn't translate laughter, light or otherwise.

Jane watched her agent laugh and saw the terminal translate the sound as unintelligible. She could see Melody was very, very nervous. She wished she could lessen Melody's concerns, but she also knew Melody performed best when nervous.

"Should we go inside?" Jane asked.

"Yes, that's a good idea. We can sit and talk."

Melody led the way and held the door open for Jane to enter. They found round couches in the lobby and after being told where Jane sat, Melody tried to hold an eye-to-eye conversation with her client. But as usual, Melody's eyes flitted from spot to spot, trying to find something on which to focus.

"I just want you to know there's no big deal about this meeting. The lawyers have been over everything; I got you a … you have a very large advance, future book deals wrapped up. It's all … good. And I told them you were in no hurry to return to writing, and they said they're prepared to wait until you're ready."

Melody was a little frustrated that she couldn't throw in a few more colourful words to emphasize how brilliant a deal she had extracted for her client. Jane had never actually admonished Melody for swearing, but Melody always thought she detected disapproval.

"That is very generous of them," Jane said.

"Ha, generous, I like that. No, I think it's their idea to milk you as long as they can. They're in no rush to bring another book to market. I'm sure they'll want to re-release your books, with new forewords by you. Probably arrange tie-ins with the movie companies. Make you do the celebrity circuit. Then when the public, and I mean the larger public and not just the Janeites, are ready, they release your next book."

"I was being droll, Melody."

"Oh, sorry Jane. But you see their strategy and I think it means you can take your time writing, as long as the first book is *The Watsons* … or something like it."

"In other words, it has to be 'Jane Austen-y.'"

"Uh, yes. Which means Jane Austen can't say things like 'Jane Austen-y.'"

"My, we are certainly being pernickety. But you have my complete faith and trust, and I shall do my best to prove my *bona fides*."

"Thanks. And that sounds more like the Jane Austen I know and love."

If she could have, Jane would have made a face.

"But I shall want something from this 'deal.' I trust I can use modern vernacular if I surround it in quotes?"

"Uh, sure. What do you want? Although I think I can guess."

"I want to be able to write something entirely new and be assured of it being published," she said. "Something … something relevant today."

"Jane, I think I could get you almost anything you want, as long as you were willing to … to …"

"Write a sequel to *Pride and Prejudice*? That I will not do. Lizzie and Darcy have had their day. But I will seriously consider *The Watsons*. Are we understood then?"

"Perfectly. OK, let's go upstairs and …" She stopped suddenly and Jane saw a spasm of pain flicker across her friend's face.

"Melody, are you all right? You look unwell."

Melody brought a hand to her mouth and belched as politely as possible when standing beside a famous author.

"No, I'm fine, just a little indigestion. And you're right, I am nervous. It just hit me again: I am Jane Austen's agent. Enough to make anyone a little queasy."

· Ripples ·
The Austen world reacts

— CHICAGO —

Alice paused outside the door to the study room in which her graduate students awaited her. She could hear their raised voices quite easily and could see through the glass that they were all looking at Stephen's iPad. Normally she'd be happy to see her students animated because young men and women embarking on a course of study of Jane Austen could be a little … well dull. They took it all so seriously and knew too much about the Corn Laws and Enclosure Movement and other capitalized nouns that sucked so much of the sheer fun out of Austen.

It didn't, however, surprise her that Stephen would be the source of whatever amusing viral video or app he'd found. Stephen was the only one of her students who seemed to find fun in what he was doing and his enjoyment was infectious. There were times when Alice found herself teaching to him and ignoring the others. He was the only one who seemed to genuinely enjoy Austen as a storyteller, even if he wasn't necessarily an enthusiastic supporter of her conjectures about the Regency author. And this despite the fact that his thesis was about Corn Laws and the Enclosure Movement.[1]

---

1   Corn Laws refers to any number of protective trade legislations that kept

She opened the door and the noise guiltily stopped.

"Oh, hi Dr Davis," Stephen said, as she walked to her chair and set her bag on the floor beside it. The other students scurried to their seats and resumed their serious looks, but Stephen kept a big stupid grin on his face.

"OK, what is it?" she asked. In response, he got up and handed her his tablet. She saw a *New York Times* article about the publication of a … she sat down.

The students resumed a low buzz of conversation at this remarkable display by their teacher.

"Pretty exciting news, isn't it?" Stephen asked.

She looked up irritably at him, but the eager look on his face softened her response.

"It's … interesting, but you all know my opinion about anointing anyone as *the* Jane Austen." They were quick to nod except for Stephen, who paused several seconds before so doing.

"But legally she is Jane Austen, right?"

Alice was about to agree, but then stopped. "Actually, I don't know how legal it is. Certainly most people seem to accept the AfterNet's word that so-and-so is who they claim to be. That's actually a good project for you Stephen, and you can report back to us what you find. Now if we can return to Ashleigh's question about … what was your question from last time?"

"It was about Sir Thomas' change of heart, but what I'd really like to know is if you've got an advance copy of *Sanditon*."

Alice looked at Ashleigh in surprise. She was the most obsequious student she'd ever had and never ventured an opinion. Like it or not, she had to admit that this pretender to the mantle of Austen had her students excited.

"OK, OK, we'll talk about it. I know we haven't met since the announcement of … this woman's identity. So Ashleigh, I assume you're not asking whether I've received a review copy."

Ashleigh shook her head and then realized her affirmation might be

---

grain prices high in Britain. Corn is a generic term for grain. The Enclosure Acts encouraged wealthy landowners to enclose common grazing lands, to the detriment of villagers who freely used the commons for centuries. Many villagers, unable to make a living, moved to cities.

confusing. "Yes, I mean I'm not asking that. I wanted to know if you had the leaked copy?"

This comment started another buzz of questions so Alice intervened. "Why don't you tell us what you know about the leaked copy? Actually, start at the beginning and its involvement in proving her identity. Assuming you know that part of it?"

Ashleigh nodded enthusiastically, eager to show her knowledge. "OK, Austen ... this woman ... had to convince the identity committee she is who she says. And as I understand it, you can go two routes: by either producing some proof or knowledge that only the person could know or by convincing the committee—sort of like defending your dissertation. It's supposed to be all very secret and the AfterNet tries to hide who's on the committee, but everyone suspects Deirdre Le Faye and Joan Ray were two of the five."[2]

"I heard you were on it, Dr Davis," said the unctuous Roy.

"I was not, Roy."

"Yeah, but you're supposed to deny it if you were," Stephen added with a mischievous grin.

"I would never lie to my students. Now stop interrupting Ashleigh. Continue."

"All right, the committee is also not supposed to divulge how they reached their decision, but I've read Austen ... this woman ... satisfied both criteria. She produced some proof and supposedly she was able to recite her continuation of *Sanditon*, while unconnected to the AfterNet. Apparently she'd had to memorize it while writing it; and the general consensus was that it's amazing." Ashleigh sat back in triumph at this, making it pretty evident she thought the claimant was the genuine Jane Austen.

"I didn't think it was that great ... I mean the part I read," said Lucy, who'd been quiet up till now. Alice turned to her, the acid smile she normally reserved for Lucy—not her favourite student—frozen on her face. She hated that Lucy might share her opinion on the matter.

"To what are you referring, Lucy?"

"The excerpt that's everywhere. I think I saw it on *Jane Austen Today*, but it ..."

---

2   Deirdre Le Faye is an eminent UK Janeite and author of *Jane Austen: A Family Record*. *Dr Joan Klingel Ray* is a past president of the Jane Austen Society of North America (JASNA) and the author of *Jane Austen for Dummies*.

"Nobody thinks that's genuine," Roy argued. "I mean that wouldn't have fooled someone like Dr Ray or ..."

"And that's not the only one out there, Lucy," Stephen offered. "All the people working on Austen continuations are coming out of the woodwork. I've even seen someone stealing from Anna Austen Lefroy's attempt[3] and claiming it as her own."

"But do you have the copy that was supposedly leaked out by one of the committee members, Dr Davis?" Ashleigh asked in an attempt to take charge of the conversation.

"No, I don't, although Stephen will probably just claim I'm supposed to deny having it. And let's face it, can you imagine any of the people who've been mentioned as being on this committee leaking it?" She gave them a stern look, hoping to end the conversation.

"Look, it's all speculation on the Internet, which is fine and it's kind of fun, but it's not scholarship."

"You don't think she is Austen, do you?" Lucy asked.

"That's a ..."—she stopped herself from saying "stupid"—"that's not the right question, Lucy. The right question would be whether I have doubts, to which I would answer that I really don't know how anyone could ever be sure. The only thing I do know for sure is that I'll end up buying a copy of her *Sanditon* and I assume all of you will as well. And I think that's the last word on this subject. Now if we could return to Sir Thomas."

Ashleigh's speculations about Sir Thomas[4] were interesting, Dr Davis had to admit, but she was distracted during the whole time with her students. She couldn't put her finger on why she so disliked the idea of a Jane Austen made ... well not flesh, but at least made identifiable. Despite all her critical analysis of Austen, she had to admit she'd somewhat deified Jane. The thought of encountering a real Jane—virtual warts and all—made her uncomfortable, and she had to admit no claimant could ever satisfy her.

Her hour with her students finally ended. As usual, Stephen remained behind but she tried her best to ignore him.

---

3 Anna Austen Lefroy's continuation is also unfinished. The Lefroy and Austen families were very close. Austen's niece married Benjamin Lefroy, a cousin of that Tom Lefroy.

4 Sir Thomas Bertram is the uncle of Fanny Price, the heroine of *Mansfield Park*, Austen's third published novel

"You really don't think she's Austen, right?" he asked when he tired of being ignored.

She sighed. "Does it matter? I'm willing to admit I could be wrong. Maybe she is the creator of six novels and a smattering of juvenile writings that have defined most of my life and my academic career. And if I'm right and she's not Jane, we'll know it when we read her book."

"Come on, doc, you've got to have a copy already. You and I know someone has the transcript of that committee and if Austen really was reciting *Sanditon* to them ..."

"I really don't, Stephen. And don't think I haven't tried to get a copy, but it's not something you can directly ask, 'Do you have an illegal copy of a book that's about to be published?' Not when you're not even sure whom to ask. But ..."

"But what?"

"I wasn't joking earlier. Do you think you could look into the whole vetting process on your own? Maybe you can find some information I've missed. I really would like to know something, anything, about the proof she offered."

Stephen promised he'd see what he could find out, a little happy to be asked; a little worried he'd find nothing. Alice left him and went back to her office and decided she could try sending another email to Deirdre and try to divine any meaning from her maddening noncommittal denials.

— AMES, IOWA —

Ajala dipped her laptop screen down at the discreet knock on her door and saw her assistant standing there. "Ajala, you said to remind you about your 'meeting.'" Becky made air quotes around the word.

"What? Oh, I think I'll have to skip it today."

That caused Becky to enter the office and sit down next to Ajala's desk. "Really, because you said you really didn't want to miss it this time." Then Becky noticed Ajala's expression. "Hey, is something the matter? You look upset."

Ajala looked at Becky and wondered what to say. She was both upset and unsettled. She had been unsettled since the announcement that Jane Austen had been recognized. It was similar to the feelings she had every time someone claimed to have found a portrait of Austen. She somehow didn't like the idea of Jane being identified, especially if it conflicted with her own idealized conception of her.

But all that took a back seat to what was really upsetting.

"Everything's ruined! Oh my God, they'll have to start from scratch."

Becky was now truly alarmed. She'd never seen her boss like this. Ajala Johnsson was famously imperturbable. She managed her department with skill and grace and treated everyone fairly and kindly. Since she'd moved into the corner office, it was like living in a Golden Age, where all the peasants were happy and the dragons had been slain. She'd protected the department from cutbacks and reorganizations and …

"Not layoffs?" Becky gasped.

"What? Oh no, it's nothing about work. It's …" Ajala flipped her laptop screen up and swivelled it around to face Becky.

Becky looked at the news story about some author … some disembodied author …

"Oh, it's your Jane Austen." Becky looked around and saw her boss's fetish displayed throughout the office as books and knickknacks and even a little Jane Austen action figure. She'd gotten used to the items, of course, but she couldn't forget that Ajala was the president of a national Jane Austen organization. Ajala was scrupulous about not making Becky do any work related to … the coffee cup on her desk reminded her of the organization's name … JASNA, but she still ended up taking messages and fielding phone calls for her boss.

"Isn't this good news? You finally get to read another of her books, right?"

"No, you don't understand," Ajala said. "We have to invite her. We have to invite Jane Austen to the AGM! Everything's going to be different!"

— ARLINGTON, TEXAS —

Cindy Wallace heard the other participants to the conference call hang up. The sound was like the slamming of a prison cell door.

"Two years planning down the drain," she said. "Two years down the drain."

Her husband chose this moment to walk into her office, having been curious why his wife had been on the phone the past two hours. He assumed it was something to do with the AGM;[5] it was always about the AGM and as he often did these days he regretted his bright idea to urge his wife to become the North Texas regional coordinator. He'd been a long-time Austen fan—not quite a Janeite—and had introduced Cindy to Jane Austen shortly after their marriage. She didn't embrace Jane as much as he'd hoped but after their children left home she had seemed to find a new relevance in Austen. Her enthusiasm grew and grew as did his and they joined JASNA. They became quite well known for their fondness of wearing costumes and their several trips to England and the various Austen shrines of Chawton, Bath and Winchester.[6]

When the regional coordinator post became vacant he suggested she run for it, which she did and was elected. At that time, the AGM was still three years off, the North Texas region having secured the honour of hosting it under the leadership of the previous coordinator.

Harry quickly learned, however, that hosting an AGM was a daunting undertaking. He hadn't realized what he'd talked his wife into. She seemed to spend less and less time enjoying Jane Austen and more and more time talking to catering managers and airlines and local businesses and cranky authors and even crankier academics.

"What's up, hon?" he asked, getting a sinking feeling even as he asked it. He of course knew the recent news of Jane Austen and suspected it might have an effect on her planning.

"Two years planning down the drain because Jane Austen's coming to the AGM!"

"But that's a good thing!" He regretted saying it immediately.

"It was supposed to be *200 Years of Sense and Sensibility*, and now all it's going to be is the Second Coming of Jane. We're going to have to scrap the whole program."

Harold knew his wife was no Mrs Bennet[7] and not given to hyperbole, but still he wondered at her reaction.

"So who were you on the phone with?"

"Everybody. Ajala Johnsson and Dick Wilson and Lorna White.

---

5 Each year, JASNA convenes in a different city for the Annual General Meeting

6 Austen is buried at Winchester Cathedral

7 The mother of Elizabeth Bennet, the heroine of *Pride and Prejudice*. Mrs Bennet was given to histrionics.

Ajala just got a call from Jane Austen's agent ... can you believe it? Jane Austen's agent! She wants to know if it would cause a bother if she attended the AGM? Ha! A bother!"

— SOMERSET, ENGLAND —

Courtney looked at the English countryside whizzing by the train, or rather the reverse, for the train was whizzing past the countryside. But to him, it certainly felt like it was the world that was whizzing past. He refreshed the Google news search on his laptop and saw another story about Jane Austen. "Chick lit author ready to ink sequel," said the cheeky headline in a British tabloid, predicting a sequel to *Pride and Prejudice* even though the Austen claimant had repeatedly said it would never happen.

He pulled his hand through his hair, destroying his carefully sculpted spiky hairstyle. *She can't really be alive, I mean dead, I mean ... you know what I mean*, he thought. *Could the timing be any worse?*

From the empty seat beside him, he picked up the mock-up of his book cover that he'd received last week. It showed a ghosted portrait of a model dressed in Regency costume superimposed over the oh-so-familiar silhouette of Jane Austen. The cover looked good, although the model seemed more endowed than he'd ever imagined the author.

Oh damn, what's she going to say about the cover. Will it flatter her or will she object? And how the hell does anyone know she's really Jane Austen?

The last question he'd asked himself time and again since he'd heard the news that Austen had managed to prove her identity.

He looked at the mock-up and quietly read out loud the title: *The Real Jane Austen: Hidden Passions and Secret Desires.*

He dropped his head and the older woman sitting on the opposite side of the aisle might have heard a small moan escape him. His ringing phone interrupted his self-pity.

"Hello?"

"Hey Courtney," he heard his agent say. He winced at the use of his full name and wondered again why he couldn't convince his own agent to call him Court.

"Yeah, Dan, what's up? I'm sorry I haven't sent my thoughts on the mock up." Courtney offered an apologetic shrug to the woman across the aisle. She returned to her perusal of a knitting magazine.

"Oh, don't worry about that. Listen, there's been a change on the publication schedule."

"What? They can't move it any closer. I still …" His voice rose and again he attracted the attention of Miss Marple. Courtney turned his head toward the window.

"No, not closer, they want to delay it. But don't worry, it's good news."

"How can it be good news they want to delay the publication? And I already bought the tickets for the book tour."

"Don't sweat it, Courtney. You can throw those tickets away. We now have a tour budget, paid for by the publisher. They want to time the release to whenever Austen publishes her book. Anything Austen is hot right now, so you're sitting pretty. Can it get any better?"

"Oh, no, I mean yeah, that's great."

"And there's a rumour going around that they want Jane Austen to be on a book tour, although I have no idea how they would manage it. Luckily I have a friend who might be able to leak me the itinerary when it comes time. Think about how great that would be for you? You could be signing your book right next to Jane Austen herself. I guess she wouldn't be signing her book, of course. Maybe they can hire an avatar to do it. There have to be copies of her autograph somewhere, right?"

Dan kept babbling away, envisioning the book tour and obviously very happy having a so-so client with his limited appeal book suddenly become a hot property. But all Courtney could think of was sitting next to an invisible Jane Austen disapproving of his book.

"You have no idea how great it is having a real touring budget. I usually have to tell my clients to book their own tickets and tell them to stay with family … hell you know what I'm talking about! Well look, got to go. I'm very happy for you, Courtney."

Courtney silently cursed after his agent hung up and as he did so, he realized he'd been looking at the woman across the aisle and she'd correctly interpreted his four-letter word. She gave him a long, disapproving look and returned to her magazine.

Courtney was embarrassed and disappointed that he'd allowed his fear and frustration to be evident to the old woman, although he certainly had justification. His book was essentially finished, and if there were no Austen claimant, it could stand on its own, but now that there was one, he desperately needed the letter. To actually know in her own words the name of Jane's Lyme Regis lover[8] would be amazing, assuming of course it corresponded with his conjectures. And it would certainly make it difficult for the Austen claimant to refute him.

He was travelling back to Bath to see if he could find proof the Gorrell family had any connection with the Austen family. And from there he hoped to trace the family forward. Unfortunately it meant nothing if he couldn't find the old lady and the letter, the trail having run cold sometime in the 1980s.

He tried to reassure himself that even if he were unable to find the letter, his book was solid enough, but he knew he might have pushed some of his suppositions a little far.

He'd weathered criticism before, of course. His Byron biography was controversial, and he had been prepared to have some hard-core Janeites take issue with the book, although he had also hoped it would appeal to the incurable romantics who wanted to think Jane had actually experienced some real passion.

Maybe I'm blowing it out of proportion. Maybe Austen won't mind me revealing her affair. After all, that was a long time ago. Maybe if I contact her, she'll give me an interview.

He decided to look up her address on the net, but of course searching for Jane Austen produced a lot of results that weren't relevant. Then he went to the AfterNet and searched for her again and found several stories about her identity being certified but that still didn't produce an email address by which he might contact the one true Jane Austen.

Then he went to facebook and the same was true again. There were several Jane Austen pages and many usernames like JaneAusten12 and janeaustenauthor and IAmJaneAusten, but he had no clue which was genuine.

He'd assumed once she had proven her identity, Jane Austen would be easy to find, but he supposed it wouldn't be any different than if he wanted to find Salman Rushdie's email address. He thought that

---

8   Austen visited Lyme Regis at least twice in her lifetime, and in a letter Jane sent to Cassandra about a dance she attended there, remarks on "a new odd-looking man who had been eyeing me for some time, and at last, without any introduction, asked me if I meant to dance again. I think he must be Irish by his ease, and because I imagine him to belong to the Honbl. Barnwalls, who are the son and son's wife of an Irish viscount, bold and queer-looking people, just fit to be quality at Lyme." There is no reason to believe the relationship involved more than the one dance.

perhaps his agent might be able to find Austen's agent and he could get a review copy to her that way. He was dialling his agent's number but stopped before the final digit.

And what if she says I'm making it all up. No, I don't want to approach her until I can authenticate the letter. After all, no one's said anything negative about the book. All the proof readers thought it well written and I made my arguments.

He tried to quell the worry that only two of the reviewers to whom he'd sent the book were scholarly Janeites and he had sent them early incomplete drafts. He'd meant to send other drafts but kept delaying, hoping he might finally gain access to the letter.

Maybe if I just found another Janeite, a real scholar, and I could explain to her about the letter. After all, we're all in the same boat now.

He looked at his folder on his laptop where he'd collected the various references he'd used in writing his book. He saw the *Persuasions*[9] articles by Dr Alice Davis. She was a respected Austen scholar, even if she did have a reputation for promoting a feminist agenda. He'd early on considered interviewing her for his book, but she also had a reputation for not suffering fools gladly.

The train was now slowing as they approached Bath. He unplugged the computer's power supply from the outlet under the seat and collected his coat. He looked for the old woman he'd offended and saw she'd already left her seat and was making for the queue to exit. He stood up as well, but waited to proceed until the train completely stopped.

It was time to return his attention to the purpose of his visit. His first stop was the Guildhall. Once he got to his bed and breakfast he would search again for Mrs Westerby ... and he would try to contact Dr Davis through the University of Chicago website.

After all, she was on the committee that identified Austen. If I can get a good review from her, that should count for something.

---

9 *Persuasions* is a journal published by JASNA

· An empty chair ·
Jane needs an avatar

"Then we are agreed," Mr Pembroke said and sat back in his chair. Jane regarded him with some amusement, charmed by his manner that seemed so like her Mr Gardiner.[1] *He is just as I imagined, a good and sensible man with just that sort of amusement.* It helped strengthen the resemblance that he was English—having lived in America a number of years—had grey hair, balding on top, and affected wire-rimmed spectacles that did not obscure his grey eyes.

It was their fourth meeting, and Jane could not complain of Melody's skills at negotiation, but to be honest, Mr Pembroke hardly objected to any of her demands. He professed to be Jane's ardent admirer, having "cut his teeth on Austen," a phrase that made him laugh just as she imagined Mr Gardiner would.

Damme, what was his first name? It won't do for me to forget the name of … wait, did I ever give him a first name?

She felt slightly foolish, foolish for again cursing and then for forgetting. *I did create him two hundred years ago. And I have created not a few characters.*

---

1 Mr Gardiner was the uncle of Elizabeth Bennet in *Pride and Prejudice*. In contrast to Elizabeth's parents, Mr Gardiner and his wife were sensible people. Their deportment helped convince Fitzwilliam Darcy that Elizabeth's relations weren't all foolish.

"... if you might consider changing the title?"

"What?"

"I'm sorry, you want to change the title?" Melody asked.

"It's just ... now I know this is just one of those marketing things that drives authors insane ... it's just your most famous novel is *Pride and Prejudice* and ..."

"I see where this is going, Mr Pembroke," Jane said, her words audible for the man through the small speaker attached to the AfterNet terminal on the table before them. "My next most famous novel is *Sense and Sensibility* and you would like another three word title that is similarly alliterative." Jane hoped the digitized voice of the terminal would convey that she wasn't upset by the suggestion.

"But it's been known as *Sanditon* for two hundred years," Melody said. "Why would you ..."

"It also has been called *Sand and Sanditon*, Melody, although I never quite understood that. And I thought of it as *The Brothers*. I will certainly consider your suggestion, Mr Pembroke." Then she thought her words sounded dismissive, and added, "After all, my first titles did not often survive and I'm sure my fame would have suffered if my first books had remained *First Impressions* and *Elinor and Marianne*."

"Excellent. Now, could we turn to the matter of the avatar?" he asked, obviously pleased at having won a small battle.

"Avatar? What avatar? Melody, did you know of this?"

Melody would not turn to meet her, but nodded her head.

"Mr Pembroke, could I have a moment alone with my client?"

The gentleman nodded and left the table, saying he would refill his coffee. After he left, Jane again addressed her friend.

"I do not recall agreeing to an avatar."

"Well, I do not recall you objecting to one."

"Who do you think I am? A dead movie star? A politician?"

"No, you're just a world famous author who's inspired a cult following. Look, lots of people have avatars, Jane. And ... well a book tour looks pretty stupid with an empty chair."

"I thought you would accompany me."

"When I can, yes, but this book tour has you going everywhere, which you agreed to."

"Yes, but ..."

"There are no buts, Jane. Look, I'm going to be awfully busy back here looking after Jane Austen Enterprises, or whatever you want to call it. And I can't be on the road with you the whole time. You're going to need somebody to be me and carry this." She pointed to the terminal on her arm. "And wouldn't it be better if instead of being me, they were being you. That way they have someone to focus on instead of an empty chair."

"Stop saying empty chair. I am here."

Melody rolled her eyes at this, a gesture Jane despised in others for all the times she had employed it herself, usually against her brother Henry.

"I know you are Jane, I'm sorry," she said, addressing the empty chair and now doing her best to appear as if she could actually see her friend and client. Jane let the moment drag on without responding and Melody did her best to look sincere and supportive. After a very few seconds, however, the look of sincerity on Melody's face gave way to the corners of her mouth lifting until finally it disappeared behind a wide smile.

"I can't keep this up, Jane. Are you going to forgive me?"

Finally Jane relented. "Yes, you are forgiven. And yes, you have made your point. Perhaps it would be as well were I to employ an avatar."

"Good, glad you see it my way," Melody said. Then she stood and went to the door, opened it and beckoned Mr Pembroke to return.

Once seated, he said, "Ahem, I hope there is no problem regarding the avatar."

"Jane is willing to consider it," Melody said, before Jane could form her response.

"It must depend on the suitability of the ... I suppose she will be an actress," Jane said.

"Yes, I have an agency in mind. They're called Stand By Me. They have supplied avatars to many celebrities who have ... passed on. Perhaps you could interview the candidates yourself, if that would make you more comfortable."

"That's an excellent idea, isn't it Jane? We wouldn't want a focus group deciding who to play you."

"Yes," Jane replied, unnerved that there had been any possibility of a focus group—whatever that was—choosing her avatar.

"Then let me send you ..."—he took out his phone and punched the screen—"... my contact at the agency. You should have it now Melody. And now unless there is anything else, we get the lawyers to finalize the contract and we can look forward to a long relationship, Miss Austen."

"Thank you Mr Pembroke."

"If I might presume, please call me Alan. I know in your day …"

"That was another time, Alan. And if you would please call me Jane."

"It would be my honour. And if I might just say, I was considering retiring. There are several people in the company who think I'm a bit long in the tooth. But the opportunity to work with you Miss Austen … Jane. Well I would say it's a lifelong dream come true, but who would have thought it possible to work with a dead … disembodied author."

"I understand perfectly your excitement, Alan. Just a very short while ago, a drop in the proverbial bucket for me, I would never have thought it possible that I might be published again as a … working author. And I understand that the publishing world is very much different from what I knew. I must take you and Melody as my guides, for this time I do not go forth anonymously. My goal is to reclaim my posterity and for that, I will depend upon you."

· Albert Ridings ·
Keeping watch for minimum wage

lbert Ridings watched the girl collect the discarded dresses from the bench of the fitting room. She'd tried on four dresses and apparently had decided that none of them suited her, although he thought the dark green dress went well with her red hair. One of the dresses would clearly be too tight, a size 12 on at least a size 16 figure. But most of the dresses seemed appropriate and flattering.

She had already redressed in her jeans, sweater and trainers[1], collected her purse from the hook provided for same and now stood there, juggling the dresses, her handbag and her coat. After some back and forth, she left with three dresses in her left hand and the green dress underneath her coat in her right hand, her purse slung over her left shoulder. She exited the dressing room stall and returned the three dresses to a rack where they would be later returned to the floor.

She left the racks displaying early spring fashions in the junior miss department and entered the aisle that led to the sales registers and the exits. She moved to her left, angling toward the exits and away from the registers.

Albert raced ahead of her and captured the AfterNet field of the terminal hanging from the arm of the loss prevention guard near the exits. Albert was about to log in when he saw the woman suddenly stop

---

1   Sneakers, athletic footwear

as she struggled to put on her coat and noticed the green dress. She turned around and Albert followed her as she returned to the dressing rooms, returned the dress and then departed the store.

Oh well, she seemed like a nice person, he thought. *But it might have been nice to have another shoplifter. It's been a slow month.*

He'd only identified 10 shoplifters so far with only a few days left in the month, down from his high of 28. Apparently the word had gotten out that it was a difficult department store from which to steal and although he doubted he'd lose his position, he might be transferred to another store. *At least I'd have more to do.*

He worked the remainder of his shift without identifying any shoplifters and left, never having spoken a word with anyone living. He had hoped that Phyllis would have been the guard at the door, who during breaks would at least natter on to Albert about her grandchildren, but instead it was the taciturn Ted whom Albert suspected was not overly fond of communicating with the dead.

He left the shopping mall and hopped a bus that would take him to the assisted living centre and the room he shared with, at last count, 15 other disembodied. It was also the games room for the living residents and he hoped he might find someone with whom to play chess. His previous regular partner, Joe, had died a week before and Albert still felt a sense of abandonment after Joe failed to appear on the AfterNet.

Probably went back to Massachusetts to plague his poor daughter. Can't say I blame him, Albert thought ruefully. After all, the only reason for Albert being in Boca Raton was to occasionally look in on his great-great granddaughter. In fact he was to visit that weekend and thought he might surprise his family by buying them a new computer, which coincidentally would improve his ability to surf the web.

The games room was empty of any living chess partners, and after logging on to the shared AfterNet terminal, he saw that none of the disembodied he might call friends were online. He did see Ronnie's name listed, and as the oldest dead person, having died in 1918, he felt some responsibility toward Ronnie, the care centre's newest resident. The 25-year-old man had died in a car crash last fall, but Albert felt he had little in common with the youngster and he thought the feeling mutual.

So instead Albert checked his inbox and found an email about the upcoming JASNA AGM. He was puzzled by the early announcement; registration didn't usually begin until late spring. Then he saw the link that explained all. He clicked the link that took him to the JASNA website and read the news.

Oh my, Jane Austen … THE Jane Austen will be at the AGM! The news came as quite a shock despite its being expected. From the moment he'd read that Jane Austen had been certified by the AfterNet, he'd hoped she would be attending the AGM.

He could barely contain his joy and immediately searched the chat rooms his Jane frequented but could find her nowhere online. He consoled himself by composing an email and hoped he might get an early reply, but she had been increasingly difficult to contact. He worried briefly, the improbable, incongruous, absurd worry of a man dead a hundred years that a woman he fancied had lost interest in him.

Stupid old man, she's probably just busy. She did say she might have a surprise for me the last time we talked. But what might keep a disembodied woman so busy he could not imagine.

His attention wandered back to the JASNA website and he saw the notice about the special disembodied rate for the AGM. It had been announced at the 2010 conference but this was the first official confirmation that it would be in effect for the 2011 AGM. It was a considerable savings on a full rate, and the web page promised AfterNet access at all the breakout sessions.

Suddenly Albert decided to take a rash step. He erased what he'd written so far to Jane and decided to make an offer that he hoped would not be considered unseemly. He worked long and hard at the email, rewriting it several times before he felt satisfied and then paused for almost five minutes before sending it to her.

Afterward he felt drained and yet … he could not help but remember the first time he had asked out Catherine all those years ago and he felt quite silly that he found himself just as excited now as he was then.

Now he must wait for a reply. He was tempted to open his copy of *Mansfield Park* and lose himself with the dysfunctional Bertram family, but instead he pinged his roommate Ronnie and inquired as to whether the young man had any knowledge of chess.

· Something Fresh ·
Something new

J ane looked at what she'd written with some frustration. It was about one in the morning and she was in Melody's apartment alone, Melody and Tamara having left for the evening to attend a Broadway play and afterward spend time with the director and his particular friend. Melody knew the director from her university days. Jane had always been puzzled that for a person with so many accomplished and famous friends, Melody was so unsuccessful. Then it would occur to her that she had been presuming on her friend and agent for six months by staying in her apartment—Melody's and Tamara's apartment she amended.

Perhaps I need not look too far to find the reason for Melody's lack of success. She is too charitable to be successful. That thought made her feel guilty because she felt she owed Melody—and herself—more success than just *Sanditon*. She had been trying to begin something new, something fresh, for weeks and had found little success. Admittedly the endless meetings with Random House and now the avatar agency had interfered with her ability to focus, but the endless nights still provided a great deal of time to write.

Her latest idea had been to write a story set during the Battle of Britain, during the darkest days of the Second World War when Hitler seemed poised to invade England, if only he could cripple the Royal Air Force.

It was war that helped ground her the most, to connect her to the living. There had been many long periods of her afterlife when her attention had drifted and she had almost lost the thread of her humanity, but she could not witness the horror of war without empathizing.

In particular, she had come to identify with a young WAAF[1] whom she had encountered one day on the Underground. The young woman, really no more than a girl, was reading *Mansfield Park* with an attention that seemed impossible to achieve in the crowded car. She stood serenely, one hand holding a strap and the other her book, kept inches away from her nose. After the woman exited the train at Westminster, she kept reading the book, giving her surroundings only the briefest of looks as she made the long way to the surface.

Jane followed her, happy to see someone enjoying her writing amidst the daily horror of the Blitz. Unfortunately the press of bodies leaving the station caused her to lose sight of the woman. Jane was very disappointed for she saw something of herself in the young woman and wondered if she were alive whether she might also serve her country.

And so the next day Jane waited at Westminster station and the next and the day after that, hoping to catch sight of her, which she finally did five days later. Jane followed her to the Cabinet War Rooms where she worked as a telephone operator. For months she became a voyeur, daily following the young woman from her shared flat in Camden Town to the war rooms.

When the young woman—Helen she was—entered the building, she would put her book away and don the glasses she needed to do her work but which she obviously thought unbecoming.

She was a dedicated reader and over the course of two months, she finished *Mansfield Park* and then *Emma* and then *Jane Eyre* and then *Tess of the d'Urbervilles* and when she could, Jane read along, mostly at night when Helen would wear her glasses and hold her book with her long arms outstretched, perhaps in compensation for those cramped times on the Underground.

Helen died the night of the 29th of December, 1940,[2] when so many

---

1   Women's Auxiliary Air Force
2   The Second Great Fire of London, when the German air force dropped more than 24,000 high explosives and over 100,000 incendiary bombs on London. The iconic image is of St Paul's Cathedral wrapped in smoke and flame, but which survived that night.

others died. She was simply in the wrong place at the wrong time, on a date with a man she had hoped for months might ask her out.

Jane had tried to write about Helen, about her hopes and dreams of the man, who also worked in the war rooms and of whom Jane did not approve. But despite her hope that the story would bring Helen back to life, that she might at least offer Helen a measure of happiness, she had not had much success.

The tone is not right, Jane thought. *Perhaps not having heard the actual speech of the time I am unable to reproduce it.*

Which thought made her again long for sound. Of all the senses she had lost, it seemed that sound might be the one she longed for the most—that is until she thought of the aroma of warm bread or the feel of cool linen on a hot night or the tartness of an orange. But for right now, to hear a voice again, to hear people speaking, would be a joy beyond compare.

She sighed her inaudible sigh. *There is no sense in wishing for what I cannot have. I have long since accepted my death; there is no point in cavilling on this minor point.*

Writing *Sanditon* had been so much easier, but then she'd written it so many years ago and in the language of her own time. Writing it in her mind was the only thing that kept her grip on sanity in the first years after her death. It was a tedious process, of course, and it was that tediousness that provided the anchor. She'd learned to memorize what she'd written and retold the story to herself again and again like an Icelandic saga, each time weeping at her faulty memory. She would be forced to reconstruct that which she'd forgotten but in the process she was honing her words razor sharp. And when, after the arrival of the AfterNet, she was finally able to write it down, she thought it the best she had ever written.

My guiding principles have always been to write what I know and to write of the here and now. But what for me is the here and now? Is it my life in Hampshire or the years I wandered in India or the time alone in the Rocky Mountains or the trenches of the Great War or my time in the Holy Land?

And do I really remember that life in Hampshire anymore? I, who am forced to look up the particulars of my own life in wikipedia when I forget the names of my own nieces and nephews.

That thought of wikipedia made Jane uncomfortable. Now when she wrote she was constantly pausing in her work to Google some fact.

She had never before attempted writing something outside her ken, but the resources of the Internet now made that possible. Before she would have never dreamed of writing about the life of a WAAF corporal, but now she had access to museums and libraries that reproduced every aspect of that life and that promised to lend a veneer of verisimilitude to her efforts.

Perhaps the here and now for me is the here and now of 2011.

Jane closed the window but did save what she'd written. She had been a novelist long enough to recognize that even her best work required considerable editing and that it was a mistake to consign anything she'd written to nonexistence. After all, when she still put pen to paper and would abandon a story, she still kept it.

Instead, as she was wont to do when frustrated or bored, she looked at her email. She maintained several accounts, the first being the one created when she first accessed the AfterNet. It was JaneAusten3@theAfterNet.net, she being the fourth person who had claimed her identity, although to be fair JaneAusten2 only chose the email address as a lark, not actually claiming to be the Regency author.

Her most recent address was JaneAusten@JaneActually.com, Jane Actually being a website that Melody had persuaded her to create once her identity was officially recognized. It consisted of little more than a domain name, a holding page and her email address. She did not care for it but Melody insisted she use it for any official correspondence.

She preferred her original address through the AfterNet. She would not presume to contact the holder of JaneAusten@theAfterNet.net and ask her (or possibly him) to relinquish the address. She was after all bemused that three people before her and countless others after her thought the mantle of Jane Austen worth claiming.

She found in her original email account a letter from Albert.

From: AARidings@theAfterNet.net
To: JaneAusten3@theAfterNet.net
Date: Jan. 31, 2011 06:15:09
Subject: Guess who's coming to the AGM?
Dear Jane,
Have you heard the news? THE Jane Austen is coming to the Fort Worth AGM. I just found out today. I'd been hoping they would invite her, what with the release of Sanditon, but I was still surprised. This certainly puts

everything the other way round. Instead of us trying to guess what she was like, we can now just ask her.

I also found confirmation that JASNA is offering the disembodied a special rate. It's a nice gesture and makes a welcome contrast from the years before the discovery when I would attend as a lonely ghost, unable to even say "boo!" and reading over the shoulders of the attendees. It's quite affordable and I hoped that I could persuade you to attend. I know it's a daft thing to say, but I would enjoy meeting you "in person."

You've been so coy and secretive of late and I thought that perhaps you were embarrassed that you couldn't afford the registration fee. Of course I know most of us don't have money or the means to make any, so I thought I might offer to stand you the fee.

Or if that makes you uncomfortable, perhaps you could attend unofficially. We could still meet at any public terminals at the hotel. Do say you'll come.

Then again, perhaps your recent silence is you giving me the "brush off" and all I've done with my offer is make the situation more awkward.

But the deed is done and my offer stands.

Albert

Jane looked at the letter in amazement and she had to admit she felt a flush of excitement. In her day, such a letter would have been an admission of love. Today it would be tantamount to little more than "let's have coffee." *Well, perhaps more than coffee. Perhaps it would be closer to ...* she couldn't actually think what it would be closer to. Two incorporeal entities could do little more than reside in the same space.

She also felt some guilt over Albert's remark of "recent silence." She hadn't intentionally been avoiding his emails; she had simply been busy, but of course this was nothing compared to the guilt over the fact that she had never mentioned to him that she was *THE* Jane Austen.

In fact she had admitted that to almost no one who knew her as JaneAusten3, apart from Melody and the committee that judged her identity. Her reasoning was simple; she hadn't wanted to be associated with those who claimed to be Napoleon, Jesus Christ or the very famous singer named Elvis from the mid twentieth century. Their claims made them look mentally unstable and she felt sorry for the actual person in question. So although she had claimed the identity of Jane Austen in her username and email address, she never made any claims in her conversations.

She had found Albert online and they were drawn together by their mutual interest in Hampshire, he claiming birth near Aldershot. Obviously from her username he thought her to be an Austen claimant, but from the first she—disingenuously perhaps—disassociated herself from any such agenda.

The other reason for avoiding the subject of her identity was her interest in Albert's life. He told her he died late in the Battle of the Somme during the Great War, which resonated deeply with her for she had been there amid the mud and the death of that horrific battle. Naturally enough he wanted to avoid talk of that time and by mutual agreement their conversation concerned mainly the period after the war.

He had returned to Hampshire after his death but like Jane eventually decided to travel as a means of forestalling the terror of his afterlife. He was somewhat more adventurous than Jane and told her stories of crossing the Himalayas and of being swept off peaks, his soul floating in the clouds for days before alighting near the Forbidden City of Peking. (She suspected some poetic license there.) He had also trekked the Amazon, hoping to catch sight of Maple White Land, a fictitious land created by Sir Arthur Conan Doyle[3] and populated with antediluvian monsters.

After decades travelling, however, he again returned to Hampshire and found that his granddaughter had left for America, the bride of an American soldier. And so he had come to the United States in 1947 so that he might be near family, although he still travelled regularly.

Jane told him of her wanderings as well, although hers was less of a *Boy's Own* tale. She had been to India as well in 1891 and again shortly after Partition. And she had visited Hong Kong and Australia, although she had to admit that last story involved enough hardships to make it a suitable adventure tale. By the 1950s, however, she had returned to England and rarely left the British Isles until her trip to the US to meet Melody.

She found Albert a charming correspondent. His background was more of the sod than of land but by his efforts he presented himself as a well-educated gentleman. They were both fond of Agatha Christie and exchanged tales of how infuriating it had been before the discovery of the afterlife to ever finish one of her stories. Albert was denied the end-

---

3　In *The Lost World*

ing of *The Murder of Roger Ackroyd* by the not untimely death of the nonagenarian whose shoulder he peered over. He claimed, however, to have puzzled out the story, although it took him another year to find his logic proved correct.

And they had both attended numerous performances of *The Mousetrap*,[4] and hampered by their inability to hear, it took many performances before they could understand how the killer could possibly be ...

A flicker of the interface notified her that she had another email. She found a message from Melody reminding her of their early meeting at the avatar agency the next day and a suggestion that she not take her customary late night stroll.

She replied immediately, a little annoyed to be told she couldn't go out. "If I wish to walk, I shall walk," she wrote back, although her high dudgeon was tempered by the knowledge that she couldn't open the door and must wait until Melody and Tamara returned.

Eventually her indignation quieted and she was left to deal with the guilt she had tried to ignore: *I shall reply to Albert at my earliest opportunity and make a clean breast of it ... tomorrow.*

---

4 A murder-mystery play by Christie that has been performed continuously since 1952. Attendees are urged not to divulge that the killer is

· Virtual Chawton ·
Jane Austen's online home

On his iPad, Stephen pawed his way through the inventory, amazed again at the detail available at Virtual Chawton. He was now looking at the section detailing what the library at Chawton House no longer had in its collection or at the nearby Chawton Cottage. He knew, for instance, that Chawton Cottage[1] had for many years been used to house estate workers and even served as a village library and that most of the Regency era belongings had been lost, sold, or pilfered. The inventory attempted to catalogue what exactly had gone missing.

The inventories of what remained and what had been lost were so extensive and so freely available, that Stephen marvelled at what information the Austen claimant could have provided that wasn't public. The philanthropist who'd funded the project had inadvertently made it quite difficult for anyone to claim Austen's identity.

There was speculation that the curators of the library and/or the cottage had withheld some crucial piece of information or that the Austen claimant knew of some memento hitherto undiscovered. But examining the inventory was ultimately a dead, if fascinating end.

He was sitting on the hallway floor, next to his advisor's office door,

---

1 Chawton Cottage was Jane's home before her death. Sadly, Virtual Chawton only exists within the pages of this book.

when he heard Dr Davis's heavy tread approaching, put his tablet to sleep and stood waiting for her. He watched with some appreciation his advisor's advance, amused how the people in the corridor shied away from her. She actually had a pleasant expression on her face, but her size and determined step ensured she had the right of way.

She merely nodded to Stephen upon reaching the door and then unlocked it and entered. Stephen followed and deposited his bag on the spare chair. He waited for Davis to put away her purse, look through the letters she had carried in and finally give him her full attention.

He was no longer frightened of her but she still did command his respect. She was a rigorous mentor who could spot a flaw in his reasoning just from his choice of adjectives and knew when he was hiding sloppy research. Unfortunately she was not quite as rigorous in her own scholarship. She attributed to Austen motives and ideals that Stephen thought heavy handed. He tended to think that most authors simply wrote and if their work exhibited themes and motifs and abstractions, that was just the happy coincidence of the author's experiences and prejudices infiltrating their writing.

But his mentor saw grand schemes in Austen, some of which Stephen begrudged, and others that he didn't. His thesis, that Austen's awareness of the political and social changes during the Regency was profound, coincided with Davis' opinion. Her argument—that Austen was pursuing a feminist agenda that would have become apparent in *Sanditon* had Austen finished it—he found less convincing.

Despite their less than perfect unanimity, he had enjoyed being her graduate student. Her recent *idée fixe*,[2] however, was becoming tiresome.

"So, Stephen, what have you learned about filing an exception to an identity?" she asked. She had folded her hands together in exactly the same way his high school principal had used when admonishing him for smoking grass underneath the stadium bleachers.

"Uh, I learned you can't really file an exception once an identity has been … bestowed. Another person can make a claim to the identity and if it's deemed credible, then a review of the previous claim can be made. But you'd have to be dead to make that claim, and I don't think you want to carry it that far." He said this last with a smile, hoping he could get her to recognize the futility of her objections.

---

2 Obsession

She ignored his attempt at humour, however, and said, "Yes, that's what I've learned as well. And what about the legal status this bestowal confers?"

Well if you already knew, why the hell did I waste all that time looking it up? he thought.

"It's kind of meaningless, legally. All her copyrights have expired. She's public domain. Some states have passed laws defining disembodied rights, but that has nothing to do with claiming her estate. There've been a few bills proposed to allow the disembodied to make an additional copyright extension, but it wouldn't affect anything published before 1923.

"And besides, she's English, although that's an abstraction that really doesn't mean anything once you're dead. UK law is also in flux, but it doesn't matter. She can't claim any proceeds from her previous work, just anything new, like *Sanditon*. What she has done is declare herself a corporation, and once she had the AfterNet's blessing, other corporations were willing to make deals with her. Ultimately, it's how well *Sanditon* sells that'll truly define whether she's accepted as Austen."

Davis nodded several times at this and Stephen got the feeling that again she already knew all this.

"And what did you learn from Virtual Chawton?"

"Look, Dr Davis, you know all this. What's the point of me telling you ..." The look on her face convinced him that his best strategy was to humour her.

"OK, Virtual Chawton, as you already know, is amazing. But I can't see how that's going to help us ... you. If anything, it makes it obvious that Austen must have known something pretty specific and obscure to prove her identity. Anyone can call up 3D plans of the cottage or the house and see the location, or the supposed location, of everything the house or the cottage ever contained. Maybe she hid a letter under a floorboard that said, 'In the event of my death, this will be proof of my existence.'"

"Don't be facetious, Stephen."

"I'm not. Face facts; for all intents and purposes, she's Austen."

She said nothing for a while and Stephen wondered if he'd angered her. His voice had risen slightly because he disliked the idea that she'd allowed herself to get fixated. And he had doubts that anyone could survive two hundred years of solitude and still be coherent enough to pose as Austen. But he admired Austen—that is the original author—

enough to hope if anyone had the proper mental makeup, it would be her.

"You're right, Stephen. I have to accept what my peers, whoever they were, have decided. I'm sorry to have wasted your time on this. You'll be happy to know I haven't completely allowed myself to be absorbed in this quixotic quest. I looked over the draft you sent and can offer a few … recommendations."

She appeared to have shrugged off her irritation at his inability to help her and threw herself into her critique of his manuscript. Far from being fooled, however, he finally recognized what lay at the foot of her objections. It was so stunningly obvious: *I didn't realize it before because I was sure she was on the committee. She's hurt she wasn't asked to help identify the most important person in her life.*

· Mary Crawford ·
It beats waiting tables

"Thank you, Miss Crawford, you're all done," the technician told her. Mary opened her eyes and blinked at the brightness of the room after he'd turned the lights back on.

"We're done?"

"Yes, you're on file now, and when we call you, you'll be ready to go."

He offered her his hand, a gallant gesture she thought, and helped her out of the comfortable chair in which he'd placed her. Then she realized it was a more than gallant gesture; the chair seemed reluctant to let her go.

Then she stood, feeling just a little sleepy after her five minutes in the dark, resting comfortably while his equipment recorded her unique field signature.

He ushered her out the door and she walked back to the reception area where she signed herself out and left the agency. She stood outside in the sun and for a moment panic gripped her.

What if they never call? What if they call me for somebody gross? What if I'm awful at it? What if they call today?

She tried to reassure herself that the agency wasn't a scam, like all the "modelling agencies" in the city. *I did hear about it on WNYC. If I can't trust NPR,[1] who can I trust?*

And so what if they don't call? I got a lunch out of it. And if they call today, I get my ass back down here and I don't care if it's … it's … She struggled to think of a truly evil woman, but realized it was a mostly male province. Which made her realize that it wouldn't be impossible that she might be asked to be the avatar of a dead man.

Wow, that would be weird. But not weirder than some of the exercises I've done in class.

She headed back to the subway station, her mind more on her crazy acting exercises than where she was going and bumped into a busy commuter who grouchily told her to watch where she was going.

Damn, get my head back in the game. She hugged her purse a little more tightly and tried to bring her awareness back to the present, the subway, her fellow commuters and the man smelling of urine scrounging for change.

She hated the city and if she was honest she hated her decision to be an actress, but that was an admission that she kept firmly squashed into a small corner of her mind.

She swiped her MetroCard through the reader on the turnstile but not in the swift assured motion of the other riders. "Please swipe again," it prompted, which she did and luckily this time her performance was considered acceptable and she was allowed to pass.

She joined the throng on the platform waiting for the train and wondered again why she did this, why she kept putting herself out there. She was not a confident performer, her teachers always instructing her to project, not to hug her body, to throw back her shoulders, to find her voice in her stomach or one of a thousand other tried and tested tricks of the trade, all of which momentarily sufficed to fool her teachers into thinking they had imparted some wisdom that would help a difficult project. But when she returned to that exercise the next day or week or month, she would fall back on her reticence and again her teachers would wonder whether they needed to have the talk with her, the talk where they would confide that not everyone is suited for the life theatrical.

Her train arrived and she entered, not moving quickly enough to

---

1   WNYC is a public radio station in New York City and an affiliate of National Public Radio

find a seat and instead grasped a pole, her mind still wallowing in her failures.

She thought several times a teacher would give her that talk and she would be released of having to follow a dream of which she no longer dreamed. But the talk never came and time and again, like right now, she realized ruefully, she would deny her doubts. She put herself out there precisely because she was afraid not to. Because if she didn't try she'd hug herself right out of existence.

Anyone watching her would have seen an actress registering determination, but privately it felt like resignation. *I will keep trying because not trying is too awful to contemplate.* And until then, she knew that she must find some work as her savings and scholarships were insufficient. *Besides, what better acting experience could there be than pretending to be someone who's dead.*

· Bath, England ·
Looking for traces of Jane

Court smiled sweetly at the woman as she waited for him to don the gloves. The very young woman returned a blank stare. Clearly his charms were wasted on her so he concentrated on squirming his large hands into the small, latex gloves. They should be cotton archivist gloves, as the box packaging indicated, and he assumed they'd run out of those gloves and substituted medical supply gloves, size small.

He could not jam his fingers completely into the gloves, leaving translucent appendages dangling from the end of each fingertip, but he held out his arms for the ledger anyway. The woman, not wearing gloves herself, put the ledger in his arms and told him he could sit at the desk behind him, and then left the counter.

"Much obliged," he said to the retreating back of the woman, who was quickly swallowed up by the stacks in the basement of the register office.

He took the book over to the indicated desk and sat with his back to the counter. He tried opening the book, but it was an almost impossible task with the flubbery worms depending from his fingers and quickly pulled off the gloves. Then he looked inside his messenger bag, found one of the individually wrapped wet wipes he kept there, tore it open and cleansed his hands. The sharp smell of alcohol reached his nose, mingled briefly with the musty smell of the book and then evaporated.

Finally he was able to open the book and feel the dry crinkle of the paper as he leafed through. He felt that little thrill that any but the most insensitive must feel when holding history. And that thrill was magnified when he reached the relevant dates in the record of births and deaths recorded in the book.

Many of the records for the Bath and North East Somerset Council were already digitized, but the cutoff was 1837, and so he found himself actually leafing through the pages of this ledger for 1775, looking for a birth sometime in …

And then he found the notice he'd sought on 23 February: the record of the birth of a son Robert to John and Mary Gorell.

It has to be him, he thought, although he expected to find the name Gorrell spelled with two "Rs", although he was hardly surprised at a minor discrepancy in spelling. He had to admit to a certain excitement. He hadn't had time to follow up the rumour of the letter on his previous visit, but he hadn't taken it seriously then. After all, precious few of Jane's letters had survived Cassandra's culling,[1] but this ledger entry actually provided an unbroken chain to Jane's lifetime. Which made it all the more important he track down the letter.

He used his camera to take a photo of the entry and reviewed it. Then he thought to take a larger photo that showed the entire ledger and then a photo of the counter with the words Bath and Somerset Council Records over it. After that, as the woman had not returned to the counter, he took the ledger from the desk, placed it on the counter and took another photo.

Finally, he rang the bell on the counter and after a minute the woman returned, holding a meat pie in one hand, and asked him, "Wotcher want?" around a mouthful of pasty.

"I need to make a copy—a certified copy—of this page. Is that possible?"

The young woman swallowed and said, "We can print out a copy. It'll take a few days and then we can mail it to you," she said.

He considered this and asked, "What will it look like. I mean will it look like a page from this book?"

---

1 Cassandra burned many of her sister's letters

"Naw, it'll look like ..." the young woman glanced around and from some recess under the counter she produced a sheet of paper. "It'll look like this."

It was a sample of a birth record with the recorded names as John and Mary Smith and their son John, printed on council letterhead and a place for the register to sign. It was legal looking enough, but hardly had the impact of what he needed.

"I would like to order that, but I was wondering ... I'm a writer and this record is important to my research. I need something a little more ... do you have a supervisor?"

The young woman looked annoyed at this and Courtney realized he had offended her, which wasn't his intent.

"Give us a minute," she said and turned, stuffing the last of her pasty into her mouth as she left.

From somewhere just out of sight, he heard the woman say, "Doris, there's an American here. He wants to talk to my supervisor."

"Oh very well. What have you done now?"

Courtney prepared his most pleasing smile before Doris arrived. He was in luck, he saw, based on the woman's appearance in her late forties, her hair swept up into a bun. She was still attractive, in an appropriately librarian manner, with immaculate makeup, and her elegant clothes hid some of the excesses of middle age.

She immediately returned his smile and again Courtney knew he was in luck.

"Yes sir, may I help you? I hope Ariel ..."—she made a little face as she pronounced the name—"... has been helpful."

"Ariel has been a delight," he said, and shot a smile at Ariel, who hovered behind Doris. He still didn't get a smile back so he returned his attention to Doris.

"I was hoping, however, that I might ask something out of the ordinary. I'm a writer and I'm doing a book about Jane Austen ..."

Bingo! he thought. Doris's smile at the mention of the author's name reassured him.

"Our most famous resident," Doris said, "although she really didn't like Bath."

He nodded, wondering why everyone in Bath was always so quick to point that out. It almost seemed a point of pride.

"So I've been informed," he said. "Well, I believe one of the names in this ledger belongs to a friend of Miss Austen's and I'd like to get a copy of the birth ..."

"Well Ariel can help you with that. We can have a copy made for you ..."

"So she said, but I'm leaving Bath tomorrow and besides, I'd like something a little more impressive than just a form on letterhead. I was wondering if you'd agree to be photographed holding the ledger open to the appropriate page, and possibly pointing to the entry."

The request flustered her. "Oh, but that's very unusual. This is for a book, about Jane Austen?"

"Yes, I think this name here ..."—he pointed to the entry—"... I think this person became a good friend of Miss Austen during her time in Bath. And it will be such a surprise when she learns I've found a record ..."

"You know Miss Austen? You've talked with her?" Doris asked, her eyes behind the half-moon progressive lenses now very bright.

"Yes I have," he lied. "And Robert Gorrell is an important part of my book. So I thought if you could hold the ledger while I take my photo ..."

"Oh, but I must look a fright!"

"Doris, you look lovely," he said, looking directly into her eyes.

Doris blushed prettily and said, "You Americans, you always think flattery will get you anything."

Behind her, Ariel was getting bored and asked, "Can I get back to my lunch, Doris?"

"Yes, yes, I'll help Mr ..."

"Blake, Court Blake," he supplied.

"Charmed," she said and actually giggled. "I suppose I can pose ... I mean hold the ledger for you."

"Great," he said, and instructed her to stand with the ledger facing outward, with her finger pointing at the entry.

He stood back a little and took several photos and then transferred one of the pictures to a USB thumb drive.

"Those were great," he told her and tried to show her the picture on the LCD screen of the camera, but she refused to look.

"Oh I never look at photos of myself. It would utterly destroy my self image."

"But why, you look lovely," he told her, and he meant it. He dropped his hand on hers, still resting on the ledger. She had to look away from the intensity of his gaze and he took the opportunity to get what he really wanted.

"Do you think you could print out one of those copies for me now, Doris?"

She nodded enthusiastically.

"And maybe you could add the spelling of your name, for the cut-line in the book."

"Of course," she said, delighted her picture would appear in the book.

"As a matter of fact, could I use your printer to print a copy of the photo I just took, and maybe you could sign that as well." He handed her the thumb drive.

"I don't know how ..." she said, confused at his request and also the process of printing directly from the thumb drive. But he recognized the printer model that stood behind the counter and directed her through the process of inserting the thumb drive, specifying the photo and printing it out.

Then he asked her to sign the photo and date it, which she did with a stamp kept behind the counter.

"And lastly Doris, could I have your phone number?"

This request surprised her more than his one for the print out.

"Why do you need that for your book?" she asked sharply, her suspicion suddenly aroused.

"As I said, I'm leaving Bath tomorrow, which means tonight I'm free."

From around the corner, he thought he heard the sound of Ariel voicing an exaggerated sound of disgust.

· First Impressions ·
Jane meets the improbably named Mary Crawford

Mary waited nervously, now the next person in line in a hallway that seemed full of women very much like her. They were all of an average or just above average height, all had brown hair of moderate length but which they all, except for Mary, wore up and most had brown or hazel eyes. Two were in costume. Most were also reading with rapt concentration Jane Austen novels, predominantly *Pride and Prejudice*. Mary was an exception, knowing little about Jane Austen except for a dim recollection of reading her in high school. She hadn't even thought of reading any of the novels when she was told she should audition to be the dead novelist's avatar.

Her lack of resolve could partly be attributed to her disinterest in Jane Austen but mostly because she frankly didn't give a damn whether she got the role. Since she'd applied to be an avatar she'd had the talk with one of her teachers where she learned that not being suited to be an actor was not a personal failing but simply a mismatch of desire and ability. She was considering leaving school and going back home and so really didn't need to land a role as an avatar, except for those outstanding debts she ought to address before leaving the city.

But the single-minded concentration of the other women auditioning did make her wonder whether she should have at least tried to remember something about the English novelist. The woman third in line was reading *Mansfield Park*, a unique choice among the group, but lying at her feet was a dog-eared paperback of *Pride and Prejudice*.

"Excuse me, do you mind if I look at your book, the one on the floor," she asked the duplicate of herself.

"Huh? No, help yourself," the woman said after a distracted glance at her questioner.

Mary reached down to pick up the book, then had to retrieve the half of the book and several individual pages that were no longer attached to the cover. That cover caught her eye as it depicted a young woman with dark black hair and sparkling eyes, younger than herself she thought, and wearing a bonnet that somehow appeared attractive, and also wearing an almost military looking jacket over a thin white gown. The artist, for it appeared to be a painting or at least made to look like a painting, had captured a woman of intelligence and some little mischief—a woman sure of herself and appearing not to have anything at all in common with Mary.

She would be fun to play, Mary thought. She turned the book over and saw from the description that the character had to be Elizabeth Bennet, the heroine. The back cover also displayed a painting of the author—really more of a sketch, apparently done by her sister.[1] Mary looked at the painting, which showed an unpleasant face, two parentheses bracketing a tight mouth and a long nose. She looked off to her right and her arms were crossed. She seemed to be sitting in judgment over something and the phrase "the suspicion that someone, somewhere is having fun"[2] came to her mind.

She turned back to the cover and saw the painting of Elizabeth and couldn't reconcile the two images. *Did her sister hate her?* she wondered. *Or maybe her sister wasn't a very good painter? Or maybe she got kind of grumpy in her old age?*

She opened the book to the foreword, which surprisingly wasn't written by a scholar of whom she'd ever heard but by Garrison Keillor,[3] whom she knew from public radio.

---

1   A rough pencil and watercolour portrait of Jane Austen by her sister Cassandra is the only known likeness of the author

2   American journalist and caustic wit HL Mencken described Puritanism thusly: "The haunting fear that someone, somewhere, may be happy."

3   The story-telling host of *A Prairie Home Companion* and author of *Lake Wobegon Days*

It's a mystery why we keep reading the works of an English spinster who died almost two hundred years ago and wrote of silly, little things like friendship and marriage and love. She didn't write about great intrigues or famous people, but she's never been out of print since 1832 so she must have found a way of finding the importance of silly little things. After all, silly little things remain the same while big important things change all the time.

I guess it's similar to the mystery of why anyone would listen to a grumpy Midwesterner talk about silly, little things like marriage and love ... and Ole and Lena jokes. To many people my voice on the radio probably seems as dusty and ancient as the words of that good woman from Hampshire, which is probably why the folks at Penguin Books thought I'd be a good choice to write this foreword, a task usually left to even dustier academic voices.

But as I write this amid all the news about the afterlife being real and provable and the possibility that maybe someday we'll get to talk to Jane Austen herself ...

"Miss Crawford, you're up." A man even younger than herself, holding a clipboard, was standing in front of her. He was smiling and motioning her to follow him, but for a second she found herself rooted to the spot. Reading Keillor's words suddenly made seem very important the role for which she was auditioning.

Finally she stood, nodded at the young man and followed him as he led her through a sea of cubicles and then into a corner office.

~

Jane looked up as this newest applicant entered the office. Despite her initial misgivings, she found herself enjoying the experience of essentially shopping for a new body. She'd never, at least in a modern sense, gone shopping before. She'd lived in a time before ready-made clothes, where usually you picked materials after seeing illustrations showing a dress design, or if you were lucky, dressmaker's dolls displaying the fashion. Afterward, you either found a woman in the village to make the dress for you, made it yourself or if you could afford it and lived in London or Bath, paid a dressmaker's shop to make it. But rarely could you try things "off the rack."

But now young women were parading before her and she had the luxury of admiring their fashion, their poise and most importantly their looks. In fact she had wanted to select the first applicant, a tall stunning beauty of auburn hair, ample bosom and striking blue eyes—much to the apoplexy of her agent.

"Jane, you can't pick her!" Melody said, after the applicant had left. "Why not?"

"She looks nothing like you. She has blue eyes, for Christ's sake. And she's stacked and taller than Shaq."[4]

"And how do you know how I looked?"

"Your sister's portrait."

Jane groaned silently. *That damn portrait.* She must as a good sister defend Cassandra's skill as an artist, *but that damn, awful portrait.*

"It was a sketch, nothing more. Cassie always said she'd ..." Jane stopped, realizing that she was whining. "I was considered tall."

Melody snorted, which Jane could not hear but suspected. "You were considered tall for a woman in the 1800s. That girl was a gigantor. You can't just buy the first dress you try on. After all, your public has an image of you ..."

"But I don't like that image. I don't want to be a 41-year-old spinster anymore."

"You don't have to be. But you can't be *Xena,*[5] *Warrior Princess* either."

The reference was lost on Jane but a quick search on YouTube showed her the absurdity of Melody's comparison, and also showed Jane the absurdity of her preference. So she remained largely noncommittal as the other candidates entered and left, keeping her notes to herself. Then Mary Crawford entered.

But then she stopped, momentarily ignoring the proffered hand of Mr Pembroke, and instead stared outward through the large windows of Mr Pembroke's office. Jane too looked out through the windows and saw the breath-taking view toward Central Park and thought how especially wonderful New York City could appear on a bright sunny day. Miss Mary Crawford—and suddenly Jane realized the import of the name—was the first applicant to appreciate the view.

"Miss Crawford?" Mr Pembroke asked, breaking the spell the view

---

4   Shaquille Rashaun O'Neal, a player for the National Basketball Association

5   Portrayed by Lucy Lawless in the television series that ran from 1995 to 2001. The titular character was said to be six feet tall.

had on the young lady. She started, then smiled and shook hands with Mr Pembroke and Melody, and then was introduced to Jane.

"Miss Crawford, I'd like you to meet Miss Jane Austen," Mr Pembroke said. He suddenly looked surprised and said, "I just realized ... Mary Crawford!"

He laughed and after a second was joined by Melody.

"Jane," she said, "that's a coincidence. Wait, that is your real name isn't it?"

Mary had no idea to what Melody referred but she realized that her name obviously had some association with the author.

"Yes, it's my real name," she said, trying to project confidence that she appreciated the coincidence.

"Mary Crawford was an enjoyable character to write, but I hope you don't share her faults," Jane said.

Mary heard the words come from a speaker attached to what looked like a smartphone. She assumed it was a portable AfterNet terminal through which the author was speaking. There was an empty chair immediately next to the terminal.

"Miss Austen? Excuse me, where are you?"

"I am in the chair before you. Forgive me, you seem somewhat uncomfortable. Please have a seat."

Mary took the seat Mr Pembroke offered.

"Do I detect that you are as new to the role of an avatar as I am to the need for one?" Jane asked, although she knew from the information provided by the agency that Mary had yet to play the part of an avatar. She was being considered primarily because of her appearance and her considerable ability to interface with an AfterNet field.

"Yes, I am new to this. I've met other disembodied people of course, but ..."

This was a partial lie. Mary had corresponded with a few disembodied people online, but had never met one in person ... so to speak.

"But talking to an empty chair is disconcerting, I understand. And you have shown me how important it is that I employ an avatar for my upcoming book tour."

"I'm sorry," Mary said nervously, understanding how wrong it would be for someone so untried to expect such an opportunity. "I think maybe it would be better if you interview the next candidate."

She made to rise.

"Please, Miss Crawford, have I offended you in some way?"

The question disconcerted Mary.

"No, of course not. I think it's the other way round. I mean you're Jane Austen and I'm just some schlub[6] who doesn't know the first thing about you auditioning to play you, well more than play you, but be you. Most of the women out there have their noses in your books and I didn't even think to look you up."

"You don't know who Jane Austen is?" Melody asked, alarmed.

"Well, yes, I do know who she is. I read her in high school, but that's about it. I don't think it qualifies me to be you."

"Why don't you let me be the judge of that." Jane said. "By the bye, do you even know the significance of your name, why we find it so surprising?"

Mary was ashamed to say, "No, I do not."

"She is a character in *Mansfield Park*, and I enjoyed creating her almost as much as I did Emma," Jane said. "Mary Crawford, my Mary Crawford, was a person who could behave well, even generously when it did not cost her anything or to be fair, even when it did not benefit her. She was in her own way genuinely a friend to poor, drab Fanny. But she also treated Fanny as a plaything, but then so did I. Sadly my Mary Crawford never had the conviction to choose happiness over status."

Mary laughed. "I know someone like that." She thought of her brother, the fair-haired child of her family. She noticed that Mr Pembroke and the agent, whose name she forgot, were waiting for her to elucidate.

"Oh, my brother," Mary supplied. "Your Mary Crawford sounds like my brother."

"Don't tell me his name is Henry," Melody said.

"Uh no, it's Nathan. I guess Henry Crawford's also in *Mansfield Park?*"

"Yes he is and he's a thoroughly rotten scoundrel," Jane said.

"Who was also a lot of fun to write, I'll bet?"

"Oh yes, quite fun. Now, Miss Crawford, perhaps you might tell me something of yourself despite your complete and utter lack of suitability for the role of yours truly."

Mary allowed herself to relax, dropping her shoulders and sitting back in her chair slightly, but careful not to slump. Somehow she had

---

6 From Yiddish, a talentless, unattractive, or boorish person

the impression that Jane Austen never slumped. For some reason, perhaps because she needed to talk, she revealed more of herself than she ought. Her words came in a torrent.

She spoke of her upbringing in Ohio; of her mother, a Briton who had grown up in Hounslow, which Mary rightly believed to be a London suburb—"I knew a very pretty young girl from Hounslow" mused Mr Pembroke; of her decision to become an actor despite her diffidence—"a young lady who leaves home and moves to New York City must have some confidence," said Jane; and of her partiality to musicals, including *West Side Story*—which occasioned Mary and Melody to relate the plot to Jane, with musical accompaniment that sadly the terminal interpreted as "unintelligible."

Mary found herself enjoying the interview, but it was finally interrupted by a knock at the door and an assistant informing them that there were still many candidates waiting in the hallway.

"Thank you for taking the time to come today, Miss Crawford," Jane said.

"Yes, it was very nice meeting you and we'll let you know soon if we'll need you to come back," Melody said.

"Good day to you, Miss Crawford," Mr Pembroke said with finality.

Mary thanked them all in turn and was led out of the office by yet another assistant and within a few minutes found herself out on the street looking up at 1745 Broadway.[7] She felt adrift after having made a connection with Melody, Mr Pembroke and most of all Jane Austen. She could have sworn it had been going so well but then they had hustled her out so quickly and efficiently, like a trapdoor had opened and dropped her body to the river below. She shrugged her shoulders and walked back to her subway stop and again contemplated that New York City and her dream of acting were to be consigned to the past.

---

7 The offices of Random House, Jane's publisher

· Planning for the future ·
Melody faces the changes in her life

Melody pondered the cities in the upcoming tour. In her office, she'd put up a large map of the US with little pushpins for each city and was even tempted to connect them with bits of string. The logistics of the whole affair was starting to overwhelm her and she knew she needed someone to help with the burden. Her former assistant had moved to the West Coast last year, ostensibly to open her own agency, but Rebecca had really left because her fiancé had taken a job there.

Rebecca's departure left Melody with no one except her ancient receptionist. Lillian only worked mornings answering the phone and occasionally ran errands and was all but retired. Melody kept her on for the pretence of being more than a one-person company and because Lillian actually knew the business.

Intellectually Melody knew that her world had changed with Jane's contract. She would either have to make Jane her only client and transition from literary agent to manager/personal representative, or she would actually need to hire associates who could handle her other clients. She glanced at the stack of unsolicited résumés from eager, young literary agents and at the enormous bags of query letters she'd received since the announcement of Jane's contract.

She looked around her cramped office, still looking almost exactly as Janet Appelbaum had left it. The walls were filled with book covers, awards and photographs, plus the detritus of personal belongings Melody had introduced over the years to make the place cozy. Lillian had also contributed with her photos of other people's cats.

I will hate to give this place up, but it's too small for Jane Austen MediaCorp or whatever. Oh God, I'm getting gloomy!

She turned her attention back to the map and the tour. She could definitely meet Jane in Seattle, where there was a particularly enthusiastic Janeite installed at a Barnes & Noble store. She'd been one of Jane's earliest supporters, in fact, and should be able to arrange a good signing. And from there to Fort Worth for the AGM.

She sighed and prayed that by Jane's arrival in Fort Worth, a higher percentage of the Austen community would accept her. A recent poll at *Jane Austen Today* showed about 50% accepted Jane as Jane. It was hardly a scientific poll, however, and could easily be swayed by Jane's supporters and detractors. And it wouldn't take much to sway opinion one way or another, she knew. If Jane should say something injudicious … the thought sent a cold shiver down her back. She thought of Henry Austen's treacly words about his late sister in his Biographical Notice that prefaced the posthumous publication of *Persuasion* and *Northanger Abbey*. It gave little indication that Jane could vent with the best, although Melody did have to allow that Jane's long afterlife might have sharpened her tongue.

I need something that will help the public identify with Jane, although that means I run the risk of making the public identify with her avatar as well.

The thought of the avatar becoming the public face of Jane had always worried Melody, because she understood her responsibility to Jane's legacy. Jane had already been famous for two hundred years and she might be famous for countless more. And who knew how many avatars might be needed over that time. It was important that Jane had an identity independent of the current avatar.

Melody suddenly worried what would happen if she died. Who would take care of Jane?

Stupid, that would be me. I might still be her agent even after I die. I might need to take someone on … Oh God!

The image of her disembodied self working with Jane through a succession of avatars over centuries made her stomach churn.

Is that what it's like to be Jane? No wonder the disembodied go crazy. Got to think of something else. Go back to the problem of how to make the public sympathize with Jane and not just her avatar. I need something to make people believe in Jane.

Those last words conjured the image of an 'I believe in Jane" button, the words superimposed on Cassandra's watercolour.

No, not the watercolour. Jane's too old in that. We should commission a new portrait that represents Jane in her prime.

She and Alan had talked about a new portrait before they'd made their decision to hire an avatar and the idea had been lost in their worry about Jane objecting to the idea. But Melody decided it was long past time that Jane had an official portrait. She made a note to ask Mr Pembroke to suggest an artist who would be up to the task.

Of more pressing concern was the choice of Jane's avatar. She had been concerned by some of Jane's preferences, including mousy Miss Crawford and the Xena look-a-like. She would have to ensure the latter preference never became known and reflected that yet again some foible of Jane's character would end up redacted.

From 23 candidates, three finalists had emerged. There was Miranda Prentiss, the bookish stammerer who seemed to know Jane's life better than Jane; Linda Holland, a museum docent by day and stand-up comedian at night; and Mary Crawford.

Melody had run a background check on Miss Crawford, not trusting the authenticity of her name, but in fact she was born Mary Crawford in Ohio to an elderly father and his comparatively younger second wife.

Mary had a half-brother, Nathan, and a half-sister, Barbara. She seemed to have few accomplishments, other than her ill-conceived notion of moving to New York City to study to be an actress; an admittedly pleasant singing voice, which Melody assumed was lost on Jane anyway; and very high marks for her ability to use an AfterNet terminal.

Not only did Melody find the coincidence of Mary Crawford's name suspicious—although it was hardly an unusual name—she was also annoyed that someone with no knowledge of the famous author should have been a finalist. True, Ms Holland did not profess a deep understanding of Austen, but Melody thought Holland's improvisational skills and museum experience made her quite attractive. Melody hoped to promote Holland at the next round of interviews.

· Finalists ·

Jane and the finalists begin training

"Now Miss Austen, I'll need you to relax. These new terminals require precise calibration." Jane glanced nervously at Melody, who kept nodding her reassurance. Even though it was still easy to see her friend, the mesh ball that enclosed her essence still felt very confining. She watched the white-coated technician fiddle with complicated electronic equipment before he said, "I have to warn you that you'll experience some sensations, both good and bad, but it will last only five seconds. In three, two, one ..."

Sensations, that would be novelty indeed. I haven't felt anything since ...

Suddenly Jane felt a whirl of emotions and feelings and most unexpectedly a flood of sense memories, the smell of hay, rain, the feel of muslin, the pain of a stinging nettle, the memory of her parents telling her of their remove to Bath, the rustling sound of the pages of the first printed copy of *Sense and Sensibility* she had ever held, the death of her father ...

And then it was over, but not before she uttered a phrase that from the look on her friend's face had been transmitted through the After-Net field.

"Jane!" Melody said. "Where did that come from?"

She could almost feel the flush that came to her so easily when alive.

To cover her embarrassment, she said, "Two of my brothers were sailors," she said, which hardly excused or explained her words.

Melody laughed and responded. "And two of them were clergymen!"

The technician appeared undisturbed by the outburst; obviously he had heard similar exclamations.

"Do the ... must the avatars endure this as well?"

The technician answered her without taking his eyes off his equipment. "What? Oh, well they did it when they first applied, although the experience isn't as intense for the living." Then he turned back to her and opened the metal mesh ball and she escaped.

"But excuse me, why is all this necessary?" Jane asked. "I did not have to endure all this when I first communicated through an After-Net terminal."

The man sighed and said, "You know they're supposed to explain this before you come down here for calibration." He fixed his gaze on Jane, which was either impressive intuition or a stroke of luck, and continued. "An avatar's terminal is a lot more advanced than a regular terminal and provides more information than just your voice in their ear. It can pick up your emotional state and adjust the speech synthesis to reflect that. It also gives clues to the wearer as to your position, so you don't have to tell him ..."—he looked at his clipboard—"... or her to turn left or walk straight ahead. They'll follow you around. You can also program the terminal as well. Honestly, they're supposed to tell you this but they never do. OK, Ms Austen, you're done here. If you and your friend will just wait outside, someone will be by to take you to the training course."

Melody and Jane left the room, both of them feeling a little overwhelmed at the brusque treatment from the technician.

"I'm sorry Jane, he shouldn't have treated you like that."

"No, no don't worry Melody. It's ... actually refreshing to be reminded just what I'm about to ... the implication of it ... I'm sorry, I am not normally so discombobulated. Perhaps it was his mention of a training course. Whatever could that mean?"

Jane and Melody were soon to find out after a rail-thin, young woman, dressed in black slacks and silk black top, led them down the hallway and through double doors into a large room resembling, in a minimalist sort of way, a television studio. There was a raised platform or stage with three chairs presumably intended for an interviewer and two guests, with very bright lights shining on the stage. There was even a television camera mounted on wheels trained on the stage. They found Mr Pembroke, the saleswoman from the avatar agency whose name Jane could not remember and one of the candidates, the stammerer, Ms Prentiss. Jane also saw two others, a man and woman, standing further back in the shadows.

"Ms Austen, so good to see you again," the saleswoman said.

"Miss Austen says hello, Ms Parker." Melody said for her friend, "and asks if you would please call her Jane. And she also says hello to you, Alan and Miranda."

"Then please call me Sharon," the saleswoman said, "which you will be able to do more directly in a moment once we ... oh, here we are."

She stopped as the technician from the calibration room arrived. She nodded to him.

"Who's this go on?" he asked abruptly.

"I think that would be me," Ms Prentiss said, stepping forward. "Good morning Miss Austen, Ms Kramer."

The technician approached Ms Prentiss, but stopped and again with uncanny accuracy looked directly at Jane and asked, "Are you right handed?"

It was a question that surprised Jane, it not having been an issue for almost two hundred years, but she answered in the affirmative, which Melody communicated. He then put an armband holding a portable terminal around Ms Prentiss' left arm and gave her two small wireless earbuds, which Ms Prentiss inserted. With her right hand she then activated the device on her left arm and after a few seconds walked to Jane's immediate right.

"Hello, Jane, with your permission, I'm ready to act as your avatar." Ms Prentiss's voice almost seemed to sound in Jane's mind; the After-Net field of the terminal was so strong and pure that it washed out the field of the less sophisticated terminal Melody wore.

"Yes please ... go ahead," Jane said.

"Actually, it's the other way round. Once you give permission, I act on your behalf. You have only to think what you want to say and I will say it for you. You only have to move and I will follow. At first I'll have to edit you to prevent my saying what I think are your private thoughts. I would suggest you asking your friend to turn off her terminal, but you'll have to speak that thought. Are you ready?"

It was then that Jane realized their conversation was silent. Ms

Prentiss did not speak out loud for her terminal to interpret, but instead could project her thoughts directly into the AfterNet field where it was relayed to Jane. This was her first experience of a living person talking directly to her.

The surprise of it slightly delayed Jane's answer. She regained her composure, however, and said, "Melody, would you please turn off your terminal?"

Jane found that the terminal interpreted her thoughts almost as easily as if she were speaking out loud. She hoped her casual thoughts would not be captured by the terminal as well, and then panicked when she thought that thought had just been captured. But a quick glance at the transcript reassured her.

Ms Prentiss spoke those words aloud a mere fraction of a second after Jane said them. Melody raised an eyebrow at the experience of Ms Prentiss, affecting an English accent, speaking for Jane. The technician, having observed Ms Prentiss closely, nodded to her and left the room.

"I believe we're ready to get started," Ms Parker said after stepping forward. She turned to look at Ms Prentiss but addressed her as Jane: "Miss Austen, we'll begin with a mock interview to see how you and Ms Prentiss interact. If you'll follow me onto the stage."

To the others, it appeared that Ms Prentiss hesitated, but in reality it was Jane who was momentarily confused by the experience of the saleswoman addressing Ms Prentiss as herself. After a second's pause, however, Jane rallied and said, "Of course, Sharon," which her avatar relayed. She then moved to the stage and her avatar dutifully followed. Ms Parker took the seat at stage right, while Ms Prentiss sat in the middle chair. Jane, suddenly understanding, sat in the chair at stage left.

The man and woman who had been in the shadows came forward. The man went behind the camera and the woman came on stage to put lapel microphones on the two seated women. Jane watched this and marvelled at the efficiency of it all. It was obvious also that Ms Parker and Ms Prentiss were well prepared for this and Jane also noticed that they wore heavier makeup than fashionable, presumably because of the filming.

After the woman stagehand left and the two women seated themselves comfortably, Ms Parker told the cameraman to begin filming.

After a slight wait, the cameraman began counting down with his fingers and then pointed at Ms Parker. At the same time, Jane noticed a red light appear on the camera, which Ms Parker addressed.

"We're here today with Jane Austen, the author of those classics you remember from high school, like *Pride and Prejudice* and *Emma*, and which have been made countless times as movies here and abroad. After an almost two hundred year absence from the new releases category, she's back with her latest novel, *Sanditon*." She then turned to Ms Prentiss and asked. "What's it like, Miss Austen, to find yourself competing in the modern world of publishing?"

Jane froze. The novelty of the situation left her bewildered. She realized now that the avatar agency had intentionally given her little instruction to see how she would cope, which raised her ire. She was about to complain about her treatment, when she found Ms Prentiss saying: "Thank you very much for asking me on your show, Ms Parker. As I'm sure you understand, this is a novel experience for me."

She's starting without me, Jane thought, and then realized that thought was probably communicated to her avatar.

"You'd better think of something to say," Ms Prentiss silently said to Jane. "I can only stall so long."

What was the question? Jane quickly looked back through the transcript of the conversation, and thought loudly of a reply.

The others in the studio might have seen Ms Prentiss wince ever so slightly, but she relayed Jane's reply after only a slight pause.

"Now as to your question, that's very interesting because I truthfully had not imagined myself in competition with anyone, other than perhaps myself ... my reputation that is."

There, that's a clever response. I have led her to a path I am more comfortable following. Jane again worried her fleeting thought might have been transmitted to Ms Prentiss but a quick look at the transcript showed that it remained unsaid.

"You mean that you're worried whether the critical response to your book will match that of your other six novels? Or that you're worried that not everyone has embraced the idea that you are in fact the real Jane Austen?"

Jane was bothered at the impertinence of the latter question and chose to address the first. The thought of the easy solution encouraged her.

"Why I am worried about the critical response, of course. When I wrote my first six novels, it was obviously a much simpler world. Even the most vitriolic critic had to put pen to paper and take that to a publisher where type would be set and a day or a week or month later that opinion would be printed. Now anyone can voice their opinion instantly, and yes I admit the thought frightens me, but not as much as the two centuries of silence I endured frightened me."

And so the interview continued, and in the questions posed by Ms Parker, Jane recognized the hands of her friend Melody and Mr Pembroke. They had obviously prepared questions designed to unnerve her and she felt a rising confidence as she found ways to avoid, deflect or rephrase questions. It was not unlike the etiquette of calming a quarrelsome relative or the deflecting the impertinence of an over ardent admirer. It was a skill to which she had grown unaccustomed, but which she found enjoyable to relearn.

After the interview, which lasted only about five minutes, Jane was led to another room they called the obstacle course, although it was nothing more than a furnished room. Jane was asked, via instructions pre-recorded on the terminal Ms Prentiss wore, to navigate the room and pick up and handle various objects, such as a brush, a television remote and a cell phone. Ms Prentiss was unaware of the pre-recorded messages and instead responded to Jane's instructions.

At first Jane moved too quickly for her avatar, but soon they were moving in unison, almost a dance. She was confused by the television remote and the cell phone but decided she could simply depend on Ms Prentiss to operate those devices.

During all this Ms Prentiss refrained from any remarks and Jane refrained from posing anything as a question. The cool efficiency of the woman impressed Jane and she recalled that Ms Prentiss had been with the agency three years. Her professionalism was apparent.

At the end of the training session, Jane finally addressed her avatar directly.

"That was very impressive, Miranda," Jane said, successfully remembering to call the woman by her first name.

"As were you, Miss Austen. Was this truly your first time partnering with an avatar?"

"Partnering, yes, that's what it is," she replied, although truthfully she meant it to be a private thought.

"I would have edited that," Ms Prentiss confirmed.

"Thank you. Yes, it was my first time and it was a very ... I don't know how to describe it ... it was very intimate."

"It should be. And Miss Austen, may I say how very honoured I am to be a finalist. I have been a fan of your stories since … well since high school. I've seen every movie and been to live productions. I truly hope you will pick me."

Ms Prentiss's professionalism fell away and Jane was confronted for the first time with an adoring fan.

"Yes, well, I'm sure you give me too much credit, but I thank you sincerely."

Afterward she reunited with Melody, happy for the moment with the more primitive terminal her agent wore.

"How was it Jane? What was it like to have an avatar?"

"Beyond anything I could imagine, but I find myself somewhat fatigued. Perhaps I could watch you take lunch."

A look at the clock on the terminal confirmed it was near 2 pm. She knew Melody would be hungry.

Melody looked at her watch and agreed. "Sure, we've got some time before the next interview, but I'm not going to eat clotted cream again just to please you. I could feel my arteries harden while I ate."

· Differing opinions ·
Jane and Melody clash on choice of avatar

"I really think your avatar should have read one of your books," Melody said. Or at least that's what Jane believed her agent had said, although it was difficult to follow Melody's words as she bounced up and down on the elliptical trainer.

"I don't see what difference that makes," Jane said in response. "The avatar is merely my mouthpiece."

"Really Jane, 'mouthpiece?' Who are you, Philip Marlowe?[1] And just yesterday you were saying your avatar had to do more than just parrot your words."

Jane could not contradict Melody, for she had said something similar while defending Mary as her choice. So she decided to change tactics.

"Then who do you suggest?" Jane asked.

"Well isn't it obvious? Miranda did a great job with you on the interview."

"Who? Oh, the stammerer." Jane immediately felt guilty for adopting this ploy of pretend ignorance and disparagement. Ms Prentiss certainly had impressed with her skills. Mary Crawford, with her inexperience, had not.

---

1 The hard-boiled detective created by author Raymond Chandler

"Oh Jane, that is beneath you. You know Miranda Prentiss was by far the best in the mock interview. She was perfect."

This surprised Jane, for she thought Melody more partial to Ms Holland, but her friend had apparently changed camps after Ms Prentiss's perfect performance.

But of course that was Jane's principal objection to Ms Prentiss. She was perfect and loudly praised and admired by everyone, even Jane. She had to admit that Ms Prentiss' skill at conveying her words so effortlessly was an amazing experience, whereas Melody said Mary Crawford looked like someone "hearing a who."[2] Jane wasn't sure what that meant, but assumed she meant Mary gave the impression she was merely reciting Jane's words transmitted through the earbuds.

Jane had to admit that her interaction with Mary was not perfect, or good or even acceptable, but by the end of the interview, they had improved. Part of Jane's preference for Mary was influenced by the fact that Mary wasn't familiar with her novels. She most enjoyed interacting with people new to her work.

"... the fact her name is Mary Crawford. You think it's some sort of sign," Melody said. Jane realized she had drifted away from Melody's terminal and had just drifted back, catching the tail end of Melody's argument.

"Nonsense, I realize it's just coincidence," Jane replied. "I know it cannot be an uncommon name."

"And it's a little too ... well it's a little too weird."

Jane detected a possibility.

"Is that why you dismiss Mary?" Jane asked. She knew Melody had a distaste for anything that smacked of the supernatural. She had an almost superstitious distaste of it.

"What? No, I just thought maybe she'd given a false name to ..." she trailed off without completing her theory.

"Is it likely the avatar agency would have allowed such an imposture?"

"No, it's not. I double-checked. It really is her name."

---

2   A reference to the Dr Seuss story *Horton Hears a Who!* In the children's story, only Horton the elephant can hear the infinitesimally small inhabitants of Whoville. He is ridiculed for believing in the existence of something only he can hear (because of his big ears).

"I really think, Melody, that it should be enough that I enjoy Miss Crawford's company and that I think I might work well with her."

"She's too young for one thing," Melody said, desperate for another argument against Mary.

"And yet you and Mr Pembroke had earlier suggested a younger avatar would make me accessible to younger readers."

Melody was ready to object to this until she remembered her private conversation with Mr Pembroke where the subject of a younger avatar had been discussed.

"I think Ms Prentiss, while very capable, might be perceived as too much of a pedant." Jane added. "She might appeal to Janeites, but I thought our intent was to attract a new audience to my novels."

"But do you think you can improve her ... Mary's ... skills enough that she won't look like she's hearing voices?"

"I think that possible, yes. But in all honesty, I think at least half the blame falls on me. Ms Prentiss overcame my own poor performance in the interview while I think Miss Crawford may have been distracted by my own nervousness. I'm sure we would improve with practice. After all, neither of us had ever done anything like this before."

Melody wanted to point out this would be one of the arguments for choosing Ms Prentiss, but Jane's comment about Miranda's pedantry was accurate. She did come off a bit academic.

"I suppose it is a matter of who you think you would work best with," Melody then conceded. "I mean ultimately it is your choice."

"But only if I have your support, Melody. I should not want to make such a decision without your support."

Melody rolled her eyes at this, knowing full well that Jane was peddling snake oil.[3]

"Of course Jane, we work best when we work as a team," Melody said.

---

3 A quack cure or remedy with no medicinal value

· Sandwich money ·
Jane chooses Mary

"Argh!" Mary cried in a voice so small no one in the library looked at her. She put down the book she held, not knowing what purpose it would serve to read it now. She'd reserved the book before her mock interview with Jane, but now she didn't know if there'd be any point in checking it out. Based on her performance, she was unlikely to be hired as the author's avatar. In fact, she'd be lucky if the agency decided to keep her on call.

She looked at the book's cover, which showed a woman painting another woman awkwardly holding a Grecian urn and the simple title at the top and the author's name. She'd enjoyed watching the movie—Gwyneth Paltrow[1] almost took her breath away she was so lovely in the role—and had decided to read *Emma* even before *Pride and Prejudice*. Despite his charms, she found Colin Firth a little too insufferable in the miniseries, and that was enough to dispose her toward *Emma*.

Mary's feelings were conflicted because though she had to admit her performance was awful, she didn't think it reflected at all on her acting ability. Being able to voice what someone was saying in your ear in a computer monotone was not a skill she'd practiced, although she thought she'd improved by the end of the interview.

What truly upset her about the interview, however, was the fact that

---

1   The actress portrayed Emma in a 1996 film

she was beginning to like Jane Austen. Her patience and kindness during the whole experience was something she'd missed since moving to New York. And she felt that by being Jane's avatar, she had a connection to all the actors who'd ever played a Jane Austen character.

She got up from her chair still undecided whether to check the book out. Looking ahead at the self-checkout kiosks, she saw they were all occupied, but as she approached, one was freed and so she stopped to swipe the book and her library card.

She left the library and stepped out into the brisk air. She turned toward the subway station that would take her home, but decided she didn't much feel like returning to the dingy flat she shared with two other women, both of whom were out of town. The flat, normally a cramped space, would, in her current mood, feel too empty. So she found a coffee shop and began reading the book, her first real introduction to Austen.

The language was remarkably modern for being almost two centuries old, although she wished her ancient brain-dead phone had a web browser so she might look up "valetudinarian."[2] She was actually making rapid progress through the book, although she realized it was coming at the expense of some retention. The paragraphs were long and complex enough that she'd started skimming, which was always her habit, especially when reading literature with a capital "L."

She was a little confused at the notion of Frank Churchill being Mr Weston's son, but being raised by his aunt for the reasons stated. And she was also confused by Harriet Smith being brought up by a woman who essentially ran either a day care centre, an orphanage or an unlicensed school. She vaguely remembered these complications from watching the movie but the full import of the vastly different world of the early 19th century struck her. The idea that if you lost your wife you could ship off your son to a relative seemed bizarre, but then she remembered the complications of Charles Dickens stories and also some of the scandals from the southern branch of her own family.

She'd read long enough to have finished her first cup of coffee, taken advantage of the one free refill and then used a shift change to sneak in an additional refill. Having seen the movie had certainly helped. She thought she would not have gotten as far reading otherwise and was already looking forward to Emma painting Harriet's portrait. Of

---

2   A person unduly anxious about their health; a hypochondriac

course the more interested she became, the more she felt the loss of not getting the job.

She was thinking she might get a sandwich to counteract the pit of coffee in her stomach, and was calculating how much money she had when her cell phone rang.

She answered it absentmindedly and heard a flat, digitized voice in response to her "hello."

"Hello Miss Crawford, this is Jane Austen."

The surprise of getting a call from a disembodied author was a little too much for Mary and she dropped her phone to the table, where it bounced and fell to the floor. Mary let out a little cry that brought the attention of others in the coffee shop. Several well-meaning people bent down to pick up the phone, which resulted in no one being able to pick it up at all. And so it took some time before Mary was handed back her phone, fortunately still working. She heard the digitized voice saying, "Hello? Hello?" with a fake interrogative accent.

"Miss Austen, hi. I'm sorry, I dropped the phone. I didn't expect … I didn't know you could …"

"Quite all right, Miss Crawford. Melody always says I shouldn't call, but I am unable to appreciate why getting a call from a disembodied person should be so much more upsetting than talking to one online. I fear the intimacy of telephonic conversation remains a mystery to me."

"No, I'm not upset," she lied, for dropping her phone to the floor certainly would indicate she had been upset. "Just surprised."

Austen's response took long enough that Mary thought perhaps her phone had been damaged. Then Mary realized the pause was the consequence of the author forming the words in her mind and then projecting them into the AfterNet field, after which the terminal translated those words into speech.

She'd already grown accustomed to the pauses while speaking to Austen in person—or whatever it could be called—but over the telephone, the pauses were more distracting.

"Well, I hope you'll find this a pleasant surprise, but I wanted to tell you that I … we have chosen you to be my avatar, if that will be convenient."

"Yes, very convenient," Mary said, and silently added: *especially as I was just wondering if I had enough change to buy a sandwich.*

"Good. Would you be available soon? I don't wish to rush you, but …"

"I can begin immediately. Or now. I could start now. I mean I can be there in …" Mary didn't finish the sentence for she realized she didn't know where there was.

"Oh, I wish I could make this thing laugh," Jane replied. "I am told the effect is rather too horrible for words. Tomorrow will suffice. I believe the avatar agency will allow us the use of a room where we might start practicing. I … I will be honest, I do not think we were at our best for the mock interview, but I do think we improved."

"I am sorry, Miss Austen. I'm afraid my acting classes didn't cover … but I really think I got better."

"No, Miss Crawford, please do not feel the need to apologize. We are both new to this and with practice we shall become accomplished, but it will be hard work. And so we begin tomorrow morning, say at 10 o'clock?"

"Yes, that will be fine, Miss Austen."

"Please call me Jane. If you are to be my voice, we must become fast friends."

"Thank you, Jane. And I would be pleased if you would call me Mary." Mary wondered at the formality of her reply and realized she was starting to slip into the role.

"Thank you, Mary. Oh, Melody reminds me you might want to arrive a little earlier for the agency will undoubtedly want you to fill out more paperwork. Until tomorrow then."

Jane rang off and Mary put away her phone, slightly dazed to have had her first phone call from a dead person and gotten a job. But after contemplating her good luck for a minute, her stomach reminded her that it was still hungry. With a smile, she decided to use her one still working credit card to get that sandwich.

· Hampshire ·

Jane compounds her lie

BertieFromHants Says:

Jane, so glad you made it.

JaneAusten3 Says:

Oh Albert, I am so sorry to have missed our last rendezvous!

BertieFromHants Says:

Amazing woman! I did not mean anything by my remark.

JaneAusten3 Says:

Oh, come now. "So glad you made it." Is there not an accusation, Albert?

BertieFromHants Says:

Very well, perhaps a little. I was disappointed you couldn't join me for our usual conversation.

JaneAusten3 Says:

I did send you an email.

BertieFromHants Says:

Yes, thank you, but it hardly made up for missing your company.

JaneAusten3 Says:

I am suitably chastened, sir. Am I forgiven?

BertieFromHants Says:

Once you tell me what made you miss our chat.

JaneAusten3 Says:

I've started employment … a job. I have a job. That's such an odd thing to say. I have a job.

BertieFromHants Says:

Jane, that's brilliant! And I know what you mean. As inane as my job is, it's great to be working again. What is it?

JaneAusten3 Says:

It's in the publishing industry. I'm editing a book.

BertieFromHants Says:

Well with a name like yours I shouldn't wonder you'd be good at it. Do you have to go to an office? And what company?

JaneAusten3 Says:

No, I can work from … well where ever I happen to be. And it's Random House.

BertieFromHants Says:

In London?

JaneAusten3 Says:

No, I'm in New York City, which I am sure my status reflects … oh, no I guess I hadn't updated that. Well, I am in America and I am staying with a friend—a living friend. So I suppose I have taken all your advice to heart.

BertieFromHants Says:

I did say you would enjoy visiting America.

JaneAusten3 Says:

And I said I had visited America, and I haven't said that I am enjoying myself.

BertieFromHants Says:

But you are, aren't you?

JaneAusten3 Says:

Very well, Mr I Am So Clever. I am enjoying myself, despite my preference for a quiet life. It certainly helps that I can't hear the traffic or smell … well I shan't say what I am spared. But bagels, I wish I might smell those. And the lox, I wish I could taste that.

BertieFromHants Says:

Well look at the shiksa now.

JaneAusten3 Says:

What is a shiksa?

BertieFromHants Says:

LOL It's a Gentile woman, a non Jew. Sorry, I've been in Florida quite some time and have successfully absorbed the culture.

JaneAusten3 Says:

Oh, so you are making fun of me—again. But I suppose I am "going native." It is the folly—or the talent—of the British to do so. But the longer I've existed and the more I've travelled, I find myself enjoying the mutability of mankind more and more. (JaneAusten3 is still typing.)

JaneAusten3 Says:

We started off with the same basic needs for food and shelter and yet we end up with the Anglican Church, Hindoos and Scientology. So many faiths, beliefs, customs, rules and accepted behaviours and all the ... well I will not be so judgmental as to call them wrong, but ...

BertieFromHants Says:

My word, Jane, you've grown philosophic from a simple jibe.

JaneAusten3 Says:

Yes, well travel has that effect on me. Restore me to the quiet and green of Hampshire and I shall promptly rusticate.

BertieFromHants Says:

Have you found yourself a small fish in a big pond?

JaneAusten3 Says:

How perceptive you are, although in fact I'll have you know I am considered a person of some importance now, but yes, perhaps I do feel myself thrust into a world of business of which I know little. Enough self pity, however, tell me of your family, especially your little Alicia. How did she perform at the school fete?

Albert talked of his granddaughter and great grandchildren and his great, great grandchildren with delight, and Jane envied him his relationship with his family. It had been relatively easy for him, a man not made famous, to be welcomed into his extended family. Jane had little contact with her family, although she had received warm wishes from Robert Knight, president of the Jane Austen Society and a descendant of her brother Edward.

She had, of course, followed the lives of those relatives alive when she had died, and even the generation that followed, but drifted away from them as she had drifted away from England. And upon her return, she found a world too changed and a family unrecognizable. By the Great War, she no longer followed her family, save for a very distant relation who she thought resembled her brother Henry and whose name he shared. And it was interest in this relative that brought her to the mud and the horror of the Somme and unbeknownst to her at the time, also to be in attendance at the death of the man who would be her friend decades later.

~

After their chat ended, Albert chuckled at the interest of his friend in the little reports of his family. She had actually corrected him on the age of Thomas and she reminded him that it had been she who recommended the *Thomas the Tank Engine* DVD as his birthday present.

He also had to laugh at how deftly she'd managed to avoid rejecting his offer to pay her admission to the AGM. He had an uncharitable thought she'd invented the job as an excuse not to accept his charity, but as she did confirm she would be attending—as a paying attendee—he had to assume her employment was genuine.

And as always after a chat with her he felt the warm glow he remembered after receiving one of the letters from his wife. And as always he felt the tug of guilt that this woman should excite in him feelings he knew were the province of his long dead wife Catherine.

He tried to push the guilt aside and instead he found additional humour in the patterns of his friend's conversation. She always began her chats in the modern vernacular but by the end of it would always devolve into the language of Hampshire. She might not actually claim to be Jane Austen, but she certainly was of Hampshire.

And she had died a long time ago, for she used expressions familiar to him from his youth. As a gentleman, he'd never pried into her age, but he had the unfounded belief that she might have died during the same epidemic that claimed him.

And then he remembered his own language, how he became far courtlier than was his wont when alive. His romance of Catherine was never as mannered as his conversations with Jane. He had fallen in love with Catherine on the spot and within a week had proposed and within a month had married. His memory of the eloquence of his proposal shamed him, it being along the lines of "Wotcher say we get married?"

She had deserved better than him, certainly better than being a widow at twenty with two babies.

Is that my compensation? I gave Catherine my passion and I give Jane what little eloquence I can command.

The thought struck him hard and brought him out of the AfterNet field and made him aware of his surroundings and the sleeping octogenarian at the card table and the brisk steps of the caregivers in the hallway and the overhead fluorescent lights of the games room, especially the one that presaged its imminent death by its annoying flicker.

I just equated Jane with Catherine. I just equated a dead woman with ... And then that thought struck him even harder. *They're both dead and so am I. I'm being a ridiculous old man. Even Mr Cardenas is more alive than me,* he thought, looking at his fellow inmate who'd fallen asleep in the games room.

Day is dead, and let us sleep.[1] *If only I could.*

---

1   From the poem of the same name by Augusta Davies Webster

· Something fresher ·
It was the best of times?

"It was hardly the best of times, but Judith had to concede it was hardly the worst. Mostly it just lay there, waiting." She laughed at her own cleverness or perhaps pretension. Truth was, she was not as enamoured of Dickens as a novelist should be. She tore the paper out of the typewriter, mashed it into a ball and threw it at the wastebasket. It did not go in but bounced off the edge and fell to the floor where it joined its compatriots of similar failed openings.

Undaunted, she pulled another sheet from the ream of crisp, white blank paper and loaded the typewriter for another attempt. She sat poised, her fingers resting lightly on the keys, a cigarette dangling from lips in what she hoped was a world weary attitude, something befitting a novelist attempting the definitive book that would capture the essence of an entire generation scarred by four years of war.

"Are you still here?" she suddenly heard. Her flatmate had entered unbeknownst to her and was looking over her shoulder. "Christ, you still haven't written a thing!"

Jane looked at what she'd written and closed the window, the mouse pointer poised above "Don't Save" in answer to the question "Do you want to save the changes to Document2?"

She didn't know how to answer the question. Her earlier thought of writing a story about the WAAF she'd followed had somehow become a story about a woman novelist trying to write about the Great War. She blamed Hemingway and Fitzgerald and Stein and all those other American expatriates who had flocked to Paris and whose writing she had at first detested and then embraced. She had met Hemingway in Paris, or rather looked over his shoulder while he wrote, and had admired the passion that drove his work, but she could not understand his spare prose that laid bare the world under a harsh and unforgiving sun. With time, though, she came to accept it as a new style for a new world and had experimented with it again and again.

She clicked "Save" after naming the document.

"Hi Jane, still at it?" Tamara asked as suddenly as the fictional flatmate she'd discarded.

"Oh, hello Tamara. I'm sorry, I didn't see you enter."

Tamara threw off her coat, which missed her target, the couch, and it landed on the floor. Then she indecorously flopped onto the couch.

"How's that even possible? I thought you saw in 360."

"I'm afraid it's still possible to be unaware even then," Jane replied. She looked at the clock on the terminal and saw that Tamara had returned early from her job and that it would still be some time before Melody might return.

Her calculations made her feel guilty. There was no real disagreement between Jane and Tamara but simply no real agreement on tastes or interests other than their mutual association with Melody. Tamara worked for the city of New York as a planner, a job Jane still found incomprehensible whenever she contemplated the vast insanity of the city. How could anything so chaotic and beautiful be planned?

They were very cordial, however, and whenever Melody was present they would have no difficulty, but without her they simply had no idea what to say.

"You look as if you've had a difficult day," Jane observed.

"But not a bad day. I got approval for a project I've been working on. It should let us get by with 15 fewer street cleaning crews just by being a little more flexible with scheduling, which is useful because they removed 18 street cleaning crews from next year's budget."

"I know next to nothing of these matters, but I imagine both numbers are significant."

"You're right. And the really amazing thing is that if other departments could apply this same kind of thinking ... hey, let me get some wine and I'll tell you about it."

Tamara got off the couch and went into the kitchen and poured herself a glass, talking loudly enough for the terminal to recognize her. She related to Jane the new schedule she'd devised, that involved 12-hour shifts with rotating days off and bemoaned the resistance that the union had mounted to her plans. But other concessions had finally won over the last resistance and the plan would be implemented in a few months time. To Jane, the plan seemed as if it might cause a major disruption in the lives of the employees, but she refrained from any negative comments, happy to have found some rapport with the lover of her agent and good friend.

Jane did her best to engage Tamara, congratulating her and asking questions where appropriate. Tamara was only too happy to talk, glad to have an audience and to hear Jane's congratulations. She was very animated in her descriptions of the various opponents of her plans. They were mostly men, of course, and Tamara offered impressions of them that emphasized their pompousness and intractability.

"Thanks very much for hearing me out, Jane. I don't usually get to go on about my victories in the planning department. Melody tends to glaze over when I talk about work; it's not very glamorous."

"But it is important. And I can understand your need to celebrate. I used to dance about the room when I had found the solution to a plot complication."

"Yeah, that's what it's like. I needed to dance about the room. So, were you working when I came in? I'm sorry if I interrupted you."

"No, the interruption was welcome. It wasn't going very well, I'm afraid."

"Oh, if you don't want to talk about it …"

"I would love to talk about it, if you don't mind."

Jane explained to Tamara her need to write something new and her attempts to write something of a little more import.

"So what are you writing?"

"It's the story of a young woman, a writer like myself, writing at the end of the Great War. She's writing about the war and her involvement."

"But she's not like a soldier, I mean not if it's World War I."

"No, she was a spy, in France," Jane said, which was a surprise to her. She had not thought that far ahead in the story; it truly was just an experiment, an exercise for the left hand. But suddenly her heroine was a spy.

"Wow, that sounds pretty interesting. I suppose she falls in love with a guy."

"Well yes, there is a romance." Jane had not specifically meant to write a romance, but she enjoyed describing a book that she thought Tamara might enjoy.

"It sounds very exciting, not like … I mean, the books you wrote …"

"That's all right Tamara. I realize I am not known for writing thrillers."

"So, do you know much about World War I? Oh, what a stupid question. You lived through it. Well I don't mean lived. I mean you experienced it, didn't you?"

"I did and it was … it was during one of those periods where, perhaps understandably, I was despairing of mankind. It was all so familiar and reminded me of our long war with France, when I was alive, I mean. And here we were at war again, only now with France against Germany, which seemed incomprehensible because England's ties with Germany were so many and so strong."

"And how's it going? The writing I mean."

Jane was tempted to answer her question with a platitude—she'd heard that one writer had responded to the same question with the phrase "it's a process." And Jane had always been a furtive writer, loathe to divulge her progress to anyone. Any dancing she might have done was away from watchful eyes. But today she decided to be honest.

"It's not going well, and please don't tell Melody because she'll worry."

"Is there anything I can do to help? To make it easier for you to work. I realize … I realize that maybe I haven't … that I haven't been as open to you as I should." Tamara put down her wine glass and sat upright. "I'm really kind of jealous you know. Or I was. I mean how can I compete with Jane Austen?"

"Oh Tamara, how could you be so foolish. Melody loves you utterly and completely. You pierce her soul."[1]

At these words Tamara's eyes grew wide and the smile on her face made clear her appreciation of the sentiment. Granted Jane felt a little

---

1 In *Persuasion*, Austen's last completed novel, Captain Wentworth says this of heroine Anne Elliot in a letter he sends her

guilty for borrowing from her own work, but she knew Tamara was not a fan.

"Thank you Jane. Melody's kind of … well she's never spoken like that … but you think that's what she really thinks?"

"You may depend on it."

Tamara reached in a pocket for a tissue and dried her eyes.

"Uh, so what I was saying before. Is there some way I can help? I mean I don't know how, but … I mean what's the problem? Is it writer's block?"

"Ha! If it only were. I will tell you something that I don't think I could tell anyone else. I've lost my voice. I don't know how to write anymore."

"But you just wrote your sequel, I mean your completion, *Sandytown*."

"I finished that a century ago. I haven't written anything new since." Of course this was an overstatement of the facts. She had written many small stories and countless undeliverable letters to Cassandra.

"Oh, OK, that's a dry spell. Was it for lack of trying?"

"Partially. I've seen so much since I died. So many wonderful and horrible things, but I've been apart from the world, just observing."

"But isn't that what a writer does? They stand back and watch. I've always found it a little creepy, to be honest. Most of the authors Melody represents are … they're kind of weird, just a little detached from reality."

Jane considered this. She knew that might be an apt description of her while alive.

"So what else is going on in the novel you're writing?"

Jane briefly considered admitting to Tamara that she had written only a few opening paragraphs, but with a ready audience, she decided to set aside her caution and made up a story for Tamara, much like she'd done when she was much, much, much younger.

· The Real Jane Austen ·
Melody learns of Court's book

Melody looked at the press release for the third time, still willing the words to be different if she just read it again:

> Courtney Blake's book examines the personality of Jane Austen with the tools of modern-day medicine, forensic psychiatry and textual analysis to expose the famous Regency author as being much more sexually aware and adventurous than her reputation as a spinster would suggest. Blake's detective work even suggests Austen did not die ignorant of carnal pleasures and identifies her possible partners, both from the usual suspects and some that will surprise and even shock Austen fans. Blake is aided by in his analysis by FBI profilers, neuro-linguistics and computer-aided analysis of the text of Austen's novels and letters.

The press release included a picture of the book cover, which showed a woman with heaving bosom more appropriate to a bodice ripper than any sort of serious examination of Austen.

Oh my God, this is horrible. Poor Jane. I have to tell her right away before she sees it. Melody was shaking from the outrage of it.

She could imagine the distress of her client and friend, further summoning her anger against this insect who would dare besmirch Jane's reputation. Her anger could not be contained and she stood from her desk and paced angrily around her office. Finally her emotions drove her from the little space, now filled with boxes of stuff waiting to be moved, and she left her office for the hallway. She walked up and down the hallway, past all the other little offices of accountants and dentists and other professionals desperate for any space in the city that wouldn't bankrupt them.

Slowly her anger cooled and her instincts as agent and publicist took over. The PRNewswire release said Blake's book was due to be released just before the AGM. It smacked of a rushed release to capitalize on *Sanditon*, hoping to ride that book's sales.

But it could work both ways, Melody realized. Sex sells and sex was something conspicuously missing from *Sanditon*. This Blake creature's book could save Jane from eternal spinsterhood, even if it isn't true.

But what if it is? Is that so bad? Why should I resent it if Jane didn't die a virgin? Of course, what really worried Melody was that "surprise and even shock" line. *Is it going to revisit the accusation that Jane was a lesbian?* The thought first angered Melody and then confused her. *How can I be mad at Jane were I to learn she's a lesbian?*

But it would be a betrayal, Melody knew. It would be the crushing realization that a very close friend had kept something from you, something that would help you understand and identify with that person. After reading and countlessly rereading Austen, Melody thought she knew everything about Jane, ignoring the very real difficulty of ever truly knowing the elusive author.

I would have something in common with her that I never knew I had, but I don't want her to change. I want my Jane Austen to be the Austen I grew up with.

And then she realized that she had—for a moment—taken this man's book seriously. She realized the danger that such a book might do. After all, even without Courtney Blake's book, the Jane Austen she thought she knew wasn't the Jane she'd come to know. The Jane who was her client could never be simply described as a spinster author. She'd often wondered at the thought that Jane had died a virgin and like many, considered the idea tragic. So another part of her hoped that Jane had found some sexual release, which just spiralled back to a basic disgust of having to talk about Jane having sex.

Melody walked back to her office but rather than go inside and see her boxed belongings, she decided to lock up and go for coffee. Perhaps caffeine would help her find a tactful way to tell Jane the news of the book.

· English country dance ·
Some experience required

"No, you're the first couple, but you have to wait one go round with your partner because we have an uneven number of pairs," the instructor said patiently, despite Mary's frequent mistakes. Mary had gotten confused when she reached the end of the line and wanted to immediately re-enter. It was the goal of the afternoon that Mary should complete one dance without any glaring error.

"Sorry," Mary said to the instructor, who nodded pleasantly, probably because of the substantial amount of money the dance group was being paid to teach Mary English country dancing.[1]

"Why don't we take a break?" the instructor suggested. "I think some of us could use water."

Some of the members of the dance group nodded enthusiastically; they had been dancing several hours and about half the members were

---

1 English country dancing generally consists of two or more pairs of couples who exchange positions in a series of figures or movements. At the beginning of the dance, partners face each other in two lines. There are odd and even couples and usually at the end of a set series of movements, a couple moves (progresses) up or down the line. When a couple reaches the end of a line, they must wait a turn until they can progress back through the line. Specific music accompanies each dance. Country dancing was popular in Jane Austen's time, but after the Napoleonic Wars was largely supplanted by new forms such as the quadrille (which became square dancing) and the waltz.

of a certain age and half were much younger. It was mostly the younger dancers who appeared winded.

Mary went to her chair for water and a towel to mop her sweat. She sat down exhausted.

"You might have said something," Mary said silently to Jane.

"You said you wanted to do this on your own," Jane replied, impressed at how easily Mary was now using the terminal. They had maintained a running commentary while Mary stepped through the dance, which might have led to Mary's inattention.

"This is a lot more tiring than I would have thought," Mary said, still silently. "I'm sweating like a pig."

"That's hardly something Jane Austen would say, Mary," Jane admonished her avatar, even though she remembered saying something similar at an assembly dance.

"Sorry," Mary said. She'd gotten used to making apologies the past few weeks of training, which involved everything from English country dancing to deportment to honing her accent with an actual Hampshire native. She was bone tired, and yet she enjoyed it all in a way she had never enjoyed her acting lessons. Having Jane beside her gave her a confidence that she lacked before.

"Why aren't the old people … I mean the elderly … tired?" she asked, noticing that the older members had not sat down.

"They move with a minimum of effort and keep better time to the music, while you are always late or early. And for now, be more aware of your partner; he knows this dance well and keeps trying to help you, but you are too absorbed in your mistakes."

"Well, aren't we the expert," Mary said, although she smiled when she said it.

"I'll have you know I was dancing when your I don't how many times removed grandmother was still in nappies." Jane instructed the terminal to convey her words with the laughing digitized voice, a sound so awful that Mary grimaced.

"Oh God, Jane, never use that voice again," she said out loud and attracted the attention of those sitting nearby.

"Sorry," she said again, pointed to her earbud and shrugged her shoulders. She pretended to be on the phone rather than be seen talking to a disembodied person. Austen's agent had asked her to remain inconspicuous and to pretend that she was a movie star who'd landed a role that required she learn country dancing. Melody wanted to keep

Mary's identity a secret. Mary suspected Melody wanted to be able to quietly pick a replacement avatar should she prove unequal to the task.

"What is wrong with that voice?" Jane asked.

"It makes you sound like a drunken hyena. A male drunken hyena. On laughing gas."

"Oh, I ... I didn't know that." Jane was a little flustered. She'd chosen the voice based on a recommendation from a disembodied support group. She'd learned the coding necessary to switch into different voices and had downloaded the voice into the terminal. She'd been so proud of her technical skills and so it was a let down to learn that she still didn't fully appreciate the limitations of communicating with her avatar.

"All right, everyone, that's enough of a water break," the instructor said. "We still need to teach Ms Crawford a triple progression and do it flawlessly." She then turned aside to Mary, "And if you would pay better attention to your partner instead of talking to your disembodied friend, we might just get this done today."

"Yes, ma'am," Mary said, surprised to learn the instructor recognized that she was an avatar. The revelation so surprised, in fact, that she didn't notice Jane's silence for the next half hour.

· Business decisions ·
A large income is the best recipe
for happiness I ever heard of

"The latest offer is from Miramax, the Weinsteins," Melody informed Jane. They were sitting in Melody's apartment, she in her old lady BarcaLounger that was out of place in Tamara's chic decor, and Jane sitting on the couch, just barely in range of the terminal on the coffee table.

Tamara was already in bed after a vexing day at work. Jane had tried to console Tamara about the inequities of women in the workplace, but the topic was so out of her ken that she feared she offered little practical advice. And yet Jane admired and even envied a little Tamara's life as a professional woman.

Jane and Melody, however, had also spent a busy day at the avatar agency, with Jane and Mary perfecting their skills and Melody pretending to be an interviewer. Melody thought Jane and Mary had improved tremendously. Mary no longer looked as if she were hearing a Who and managed to simply look thoughtful while waiting for Jane to tell her what to say. Mary also had gained enough confidence to start talking before Jane completely finished her reply, although that predictably resulted in a few missteps.

Jane's performance was still uncertain and this puzzled Melody, until Mary suggested that perhaps Jane could start employing texting shorthand.

"Every one of her responses is grammatical and well thought out, with the proper punctuation, but it takes a while," Mary said, which for her was close to complaining. Actually, Melody thought Mary's skill considerable and her attitude exemplary. She never complained at the demands placed on her, which Melody attributed to her theatrical training. She felt chagrin at having objected to Mary.

Jane, however, was getting crankier and crankier. Jane had assumed she could assemble her thoughts quickly and coherently, not unlike her ability in various chat rooms and instant messaging. She prided herself on forming complete, complex sentences that Elizabeth would be proud to utter, or pithy epigrams—"My good opinion once lost, is lost forever"—that Darcy would toss.

"You're trying too hard," Melody said later, after Mary left. "Stop trying to write dialogue and just talk like you normally do and let Mary make it sound clever."

"What?"

"She's pretty good at the accent and we're Americans. We're programmed to think anyone with a British accent is smarter than us."

"Do I have an accent? I really don't know what my digitized voice sounds like."

Melody laughed, which Jane saw but of course could not hear. "Yes you do, because I downloaded and installed a new voice for my terminal. It's called 'Elizabeth' appropriately enough, and it does kinda sorta have a British accent."

Melody looked a little embarrassed at this revelation.

"You can change my voice, whenever you like?" Jane asked.

"Yes, although I've only changed it the once. The default voice and the other voices that come with the terminal ... well none of them sounded right." The admission made Melody recall the shock the first time she heard Jane's digitized voice come through her terminal. She'd emailed and chatted with Jane and become friends and then took her on as a client without ever hearing her voice. She'd accepted Jane's claim that she was the real Jane Austen almost from the first. She had to admit she'd made her decision on purely subjective and emotional reasons that were happily later substantiated by fact. But the first time she heard the flat digitized voice, she suddenly doubted her support of Jane.

Which led to the search for a better-digitized voice and specifically one with a British accent. "Elizabeth" was a rather posh, frosty voice and was correspondingly expensive, but the first time Melody heard it, she knew she'd found the perfect voice for Jane, and her misgivings vanished.

"What voice does Mary's terminal use?"

"Gosh, I don't know," Melody replied. "We should ask. It makes a big difference."

Jane was silent for a space, thinking ruefully of her recent attempt at programming the terminal and Mary's reaction. She returned to their previous topic: "Sorry, I was just looking at the transcript. You said we had another movie offer for *Sanditon* from Miramax. That is another production company?"

"Well, it's essentially Walt Disney nowadays, unless they sell it off, like all the rumours say will happen. They make a lot of the 'quality' movies—including several of yours."

"Oh, which ones?"

"The Gwyneth Paltrow *Emma*."

"I liked that one."

"*Mansfield Park*, the '99 one." Melody made a face.

"The slavery one? I did not care for that."

"Neither did I. And the Weinsteins were trying to make a movie out of *Becoming Jane Austen* ... did you ever read that?"

"No, I did not, although I understand it was well received."

"I bet Spence wishes he'd had you to talk to. Then again ... anyway, it never got made, but God knows what they would have done with it. So now they've made an offer for *Sanditon*."

"And what is your thought?" Jane asked.

Melody paused before answering. "You do know I'm out of my depth here. It really would be a good idea ..."

"We are not having this discussion again, Melody. You are my agent; I will consider no other. Hire whomever you need and increase your commission."

"Jane, you can't just ... if I make a mistake ... it could cost you millions."

"What difference does it make? I hardly need the money. As long as I see my name on the title or in the movie's credits and ... well, naturally I wouldn't want my name associated with ..."

"You see? It is important. And talking about hiring people, I am getting you a publicist."

"A what?"

"Someone to promote you in the press, who makes sure your name is out there."

"I thought you did that?"

"Not really. I sell you to publishers and movie studios and if someone wants to sell a Jane Austen perfume and so on, but I don't really promote you the same way a publicist would."

"Why ever would I want this?"

Melody sighed. She knew this would not be an easy task. "Your name, your reputation ... well there'll be people who'll want to tarnish it, or who want to leverage off your fame for whatever reason. Look, you of all people should know there are some nasty people out there; you certainly created some fine examples."

Jane did not respond so Melody continued. "Let's say somebody unearths some scandal about you. Maybe something about Tom Lefroy and you ..."

"There is ... there was nothing salacious about my relationship with Mr Lefroy, and surely that is ancient history."

"I don't know how someone would spin it to make it ... tawdry ... or relevant. But believe me, there are nasty people out there who could. If you have a publicist, well it's someone who can ..."

"Lie for me?"

"Massage the truth. Or at least someone who can draft a response for you. You can get snitty, Jane, and occasionally you can say ..."

"Is there something you are withholding from me, Melody?"

"Well, yes, there is. There's a book coming out from someone named Courtney Blake. It's a biography of you."

"It is unflattering?"

"I don't know, I haven't read it, but I did get word what it's about."

"Which is?" Jane prompted after Melody fell silent.

"It re-evaluates you ... and all your novels ... from a psychological basis ... and a sexual basis. It speculates if you had sex and if so, with whom you had it." Melody spoke the last sentence quickly.

"What, like that horrid book from the nineties?"

"You knew about that?"

"Not at the time, but after the discovery of the afterlife. I gather it made a little furore coming about the same time as the BBC miniseries. I was dismayed that the same old prejudice against spinsters prevailed, but it was not well received and is largely forgotten, although I know you have a copy."

Melody looked embarrassed and she rushed to defend herself. "How did you ... it was ... it made you ... I never believed it."

"It doesn't matter. And now this person has revisited those accusations."

"No, it's much more than that. Apparently he's examined everything you've written, things your characters say. He's talked to psychiatrists and FBI profilers to make up a picture of you. I've also heard, and this is largely rumour because the book isn't out yet, that he speculates you rejected Harris Bigg-Wither ... because you preferred the company of women."

Jane was silent for a second before answering. "Ah well, at least he doesn't accuse me of congress with my sister. I can assure you, Melody, I was no Gentleman Jack or lady of Llangollen,[1] but even if I was, surely it no longer matters today. Why I even believe my best friend prefers the company of women."

Melody paused before answering. "I don't really know, Jane. There're a lot of people who read you because there's no sex in your books. I mean you're a clergyman's daughter. You might lose some readers if they thought you were a lesbian. And then there's the whole spinster thing. You're not such a tragic figure anymore if you ... you know, did it. I don't really know how this will play out. I mean if this book came out at any other time, it would probably disappear like the other one, but you can bet they're going to capitalize on your book launch. This is why it would be a good idea to get you a full-time publicist."

"Very well, Melody, I certainly cannot fault any of your decisions to date. If you think it necessary, then I agree."

Melody looked to the empty couch and asked, "You're not being sarcastic, are you?"

---

1 The Ladies of Llangollen (in Wales): Eleanor Charlotte Butler and Sarah Ponsonby were two Irish women who lived during the reigns of George III and IV. There was speculation as to the nature of their relationship. Gentleman Jack: Anne Lister was a contemporary of the Ladies and earned her sobriquet for her manly interests and the fact she had female lovers. Coming from the landed classes and being wealthy, the peculiarities of these women were tolerated and to a certain extent even celebrated. There have been speculations that Austen was a lesbian and that she had sexual liaisons with her sister, but these speculations came about because of a misunderstanding of the intent of a review of a book on Austen's letters.

"No, if I were being sarcastic, I would have wrapped my comments with sarcastic tags."

Melody didn't understand and simply said, "Whatever," and then sighed deeply and relaxed into her decrepit armchair. She'd managed to convince Jane of the need for a publicist and broke the news to her about Courtney Blake's book, two tasks she'd dreaded that had gone reasonably well. *I am Jane Austen's agent, and I think I'm finally getting the hang of it.*

· The secret fear of Janeites ·
"Will the AGM become the equivalent of a Star Trek convention?"

Jane left Melody's apartment early, even though she wouldn't be meeting Mary at the avatar agency until late that afternoon. She needed to walk after spending the night in the living room while Melody and Tamara slept. She had spent the whole night researching Courtney Blake and reflecting on the unlikely home and friends she'd found in light of her offhand remark that "her best friend prefers the company of women." It was something of a surprise that she considered Melody her best friend and yet it was true nonetheless. Despite the different worlds that had shaped them, Jane considered Melody her friend and felt indignation that in some way, Courtney Blake's book was an attack on both her and her friend.

Jane had to admit that when she first learned Melody was a lesbian, she was taken aback. The concept was hardly unknown to her, however, and in time, she came to recognize the love that existed between Melody and Tamara. There was also nothing like the experience of the afterlife to make clear that love, no matter what form it took, was a precious gift.

And from her investigation of Blake's book, it became clear that it took a prurient interest in her supposed sexual liaisons. From her study of his previous books, it was clear this was his preferred tactic—to expose the deviant behaviour of famous authors including Lord Byron and Charles Dickens. Why she deserved the same attention was a mystery. *He did say I was a particular favourite of his—lucky me.*

She had wandered several blocks from home and found herself in Provenza's, a pizzeria her friends frequented. She was using an ancient AfterNet terminal (in the back on a small table with a single chair) to search for reaction to Blake's book. In the process, she visited austenonly.com, one of the popular blogs devoted to her. She had enjoyed her visits to the site in the past as it often featured objects that were known to her in life or told of her visits to Stoneleigh Abbey or even images of the booksellers she once frequented.

Unfortunately what she found there today was almost as upsetting as the news of Blake's book.

The article in question was the most recent guest post by "an anonymous Austen scholar."

Is Austen scholarship dead?

In all the excitement over the announcement that the AfterNet has certified someone as being *the* Jane Austen, I think it's gone unnoticed that we may well be seeing the death of Austen scholarship, and I think that a very sad thing.

For in future when a question arises as to an incident in Miss Austen's life, we need merely ask her the question and her answer will settle the matter. We need no longer scour the letters of Cassandra or Jane. We need no longer look at a registrar's records to see who has been born or married or died on such and such a date. We need no longer search the periodicals of the day to see what news Miss Austen had just read. We can simply ask her.

And by asking her, we need no longer write our learned papers and await their publication in *Persuasions*. We need no longer await the hue and cry caused by promoting this theory or that and then defend those theories before graduate committees or on blogs and forums because any answer Miss Austen provides will be definitive.

I had never thought of this wrinkle. I've always dreamed of asking Jane Austen why she accepted Harris Bigg-Wither in the first place or who was the mystery man from Devon. But I never dreamed that knowing the answer would take all the fun out of it.

Sadly we may be reduced to nothing more than a fan base. Will the Annual General Meeting become the equivalent of a Star Trek convention where we line up behind a microphone to ask Miss Austen one inane question after another?

And I can't see a way out of this dilemma. To ignore Jane Austen as a resource would be unimaginable, but with each answer another graduate student finds his thesis confirmed, denied or made irrelevant.

Of course I am thrilled beyond words that Jane—I mean Miss Austen, for now that she is among us it seem presumptuous to address her so informally—has regained her voice. To read her completed *Sanditon* is a joy I eagerly await, but I cannot help but mourn the loss of her heretofore essential unknowableness that allowed her to be my best friend. Previously I had no fear whether she was a conservative or a liberal, preferred dogs to cats or thought Benny Hill superior to Monty Python, but now I might learn that she doesn't share my values and opinions. I may learn that she may think my writings about her an awful cheek and so inaccurate as to be laughable.

Or I can hope the wisdom she has acquired all these years has led her to a calm acceptance of our interest in her. Perhaps she will choose to keep her life a close secret, just as she did when she titled her first book "By a Lady." But in this day and age of podcasts, blogs and a 24-hour news cycle, I think that unlikely.

Jane did not know what to think after reading this obviously heartfelt appeal. Her immediate reaction was to leave a comment saying that she had no intention of denying anyone who wanted to continue studying her life, but then realized that even leaving a comment might be construed as her trying to wield her influence.

She'd never given much thought that her very existence would threaten the industry that had evolved around her life and novels, and it also made her realize how far she had come from that author who had been content with anonymity.

In her lifetime, she did not want the notoriety associated with being a woman novelist, but at the same time she wanted the respect due her as an author. Had she lived longer, she would have had to reconcile those two desires. But over the long years of seeing first her fame decline and then slowly rise to heights she could never have imagined, she had come to accept herself as a famous author.

By now she'd already given several interviews and soon would be going on book tour and doubtless would be answering endless questions about her life and her writing. She had never given a thought that her answers might affect people who had made her life their life's work.

And there were many misconceptions and fallacies about her life that she had fully intended to address. Some of the comments her brother Henry made after her death made her sound so good and simple a soul that she could hardly recognize herself. In fact, she would not care to know someone who "never uttered a silly or severe thought" or some such nonsense. Such a person would be entirely too dull. And to be said that she sought neither fame nor profit flew in the face of all those careful calculations she had entered into with Henry,[1] down to the thickness of the paper and the size of the type, so that she might maximize her profits.

Am I to be kept in silence so the Jane Austen industry might continue unabated? Have I not the right to say what I want, to explain myself, my motives, my inspirations and my desires?

Jane suddenly realized that her opinions had suddenly gone the other way, from sympathy toward those who had built their careers around her and then anger that she should be cajoled into a meek silence.

She looked around her then. As always, the turmoil she felt went unnoticed by the lunchtime crowd in the pizzeria. She watched as the wait staff burst out through the swinging kitchen doors, almost hitting the table where the terminal and Jane sat alone.

Or so she thought, because when she glanced at the display she saw that not only was she not alone, but there was a request to chat, which she answered.

JaneAusten3 has entered the room

JaneAusten3 says:

Hello?

bobkirkendorf says:

Hi, just saw your username and I had to ask

JaneAusten3 says:

Pardon?

bobkirkendorf says:

OK, this seems silly now, but all the news about Jane Austen and this is NYC and I read she's here working with Random House where I work and I was just wondering … is it you?

---

1   Henry Austen provided his sister with the money to publish *Sense and Sensibility*. They adjusted type size and line leading to reduce the number of printed pages, just like the publisher of this book chose 10.5 point type with 2.1 points of leading.

Jane stared at the question, wondering how to answer. She had not logged into the terminal anonymously or privately. Instead she was listed as JaneAusten3 for all the world—or at least this one other user—to see.

She was annoyed because Melody had finally convinced her of the need for discretion, especially if she had any hope of maintaining the privacy of her JaneAusten3 account.

bobkirkendorf says:
  I'm sorry, I shouldn't have asked. I've worked with enough authors over the years to learn not to gush
JaneAusten3 says:
  No, there is no offense. Yes, I am that Jane Austen, although I would appreciate your discretion

As they were talking, Jane quickly Googled the man's name and found that he did purport to work at Random House as an editorial assistant and that very surprisingly, he was living. She went back to the terminal's list of users online and saw that he was directly connected to the terminal's AfterNet field. The listing confirmed that he was living.

JaneAusten3 says:
  Excuse me, you are in this restaurant?
bobkirkendorf says:
  That's me waving

Jane looked around and saw a man a few tables away waving his arm. He was a young man with close cut black hair, wearing the uniform of the young, urban male, middle class: baggy cargo shorts and a T-shirt proclaiming his preference for the New York Mets baseball club.

JaneAusten3 says:
  How is it that you are using the terminal directly?
bobkirkendorf says:
  Well, I'm one of those freaks who can read an AfterNet field with no problem. It's very handy because I have a disembodied girlfriend. She's the one who turned me on to you.

The man smiled apologetically at his admission. She could see that his lips did not move during their conversation and he was not typing so there was no question of his communicating through speech recognition. He apparently could project his thoughts as easily as Mary.

JaneAusten3 says:
You should be an avatar. Wait, did you say your girlfriend is disembodied?
bobkirkendorf says:
I know, crazy right? How's it going to work out? Do you hope to have children? How do you even know she's a woman? That's all my parents and friends can say. And I don't know if it's going to work out, but Karen's … I'm sorry. I'm venting.
JaneAusten3 says:
There's no need to apologize. Please, may I join you at your table?
bobkirkendorf says:
I would be honored.

Jane left her spot by the terminal and joined him, surprised at how weak the terminal's field was at this distance. That he could still use the terminal was astounding.

She quickly learned the young man was one of the editorial assistants who read through the "slush pile" of unsolicited manuscripts. His girlfriend had recommended he read her novels and she found delightful his comments about them, especially *Emma*.

bobkirkendorf says:
I remember seeing Clueless on a movie date and I thought Emma was an airhead, so I was surprised when I read it that she's not a materialistic valley girl. She's just young is all, and we all think we know everything.

They talked about an hour until Bob realized he'd taken an hour and a half lunch. Jane jokingly promised to vouch for him if he was in trouble in exchange for his promise that he would keep her username a secret.

After he left, Jane remained for a time, thinking how much she enjoyed speaking with a fan. She realized, of course, that not every interaction would be as enjoyable. She did not give away much of herself; they mostly talked about his relationship with Karen. She wondered at the advisability of his forming an attachment with her, especially since he had met her online when he was seventeen, at the very dawn of the AfterNet, and Karen purported to be thirty-five years old when she died in 1960.

The maths was not that different from those of Knightley and Emma, of course, and apparently Karen had resided in the Kirkendorf home unbeknownst to Bob's parents.

Jane had felt tempted to step into the role of maiden aunt and advise him of the dangers of such a relationship, but she had refrained, although she exchanged email addresses with him and might offer her advice in the future.

Finally she left the pizzeria, realizing that she was now late for her training with Mary and would have to hurry. Her time, however, had been well spent. Her conversation with her new friend made her realize that more than ever she felt very much a part of the twenty-first century and was not content to sit back while her life was the plaything of every scholar and voyeur with a publishing contract.

· An open letter ·
Jane responds online

Dear friends,

Oh that salutation will not do at all, for I wish to address all my friends, critics, detractors, admirers, apologists and scholars of my works and life. I want you to know I appreciate that my "reappearance" has come as a surprise, if not a shock, to many.

During my time away, many have stepped in to keep my voice alive, so much so that almost two hundred years later, my name and my novels have greater currency now than during my corporeal existence. I am continually amazed that in this day of reality television, 24-hour news and science fiction blockbuster movies, there is still a desire to read of "three or four families in a country village."[1]

---

1 In a letter to a relative, Austen offered this writing advice: "You are now collecting your people delightfully, getting them exactly into such a spot as is the delight of my life. Three or four families in a country village is the very thing to work on, and I hope you will do a great deal more, and make full use of them while they are so very favourably arranged."

But of course my "little bits of ivory"[2]—oh how I regret how twee[3] that now sounds—have been enlarged to include zombies and vampires and my characters have even travelled through time and space.

And organizations such as the societies in my homeland and in North America have done much to make my stories more accessible, both by promoting my work and by providing the context of the world in which I lived and wrote. I am sometimes surprised by learning how clever I was, but I must protest that my understanding of the politics and economics of Regency England was rudimentary at best. I do, however, admit I had a subtext in my choice of characters, names, locations and behaviours that I am glad is still appreciated.

Movies and television have also done much to keep Elizabeth and Darcy and Emma and even poor Fanny relevant to the era in which they were created, often adding elements that I had never intended (or in some cases would never have approved of) and yet I understand the considerations of producers and directors and the arithmetic of box office and television ratings.

Scholars have also found my life and times of great interest, although why is a mystery. Perhaps by editing and withholding many of my letters, my sister Cassandra unknowingly contributed to making it a mystery and scholars find mysteries very tempting. That may explain efforts to bend my temperament and sympathies this way and that and often back and forth as theories are advanced to match current sensibilities, each generation understandably at odds with the interpretations of the previous.

Recently I've become aware that some scholars and authors are worried that "the real Jane Austen" might object to these speculations, biographies, pastiches, parodies, reboots and continuations, but despite my identity being certified by the AfterNet, I assure you I am no longer "the real Jane

---

2   In a letter to a different relative, Austen wrote: "What should I do with your strong, manly, spirited sketches, full of variety and glow? How could I possibly join them on to the little bit (two inches wide) of ivory on which I work with so fine a brush, as produces little effect after much labour?" Austen wrote on small pieces of paper, examples of which you can see at http://www.janeausten.ac.uk/.

3   Excessively or affectedly quaint, pretty, or sentimental

Austen"—or rather I am not that little travelled Regency author, unnamed during her lifetime who preferred the simple life of Hampshire. As I write this, I am in New York City in America and these words will appear on my blog and you will read them on your computer or your smartphone. I am about to embark on a book tour of the United Kingdom, Europe and the United States. So I cannot in all good conscience pretend that I speak for that Jane Austen of so long ago and I look forward to the next biography, the next continuation and the next movie.

That said, I do owe a debt to that Jane from so long ago and to the Austen name and the great and the good of my family and of my country. I cannot stand by if untruths or rumours can be corrected by me. And as much as modesty, propriety and my natural reserve permit, I will speak truthfully of my life when asked, even though it might cast my character in a bad light, destroy a thesis or contradict a biographer. I still claim ownership of my life, even though I am willing to share it.

Some may also worry that my presence means an end to Austen scholarship, thinking me the final arbiter of my own story, but I assure you, I am not. Two hundred years is too short a period to achieve true self-awareness and yet it is long enough that I have forgotten much. Remember that I was just a maiden aunt in a small corner of England and although I read widely and had some small knowledge of the larger world, I truly knew very little. In fact, it is surprising what I did not know ... but that can be said of many.

I remain your humble and obedient servant,

Jane Austen

"What possessed you, Jane? Did you suddenly think I had too much time on my hands?"

Jane sat opposite her excited agent and Mr Pembroke from Random House. She had excused Mary from attending, not thinking it fair to make her avatar be the target of Melody's predicted ire. Fortunately Mr Pembroke was there to calm Melody, reminding her that the other diners at the restaurant were observing her raised words. Jane, however, suspected Mr Pembroke was almost as concerned as Melody.

"I'm sure Jane just didn't consider public reaction to her post."

"Oh she knew, all right. That's why she did it without asking me."

"Am I to seek your permission first, Melody?" Jane asked, her voice coming over the speaker attached to Melody's terminal. Mr Pembroke reached over to reduce the volume.

Melody said nothing, perhaps wisely, but her silence made clear her opinion that Jane should have asked permission.

"No, I'm sure that's not what Melody meant," Mr Pembroke said. He smiled, as broadly and as affably as he could, which was considerable. He began to regret his suggestion of a dinner meeting. "But you have to understand ... if we'd known what you were ... if you had said something, we could ..."

"Have stopped you from doing something so stupid," Melody said. "Did you even think for one second ..."

"Because I knew you would do your best to ..."

"Melody, Jane, shut up!" Mr Pembroke said, in a loud stage whisper. He pointed to Melody and the invisible Jane in turn.

"You are obviously friends who have come to an impasse and it falls to me to make you realize you are still friends. First, Melody apologize to Jane for calling her actions stupid."

"But I ... yes, I apologize," Melody said.

"Second, Jane, admit the reaction to your posting has caused far more controversy than you had intended."

Oh very skilfully handled, Jane thought. *He first gets us to admit what we cannot deny.*

"Very well, I admit ... there are wider ... yes, I never thought it would cause so much trouble."

This was an understatement. For most of the day, Jane's reply at austenonly had occasioned mostly positive comments, but then some had decided that Jane was asking for a moratorium on further biographies. Predictably Jane had supporters who said that Jane had every right to defend her name against slander and soon the back and forth of postings spread to other Austen blogs. Jane's actual words were soon lost in the tumult.

The controversy was also reported in the press, which had been closely watching how the most prominent disembodied author to date would handle the treacherous world of social media.

"Very good, Jane. Now Melody, admit that Jane's original post was very balanced. I first read it and thought nothing very alarming about it."

"No, there's nothing wrong with the post. But if she'd only ..."

"Stop. Now Jane, is it possible that you forgot that one of the responsibilities of an agent is to represent and protect her client?"

As he said this, he lost his stern look of admonition and returned to his more natural avuncular manner. He again smiled so broadly and earnestly that Jane forgot her anger.

"Yes, I should have asked Melody's ... advice," Jane said.

"Then let us leave rancour and blame behind us and move on to crafting a strategy to address the problem."

Melody replied by nodding her head in agreement. "And I'm sorry I ... your post wasn't ... I shouldn't have ..."

Jane knew this amounted to an abject apology from her friend and to stop her train of elliptical contrition, Jane said, "I hope you can quickly hire a publicist to repair the damage."

Melody looked embarrassed and answered, "Actually I hired her two days ago. She starts tomorrow."

"That is fortuitous timing," Jane said. "I am sure she will be a great asset."

Mr Pembroke looked to Melody and then to Jane's empty chair, wondering what dynamic he was missing. He decided to ignore it, happy that he had reconciled the two friends and added, "I'm pretty sure this will die down shortly and then perhaps I could approach a few academics that might come to Jane's defence. They might help explain that Jane doesn't want a moratorium on Austen scholarship. There's a Dr Davis in Chicago who's writing a book right now. I'm sure we can count her on our side."

• Shared interests •

She looked fully capable of ripping most men in half

Courtney couldn't get comfortable in his chair or quit his worry that he was in the wrong place. He'd told the taxi driver to take him to Jimmy's Bar on 55th Street and the driver assured him he knew the place, but had deposited him at a nondescript looking building labelled Woodlawn Tap. Inside the almost empty bar it was dark and smelled of decades of cigarettes, fried foods and spilled beer. A large print of Nighthawks was by the entrance, several band posters adorned a small stage and a bartender had assured him he was in the right place and that he should sit anywhere.

He rubbed his sweaty palms on his pants, tried to think good thoughts and took another sip of his rum and Coke. He'd been surprised when Davis had replied to his email and had suggested meeting. Fortunately the timing had worked out, he having just returned from England to meet with his agent, and could stop in Chicago on the way. He'd frankly given up hope of hearing from her, but obviously the news that he was very close to obtaining the letter must have persuaded her.

Then he saw her enter the bar and thought of the description of Liesl from Robertson Davies' *The Manticore*. She was a large domineering sort of woman whom one might uncharitably describe as ugly. She had not that regularity or fineness of features or smoothness of complexion so admired in Austen novels. She was square jawed and her nose was bulbous and she looked fully capable of ripping most men in half. But in her elegant yet eccentric green tartan wool dress, she exuded confidence as she scanned the room looking for him. Her thick reddish hair that ended in a war club-like braid whipped about her head when she turned sharply at the sound of the bartender laughing at something on the television.

"Is Jimmy here today?" she asked the bartender. He looked over his shoulder at her and said, "Not today. He said he'd be in later."

She nodded, asked for a club soda, and returned to her observation of the room. Her eyes locked on Courtney and he answered with a timid wave.

As she strode toward him Courtney stood, which caused her to break stride momentarily.

"Dr Davis?"

"Mr Blake," she said, not feeling the need to confirm her identity.

He extended his hand, which she took in a firm, quick grip. She started to take her chair, but Courtney quickly pulled it out for her.

"Thank you," she said in her husky voice.

He quickly took his seat and said, "No, thank you Dr Davis for agreeing to see me."

"It's no great favour, Mr Blake. I am understandably interested in meeting someone who's written such a book."

He looked at her to see whether her face betrayed any distaste at what he'd written but he saw nothing other than her dark brown eyes staring directly back at him. He wanted to look away to avoid their penetration but he held firm.

"Please call me Court. And 'such a book' is a noncommittal phrase," he said. "I wonder if it masks a dislike or …"

"I do not mince words, Court. I dislike your book for the same reason I dislike any book that tries to re-evaluate Jane—or any historical figure for that matter—based on the pop psychology of the present day. You have to view people in the context of their times and so I detest your argument for the same reasons that I dislike attempts to cast Abraham Lincoln as gay, claims the pyramids could only have been built by aliens or doubts that Shakespeare wrote his plays."

Courtney was taken aback by her blunt words and he realized he must be equally blunt to gain her respect.

"But it's OK to cast Austen as a feminist or a social commentator? Let's face it, Dr Davis, we're both using Austen for our own purposes.

I want to give Austen a sex life so I can sell books; you want to give Austen some noble purpose so she's not just some sad spinster who writes romances without ever having had one. So let's not pretend indignation, considering you asked me to meet you."

Davis said nothing for a beat and then answered, "Point taken, Court. I admit I dismissed you when I received your first email. I thought you were exaggerating the threat posed by the person claiming to be Austen, but now ..."

"You mean her challenge on austenonly?"

"Yes, I never expected ..."

The bartender interrupted her reply. "Do you want food?" he asked from behind the bar.

"I recommend a Swiss burger," she said to Courtney, "but the brats are good too."

"Uh, yeah," he said. "The burger, medium rare."

"Two Swiss burgers," she called out to the bartender, ignoring the cooking instructions.

"Where was I?" she asked. "Ah, the truth is that six months from now I will find myself in your position. I have a book ready for publication and although I will not be making your extraordinary claims, nevertheless I now have the prospect of having the subject of my research raise objections to what I have written. It's very disconcerting."

Courtney shifted uncomfortably when he realized his assumptions were incorrect. "I guess I'm confused. I thought you were on the committee that identified Austen. I would think that would give you some ... that she might be indebted to you ..."

But she was shaking her head no. "I was not a member of that committee, Court. I was not asked."

"Oh, I presumed you were."

She sighed. "You and everyone else. It's very annoying. Everyone thinks I approve of ..."

Courtney waited for her to finish the sentence and when he realized she wouldn't, he asked, "And do you?"

"I have to respect my peers, whoever they were. They take their secrecy very seriously, I'm afraid."

"So you have no idea how Austen proved her identity?"

She looked away from Courtney and to the two students nursing beers at the bar. "None at all, other than the rumours of her producing

Sanditon from memory, but I presume there had to be some piece of concrete evidence. That's why your most recent letter intrigued me."

"I thought that was the reason you finally answered me."

"It was intriguing. If you actually think you've found an Austen letter that Cassandra didn't destroy then perhaps we can use it to …" Davis was reluctant to finish her sentence.

"To expose Austen as a fraud?" Courtney suggested. "Yeah, I thought of that. If I can find it and if we can prove it's genuine and if we're sure faux Austen has never seen it … It's dangerous and it could backfire on us. If she doesn't know what it says, we've exposed her and maybe made a lot of Janeites mad at us. If she does know the contents of the letter … well then it looks like we were attacking her."

To hear Courtney elucidate the risks shook Davis, but then she thought of Austen's reply to her posting at austenonly.

"Then we have to make sure we're absolutely certain of the authenticity of the letter before we make it public. And after all, if Austen confirms the contents of the letter, then all we've done is strengthen her claim. We have to present this as the result of research and commitment to Austen studies."

Courtney was a little surprised at how quickly his discovery of the letter—well, imminent discovery of the letter—had become a joint project, but he realized how important an ally Davis could be and he also wondered if Davis weren't a little upset that she hadn't been asked to be on that committee.

And finally, he realized that he now considered Davis quite attractive. And that she had never asked him to call her Alice.

VOLUME II

Titbits II
A God-shaped vacuum

RADIO FOUR TRANSCRIPT
BROADCAST: 8 JULY 2013
SHOW: ROOMFUL OF MONKEYS
PRODUCER: JONATHAN THACKER

ROGER HAWKINS: Good evening and welcome to Roomful of Monkeys, the show that tackles thought provoking questions in a way that makes them sound silly. I'm your moderator, Roger Hawkins and this week we're going to examine the state of God since the discovery of the afterlife and we have some very exciting guests to discuss this topic. From the very popular show on state sponsored television we have that guest extraordinaire, comedian Stephen Fry. How often have you been on Idiotic Question, Stephen?

STEPHEN FRY: Every episode but one when I broke my arm, Roger, as you well know and thank you for reminding me of a painful injury. I understand you stand ready to substitute for me again?

HAWKINS: Just as soon as I can arrange it, Stephen ... I mean should the need arise again. And from the world of science, we have physicist and presenter Dr. Brian Cox, just back from circling the globe in pursuit of one of the truly staggering questions of the universe, How many times can I get the BBC to fly me to Hawaii for a documentary about a theoretical particle that has nothing to do with Hawaii?

BRIAN COX: Oh but it has everything to do with it because dark matter is invisible to even the most powerful telescopes, one of which happens to be in Hawaii, and I needed three minutes of footage of me on a beach in Hawaii and two minutes of me talking to astronomers at the Keck Observatory.

HAWKINS: It's all how you write the script then, which is why next week's podcast will be direct from the Bahamas. And our final guest may seem an odd choice but she has had a long time—almost two hundred years—to ponder the question of God, the author of *Pride and Prejudice* and *Sense and Sensibility*, Miss Jane Austen.

JANE AUSTEN: I am delighted to appear on your show, although I wonder if the odds are against me. I think Dr Cox and Mr Fry are both on record as atheists.

COX: I've been persuaded to play devil's advocate today, ma'am. Well the opposite, actually. You can think of me as an agnostic today.

AUSTEN: I still think that puts the onus on me. After two hundred years, you will expect something very clever of me, but I'm afraid all I can offer is that I think the "state of God" as you put it remains as it was before the discovery of the afterlife.

FRY: All you can expect from me are three things very dull indeed. And I am famously also on record as being a Janeite, nevertheless I have to question your remark. Isn't two hundred years of the living hell that is the afterlife proof that God does not exist?

HAWKINS: Now hold on Stephen, you know that's not our remit today. We're here to talk about the state of God, that is, about the impression among the general public about God, not about the existence of a supernatural being.

FRY: I do apologize. Let me rephrase then. Has two hundred years of solitude not changed your opinions about God, Miss Austen? And can we not also assume the general public have changed their opinions?

AUSTEN: Of course the experience of dying and awakening to the reality of the afterlife shook my view of everything that I held dear, Mr Fry. But faith ultimately sustained me. I was never one to believe that God worked on a timetable understandable to us poor mortals

... to say nothing of poor Bishop Usher who usually gets trotted out about now.

COX: I've been guilty about that. I suppose using him to discredit believers is almost as bad as comparing someone to Hitler. Mind you, there are still people who literally believe in the timetable of the Bible. Oh, and there I've gone and lost the argument.

HAWKINS: But back to the question of the general public's view of God, and not to further question Miss Austen.

FRY: I admit God is still part of our society and probably will be for a long time. We still say we dial a phone even though no one's put their finger in a phone dial for ages. So who knows how much longer we're going to say "For God's sake" or "Lord love a duck." But I'm afraid the reality of the afterlife will all but kill any belief in the jiggery-pokery of heaven or an eternal reward.

AUSTEN: Mr Fry ...

FRY: Please, my dear lady, call me Stephen.

AUSTEN: Stephen then, how can you believe the discovery of the afterlife explains anything? Professor Cox ...

COX: Brian, please.

AUSTEN: And you may all call me Jane. Brian, can science explain how it is that I slipped my mortal coil and ended up on facebook, or how I can see X-rays or how I see in 360 degrees without eyes?

COX: I'm afraid not. Theories range from the soul being intelligent dark matter to ... well the joke about "then a miracle happens" still seems appropriate. There are no credible explanations for the soul.

AUSTEN: Precisely. There still remains that God-shaped vacuum[1] in the hearts of men, Stephen. With all the unanswered questions about the afterlife, doesn't it make sense that many will choose to live their lives in accordance with their beliefs from before.

FRY: Oh, so you'll throw Pascal's wager[2] at me, dear lady? I might remind you that many have thrown off this belt and braces caution,

---

1 If Blaise Pascal didn't say—"There is a God-shaped vacuum in the heart of every man which cannot be filled by any created thing, but only by God, the Creator, made known through Jesus"—then he should have.

2 Pascal's wager posits that humans all bet with their lives either that God exists or does not exist. Given the possibility that God actually does exist, a rational person should live as though God exists and seek to believe in

even in America, where the Pew Forum on Religion and Public Life has shown that belief in God and religion has hit an all time low.

AUSTEN: Faith certainly has cycles, but I think the 'reality' of the afterlife only raises questions that can't be answered.

FRY: Brian, help me out here. Surely science has shown there's no reason to believe in God's hand in the afterlife.

COX: What, you mean by introducing yet another mysterious particle/energy that is intelligent and that can't be explained? Yes, we can measure an AfterNet field and even weigh what to all intents and purposes is a soul, but we can't divine what makes Miss Austen's intellect survive her death.

HAWKINS: Miss Austen, maybe you could relate—and I'm sorry for asking this because I know you've been asked many times to do this—your experience after dying?

AUSTEN: It is no imposition. The passage of time has softened the memory. Like most people before the discovery, I thought my condition was unique to me and I thought myself a ghost, which essentially affronted the very practical Anglican beliefs inherited from my father.

HAWKINS: You didn't feel you were abandoned by God?

AUSTEN: No, not at all. I believe my recollection was that I attributed my situation to my own failings, not knowing of course that my fate was shared by all of humanity.

COX: Can we go back to being a ghost contradicting your father's beliefs? He didn't believe in ghosts?

AUSTEN: In a romantic way, of course he did. He even told me ghost stories, but he didn't believe … no that's not the right way to describe it. His was a practical faith and didn't include what Stephen labelled the jiggery-pokery of the church. Miracles and the supernatural were part of Biblical times and apart from the miracle of birth and his many superstitions—which I think he invented to make him a more colourful character—he thought God worked in a … well, in a workmanlike manner. And ghosts, to his mind, would have been God showing off.

God. If God does not actually exist, such a person will only have suffered a momentary (a lifetime's worth) loss of pleasures and indulgences.

· Deeper still ·
Jane's fantasy expands

Jane waited as patiently as she could, but she was beginning to think Albert hadn't received her message asking him to join her. She paced around the busy coffee shop in the West Village, having fled Melody's apartment rather than risk displaying her anger in a cutting remark.

It had been a frustrating day of rehearsing for the launch parties, with Melody giving Mary instructions on how to act like Jane Austen that often ran counter to Jane's advice.

"I would never say that," she objected, when Melody suggested Mary employ a double-entendre joke.

"Oh right, like I couldn't find worse in any of the emails you've sent me."

"Those are in private conversation. I would not make such a joke in public. And what are you laughing about?" Jane caught sight of Mary trying hard to suppress laughter.

"Sorry, but it was funny."

That Mary sided with Melody added to Jane's frustration. After all, she had chosen Mary to be her avatar, but now Melody acted as if it was her brilliant choice to employ Mary. And Mary seemed to recognize that, at present, appeasing Melody rather than Jane was in her best interest.

All this was complicated by the lingering resentment between Jane and Melody after Jane's social media broadside. Despite Mr Pembroke's intervention, Jane and Melody were still nursing their grievances.

Of course Jane knew her complaints were just a symptom of the pressures under which they were working, but she still needed to vent and the one person to whom she could turn was Albert. And so she was delighted when she saw the message: "BertieFromHants has entered the room."

"Albert, thank goodness. I could not remember whether you worked today."

"I am at work. This store's changing rooms are just on the edge of the hotspot of the restaurant next door, so I may lose you from time to time. But after getting your email, I thought I should meet you."

"I don't want to take you from your work," Jane said, although she was hoping that Albert would do just that.

"I am entitled to lunch breaks, which I often take," he said, although that was a lie. He actually didn't mind his job or his time away from being online, but technically he was permitted lunch and two fifteen minutes breaks. He was simply taking his break in the changing room, where he could still look out for shoplifters and chat with Jane.

"Thank you," Jane replied, "I needed your company."

"You mentioned frustration at work. I don't have a shoulder to cry on, but you can vent your frustrations and I promise to be sympathetic."

Jane, however, had spent the last thirty minutes imagining what she would say to Albert and now that he had joined her, she realized how petty was her complaint.

"Actually talking with you has already improved my mood. I realize how silly I would sound if I told you my complaint." She also realized that it would require considerable obfuscation to voice her complaint without compromising the fiction she had created.

"Well, I'm glad that's sorted," he said. "I guess I'll get back to work."

"Don't you dare! This is our first chat in days and yes, I know the fault lies with me."

Albert refrained from saying it was their first chat in almost two weeks and how much he had missed their conversations. Last year they spoke almost daily and at length via instant messaging. This year most of their communication was by email.

"It's perfectly understandable. Your job has overwhelmed you. You recall my behaviour when I started working?"

The question surprised Jane. "Oh, yes. I had forgotten that." She suddenly realized her situation was not unique.

"Both us have spent a very long time alone and without the companionship of the living. To be suddenly working and facing the demands of a schedule again can be … actually, I'm more than a little envious of you." As he sent his reply, he noticed a man enter the changing rooms with several trousers draped over his arm, an unusual thing for a man. Women were more likely to try multiple frocks and blouses. Men usually shopped for a specific item. The man also held a carrier bag from another store, which attracted Albert's attention.

"Really?" Jane replied.

Albert took some time before replying as he followed the man to one of the booths. The man looked casual and didn't seem to be on the lookout for security cameras. Albert returned his attention to Jane. "Uh, yes. First, I dislike anything that robs me of your company. Now our time together is dictated by your schedule and mine, but I know this complaint is shared by millions of … uh, many people have this problem. But I am also envious because you have co-workers, whilst mine is a solitary occupation. That's why I feel the loss of your conversation so keenly."

"And that's how I felt when you started working. I felt … abandoned. I am sorry that the pressures of work make it difficult for us to talk. And I warn you that I see … I think it will only get worse before it gets better. And I am sorry that your occupation is a lonely one. Perhaps you should look for another job."

"I didn't mean to sound so deprived. I see hundreds of people every day and that makes my job interesting. I just wish that I might … talk to them, well some of them. But I'm … I wouldn't want to go job hunting again, not in this economy."

"Isn't there something else you could do? A man like you …"

"What skills do I have? I was a soldier longer than I was a carpenter. And though the military has uses for the disembodied … and a carpenter who can't hold a hammer is useless."

"I only meant … you're an educated man."

"No, I'm not. I only know how to talk above my station. Please Jane, I am content with my lot. Tell me about your job and about your co-workers."

This request was exactly what Jane feared, not that she hadn't prepared for it, of course. She had already populated her imaginary workplace with all manner of endearing characters culled from the many professional people she had met recently. No, her real worry was that she was compounding her minor fiction into a full novel.

"Well, I work for a woman named Melody who's really a lovely woman, but she does think she knows the answer to everything and … well I shouldn't tell tales out of school, but she sometimes takes credit for things she didn't do."

"That is the purview of every manager," Albert said. "Our lieutenant was forever doing that and the sergeant would complain he'd take credit for the sun shining up … for the sun rising in the morning."

"And then there's the new girl, Mary," Jane said and stopped when she realized her mistake.

"I thought you were the new girl, Jane," Albert observed.

"I was the new girl, until Mary was hired."

"O ho, I sense some resentment."

"Perhaps a little, but you make me realize how fortunate I am to have a job and to have co-workers who are really very nice people. Thank you."

"But I've done nothing except complain about my own job. You apparently resolved your problems without my help, despite the deep frustration I detected in your email."

Had she a face, it would be crimson with embarrassment at this. "I fell prey to the curse of email. I wrote and sent it while still angry. And you still helped me because I imagined what I would say to you and what advice you would give me. And my imaginary Albert gave me very good advice indeed."

"Better than the real thing, no doubt," he replied. "I think I'm jealous of this better me." He would have expanded on this theme, but the man who'd entered the booth with the several pairs of trousers exited with no trousers but with his carrier bag noticeably heavier.

"Oh, must dash. I've found my first shoplifter of the day. Please tell me when we can chat again. I don't want another two weeks to go by without hearing from you."

· A new portrait ·
Creating a likeness of Jane Austen

"My lips might be a little fuller," Jane told the artist, feeling quite weary. She wondered whether Mary conveyed her comment with the same weariness. They had been working with the artist for hours and it was clear Melody was losing her patience.

"You're not Julia Roberts, Jane," Melody said with clear frustration in her voice. Mary had to agree to a certain resemblance between the actress and the portrait that was emerging. But she was acting as Jane's avatar and kept her mouth shut, or rather she spoke only what Jane told her to say. Every day she was finding it easier to both speak for Jane and protect the author at the same time. She knew Jane's patience was also wearing thin, but she did her best not to sound exasperated. That is until …

"You have no idea what I looked like," Mary said, speaking for Jane.

Melody replied: "This looks nothing like Cassandra's portrait. Oh, you did not just roll your eyes at me. Wait, Mary, did Jane tell you to roll your eyes?"

"She … I only do … she only did what I tell her. If you say it looks nothing like Cassandra's painting, then it is a marked improvement. Once there's a cap and she adds some curls …"

"Then it will look like Julia Roberts with curly hair wearing a cap,"

Melody said with finality. "Argh! Why is this so hard? And why do you end up looking like somebody else every time we do this?"

Mary waited for Jane's reply, which was slow in coming. "Because I can't quite remember what I looked like," she said finally, which Mary relayed.

"Oh! I ... I uh, I hadn't thought of that," Melody said, all her frustration evaporated after that disclosure. "Hey, Barb, could you give us a minute alone?" she asked the computer artist, which was a bit of cheek for they were sitting in the woman's cubicle.

"No problem. You two ... or three ... work it out; I'm going outside for a smoke," the young woman said, collecting her purse. She left them alone and Melody said, "OK, campfire," and from her voluminous purse she pulled out the small speaker she carried to plug into her AfterNet terminal.

Mary always felt uncomfortable about Melody's campfires because by now she had become accustomed to acting as Jane's avatar and felt a proprietary interest in being the author's voice. She suspected that Melody similarly felt the loss of being Jane's conduit, as evidenced by the fact that Melody still kept her own terminal to talk to Jane. However, if Melody insisted on addressing both her and Jane at the same time, perhaps the campfire was a good idea.

"OK, so maybe you might have mentioned this at some point Jane?" Melody asked, still disconcertingly looking at Mary. Mary looked up at the ceiling to remind Melody that it was her decision to talk to Jane directly.

"It isn't ... it's something I hadn't realized," Jane replied through the speakers.

"How can you not know what you looked liked?" Melody asked. Melody's words were more blunt than she had intended, but she was truly annoyed at the time they had wasted.

"I have not seen my face for almost two hundred years, Melody. And even when alive, I never saw my face reflected back to me with the frequency to which you're accustomed. There were no photographs, no YouTube videos or facebook to remind me several times a day of my own appearance. And I only ever saw myself face on, in the mirror. Rarely did I ever see myself from the side. I am sorry for wasting your time."

Mary felt the ache of Jane's words, even through the flat tone of the terminal's digitized voice, and it was obvious Melody did as well.

"I'm sorry, Jane. I should have realized. This explains your reluctance with the project," Melody said.

"No, it is not entirely ... I tried to ignore my inability to recall my features and it ... it may explain my dissatisfaction with Cassandra's portrait. I truly do not know if it is accurate."

Jane fell silent, as did Melody. Melody obviously felt embarrassed that she had forced this admission from Jane. And Mary could only imagine how sad it must be to forget your own face. The silence continued uncomfortably.

"Why don't you just make something up then?" Mary suggested.

"What?" Melody asked.

"Just make something up. Part of the problem is that Jane is trying to recall something she can't, so she's just picking famous faces. So instead we ask your 3D artist to make up an attractive face with the appropriate dark, curly hair, hazel eyes and flawless complexion and we say that's what you look like."

"How is this possible?" Jane asked.

Mary was about to answer but Melody interrupted her. "That's brilliant. You see it on cop shows all the time. They dig up a skull and some forensic artist makes a face from it. We could have Barb do the same thing."

"I do not relish the idea of digging up my skull."

"Sorry, that was a bad choice of words. I mean Barb just starts with a standard Northern European skull shape and works from there. We give her free rein."

"But wouldn't it be a lie?"

"Maybe a little, but who's to know. And the only one who can really object to it is you. I mean do you?"

"Well, I confess I am vain enough to not want to be represented in a poor light."

"Being your agent, I also would not want you to be hideous; it could negatively impact book sales. We just can't make you too gorgeous."

When Barb returned, the concept was proposed to her. The 25-year-old tattooed computer artist with the spiky black hair seemed to listen with disinterest as they explained their proposal. With her right hand, she was doing something with her computer, apparently searching for a file, while with her left hand she was playing with the ring pierced through her left eyebrow.

Melody's patience was evaporating as she tried to explain the concept. "You can feel free to do what you want because you can just make an idealized portrait ... excuse me, are you listening to me?"

"Maybe something like this?" Barb asked, after she had finally found the file she sought and double clicked it. The window that opened caught the attention of Melody, Mary and Jane.

"Oh my God, that's perfect," Mary said, and then felt guilty because it was Jane's decision and shouldn't try to influence her.

"The nose is ... prominent," Melody said.

You should talk, Mary thought. But Jane said, "No, it is the Austen nose, Melody."

"It's still a little big," Melody countered.

"Then how about this one?" Barb asked. She opened another file and the same image appeared, except for a slightly less prominent nose.

"Now that's more like it," Melody said. "I like that."

"But when did you do this?" Jane asked.

"Yes, why didn't you show us these before?" Melody demanded.

"Well, A, that's not what you asked for. You wanted to reproduce what Jane Austen looked like when alive. And B, my boss said I shouldn't show you work I did on my own time."

"You did these on your own time?" Jane asked.

"Yeah, as soon as I heard you'd been found, I mean identified. I've been a fan since high school, ever since *Pride and Prejudice*," she said, the last with some defiance.

Melody, Mary and Jane looked at this pierced, tattooed, fierce young woman professing her love for Jane. Apparently the incongruity was not lost on Barb.

"I know I don't look like a fan, but I fell in love with Elizabeth and Darcy all the same, Miss Austen. Then I read all your books, but I probably still like *P&P* the best."

"But what prompted you to create these?"

"It was that horrible portrait of you they discovered, the pencil sketch with the cat.[1] I thought you looked awful and nothing like Cassandra's portrait, which I actually sort of like. Everyone was going on about the new portrait and I thought I could do better. I'd always

---

1 In 2011, Paula Byrne, who would later write *The Real Jane Austen: A Life in Small Things,* announced that she had what might be a heretofore unknown pencil sketch of Jane Austen. The nose of the face in the sketch was prominent. Opinion is divided as to the authenticity of the sketch.

imagined what you looked like, especially when you were my age. I tried to base it on your family resemblance—that's the one with the nose—but I didn't like that one so I modified it to what I wanted you to look like." She broke eye contact and looked down, "How'd I do?"

"It's lovely," Jane said. "I can't honestly say that's exactly what I looked like, but I certainly wish I had."

"You look like Emma," Melody said.

"Beg pardon?" Jane asked. "Do you mean by this I look like Gwyneth Paltrow?"

"No, don't be facetious, Jane. No I mean you look like fun. You've got that look I always imagined Emma would have, an expectation that the world would offer you amusement and you were looking forward to it."

Jane paused before answering. "I think that at this age ... I still did expect that of the world, before we moved to Bath and before my father died."

None of the women said anything after that until Mary said privately to Jane through her own terminal, "Well that was a downer, Jane. You might want to lighten the mood."

Jane could not reply to Mary directly for fear that Melody's terminal might translate her response. Instead she said to them all: "I think your portrait is perfect Barb, with the exception that you have shown me outdoors and I would not be without a cap or bonnet. I suggest a light cap, no more than a wisp for modesty."

"And do you think we can make her eye colour a little more hazel?" Melody asked.

"Oh, that is important Melody," Jane agreed.

"And do you not think that as she seems to be sitting out of doors with not even a shawl that she looks like she might be a little cold," Barb asked with a querulous voice that Melody and Mary appreciated.

"Hush, Mr Woodhouse[2]," Jane said to Barb, who smiled, pleased

---

2 Mr Woodhouse is the hypochondriacal father of the titular character in *Emma*. He fears the cold and assumes others are similarly afflicted. When Emma paints a portrait of her friend Harriet Smith, Mr Woodhouse observes: "The only thing I do not thoroughly like is, that she seems to be sitting out of doors, with only a little shawl over her shoulders—and it makes one think she must catch cold."

that her reference had not been lost. Then Barb turned back to her computer and muttered under her breath: "Clients, sheesh."

· Launching Sanditon ·
Planning the NYC/London book launches

M elody rubbed her temples and then her eyes. She couldn't believe the difficulties of scheduling the London launch party and
why she needed to be here at the meeting, but consoled herself
with the thought that it was just one of the responsibilities of
being Jane Austen's agent.

She was tired from worrying about the tension that had developed
between herself and Jane. Melody felt some measure of responsibility—perhaps she had taken a little too seriously her new role as Jane's
business manager and maybe she had been trying to use Mary as leverage with Jane, but everything she'd done had been in their best interests.

Thankfully relations had warmed lately and Jane seemed to take
her suggestions as intended and Melody had tried to not interfere with
Jane's relationship with Mary. It was, after all, in their best interests
that Jane and Mary should be the closest of friends, although that
might make it all the harder once they no longer needed Mary as an
avatar.

The other headache had been moving into the office space for the
combined Kramer Associates/Austen Enterprises; and interviewing
candidates for the job of her assistant. That last task might be put
aside, however. She'd just heard from Rebecca, her former assistant.
She was affianced no longer and had called Melody for support and

sympathy and Melody had surprised herself by mentioning the possibility of Rebecca returning to New York.

She was surprised because she thought she still held resentment over Rebecca's abandonment. Rebecca had gotten engaged without telling Melody, and it was something of a surprise when Rebecca announced she was moving to California to start her own agency and get married. During their conversation, however, Melody was reminded how much she had depended on Rebecca. Unfortunately she wasn't quite sure if she'd actually offered the job to Rebecca and thought maybe ...

"What about Tuesday? Would that work for Miss Austen?" Mr Laurence asked, his voice surprisingly clear over the conference call speaker in Mr Pembroke's office.

Melody had a moment of confusion, trying to remember what they'd been talking about.

"Excuse me, I didn't quite hear that," she said.

"Can we nail down Tuesday as the book launch and have the party that evening?" the voice over the speaker said.

"Uh, yes, that will be fine," Melody said. Actually, she'd hoped to be doing some of her own sightseeing on Tuesday, but obviously the book launch was the most important thing they would be doing in London.

"That's a horrible day for a launch party. Wednesday is better," someone else said in the London office, the newcomer's voice overstepping Melody's remarks in that annoying half-second lag of trans-Atlantic calls done through Skype.

"Wednesday would also be fine for Miss Austen," Melody said, eager to move on.

Mr Pembroke, perhaps sensing Melody's annoyance, suggested, "Perhaps we could move on to the venue. The last we heard you were suggesting the Savoy."

There was longer than the half-second silence from the other end. "Well, that was floated here, but the expense ... value for money ..."

Mr Pembroke smiled, not surprised at that reaction, and interjected, "The expense should not be a consideration, not where Jane Austen is concerned."

"Well of course," the other side of the Atlantic confirmed. "No, we were just thinking ... a false economy of course ... yes the Savoy would be perfect. Or the Ritz. We can get a good price at the Ritz."

"I'm sure the Ritz would be fine as well," Mr Pembroke confirmed. He pressed the mute button on the speaker.

"I thought they might try to low ball this," he confided to Melody. He was smiling broadly though, evidently enjoying promoting his last and most famous author. Melody smiled back at him, not sure whether the Ritz was a step up or down from the Savoy; both hotels sounded wonderful to her and she remembered them from *Notting Hill*.

He unmuted and continued: "By the bye, I don't think we've gotten the invite list yet."

Again a pause from the other side that went on long enough that Mr Pembroke added, "I'm sure Miss Kramer will want to make any notes that will help Miss Austen during introductions."

"Jane doesn't follow gossip," Melody said, blatantly lying but wanting to defend the impression of Jane as a high-minded individual. In fact, she looked forward to sitting with Jane and dishing dirt on the celebrities they hoped would attend. Jane would pretend to that high-minded tone, but in fact she followed the careers of those actors who had played her characters. But it was true that she knew almost nothing of contemporary British comedians and actors and television outside her interests. She recalled her attempt at explaining *Doctor Who* to her—a difficult task because Melody didn't really understand *Doctor Who*—and the fascination with whatever actor was the latest to portray the famous Time Lord. Fortunately Mary was able to help with that topic.

"So it really would help if I could give her a head's up on who's sleeping with who ... I mean whom," she added.

"Er, yes, we'll send you something today. Problem is the list keeps growing because the launch party is already an open secret and everyone wants to make sure they're invited," Mr Laurence admitted.

Mr Pembroke rolled his eyes, annoyed the London office wanted to economize when the book launch was drawing this much attention. Still, he was glad it wasn't coming out of his budget. The New York launch was already causing grumbling.

"I know how it is William," Mr Pembroke said to his counterpart. "We're having the same problem and we've had to change hotels here to accommodate the larger group. We'll need Lincoln Center by the time we're done.

"Now can we move on to the poster for the launch party. I notice your latest mockup uses Goudy Old Style for the title."

Oh God, kill me now, Melody thought. Once Alan started going on the topic of fonts, she knew she was doomed. Problem was that he'd started out in life as a typographer, back in the day when Helvetica was considered avante garde—*crap, that was practically a type joke*—and had no taste for modern typography. Which made him a pretty good choice for working with a Jane Austen novel, but didn't endear him to graphic designers on either side of the Atlantic.

She decided it might be a good time to sneak out for a bathroom break and whispered to him—"I am just going outside and may be some time"—and stole from his office, he little caring for he was busy debating the fine points of the kerning of the words "You're invited to:"

Melody did use the opportunity to visit the lavatory and then found the break room where she topped off her travel mug. She nodded pleasantly at the receptionist who was heating her microwave diet meal and confessed her fondness for her frozen chicken parmigiana entrée, the pathetic aroma of which failed to arouse any hunger from Melody, but she still enjoyed the conversation. Because of the weeks and months of the book negotiations and then the planning for the book tour, she had become almost a fixture in the office.

Fortunately the receptionist was taking her meal back to eat at her desk, leaving Melody alone. She used the time to call Tamara.

"What are you doing?" Melody asked her partner when a breathless Tamara answered the phone amid the clamour of rattling pans.

"I just thought I'd try making something a little special for tonight," Tamara answered. She had thought about spaghetti bolognese.

"What about chicken parmigiana?" Melody suggested.

"Oh, I've never tried that before," Tamara replied, surprised at the request. She was celebrating the success of the new work schedule implementation and finally had some time on her hands. She and Melody had been living on takeout for weeks—that is when Melody was actually home.

"But I'm sure it's not much more difficult than the spaghetti," she lied. There were chicken breasts in the freezer, and she'd need to get some real parmigiana and mozzarella, and Panko bread crumbs for the chicken breast and she'd need to make marinara sauce instead of the bolognese sauce and that meant she'd need white wine instead of red; and all these thoughts were going round in her head alongside the guilt of a kept woman.

The kept woman guilt had finally struck her the other day when she caught a glimpse of one of the movie offers for *Sanditon*. Melody had written down some quick figures that Tamara had interpreted as the offer and was struck by the amount. Then she realized that what Melody had written down was her percentage as Jane's agent.

Their conversation turned to other topics; the daily back and forth of two people who loved each other and had been in love for quite some time. Eventually, however, Melody decided she'd been away from Mr Pembroke too long and resigned herself to returning to discussions of the minutiae of the book launch. She said goodbye to Tamara and thought yet again how fortunate she was to find someone so lucky and talented.

And Tamara thought she'd better look up a chicken parmigiana recipe online.

· Roommates ·
Stephen and Albert meet online

Stephen tried to ignore the distractions his computer continually offered while he was writing his speech for the upcoming romance conference in Colorado Springs, but the bookmark for Virtual Chawton kept tempting him.

He was no longer actively helping Dr Davis and frankly thought her obsession a waste of time. It wasn't like this Jane Austen suddenly emerged out of nowhere. The AfterNet had announced it was examining a claimant to Jane Austen's legacy for months before they made their decision. So if this person was not really her, then the real Jane Austen had had ample time to make a counterclaim. That no one had done so meant either that there were no legitimate claimants or the real Jane Austen had over the course of nearly two hundred years withdrawn from the world of flesh and blood so much that she no longer cared about her identity and her legacy.

So if he had to choose between a Jane Austen who seemed to be living up to the reputation—and that certainly seemed to be the impression of those few familiar with her completion of *Sanditon*—or a Jane Austen so lost to dementia that she couldn't be bothered to claim her identity, then his choice was simple.

But just as an intellectual exercise, he was still curious how Austen had proven her identity. As he'd told Davis, the mapping project, the 3D reconstructions and the inventories of both Chawton House and

Chawton Cottage meant it was pretty difficult for anyone to claim secret knowledge.

He had been wondering if the answer lay in Edward Austen-Knight's other home, Godmersham Park. Perhaps Austen knew some detail at that house, which was now the home of a medical college. And soon he was reflecting on the parallels between his life and Edward's.

Jane's brother was the third oldest sibling, one of Jane's six brothers. And he had been borrowed by his father's cousin, Thomas Knight and his wife, and later adopted by them as they had no children of their own. The Reverend George Austen and his wife must understandably have hated to relinquish their rights to their son, but in the practical calculations of the day, it made sense to offer Edward a much better life with the wealthy Knights. After all, the Austens regularly visited their son at his several homes after the death of his adoptive parents and it was Edward who allowed Mrs Austen, Cassandra, Jane and their friend Martha Lloyd to live at Chawton Cottage, a house near his estate Chawton House. In that light, allowing Edward to be adopted certainly paid off.

Edward's life closely resembled that of a character in *Emma*. In that novel, Mr Weston, left unable by grief and genteel poverty to raise his son after the death of his first wife, allowed his brother-in-law and his wife to adopt his son, Frank. And in *Mansfield Park,* Fanny Price is not quite adopted but is raised by the Bertrams. And again in *Emma*, Jane Fairfax is cared for by the Campbells after the death of her father.

So repeatedly, Stephen found that Austen's definition of family ties was quite mutable, something he appreciated, as he was also to some extent a loaned son. At sixteen, he'd gone to Evanston, Illinois, to live with his childless uncle and aunt. He'd enrolled in prep school there, paid for by his uncle, and then went to Northwestern University, also partly paid for by his uncle and the scholarships Stephen had been awarded. He regularly went home to Bloomington, however, and didn't need to change his name, but in many ways, he felt the same divided loyalties that he imagined Edward had experienced. And now he also felt guilt in not being able to support Davis in her quest to unseat Austen.

Lost in these conflicting thoughts and emotions, he was happy when his computer distracted him with new mail.

From: AARidings@theAfterNet.net
To: StephenAbrams@uchicago.edu
Date: Mar. 10, 2011 09:31:11
Subject: AGM roommates

Greetings Mr Abrams,
I learn from JASNA that you have graciously volunteered to be one of the
living roommates for the disembodied attendees of the upcoming AGM
and I have been fortunate enough to be assigned to your care.
Please allow me to thank you for your kind offer. You must be very
understanding of the concerns of the disembodied and I very much
appreciate your willingness to act as our—well I abhor the word
facilitator as was stated in the email I received—guide, perhaps.
I assure you I am a man of modest habits and do not snore and will respect
your privacy, although that may be difficult for a little research shows that
you are a student of Dr Alice Davis and surely you must have opinions to
offer us regarding the special guest at the AGM.
If there is any information you require of me, please do not hesitate to
ask. I assume as the time draws near, you will provide us with more
information about the arrangements and until that time,
I remain your humble servant,
Albert Ridings

Stephen read this with a grin, amused at Albert's elaborate tone. Stephen had a fair number of disembodied friends, and some of them had
definitely crafted affectations. He suspected many were not authenti-
cally of their era and he wondered if Albert were playing up his part.
He decided to reply in kind:

Dear Mr Ridings,
Thank you for your many compliments. I look forward to meeting you
at the AGM and you are correct that I will provide more information
as the date draws near. You have the distinction of being the first of
my disembodied roommates to reply, however, so I will gladly take any
suggestions from you as to what information you would require.
It may help you to know my appearance and to that end I include this link
to my facebook page where I hope you might ask me to be your friend.
And yes the news that Jane Austen will be addressing the AGM certainly
has kept me busy. You can imagine for someone like me the appeal of

being able to directly ask Miss Austen questions, rather than sifting through family records, divining answers from diary entries and casual observations or traveling to England to examine museum inventories. Well, the last actually has a certain appeal.

Of course, even if this is the actual Jane Austen—something which I am ready to accept—the passage of time may have affected her recollections and will still need to be verified independently if possible.

I look forward to your reply and again any suggestions as to how I may make your attendance at the AGM more enjoyable.

In kind, I offer myself as your humble and obedient servant.

Stephen James Abrams, esq

Stephen smirked when adding the esquire, especially as his only pretension to the landed gentry was his one-year lease on a studio apartment, but he thought himself equal to Albert's flowery flummery. He forced himself to return to his task of writing his speech when his email chimed again and found that Albert had asked him to be his friend on facebook.

He confirmed Albert, which allowed him to view Albert's page. He found an old photo that showed a typical Tommy[1] from World War I, posed in front of some painted backdrop with his hat sitting on a waist high plinth next to him. He could make out little other than that the man appeared older than the typical soldier, although that may have been the effect of the man's smart moustache and by his sergeant's stripes. Clicking about also revealed references to the Battle of the Somme, the 1st Battalion of the Hampshire Regiment, JASNA and Boca Raton, Florida, Albert's current home. It was clear from the context that Albert claimed to be someone who'd died during World War I, presumably at the Battle of the Somme, although Stephen could also see that Albert did not have a verified identity.

Judging from the postings on his page, however, that did not stop Albert from having connected with the descendants of his family. He found numerous photos and videos of grandchildren and great-grandchildren. Stephen also assumed his descendants were the source of Albert's photograph. Taken as a whole, it seemed a pretty convincing portrait of a man who'd died during the Great War and had successfully reconnected with his very extensive family.

---

1 Slang for British soldiers, especially during World War I

But somehow the story of Albert discovering Jane Austen while convalescing from his wounds just seemed too ridiculously based on Rudyard Kipling's *The Janeite*. Of course he knew there was a basis for the story. A soldier, returned to England and recovering from his wounds at a manor house pressed into service as a hospital, might well be given a copy of *Pride and Prejudice* by a kind-hearted nurse.

OK, that's the romance author in me. I've created an elaborate background story of a man I've just met and of whose identity I am uncertain. Oh well, what does it matter if he truly is a Tommy that died in World War I or an accountant who died in Ipswich in 1988? He's still my roommate.

· Where to put Jane ·
Accommodating the author at the AGM

"Shouldn't she open the AGM?" Beth Ann asked for possibly the third time since their lunch began. The organizing committee was busy trying to rearrange the schedule. Dr Joan Klingel Ray, former JASNA president, had been their original choice to open with her talk: "Sense and Sensibility as The Problem Novel." Dr Ray was a popular choice, back when the theme was simply two hundred years of *Sense and Sensibility*.

"The first plenary session? No, then everything else is a letdown," Cindy told her friend.

"But everyone will be clamouring for it."

"Then all the more reason to delay it for Saturday," said Megan, the other coordinator. "Besides, not everyone can make it on Friday."

"Oh right," Beth Ann conceded, and then added, "but if it were Friday, then everyone can be talking about it the whole weekend."

"It's not like we won't be talking about it the whole weekend either way. Actually having Jane Austen at the AGM? How wild is that?" Megan asked her friends.

"Would you ladies care for another round?" their waiter asked, interrupting Cindy, who was about to reply to Megan's remark.

All three ladies agreed and also asked for another basket of chips and salsa, which the waiter immediately brought to their table, spurring another round of dipping and munching.

"It's actually a bit of an imposition, though," Cindy said as she knocked back the remainder of her margarita and looked in vain for the waiter to bring the second round. She followed this with ice water, cursing that she'd allowed herself to be tricked into the endless cycle of salty, spicy food and salty drink and then ice water followed by a massive Mexican dinner. It was her fault for agreeing to discuss their planning at a restaurant instead of at one of their homes.

"What's an imposition?" Beth Ann asked.

"You know, what Megan said," she replied.

"What? I just said it'll be wild to have Jane Austen there."

"Don't you want Jane Austen to come?" Beth Ann asked.

"Well, sure, but let's face it, we have to change everything to do it … move everyone's schedules around … I mean if we move someone to Friday, well Dr Davis had planned to fly in Saturday morning."

"That's why I wanted Jane to talk Friday. My friend Carol, she's the one who introduced me to Jane, she wasn't planning to come to the AGM this year because of her nephew's wedding, but she thought she might fly in Thursday night and …"

"It's not just the inconvenience," Cindy said, a little more loudly than she'd intended, and then regretted saying it. "No sorry, forget I said anything. She'll have to go on Saturday and …"

She realized her two friends were looking at her. They'd been friends in the North Texas chapter for years, all of them joining JASNA about the same time, and by now they knew each other pretty well, and they'd caught Cindy's tone.

"What's up, Cindy?" Beth Ann asked.

"Yeah, you've got that tone."

Cindy looked at her friends and decided to confess her misgivings. "I mean how do we know it really is Jane? Won't we feel incredibly stupid if it's not her?"

Beth Ann's confusion was evident. "But she is Jane Austen. The AfterNet says she is."

"What, the AfterNet is always right? I mean how can anyone really be sure?"

"Well, legally she's Jane Austen, right? So what difference does it make?"

Cindy shook her head. "No, that's not what it means at all."

"Huh?" Megan and Beth Ann said in unison.

"I've been looking into it. All it means is that the AfterNet has recognized her as Jane Austen. But it's just like a company policy, or a quasi-governmental agency's policy, or whatever the AfterNet is. But legally, I don't think it means anything."

"Well, it meant enough for ... who's publishing her book?"

"Random House," Megan supplied.

"Yeah, well it was enough for Random House to sign her up for a bazillion dollars and for whoever it is to make a *Sanditon* movie."

Megan agreed. "Uh huh, it has to be a pretty good book for them to pay her for it. They wouldn't pay her if it doesn't read like the real thing."

"I don't know about that," Cindy objected. "How many times have we heard about some famous author writing some amazing continuation and it reads like crap?"

"I really liked the excerpt I read," Beth Ann countered. "What about you, Megan?"

"Well ... it was good, but ... well it was just an excerpt. I mean I liked it and all, but ..."

Megan's comments trailed off and she looked thoughtful.

"Sorry about the drinks," their waiter said, again interrupting their conversation, placing their margaritas and Beth Ann's daiquiri from the small tray he held, while a busboy behind them scurried over to their table with a much larger tray, holding a combination enchilada plate, chicken fajitas and a taco salad. Together, they completely covered their table with food.

"Is there anything else you need? More salsa?" the waiter asked, eager to make up for the late drink order.

The women assured him they were fine and were eager to be left alone to continue their conversation.

"Sorry, I shouldn't have said anything," Cindy said. "Of course it's big news Jane's coming ... I'm just bitching about it messing with our schedule."

"No, that's OK," Beth Ann said. "But I guess I feel a little stupid for not even thinking it's possible that she isn't the real Jane Austen. I mean it would be great if she is Jane, wouldn't it? I've got like a million questions. Which reminds me we should plan for a really long Q&A period."

"What do you think most people think?" Megan asked, ignoring Beth Ann's enthusiasm.

"I don't know," Cindy replied, now very upset for having voiced her doubts.

"There was a poll on Jane Austen Today, when it was announced on her birthday she'd been identified," Beth Ann said. "I think it was about 50-50, but you know something like that's not scientific. I didn't pay it much attention."

"OK, enough about this. Let's get back to planning this. I like your thought about the Q&A, Beth Ann. I also think we've got to make sure we include Jane … and her avatar … does anyone know her name? When Ajala called, she just said Jane and her avatar."

"Well, you're not going to believe this, but I read that her avatar's real name is Mary Crawford."

That information understandably generated further discussion among the three women, another round of drinks and ensured that little was actually accomplished that night with regards to the planning for the AGM.

· White soup for the soul ·
Regency medicine

Mary tried counting to ten but only got to three. Melody had been criticising her performance all morning in the still bare conference room of Melody's new office.

"If you have some problem with my reading, just say so," she finally told Melody. "Don't just sit there with that sour look on your face!"

Melody, who'd been trying to remember how many antacids she'd taken that morning, was surprised by Mary's outburst.

"What? I don't have a problem."

"Yes you do. You do nothing but look at me and wince, and it's been that way all week. I think I'm doing a damn good job, but if you don't like it …"

But now Melody winced yet again and Mary realized she was in some pain.

"Hush, Mary. Have you still not seen a doctor?" Jane asked.

"What doctor?" Mary inquired.

"She suffers from indigestion and should see her doctor."

"I haven't got time to make an appointment," Melody protested.

"Then at the very least take one of the over the counter medications containing a proton pump inhibitor such as omeprazole."

Jane's statement surprised Mary and Melody, who looked at each other and suddenly laughed.

"Oh that's great. I'm getting my health care advice from Jane Austen."

"I think that's a whole new untapped market, Melody. Health advice from Jane Austen."

"White soup[1] for the soul," Melody suggested.

"Pardon me for taking an interest in your problem," Jane said, "but if you fail to understand the perils of gastroesophageal reflux diseases and its attendant risk …"

But Jane's attempt to describe the risk of erosive esophagitis only made Mary and Melody laugh again.

"I'm sorry, Jane," Melody finally said after her laughter subsided. "It's just a little weird to hear you talking about modern medicine. I keep expecting you to suggest leeches."

"No, I suggest Prilosec, but knowing your inherent miserly-ness, I suspect you will opt for a generic."

Melody paused to belch delicately before responding. "OK, you sold me. I think I'll go get some right now."

"Do you not have a very able assistant named Sarah who could run such an errand?" Jane suggested. Sarah had been hired only the week before after Melody had finally convinced her ancient receptionist Lillian to retire.

---

1   For whatever reason, white soup was often served at Regency assemblies—public dances that often went into the wee hours. In *Pride and Prejudice*, Charles Bingley says: "As for the ball, it is quite a settled thing; and as soon as Nicholls has made white soup enough I shall send round my cards."

Here's a recipe from John Farley's *London Art of Cooking* (1783):

Put a knuckle of veal into six quarts of water, with a large fowl, and a pound of lean bacon, half a pound of rice, two anchovies, a few pepper corns, a bundle of sweet herbs, two or three onions, and three or four heads of celery cut in slices. Stew them all together, till the soup be as strong as you would have it, and then strain it through a hair sieve into a clean earthen pot. Having let it stand all night, the next day take off the scum, and pour it clean off into a tossing-pan. Put in half a pound of Jordan almonds beat fine, boil it a little, and run it through a lawn [fine cloth] sieve. Then put in a pint of cream, and the yolk of an egg, and send it up hot.

Today, of course, it would seem strange to serve a hot, creamy soup to young people flushed from dancing.

Jane's suggestion caught Melody by surprise.

"Oh yeah, I do." She made to rise to walk and ask Sarah, but then thought to pick up the phone in the conference room. She paused in doubt, however, looking at the unlabelled buttons.

"It is the second speed dial button," Jane said. Melody gave Jane a wry look.

"I know, I know that." She connected with Sarah and gave her the errand.

"Some food might also relieve your symptoms," Jane said.

Melody also ordered lunch for herself and Mary.

After she hung up, she turned to Mary.

"I'm sorry if you got the impression I was upset with your reading. You're actually doing a great job."

"Oh. I just thought ... really? Sometimes I don't think you're paying any attention to me and then you'd make those faces."

"No, that's just the sour stomach. And if my mind's elsewhere ... well, it's just the survey numbers."

"What survey numbers?" Jane asked.

"I paid a polling company to see what percentage of Janeites accept you."

"Oh, and the results?"

"Unchanged. About half do and half don't."

"I'm sure that will change once the book's on sale," Mary said.

"Does it truly matter?" Jane asked.

"Of course it matters," Melody answered, accompanied by a little grimace.

"Whatever may be the opinion of me, or even of *Sanditon*, ultimately means little."

"Oh, I know what this is. I've seen it before."

"Seen what before?" Mary asked.

"She's in that 'what have I done lately funk' and that 'my best work is behind me' blues. Seriously, Jane, *Sanditon* is your best ever, and I think for the same reason that *P&P* and *S&S* are so good. You've been thinking about and working at it for so long that it's perfect.

"And as a matter of fact, that would apply to you, Mary. You've got Jane down perfectly and you're right to tell me off."

"Oh, OK, thanks."

"No, I mean it. I had my doubts, but now I can't imagine anyone else representing Jane."

"I must agree," Jane said. "I cannot speak to your ability to sound like me, but I have definitely seen your confidence increase."

"Thank you. I guess I have gotten … I am a lot more confident. I think for the first time, I really know what it means to inhabit a role."

"Perhaps we have been working a little too hard, Melody."

Melody had been smiling and nodding during this exchange, but Jane's last words brought her back to reality.

"Are you serious? Our first reading is two days away. We're going to eat our lunch, I'll take a proton pump what's it and then we're going to go through it again until it's perfect."

· A sneak peek ·
Jane and Mary's first book reading

J ane looked nervously to the book-lined corridor as Mr Pembroke continued his lengthy story about the drunken author he once had to extricate from a jail in the southern American state of Georgia. A long life spent in publishing had given him a vast fund of stories and he was entertaining Jane, Melody and Mary with those stories while they waited for more people to arrive at the Strand for the book signing.

But Jane could not keep her mind on the story. She kept hoping to see another attendee to supplement the seven people who'd arrived so far. All seven were seated alone, spread out over the two sections, five rows and 49 chairs, one chair in the last row gone missing. She'd had time to count.

It all looked so horribly empty to Jane and she wondered if there were some way to better distribute the six women and one man, but decided short of a miracle of the loaves and fishes variety that there was little to be done.

"I finally found a judge to set bail but by then it was too late. But it didn't matter; he used the story as his own *Reading Gaol*[1] opportunity

---

1   Oscar Wilde wrote his poem *The Ballad of Reading Gaol* after his incarceration at that jail. Wilde had been convicted of homosexual offences in 1895 and sentenced to two years hard labour.

and created a particularly pornographic ballad that I cannot possibly repeat. He would recite it at any literary party after his fourth or fifth martini. He never could hold his liquor. Which reminds me of ..."

Jane decided she could take the opportunity while he related yet another publishing story to see if there were people in the store who might look as if they had come to the book signing but had gotten lost.

She was philosophic about the turnout, of course, and had said that ten people or a hundred made no difference to her, but seven! She left Mary's side and navigated the maze to the middle of the store, which was doing good business on a Saturday morning. Coffee sipping customers were in line at the registers and the table of bargain advance reading copies was mobbed.

It was quite a scene and Jane thought briefly of the circulating libraries of her day, where she often met with people to gossip, buy postcards and had attended several book readings. She tried to imagine herself at Marshall's on Milsom Street in Bath, a venti cappuccino in hand, listening to Ann Radcliffe read from *The Mysteries of Udolpho*[2] while following along on her e-reader.

Unfortunately her recce failed to make her aware of any individuals obviously there for her appearance and she retreated back to the reading area.

She reacquired the AfterNet field of Mary's terminal and realized her avatar was speaking for her to the store manager, who had just rejoined them.

"Please don't concern yourself, Mr Britten. A low turnout might be a blessing for I am already nervous," Mary said to the worried young store employee. Jane looked at the transcript of their conversation and saw that he had apologized for the low turnout.

"Where have you been?" Mary asked of Jane. "I've been tap dancing while you were gone."

Jane wasn't familiar with the expression but guessed its meaning.

"Sorry, I just looked in the hallway. And also through the store to see ..."

But Jane's reply was cut short by Mr Britten holding up one hand while talking into the phone he held up to his ear.

---

2   Austen parodied Radcliffe's gothic story in *Northanger Abbey*. Radcliffe was a contemporary, although *The Mysteries of Udolpho* was published in 1794, long before Austen's novel.

"Oh, wait a minute," he said to Mary and Melody. "It looks like we have some people waiting outside on the sidewalk. I think someone put up the overflow sign. Let me take care of this." He and Mr Pembroke hurriedly left to investigate, leaving Jane, Mary and Melody able to converse.

"I told you there was nothing to worry about," Melody said, but the relief in her voice made clear that she'd been worried as well. Melody had advocated this book signing a week ahead of the official start of the book tour as a "shakedown cruise" and it was put together with almost no publicity or advertising. Instead they decided to see how much of a turnout could be achieved just by word of mouth.

"Well, as Mary said, a low turnout might be preferable," Jane said. Mary spoke these words for Jane, feeling odd to be referring to herself in the third person.

"Are you nervous, Jane?" Melody asked.

"Not as nervous as Mary must be, is that not so?"

Mary said these last words uncertain how to answer. Finally she said, "I thought we agreed I shouldn't break out of character, Jane. And if you're going to address me while I'm speaking as you, I think you will make me nervous."

"Quite right, Mary," Melody said. "I'm glad you at least understand how this must work."

Mary smiled at this, happy for once to be the target of Melody's praise. Just last night, Melody had been quizzing Mary about the details of Jane's life until she knew them better than the author herself.

Her biggest challenge was remembering Jane's family tree, which included Lloyds, Perrots, Lefroys, de Feuillides, Leighs and Knights. Fortunately Jane could untangle the most complicated family ties, but Melody insisted Mary memorize Jane's genealogy for those times when she was speaking extemporaneously—without Jane being present.

Jane's task to prepare for the book tour was to answer inane questions posed to her by Melody: What was your favourite food? Who was your favourite brother? Did you ever fire a weapon?

She also asked Jane considerably more personal and delicate questions: How did you get along with your mother? Did you ever fall in love? Were you ever attracted to women? Did you ever have sex?

Melody asked these "gotcha" questions as she called them only when Mary was actively representing Jane and usually at the most inopportune moments. She said Jane and Mary had to be prepared to deal with rude questions, but Mary sometimes wondered whether Melody secretly wanted the answers and was using their training as an excuse to ask.

Therefore it didn't surprise Mary when Melody asked, "So Jane, did you and Tom Lefroy ever do it?"

Mary was prepared to use one of their stock responses, perhaps: "Does impertinence pass for cleverness in this day and age?" And so she was amused when Jane directed her to say, "Yes we did, regularly and with gusto. We often did it in the library while reading *Tom Jones*."[3]

The look on Melody's face was priceless, and Mary had the further joy that she was behaving as Melody had asked, conveying Jane's words exactly.

Melody was trying to respond when they heard a commotion from the hallway and then Mr Britten returned followed by a stream of people

"Apparently we had quite a few waiting outside," he told them. "And some were shopping, so we made an announcement in the store. Sorry about the confusion."

Melody accepted his apology with ill humour but Mary again responded graciously for Jane.

"Please do not concern yourself, Mr Britten, especially as you have supplied a multitude."

That might have been a slight exaggeration, but there were now about twenty people in the lecture room and the noise level rose considerably. The people who'd been waiting outside were especially vocal, as they'd already formed friendships from waiting.

"Excuse me, Miss Austen, Ms Kramer?" a woman asked. Melody and Mary turned to see an additional group of five women and one man enter the room. The man, and the woman immediately next to him, was dressed in Regency costume and all were wearing JASNA badges or pins or some other device that identified them as Janeites.

Melody put on her professional smile and addressed the tall black

---

3 In a letter to her sister, Austen wrote of Tom Lefroy: "He is a very great admirer of Tom Jones, and therefore wears the same coloured clothes, I imagine, which he did when he was wounded." *The History of Tom Jones, a Foundling*, is a novel by Henry Fielding published in 1749. The novel's tales of sexual promiscuity and Jones's status as a bastard made it scandalous.

woman who had spoken. "Ms Hawkins, I'm so glad you could make it."

"So sorry we're late. We met up at a restaurant before coming and the service was abysmal and ... you know how it is."

While she was talking to Melody, her eyes were of course on Mary, who was conspicuous for her youth, beauty and her dress, which suggested a Regency costume. It was actually Melody's idea to give Mary a high-waisted wrap around muslin skirt that she could wear over her mid-length empire waist dress. This allowed Mary to travel to an event somewhat inconspicuously and by adding the wrap around skirt she suddenly became Jane Austen.

Melody could see the women wished to address Mary, but were clearly reluctant to put themselves forward.

"Ms Hawkins, ladies, sir," Melody said with the sudden inspiration that formality seemed advisable, "may I introduce you to Miss Jane Austen."

Almost as one the ladies half curtseyed[4] (or bowed or nodded) and the gentleman gave a bow. Mary responded with a wide smile and a curtsey and then said, "I am very glad to meet you, Ms Hawkins." And then with an inspiration of her own, Mary advanced to each member of the group and offered her hand, but not with the thumb up. Instead with the women she took the extended hand and clasped it in her own and to the gentlemen she offered her hand, which he took and offered another slight bow. Mary thought of a politician working a rope line and wondered if this would be a template for future introductions.

Jane limited herself to following Mary as the introductions were made. She thought perhaps she should offer suggestions to Mary but quickly realized that her avatar did fine without her.

During the introductions, more and more people arrived and soon Jane saw the chairs were fast disappearing. Mr Britten approached them and caught Melody's attention.

"Are these the ladies from JASNA you were expecting?" he asked?

"Yes, Ms Hawkins ..." Melody began.

"Please call me Sarah," she interjected.

---

4 An informal or half curtsey in Austen's time was little more than putting the right foot immediately behind the left foot and bending the knees, timed with a nod of the head.

"Sarah," Melody continued, "has offered to introduce Jane, after your own opening comments, of course."

Melody introduced them and the store manager and the JASNA member walked off to confer. Melody then led Mary away from the other JASNA members.

"OK, now it's my turn to break protocol. I just wanted to wish you luck, Mary. I'm sure you'll be great. And Jane, try not to wander off. I know you won't have much to do during the reading, so don't start surfing the web because we'll need you for the Q&A."

Jane was indignant that her agent would so chide her, but then she had to admit she was eager to update her blog and might have been tempted to do so. After all, Mary would largely be reciting the script Jane had written for the talk and they'd rehearsed it so many times it was now boringly familiar.

Mary, however, was happy for Melody's praise and warning.

"Don't worry, I won't let either of you down," Mary said.

Mr Britten now tapped the microphone at the lectern to get the audience's attention.

"Excuse me, if we could all take our seats now? Thank you, and welcome to the Strand and to this very exciting sneak peek into the latest book by none other than Jane Austen."

The audience's applause almost drowned out his pronunciation of Jane's name. Mr Britten was pleased and obviously surprised at the intensity of the applause, especially after the audience stood and turned to look to Mary.

Mary felt the gaze of the audience lock onto her and felt such a rush of warmth as she'd never felt before. She knew a flush was colouring her face and had no idea what to do. Jane was also nonplussed and also desperately wanting again to hear. She had never lived for adulation from a crowd, but how cruel that now, when that adulation was freely offered, she could not hear it. Jane did, however, have the presence of mind to suggest to Mary, "A regal nod would not be amiss."

Mary did as bid, but the applause continued. Finally she thought to motion that they should resume their seats and once settled, she looked to Mr Britten and offered him a nod as well, which he took as a sign to continue.

"Obviously you know who she is," he said, deadpan, which occasioned a round of laughter. "But if by some miracle you don't, here is ..."—he paused to look at the note he held in his hand—"Sarah

Hawkins with the local chapter of the Jane Austen Society of North America to introduce her."

He stepped back and the JASNA member approached the lectern to her own quick round of applause.

"I think a lot of us hoped this day might come, but I don't think any of us thought it would happen, to actually meet our Jane, who gave us Elizabeth and Darcy, Elinor and Marianne ... uh ... Anne Elliot and Captain Wentworth, Emma and Knightley, uh ... Catherine and Henry and ... and ... who did I forget?"

Several people shouted out, "Fanny and Edmund!"[5]

"Oh, how could I forget Fanny and Edmund?"

The audience laughed at this, of course, although it caused Ms Hawkins some embarrassment.

"Thank you. Anyway, I'm guessing quite a few of you here can say that 'Jane Austen changed my life' and I'm sure that number will rise exponentially with the release of *Sanditon*, her finally released novel. I've been fortunate enough to have an advance reading copy and I can tell you it's the most wonderful thing I've ever read and ... oh enough of me talking, I am honoured to introduce Miss Jane Austen, author of *Pride and Prejudice, Emma, Sense and Sensibility, Northanger Abbey, Persuasion, Mansfield Park* and now *Sanditon*."

Mary walked to the lectern as the audience again stood and applauded, but she carefully stood slightly to one side and then turned and joined the audience to applaud the empty space. She and Melody had planned this tribute without telling Jane. Unfortunately the effect was somewhat lessened because Jane was not actually in that spot, but she quickly slid into place.

The audience also took a beat before realizing what Mary was doing, but then the applause got louder. Finally Mary turned and took her place behind the lectern.

"Thank you, thank you. I am very happy for the first time in almost two centuries to acknowledge those of you who have been kind enough to read my stories. It is a sobering experience. In my lifetime, I

---

5   Edmund Bertram is the cousin of Fanny Price, the heroine of *Mansfield Park*. Fanny loved Edmund since the time they were children, but Edmund only realizes he loves Fanny after he understands the true nature of Mary Crawford.

did not seek fame—in fact I fled from it, but I would be lying if I did not admit that at this moment, I am quite enjoying it.

"Now I had planned to make some extemporaneous remarks, but my agent, Melody Kramer, whom you may notice standing there shaking her head, has reminded me of the folly of extemporaneous remarks, and so I will instead simply proceed to the reading of an excerpt from *Sanditon*.

"This excerpt will require some explanation, of course. It is a dark and stormy night and the rain is, in fact, falling in torrents onto Trafalgar House, Mr Parker's new home in Sanditon. Miss Charlotte Heywood is there, with Mr and Mrs Parker, Mr Sidney Parker and Miss Diana and Susan Parker. Charlotte has only just met Sidney and as with all my heroines, she already has a decided opinion of him."

· Excerpt I ·
A dark and stormy night

Charlotte sat close with Mrs Parker, their arms locked together and with each howl of wind and each rattle of a shutter, their hands would squeeze tightly. Across from her she could see Miss Parker and Miss Susan also sitting closely together, any complaints of their ailments forgotten in the violence of the storm.

"It is only the wind, my dear," Mr Parker said to his wife. "And think how much more fearsome it must be in the valley."

At these words, however, the lashing of the rain on the roof grew louder and now came a shriek, as some part of the house broke loose.

Mrs Parker gasped and would rise, but Charlotte's grip was firm. She would be strong for her hostess, although in truth she was quite frightened. She was used to the wind in Willingden, of course, for it would crest the top of their hill and moan, and yet it compared nothing to the storm this night. Her last image before the shutters were closed seemed to show the sea just outside the house instead of its quarter mile distance. She composed herself before answering: "Mr Parker is quite right, it is only the wind and cannot hurt us. What do you say, Mr Sidney?"

"Yes," he said, with a smile, and his smile seemed to give no hint of anxiety. "It is full of sound and fury but it signifies nothing. In fact, I think it is already spent."

A flash of lightning that shone through the cracks of the shutters and an almost simultaneous boom of thunder gave lie to his observation.

"Or nearly spent," he amended. Charlotte gave him a faint smile, which she begrudged immediately. She still felt the sting of his inadvertent slight, despite his earnest apologies. It was clear his belief in the "bumpkin nature of our country cousins" coloured his opinion of her. And how could it not be so? He had knowledge of so much of the world, moving from place to place whenever he had found "so much to bore oneself with the same people, the same buildings and the same pervading sense of ordinariness."

He must have sensed something change in her manner, which he perceived as renewed agitation about the storm.

"Perhaps we should play a game," he said. "Do you know Ghost, Miss Heywood?"

"What, Ghost in the Graveyard?" Mrs Parker asked. Charlotte felt her partner's grip relax and also saw Mr Parker nod approvingly. He knew his wife's fondness for games.

"No, I hardly think we can play that," Mr Sidney Parker said, although he smiled at the thought of the childhood game and at the thought of Mrs Parker chasing them about her drawing-room and shouting "You're the ghost!"

"No, sister," Miss Parker said. "Sidney would have us play Ghost where we start a word with a letter and each player supplies another letter and the player who completes a word loses that round. We played this game when children. Sidney always won."

"Oh yes," Mrs Parker said, although Charlotte thought with less than enthusiasm. She suspected her hostess would prefer some simpler game like Bullet Pudding or perhaps cards. But Charlotte approved of his suggestion for the mental occupation of Ghost should prove a superior divertissement. She thought, however, of an improvement.

"Perhaps we might play Ghost Magna," she said, and was pleased when she saw his eyebrow rise.

"And how is that played?" he asked.

"Almost exactly the same, but the player can add a letter both after and before."

"That does sound fun and may give us an advantage over Sidney," Mr Parker said. "His mind does move from one thing to the next and never back."

"Then Miss Heywood should start, for it is her suggestion," Mr Sidney Parker said.

She nodded and said, "Very well. I begin with 'O.' Shall we go counter-clockwise?"

She made that suggestion because then Mrs Parker would be next, making it an easy round for her.

Mrs Parker supplied the letter "G," obviously relieved that she would not be challenged.

"Is that before or after?" Miss Parker asked.

"Oh, I don't ... after. 'O-G.'"

Miss Susan Parker supplied "O-G-Y," and Miss Parker supplied "L-O-G-Y."

Mr Parker predictably prefixed another "O" and then Mr Sidney Parker said, "My apology, Miss Heywood, if you will accept it. 'P-O-L-O-G-Y.'"

"I do not accept it, sir, for I can preface it with another 'O.'" She smiled broadly at this and thought if she were still with long curls and he were her brother she would stick out her tongue at him.

Mrs Parker thought for a second, and then another, before she said brightly, "'R-O-P-L' ... no, that is not right. 'R-O-P-O-L-O-G-Y!'"

Miss Susan Parker made it "H-R-O-P-O-L-O-G-Y" and attempted to pronounce it, much to her own amusement. Miss Parker made it "T-H-R-O-P-O-L-O-G-Y." Mr Parker supplied the "N" and Mr Sidney Parker sighed with mock tragedy and completed the word as "A-N-T-H-R-O-P-O-L-O-G-Y."

"I appear to be the ghost," he said ruefully.

"That is the 'G' for you, Mr Sidney," Charlotte said, unnecessarily confirming what he'd already said.

"But in Ghost Magna, one must collect ten letters before one is out," he said, betraying his knowledge of the variant.

"Oh Lord, is that true?" Mr Parker asked with laughter. "We'll be here all night."

To which they all laughed and their laughter made them ignore the wind and the rain and the lightning and the thunder.

· Persuasion ·
Somewhere there must be cats

"Yes, I would love another cookie," Courtney said, wondering how he would choke down another indigestible digestive biscuit.[1]

"No dear, it's a biscuit," Mrs Westerby said for the third time, charmed by her American visitor. He had already eaten four biscuits and she hoped he might have another, which would finish the bag. After all, it had been opened some time ago and what with the damp, the biscuits had lost some of their crisp.

Courtney sipped his weak tea to help wash down the biscuit, and hoped he could get the old woman back on track.

"So your mother got the letter from who?"

"From whom, dear. Let's see, that was Major Gorrell-Barmes. That's with an 'M,'" she specified for Courtney who was trying to write this on a notepad while balancing his cup of tea.

"And it's been in the frame for how long?"

"Oh, as far as I can remember, and mother says ... well said, it had been in the frame since forever."

Courtney looked at the letter in its frame, sitting on the low table with the tea things Mrs Westerby had laid out.

---

1 Perhaps the closest American analogue would be a graham cracker; perhaps not

"And your mother was Amelia Corwain?"

"After she married my father, of course, but she was born Amelia Cavendish."

"And this Gorrell-Barnes ..."

"No, Barmes, dear, with an 'M.'"

"Gorrell-Barmes was a friend of your mother?"

"Oh more than that, they were engaged, but he died very tragically."

"In the war?"

"Oh no, he was killed by a lorry. It's still tragic."

"Yes, I guess it was to your mother," Courtney admitted. "And do you know where he got it from?"

"Mother might have known, I suppose, and maybe she told me, but I've forgotten. It's been sitting on the wall all these years, you see and I've not given it much mind. I'm more partial to the Brontës. Austen's a bit of a bore, but mother adored her."

"May I take another look at it?"

"Please do," she said pleasantly. She had few enough visitors and still felt the loss of her mother, although she did enjoy her independence again, now that she was relieved of the drudgery of caring for the bed-ridden old woman. So she welcomed the well-dressed American, especially if he knew the worth of the letter.

Courtney set down his teacup and took up the frame. It wasn't much bigger than five by eight inches and the letter had been folded to fit in the frame. It showed the name of the intended recipient, Harris Bigg-Wither at Manydown Park, but it didn't seem to be either franked or postmarked. The handwriting seemed to be Jane's, but it was difficult to make out. He looked up at the wall where the frame had hung, and although it was overcast now, he knew that on many days it would have been exposed to sunlight. Sunlight and the ink of the day would account for a lot of the fading. It was also difficult to make out because writing from the backside of the paper showed through.

The paper to his inexpert eye looked authentic. Unfortunately it appeared that water had seeped into the frame, allowing some mould to grow under the glass and some of the letter looked glued to the glass. Another glance at the wall confirmed what looked to be a large stain on the wallpaper.

Frankly the front of the frame wasn't very promising. Apart from the name of the recipient, he couldn't make out much. The backside was far more promising. A typed note explained: "An unsent letter from Jane Austen addressed to Harris Bigg-Wither explaining why she refused his offer of marriage after first accepting it. Fred Barmes 1923."

The note had been glued to the paper backing of the frame.

"Do you have any idea what the letter says?"

The old woman shook her head no. "I just remember Mum saying 'Good on her,' talking about it with my father once. I think she approved of whatever it was Austen said in the letter."

Courtney put the frame back on the table. His fingers felt grimy from touching it. The whole house, in fact, triggered a shudder reaction from him. The smell of rising damp made him worry for his sinuses and he also felt itchy from the suspicion that somewhere there must be cats. He wiped his hands on his pants, although he really longed to fetch a wet wipe from his shoulder bag.

"Well, as I said on the phone, I'm not an expert on documents, just Jane Austen, but if it's genuine, then I really think it's worth a lot of money, easily thousands of dollars ... I mean pounds. You'll just need to get it conserved and authenticated."

"Will that be expensive?"

"Um, yes, well I don't really know. But like I said, if it is genuine ... I'm sure you could sell it for a lot."

"That would be nice," Mrs Westerby said. "I want to sell and move into care, now that Mum's passed on. Only, you see, she said I could never sell it if Jane Austen ever appeared on the AfterNet."

Her words left Courtney a little light headed. He could feel the prize slipping from his fingers.

"Uh, did she say why the restriction?"

"She said if Jane Austen were to come forward, then the letter really belonged to her."

"That's a noble sentiment, of course," Courtney began.

"She made me promise her."

This can't be happening, he thought. *This could prove Austen had a lover and that's why she rejected Bigg-Wither.* Or it could disprove it; he had to admit the possibility, but even so, he still would be a party to uncovering a major piece of Austen memorabilia. And it could help to disprove Austen's identity.

Or, on the other hand, it might help prove it. The more he'd thought of it, the more he wondered if he might find himself in Austen's good graces by finding additional proof of her identity. Either way, he would come out ahead.

"But Mum left all these bills," Mrs Westerby added, and after a pregnant pause, "although how I could afford to conserve and authenticate the letter ..."

"Maybe if you were to explain this to your mother. Have you talked to her since she died?"

"Oh no, I've never had any interest in the Internet."

Her statement baffled Courtney. He'd gotten the impression mother and daughter were close—a natural assumption when he'd learned Mrs Westerby, an elderly, widowed, childless woman was living at home and taking care of her even more ancient mother. It seemed impossible that any person facing death nowadays wouldn't have made some arrangement to communicate with the family they'd be leaving behind.

"Oh, well perhaps I can talk to your mother."

"You can certainly try, but she had no interest in the Internet either."

"Then I suppose ... she never had her identity recorded before her death?"

"What's that?"

"Never mind," he said. That information gave him some comfort. If Mrs Westerby's mother didn't record her identity, then she'd be in a poor position to object to a sale. Perhaps he only needed to convince one old lady.

"Well, as to the costs of authentication and preservation ... that might not be a problem," he said. "Perhaps if we were to talk to the British Museum ... or more likely the British Library ... if some institution was to buy the letter, well that would be like giving it to the great British public, wouldn't it?" He remembered reading somewhere that you could convince a Brit of anything if you just referred to the great British public.

"And I'm sure we can find someone to help with the authentication. I have a friend with the University of Chicago in America, a great Janeite scholar, who might know what to do. And an auction house like Sotheby's might just defray any fees from the eventual purchase price."

"Well, isn't that clever. I would never have thought of that. But I still don't know that Mum ..."

"Maybe it's too early to worry about that. The first step is to decide if ... to get the letter authenticated."

"Oh dear, I suppose that won't be here in Glooston."

"No, it probably won't."

"I do hate travelling so. I can't remember the last time I left the village. I don't suppose ... could you run it up for me?"

Courtney paused before answering, trying his best to contain his pleasure at her request.

"I suppose I could, although I hadn't planned to leave quite yet."

"There's no hurry, of course," she said.

"But I could leave tomorrow," he said, although he realized he in fact had no idea where he might take the letter. "Then again I should do a little research before I take it from ... take it for you. Once I get back to the hotel, I can get on the Internet and plan the next step."

"That sounds a plan, but you don't have to leave right now. I can open another box of biscuits."

"That's very kind of you, but ..."

"Then you can look at the boxes."

"What boxes?"

"That's not the only thing of Austen's that Mum left. There are more in the loft."

Courtney smiled and said, "You know, those digestive biscuits might just hit the spot."

⋅ Despatch boxes ⋅
Journal of Jane Bigg-Wither

"It's a tin despatch box. Well, it's three boxes," Courtney said. He was obviously extremely excited and his head was jerking around animatedly, but some of that could be attributed to the quality of the Skype call.

"What's a despatch box? What are you talking about?" Alice asked irritably. His call came at 6 am and awakened her because she'd forgotten to turn off her smartphone. She'd heard an unfamiliar buzzing and when she'd activated her phone, discovered it was receiving a Skype call.

She'd forgotten she'd installed the application at the insistence of Courtney before he'd left for England.

Courtney had been so excited about his discovery and had wanted to call her immediately, but an indifferent Wi-Fi connection at the hotel delayed him and it was only now back in London that he could call her. He surveyed the still groggy professor, her normally constrained red hair now an ochre nimbus lit by morning sun. She appeared to sleep in a University of Chicago T-shirt, which surprised him. Not that he'd previously thought of it, but he would have guessed she'd sleep in something more elegant.

He debated telling her that her phone was transmitting video, not sure if she was aware of the fact, but decided against it.

"Mrs Westerby has these boxes, just like Dr. Watson's[1]. They're full of journals—Jane's journals. Take a look."

She muttered, "Jane never kept a journal," but not loudly enough for Courtney to hear.

Alice rubbed the sleep from her eyes and then reached for her glasses on the bedside table. She put them on and looked again at the screen and also noticed a tiny window displaying video of her. She quickly turned off the outgoing video and then paid attention to the image Courtney was sending her.

She saw three dusty looking boxes, looking very much like the metal lunchboxes kids took to school but without pictures of Scooby-doo or My Little Pony. These boxes contained the same metal clasps with the addition of leather straps and buckles. To her eye, they didn't look remotely Regency. One box was open and she saw a thick pile of paper inside fastened with what looked like red ribbon. Unfortunately the video couldn't stay in focus enough for her to make out much, other than that there appeared to be writing on the paper.

"What does it say?"

"It says 'Journal of Jane Bigg-Wither,' or anyway I think it does," Courtney said. He turned the camera back to face him. "I've only opened one box, the other two the latches have rusted shut. The second I saw the writing, I didn't want to open them or untie the ribbon. I'm in London now and I've got to get them to an appraiser."

"Wait, Jane Bigg-Wither? Are you saying …"

"It looks like Jane's hand writing. I'm sending you a photo."

"Sotheby's. They've done all the recent Austen auctions," she said. She was quickly waking up. She tried to sound knowledgeable, but admittedly it was the only auction house in England she knew, but it was true that they'd handled the recent sale of *The Watsons* manuscript.

"That's what I thought," he said. His words coincided with the sound of her phone indicating an email had arrived. She switched to her mail application and found the photo Courtney had sent and saw Jane's handwriting. The "Jane" was clearly visible but the "Bigg-Wither" was harder to make out, although still recognizable.

"Oh my God," she said, "oh my God. But you went there to look

---

1   Famously, Dr John H Watson, friend and biographer of Sherlock Holmes, kept a battered tin despatch box in the bank vaults of Cox & Co. The box contained his unpublished adventures with the Great Detective.

at a letter?" Courtney said nothing in response and then she switched back to Skype.

"You went there to look at a letter."

"Yes, and here it is." He turned his camera, apparently the camera in his laptop, back around and trained it at a picture frame. She again saw Jane's handwriting and the name and address of Harris Bigg-Wither. The letter, if that's what it was, seemed in much worse shape than the papers in the box.

"Bring me up to speed here, Court. Tell me everything that's happened."

He turned the laptop back to face him and related the story of meeting the old woman and that he was ready to leave when she told him of the boxes in the attic.

"Did you take photos of the attic?" she asked.

"Yes, every step of the way. And I recorded a video of Mrs Westerby telling me about it and even of me carrying the first box downstairs and opening it."

"Good, smart thinking, Court. OK, what time is it there?"

"About 11:30. Sorry, I didn't think about the time."

"For this, you don't need to apologize. Did you have a chance to contact Sotheby's?"

"No, the cell reception in Glooston was non-existent. And once I saw what I had, I thought I'd better get it to London."

"Mrs What's-her-name let you take it?"

"Yes, the old dear doesn't get out much and she was practically pushing me out the door with it. I think she wants the money from a sale. The house is practically falling apart."

"God, we can't let it go to a private sale."

"Just what I was thinking."

"OK, I'll start making calls. This is … this is big, Court. Congratulations."

She finished the call with her adrenaline pumping. "Jane Bigg-Wither" was hardly a combination she'd expected to see. Harris had married Ann Frith two years after Jane had rejected him. She couldn't begin to imagine why Jane, if in fact it were her handwriting, would have written "Journal of Jane Bigg-Wither." She looked at the photo again, trying to see whether in anyway the "Jane" was actually "Ann," but Austen's first name was unmistakable.

· London ·
Jane and Mary arrive at Heathrow

The young man holding the sign that said "Jane Austin" reminded Mary and Jane of the absurdity of their situation. For Mary, of course, it was an absurdity made even more unreal by the tiredness she felt after her long plane flight and then the long wait in customs while enviously watching frequent and first-class passengers jump ahead in the queue. But now to find a chauffeur holding a sign reading "Jane Austin" when she was specifically instructed to travel incognito and dress in casual clothing seemed particularly absurd.

"I think I may be the Miss Austen you're looking for," she told the dark-skinned man holding the sign.

"You the novelist?" he asked.

"I am indeed," she answered.

"Cool. Let me take your bags."

She thanked him and handed him her two bags and he led them on their way to the ground transportation level at Heathrow where he'd left the limo. Jane followed close behind during all this, a little annoyed at being forced to follow the rules of the living. She never had to wait in line for customs and rather than walk anywhere in an airport she simply waited for one of those trolleys that shuttled the elderly and infirm and hopped on board. Of course, she'd never had a reserved seat on a flight before or a companion who looked out for her, and so must be content to follow Mary and the driver as they walked through the terminal. Consequently, she was constantly buffeted by the crowd and was thankful when they finally entered the privacy of the vehicle.

After the driver entered, he looked into the rear-view mirror at his passenger. "I'm taking you to the …"—he looked down at a print-out—"… Park International in Kensington?"

"That's right," Mary confirmed with a smile to the driver. "Excuse me, what's your name?"

"I'm Tony."

"OK, thanks Tony. I hope you don't mind, but I've got to make a phone call, tell my friend I landed safely."

"Oh sure, you go ahead."

Mary pretended to make a call so that she might talk to Jane without it looking odd.

"Hi there. I landed safe in London, how about you?"

"Really Mary? Is this charade truly necessary?" asked Jane's voice through the earbuds.

Mary sank bank in her seat and lowered her voice.

"No, I already texted Melody that we'd landed. Oh, you mean the fake phone call! I get so tired of the odd looks I get when I'm talking to you. I guess my expression is different from someone talking on a phone, maybe because I keep looking at you. This helps disguise it a little bit."

"Very well, but do you not think the driver will eventually notice."

Mary looked up at the rear-view mirror and saw that Tony was already concentrating on his driving and also, judging from his rhythmic swaying, the music coming from whatever phone or music player was connected to the earphones he was wearing.

"No, I think we're safe. So, tell me a little something of where we're staying."

"Do you refer to the hotel or the neighbourhood, for I know nothing of the former?"

"The neighbourhood, Kensington. Isn't it hoity-toity?"

"No, not at all, although it does have a reputation for culture with the Albert Hall, the Victoria and Albert, the Natural History Museum and the Brompton Oratory."[1]

---

1   Kensington is a town and district of west and central London, within the
    Royal Borough of Kensington and Chelsea. It is home to many foreign

"Wow, I have no idea what those are, but they sound hoity-toity to me."

"I am only sorry that instead of staying at the Ritz or the Savoy you must stay at this unnamed hotel."

"My goodness, Jane, I never knew you were a snob. Besides, wasn't it your decision to put us up at the Park International?"

"Not my decision. You may thank Melody for that. I would have you stay somewhere nice. I think Melody still hasn't adjusted to the idea of a large promotion budget."

"I'm happy wherever I stay. I got a free trip to London out of this so you don't hear me complaining. And I'm sure the hotel will be nice," Mary said, trying to act the adult. She then caught the eye of the driver who had noticed her apparently having a conversation with the empty seat beside her.

"My friend says hi, Tony."

"Uh, yes ma'am, anything you say."

Mary looked out the window of the limo, marvelling at the novelty of being in another country, amazed at the familiarity and the strangeness of it. Being on a highway was familiar, the M4 in this case, and she didn't even really pay attention to the fact they were on the wrong side of the road, it being a divided motorway. But the look of the cars was different; very few SUVs, many more compacts and sub compacts and even the trucks—*they call them lorries*, she reminded herself—seemed on a smaller scale.

She was reminded of a documentary she'd seen about dinosaurs that had evolved on a small island, and were consequently small. The houses they passed, which practically touched the highway, were all in a row with their neat little backyards facing the road. They reminded her of the New Jersey neighbourhoods she saw from the subway.

"Where did you live in England? I mean just before you came to the US."

"I suppose just before I left for America, I was in Bradford-on-Avon, which is near Bath. It would be more romantic to pretend I haunted Steventon or Chawton, but those are still small villages. Even Alton[2] is

---

embassies, Harrods department store and, of course, Kensington Palace. Neither the Ritz nor Savoy hotels are in Kensington.

2   Alton is a small town nearby the smaller village of Chawton

very small and has terrible AfterNet access and is frankly uninteresting to a disembodied person."

"Bradford-on-Avon is more interesting?"

"Oh yes, the Avon Valley is lovely and the town is charming, although the traffic is dreadful. But I find the tourists interesting and if I desire something more cosmopolitan, there's always Bath."

"You hated Bath."

"Once. You should know by now that I can no longer be defined by my words or actions from when I was alive."

"Do you have a disembodied person with you?" their driver suddenly asked.

"What? Oh, yes I do," Mary confessed. "Is there a problem?"

"Course not. I just like to know who my passengers are. I don't want to close the door on anyone or leave someone locked inside. So which one of you is Jane Austin?"

"She is, I mean we are," Mary said. "Actually I'm Mary Crawford, but I'm her avatar, so it would be good if you think of us both as Jane."

"Gotcha."

"You're American, right?" Mary asked.

"Better than. I'm Canadian, so don't worry, I'll make sure I call you Jane Austin outside the cab. You're not my first avatar."

"Thanks Tony, and that's Austen with an 'E.'"

· Walkabout ·
Jane feels restless

"Jane, it's almost midnight. Don't you think it's a little late to start your night-time wanderings?" Mary said this while preparing for bed, thoroughly knackered from the flight. She had exaggerated; it was only 10 pm, but Jane was understandably bored, especially after watching Mary nap for three hours immediately after checking in.

"I'm sorry, Mary, I am more than a little anxious tonight and would like the night air to settle me."

"Is there anything wrong?"

"No, nothing more than the usual worries of an old ghost. Perhaps it is this city that affects me."

"OK, you will be careful. You know Melody wouldn't approve of this. What if you get trapped somewhere?"

"I am quite capable of looking after myself and have done so …"

"I know, for two hundred years. OK, suit yourself." Mary opened the door and waited for Jane to leave.

"The fire door in the lobby hallway will be closed at this hour as well. I am afraid you will need to open that for me," Jane said. She'd naturally observed all the exits when they'd arrived, not eager to find herself stuck in a stairwell.

"OK." Mary found her coat and put it on over her T-shirt, made sure she had her room card and walked out the door.

She looked around and saw no one and in her bare feet she went down the stairs and walked the short distance to the fire door. She opened it for Jane.

"When will you be back?"

"I shall return at eight. These doors should be open by then. Have a good night, Mary."

"'Night Jane."

Mary stood for a minute with the door open and then allowed it to close and returned to her room.

~

Jane travelled the hallway and into the lobby. Naturally the night receptionist didn't look up when she entered. She suddenly realized that she could not leave the lobby without someone to open the front doors.

I haven't made a mistake like this in some time, she thought. *I've become too accustomed to having a living companion.*

She now regretted her earlier self congratulation about checking the exits, but as she walked toward the reception desk, she caught an After-Net field and realized it was her way to communicate to the receptionist. A cheerful "Welcome to the Park International Hotel" message was immediately triggered, followed by another message that said, "The following information is meant for the site developer for debugging purposes. Error Occurred While Processing Request. Corrupt table."

Then she noticed the sign on the front desk that said, "Oops, our AfterNet server is down. The nearest public terminal is in the Sainsbury's."[1]

No matter. Surely someone will leave or arrive and I can escape. But she waited fifteen minutes before the front doors opened to admit a returning hotel guest. She raced for the opening and just missed being caught as the doors closed behind her. She found herself on the sidewalk and glided in the direction of the Gloucester Road tube station.

Traffic was still busy on the Cromwell Road but of course for Jane it was all silence. She could imagine the sounds of the people as they walked by but she could not imagine what motorized traffic must sound like. She could only guess that cars and trucks must be louder

---

1   Sainsbury's is a UK grocery store chain

than the carriages she knew. She had never actually heard a self-powered mechanical device such as a steam engine, which she thought would be the closest equivalent in her time.

She moved quickly for she knew that because of planned disruptions—she did have the sense earlier to check the Transport for London website—service on the Circle and District lines would end about a quarter to eleven.

She thought she made it to the Gloucester Road station in good time but still worried, so she flew through the turnstiles and down the stairs to the platform and luckily found a District Line train just arriving. Only a handful of people left the train and only three people got on, and none into the car she had chosen. She marvelled at the lack of crowding, which she could only attribute to it being Monday.

The train remained still almost a full minute, however, with the doors still open. She began to worry that service had ended when finally the doors closed and the train began to move.

Her car contained only five passengers and so she had plenty of room to herself and could ride in comfort to Westminster station. She was able to exit without difficulty. Even riding up the escalators was easy.

Because of her recent efforts at writing something fresh, she thought of the young woman she'd followed to the Cabinet War Rooms all those years ago and wondered if it were possible to visit the attraction.

~

Mary lay in bed, wondering how much trouble Jane might get in. It's true she could have refused to open the door, but Mary worked for Jane, not Melody. She was more frightened of Melody, but Jane was the one who could fire her.

Although good luck getting an avatar by tomorrow. And say goodbye to all the publicity photos we've taken. I guess I have a little more leverage than I thought. Damn, I shouldn't have let her go out on her own. But it's not like I could have tailed her. Ah crap, I should have put my foot down.

The real reason she was upset had nothing to do with being blamed. She was just worried about Jane on her own. There were always stories about the disembodied going missing or being trapped in a closet or a bathroom for days or weeks—or in a storage room for months or years.

She's survived on her own without my help for a very long time. She'll be fine.

She got up from the bed and retrieved the remote from the little writing desk. Despite Jane's disparagement, the hotel on Cromwell Road was quite nice. It was actually three merged Georgian row houses. She thought it looked very grand and imposing from the outside, but inside their room was miniscule. Jane joked it must have been servants' quarters, although as it was on the British first floor, that was unlikely. The bed was so large and the room so narrow that you could only get to the other end of the room by crawling over the bed, making sure to avoid the flat screen television that hung on the wall at the foot of the bed. She wondered how the maid ever changed the linens.

But the room was immaculate and obviously just renovated. After she opened the window, by clambering over the bed, she heard the sounds of Kensington, not too different from the noise of Brooklyn. She turned on the telly, too worried about Jane to sleep.

She found a documentary about Morris dancers, whatever those were, an episode of *Law and Order,* the UK version, a bizarre quiz show that didn't seem to have a point or any logic to the scoring, something called *Horrible Histories* that seemed to be mock music videos about historic figures (because of Jane, she was actually able to appreciate the four Georges), and finally …

"… lined up around the block at this Waterstones.[2] Excuse me, might I have a word?"

Mary saw the Sky TV reporter approaching a woman wearing Regency costume camped outside a bookstore somewhere in London.

"I see you're in the proper attire, so you must be waiting for it to go on sale."

"Yes, I've been here since seven and I can't wait to get my copy."

"What's so special about it?"

"It's the first Jane Austen in two hundred years. Do you know how many times I've read *Pride and Prejudice*? I don't because I stopped counting after the tenth. To have a new Jane Austen is Christmas and my birthday and the Queen's Birthday all wrapped up in one."

"And that's the scene here on Piccadilly, Steve. At least they'll have a pleasant night, but it will be a long time until morning and the new Jane Austen novel goes on sale."

---

2 Waterstones is a UK bookseller chain

The camera pulled back and Mary could see the long line of people outside the store. Then they switched back to the studio and the newsreader.

"Well, certainly a lot of interest in the new novel, thank you Barbara. And the book launch party tomorrow has turned into the social event of the literary world, with politicians, actors and pop stars and yes, even other authors, all trying ..."

Mary turned off the television.

I knew it was going to be like this. The agency and Melody prepared me for it. I can handle it. Oh God, why did I ever let her leave?

· In her own hand ·
"Yes, very providential"

Courtney waited nervously in the reception area, tapping his foot against the metal leg of the coffee table in front of him. The only other person in the reception area, a sharp-looking woman with her black Louis Vuitton bag on the couch next to her, coughed and glanced sharply at him. He stopped kicking the leg and smiled weakly at her. She did not return his smile.

"Mr Blake," he heard his name called and looking up saw the appraiser approaching him with his hand already outstretched.

"I'm so sorry you were kept waiting," Mr Handy said solicitously. "I should have been called the instant you arrived."

Mr Handy's manner caught the attention of the sharp-looking woman, who now wondered if Courtney were someone important after all.

"Not at all Mr Handy, I've only been waiting a few minutes," Courtney said in a voice directed to the woman.

"Call me Jim, call me Jim. Let's go back to my office. I think I have some exciting news for you." Courtney followed Handy after tossing another smile at the woman, who this time returned it.

Handy ushered Courtney into his office and then closed the door. He urged Courtney to sit and then sat across from him in one of the two client chairs in front of his desk. He leaned forward eagerly to talk.

"All the lab work is done and it's all good news. The paper of the letter is genuinely from the time period, although the margin of error and Miss Austen's life span isn't much different. The ink is of the period as well and all the handwriting analysis ... it's in her hand; there's no doubt.

"I'm sorry the letter doesn't address the topic you'd expected, however."

Courtney nodded. He'd already come to terms with the knowledge that the letter had nothing to do with Jane's time in Lyme Regis.

"It's a disappointment, but obviously it's still ... well it's still pretty revealing about Jane's temper," Courtney said.

"I agree. It's amazing to have a new Austen document, regardless. I'm more partial to the Brontës myself, but I can understand what it would mean to Janeites. Of course the content ... well, that's your business."

"Needless to say we're very excited and when Mrs Westerby should bring this to market ..."

"Yes, well that's not decided yet. And the journal?"

"That's more difficult. Despite being in boxes, those papers are in much worse condition. The pages are quite brittle and stuck together. You really shouldn't have opened the box. And unless we know that you definitely mean to bring those to sale ... it would be a considerable expense to converse and authenticate those."

"So you can't say whether the journal is ... genuine."

"All I can say is that the undoubted authenticity of the one ... makes one hopeful. We're able to read a few of the pages of the journal ... here's a report," Mr Handy said, sliding it to Courtney. He looked them over eagerly.

"It's a diary," Courtney said, "of her married life to Harris Bigg-Wither."

"So it would seem, but again, this is only three pages of what we expect to be about 350."

"This is ... it's just amazing. But the cost of restoration and authentication ... what is your estimate?"

Silently Mr Handy handed Courtney another piece of paper.

"Oh my," he said.

But sensing a potential sale slipping through his fingers, Mr Handy quickly added, "The authenticators are reasonably certain the despatch boxes were used by the Ministry of Defence during the war, possibly by military intelligence. That adds an air of mystery that should affect

the sale price. And as it would be part of a larger Jane Austen collection
… well your Mrs Westerby could find herself quite rich. Mind you we
don't exactly know how the identification of Jane Austen will affect the
price. She's got a book coming out this week in fact."

"Today, actually," Courtney said.

"Yes, very providential," Mr Handy added.

· Feeling silly ·
Pursuing a girl

lbert closed the window and his newly purchased copy of *Sanditon* disappeared. He honestly did not know what to think. Austen's unfinished novel had been a favourite of his because he'd read it so late in his afterlife. Being an unfinished work, it had been difficult to find someone reading it over whose shoulder he could peer; consequently he'd never had the opportunity to read it uninterrupted until the birth of the AfterNet. He could never make it past chapter two and Jane had only written about eleven chapters before her death.

So the incomplete story had become a favourite both because it had been elusive and because once he'd finally read it, it seemed so full of possibility. He'd often wondered what Austen's intent had been. Would Charlotte Heywood, from whose viewpoint the story was related, prove to be the heroine? and would romance be her reward?

Upon finishing this completed *Sanditon*, he could not honestly say whether either of those questions had been answered. It ended so abruptly (for Austen) and the ending was so pregnant with possibilities that he was overwhelmed with emotions and questions. He was reminded of his wife telling him that he would be a father—for a second time had stopped, his legs had left him and he'd been unable to speak for half a minute.

He certainly had not anticipated, that like Emma, Charlotte would be a matchmaker, or that unlike Emma, she would prove to be quite a capable one. Nor had he anticipated that Lady Denham should get her just deserts. He could not recall any of Austen's villains ever getting their comeuppance, although the humour of Lady Denham's downfall took some of its sting.[1]

Humour, in fact, was the hallmark of the completed *Sanditon*, he realized. Austen's previous novels breathed with humour, of course, but in this story it was a ever present ocean breeze that swept and swirled around every character and every character's folly. That they were such laughable creations made them all the more endearing.

He so much wanted to discuss the novel with his Jane, but she had of late been rather uncommunicative and some of his emails had gone unanswered, which was very unlike her.

Not for the first time he wondered about her and also not for the first time did he worry about those details he knew or thought he knew about her. She had become more and more important to him since their first meeting four years ago, when they had argued on some forum: he defending Edward Ferrars in *Sense and Sensibility* and she ridiculing Edward's passivity.

He lost his temper, he now admitted, and he recalled how like an Austen character he called her an "insufferable woman," a phrase that made him smile and realize that it was he who had overreacted. All her arguments had been calm and reasoned while he argued with emotion. He sought her out and apologized and they had become fast friends. She later admitted that her regard for Edward was not reflected in her arguments. She liked Edward in general, but did not wholly condone his character.

All this was new to Albert, this dissection of Austen. He had enjoyed Austen since his discovery of her while in hospital. His memory was that he held *Persuasion* in his hands as he drew his last breath, and that he died without the knowledge of the reunion of Anne Elliot and Captain Wentworth. It was not until two years later that he could con-

---

1   Proofreader Maryann O'Brien has thought of two Austen characters who got what they deserved. Aunt Norris resolves to quit Mansfield Park with Mrs Rushworth (Maria Bertram who was), following that woman's disgrace—"... where, shut up together with little society, on one side no affection, on the other no judgment, it may be reasonably supposed that their tempers became their mutual punishment."

firm their happiness and it was one of the few joys he could remember from those dark days.

It was understandable then, that his enjoyment of Austen was uncritical. She gave him joy and beauty at a time when he languished in the hell of the trenches and finally as he lay dying in the influenza wards. And over the decades, he had reread those six novels whenever he found someone enjoying them. He recalled the joy of finding someone reading Austen for the first time and enjoying her; and the misery of some dull elf[2] reading her who did not understand her and did not appreciate her beauty.

And so he was her champion, but he quickly found himself no match against a skilled opponent who might dismiss her as a romance novelist or a creator of simplistic plots that had only the inconsequential goal of marrying young girls of moderate means to slightly older men of substantial means.

It was those insights he most desired now. *What does she think of Charlotte emulating Emma? Does she agree that Sidney Parker is unsuitable?* He decided to send his Jane another email, feeling foolish at this point in his life to be pursuing a girl.

---

2   In a letter to her sister, regarding some lapses in attribution she had found
     in the proof of *Pride and Prejudice*, Austen wrote: "There are a few typical
     [typographic] errors; and a 'said he,' or a 'said she,' would sometimes make
     the dialogue more immediately clear; but 'I do not write for such dull elves,
     as have not a great deal of ingenuity themselves.'" "Dull elves" is probably
     an allusion to a line from Sir Walter Scott's epic poem *Marmion*: "I do not
     rhyme to that dull elf/ Who cannot image to himself/"

· UK book launch ·
May I introduce Mr Colin Firth?

"Hey Miss Austen," Tony her driver said. "Now I know who you are! You're famous!" He was waiting for her with the limo door open and a copy of *The Daily Mail* with its story of the book launch. Mary looked at it in amazement while he took her garment bag from her.

The story included their new portrait of Jane and also a photo of herself as Jane at the New York book signing last week.

And so Mary now saw herself publicly identified as Jane Austen for the first time. Naturally she had mixed emotions. It was irritating to be considered famous for being someone else. At least an actress would be credited for her work, but she must toil away in obscurity. She'd been warned of that when she had applied for the job, but she never imagined she'd be someone famous on two continents.

She sighed, just a little sigh that she hoped Jane wouldn't notice, and thanked Tony.

"Could you please sign it for me? I bought one of your books but I forgot to bring it with me."

"Sure Tony," Mary said, lapsing into American, and then catching herself and adding, "it would be a pleasure."

He opened the car door for her and waited an extra few seconds for Jane to enter, although she had preceded Mary. She'd been caught in car doors often enough that she'd learned to enter first. Tony finally closed the door, put the garment bag in the boot and ran around to the driver's door. Mary took the opportunity to get a pen from her bag and waited for inspiration to strike.

"Make it, 'To Tony,'" her inspiration said, "'whose peerless skills behind the wheel have made me feel safe amid the hustle' … no, make that 'tumult of London traffic. Jane Austen.' Oh, better remind him, Mary."

"Tony, don't forget we're to collect Miss Kramer," Mary said as she handed him the signed newspaper.

"Don't worry, I haven't forgotten, Miss Austen. Oh, and I already started reading your book."

"I am impressed. Did you stand in line for *Sanditon*?"

"No, not that one, *Pride and Prejudice and Zombies*. Cracking good story."

Mary smiled weakly at him in the rear-view mirror.

"I'm glad you're enjoying it," she said with a nod. He smiled back at her and then put his attention to getting underway.

"Do you really think he understands who we are?" Jane asked.

Mary flicked her eyes toward the rear-view mirror. Tony seemed intent on his driving so she softly asked, "What do you mean?"

"That we are a dead novelist, or do you think he simply thinks we are a person whose picture is in the newspaper."

"I don't know, Jane," Mary answered, intrigued by Jane's use of "we," which she had never done before. "He seems like a smart enough young man but like so many of the young today gets his information more from the Internet than from newspapers."

"Ha! I have infected you. He is your age, Mary. You begin to complain as I would."

That took Mary aback. *My God she's right. I'm losing myself in the part so much my opinions are becoming that of Jane. Soon I'll start kvetching about baggy jeans and backward baseball caps.*

"Just immersing myself in the role. Oh, look at the time," Mary said, a none too subtle remark about Jane's late return that morning. Fortunately Mary had been spared fretting about Jane's late return because she had slept right through her alarm. A knock at her door had finally awakened her.

She'd jumped out of bed after a quick look at the bedside clock and ran to the door, wearing just her Yankees[1] T-shirt. She opened the door a crack and saw a young woman wearing the same jacket as the hotel staff.

"Good morning, Miss Crawford. I believe I have a guest with me who needs to return to her room."

Mary, confused, looked for someone with the young woman, but the woman noticed Mary's inquisitive eye.

"It's your roommate," she said. "She needs to get back inside."

"Oh, thank you."

Mary opened the door wide enough to permit Jane to enter.

"You're very welcome," the young lady said, betraying no amusement at the sight of the dishevelled American.

Fortunately for Jane, Mary was so busy with her morning ablutions that she had little time to berate her employer for her late return. All Mary learned was that Jane had so enjoyed herself that she had lost track of time.

As a consequence, they were fully twenty minutes behind schedule as Tony pulled up to the house where Melody was staying, the home of one of Tamara's relatives who was working in London. Melody was already waiting on the street, her body posture revealing her irritation. Tony stopped the limo, got out, took her garment bag, helped her inside and put the bag in the boot.

"You're late," she complained as she got in.

"By a whole fifteen minutes," Mary said.

"It is my fault; I was chatting," Jane said, to both Melody and Mary through their terminals. Mary was glad Jane said nothing about her walkabout.

"Driver, take us to the Savoy," Melody said imperiously once Tony was behind the wheel again. Tony, instantly comprehending who was in charge, acknowledged Melody's command.

"He already knows that, Melody," Mary said.

"I know; I just wanted to say it."

Her confession made them laugh and for a moment all the worry faded as the three of them simply enjoyed the moment.

"Can you believe we're going to the Savoy Hotel for a book launch? In my wildest dreams, I could never have thought this would happen," Melody said.

---

1 The New York Yankees professional baseball team

"Does this mean you lied to me when you promised me success?" Jane asked of her agent.

Melody was about to reply but was saved by her ringing phone.

"Hi Rebecca, what's up? Uh huh. Yes, we're on our way to the Savoy right now, running just a little late. Who? Oh, that's great. Wow, OK, thanks."

Melody hung up and was silent, which was unusual enough to get their attention.

"What was that?" Jane finally asked.

"We had another confirmation," Melody said. "Elton John will be there. Sir Elton John. I'm going to meet Elton John."

"Who?" Jane asked. "Oh, the musician. But I am more excited to meet Andrew Davies.[2] I have a mind to take him to task for a few liberties, but mostly to thank him. I have seen him talk several times, but was never able to ask my questions."

"Elton John will be there? Really? Who else, the queen?" Mary joked, ignoring Jane's comment.

"No, she can't make it," Melody said, "but we might get Charles and Camilla. Doesn't really matter. I'm going to meet Elton John."

~

They spent the day at the Savoy, met there by Mr Pembroke's counterparts at the London Random House office. Melody went through the latest guest list and saw names from the mayor of London to Oscar winning actors to the prime minister. She made some last minute suggestions to move up people from the Jane Austen Society of the UK to the head of the receiving line.

She also learned of the extensive efforts to make the event accessible to the disembodied. The hotel had already installed AfterNet hotspots in the lobby and most of the ballrooms and conference areas in a recent renovation. She made sure that Jane was already registered to join all the chat rooms, an oversight that embarrassed the hotel and Mr Laurence from Random House.

Mary and Jane were taken on a tour of the hotel and acquainted

---

2   Andrew Davies wrote the script for several Austen adaptations, including the 1995 BBC production of *Pride and Prejudice*

with where they would stand. Afterward, Mary was taken to the hotel spa, much to the amusement of Jane. She found Mary's male masseuse quite shocking. Mary found his ministrations very soothing. About 4 pm, a hairstylist and makeup artist took Mary away to provide her with a mountain of curls and the appearance of not wearing makeup. By half past six, Mary was ready.

~

Mary almost staggered at the crescendo of camera flashes. She briefly felt Melody's hand behind her back as they watched the next guest approach. Mary thought she heard Melody whisper "Darcy!"

Mary, at twenty-five, thought he looked very handsome but older than she'd expected. Mary stepped forward to greet him. Just behind him stood a beautiful woman she knew to be his wife.

Mr Laurence confirmed this in his introduction, "Miss Austen, may I introduce you to Mr Colin Firth and his wife, Livia Giuggioli." Then Mr Laurence stepped back, leaving Firth, his wife and Mary alone.

His expression seemed unusually grim, like a man annoyed that people were laughing and he couldn't understand the joke, and then she realized that he was briefly in character.

She curtseyed and extended her hand, which he took and bowed over, his head almost coming close enough to kiss her hand. The camera flashes lit the room like daylight.

As he straightened, he smiled and in that smile, Mary was momentarily lost. She'd only been vaguely aware of him as a movie star before becoming Jane's avatar, but since then, just as everyone had, she'd accepted him as Darcy. She felt herself falling under his spell.

"It is a very great honour to finally meet you, Miss Austen. I have you to thank for making my career," he said.

"On the contrary Mr Firth, I believe I owe you even more," she replied with a regal nod. "I am sure I had only a middling sort of popularity before your efforts."

He chuckled at her joke and she thought, *Wow, this is fun. We're both hamming it up.*

"May I introduce my wife, Livia," he said, his voice almost lost in the buzz of the crowd and the whir of the cameras. Firth put his hand behind his wife's back and brought her forward and together Mary and she curtseyed, again to an explosion of light.

"You do know you're the only woman I share him with. He stayed up late with you last night," she told Mary.

"That is very generous of you. May I sign those?"

Mary pointed to the two copies of *Sanditon* Mrs Firth held. As Mrs Firth presented them, someone, doubtless one of the many Random House employees, took them from her. He handed one copy to Mary with a pen.

"Write: To Colin Firth, whose good opinion I hope never to lose. A devoted fan, Jane Austen." Mary did as she was bid and guessed that Jane had prepared that in advance.

She handed the copy back to Mrs Firth, who looked at the inscription and gave it to her husband, who smiled all the more broadly after reading it. Mary was given the next copy to sign.

"Write: To Livia Giuggioli, whose generosity of spirit is matched only by her beauty and charm. Forever envious, Jane Austen."

Mary returned that copy as well and then could no longer ignore the many throat clearings of her friend.

"Mr and Mrs Firth, may I introduce you to my best friend, my manager and agent, Melody Kramer?"

Melody almost leapt from behind and Firth honoured her with the same low bow he gave Mary. Melody actually tittered with delight.

Afterward, various pictures were taken including one with a space for Jane to stand. Hands were shaken and air kisses exchanged and finally, every photographic opportunity exhausted they left, and Mary suddenly felt tired.

"Oh my," Jane said. "I believe Hugh Grant is next in line."

· Chicago ·
Eighties hair

Mary yawned. She was still recovering from the excitement of the New York launch the week before. It had been a repeat of the London book launch with different celebrities but the same receiving line, balls and endless photographs.

This week, however, Mary and Jane were in Chicago without an entourage, driving to a mega Barnes & Noble store in the suburbs. Mary kept looking nervously at the empty seat beside her where sat, hopefully, Jane.

"I'm still here, Mary. I simply haven't said anything since the last time you asked if I was all right."

"Yeah, sorry, just a little nervous. And I don't drive much."

"And it shows."

Mary turned to look at Jane, stung by her rebuke.

"Keep your eyes on the road, Mary. I am sorry, but you handed me a straight line."

"A straight line? Is that proper Regency?"

"No, I learned of the term from television. I do watch television, you know; I did even before the discovery, although it wasn't until subtitles became common that I could enjoy it properly. I was quite addicted to murder mysteries, especially *Inspector Morse*. Oh, and American soap operas like *Dallas* and *Dynasty* were delightfully silly things. They reminded me of the theatricals of my youth with everyone declaiming."

Mary was surprised to hear the *doyenne* of English literature confessing her fondness for American trash TV, but it also suddenly gave her a connection to Jane.

"I used to watch *Dynasty* on DVDs with my mom. It was pretty awful but she loved it. I mean the hair."

"And the clothes," Jane concurred. "Those shoulder pads."

Almost in unison they said, "And the catfights!"

"See, you are more relaxed now," Jane said.

Her words caught Mary by surprise. "What, all that was just to get me to relax?"

"And it worked."

"You don't really like *Dynasty?*"

"My dear, I am Jane Austen whose works have never been out of print since, well since some year that I'm sure some Janeite can recall, but I am sure it has been a very long time. Do you seriously suppose that I sat around after death watching Krystle and Alexis pull each other's hair?"

"No, no I suppose not. Well thanks, like I said, I was nervous."

"Might I ask why? I thought we had established a rapport."

"Oh sure, only now, you know, I'm responsible for you," Mary said as she merged into traffic. Melody had not accompanied them on this trip, and now Mary was nervous about her charge. Jane had a habit of wandering off, which made navigating Midway Airport a nightmare. She could just imagine having to call Melody in a panic and saying, "I've lost Jane!" Being in the car with her was actually the calmest Mary had been in some time.

"You were responsible for me in London. Were you not nervous then?"

"Yes ... but I was a lot more nervous about being you in front of movie stars and politicians and actual royalty. I'm just getting over that so now I have more time to worry about you."

"Excuse me, am I an invalid that you should be so concerned for me?"

Mary turned her head to make sure there was no one in her lane and accelerated.

"It's like those parenting exercises in high school," she said, not having paid adequate attention to Jane's response.

"Then I am a child for which you are responsible."

"What? No, oh God no." Despite her worry that she had offended Jane she had to smile at the thought that Jane's words recalled.

"You look nothing like an egg," she said after a moment.

"An egg? You confuse me."

"Sorry, I couldn't help thinking of those exercises. They give you an egg that you're supposed to take care of for a week. It's supposed to give you an idea of what it's like to take care of a baby."

"That's absurd. The proper way to learn what it is to care for an infant is to have four brothers who among them have more children than a foundling hospital.[1] How many cousins and nieces and nephews have you?"

"Uh, none. My parents were only children, even Dad's first wife was an only child, and my brother and sister don't have kids yet. I'm sure I have second cousins or whatever, but we didn't keep track."

"Oh!" Jane was taken aback. Of course she knew that modern families were small, especially in America. She didn't know whether to feel pity for or envy of Mary.

"I was sort of an only child as well because my brother and sister are a lot older than me and they're only half relations. And because my father was in the military, we travelled a lot so I never really had many close friends."

"Then I am sorry for you, Mary. My family was my comfort. And a trial at times, certainly, but … your egg, how did it fare?"

"I sat on it about thirty minutes after I got it."

"Then you failed in your parenting exercise?"

"Oh no, the teacher just gave me another one."

"Well in that respect I should prove more durable than your egg for you cannot sit on me. No, I lie, you can sit on me but it will do me no harm."

Mary suddenly worried. "I haven't ever sat on you, have I?"

"No, either your good manners or I presume your training at the agency have resulted in the utmost concern for my person. And I believe you should have taken a right turn here. But no matter, you may turn right at the next street. No pardon me, the street after that. I must make allowance for one-way streets."

"Huh? Oh, thanks. You're better than a voice navigation system. I'd be lost without you."

---

1 Of her six brothers, four had children. Francis and Edward had eleven apiece

"Nonsense, despite my previous unkindness, I have to judge you are an excellent driver. I am quite envious."

"Why? Oh, of course, you can't … maybe someday the disembodied …" Mary stopped, embarrassed that for a second she had forgotten her friend was disembodied.

"Your confusion is very charming, Mary. You blush quite easily. It may almost become a game with me to elicit it. No, I do not refer to the present. I remember from my time when alive and how proscribed I was. Often my visits to Godmersham Park exceeded the length of my desire for I could not return home alone."

"Oh, yes, I remember that. Sounds like Saudi Arabia."

Jane ignored the reference she did not understand and said, "Although I could have *in extremis* travelled alone …"

"Like Catherine Morland in *Northanger Abbey*."

"Precisely. Does this mean you've read it?" Mary already knew the characters and plots of the six novels and Juvenilia—in many ways she knew it better than Jane—but she hadn't finished actually reading all of them.

"Yes, I enjoyed that. I'm reading *Emma* now. Well, you already know that." Her last words betrayed a little of the unease she felt at having a disembodied friend who observed everything she did.

Jane did know Mary was reading *Emma* and had been for some time, and knew that Mary was having difficulty.

"And do you like the story?"

Mary was relieved Jane posed her question this way.

"I adore the story and I love Emma. It's just … it's just kind of hard to read. I mean compared to *P&P*."

Jane had heard this complaint before and had feared that some would have trouble appreciating her heroine and she told Mary this.

"Duh! 'I am going to take a heroine whom no one but myself will much like.' But I actually like Emma. It's Miss Bates who drives me insane. She was boring."

Jane wished she could have smiled at this. "Poor Miss Bates. I was mean to her at the same time I delighted in making her dull, but there may come a day when you learn to appreciate her. And turn left here, for that is the book store car park."

"I need to get a bumper sticker."

"A what?"

Jane's question made Mary realize the vast gulf that sometimes separated them as she tried to quickly explain the concept of a bumper sticker.

"It's a slogan printed on adhesive backed paper affixed to the back of a ..."

"Oh those, I didn't know that is what they were called. Why, what sentiment do you wish to convey?"

"Jane Austen is my co-pilot," Mary answered, and laughed, much to the confusion of Jane.

· The Fellowship of Austen ·
Stephen gets his copy of Sanditon

Stephen opened the door to the bookstore and immediately heard the very excited conversation of those wanting to meet the famous author and then the voice of a store employee shouting to be heard above the din.

"Please, if those of you waiting for the book signing could start forming a line outside," the harried older man said, standing on a chair to be seen. The conversation rose louder with some voices heard in objection that the books would run out or the author would leave.

"We've got enough books for everyone," the man said. "And Miss Austen has promised that everyone in the store now will get their book signed. Just collect the stamped bookmarks on your way out. They look like these ..."—he held up a store bookmark—"... and they're stamped VOID on the backside. It's the best we could do on short notice," he added, somewhat apologetically.

"I just want to buy the book. Do I have to go outside?" someone asked.

The man was already stepping off his chair and had to step back on. "No, just if you want it signed."

"What time does it start?" another voice asked.

"One pm" or "one o'clock" the crowd answered back before the man could respond. Several other questions were asked and answered, but Stephen tuned them out.

He was relieved he'd be able to get a signed copy as Dr Davis had rather specifically laid that task before him. "I want a signed copy, Stephen. This person may well be a fraud, but I want it for my collection nevertheless," she had told him, and he didn't dare disappoint her.

But he worried that being last in, he'd be at the back of the line. He thought his best strategy might be to hurry outside and try to be at the head of the line, but others had this same thought. After he collected his stamped bookmark and went outside, he was relieved to see the crowd wasn't quite as large as it appeared inside. The crowd was also a lot less noisy.

"We're sorry about making you stand outside and we're going to get everyone who needs it some water," another store employee told them.

Fortunately no one seemed to mind being outside and the shade of the store awning provided protection from the warm spring sun. Soon the noise increased as people began posing questions.

"How are you supposed to address her?" an older woman with thinning white hair asked a rail thin twenty something Goth girl with multiple piercings. Stephen noticed she wore a large badge with the slogan "I Believe in Jane" surrounding the representation of Austen that had appeared in *Time* magazine.

"I read you should treat avatars as the person they represent, so I guess Miss Austen."

"But it's just an actress, right. I mean Jane Austen isn't really here," an older man, looking ridiculously tweedy, asked the Goth girl, whom the older generation apparently looked to for definitive information on the subject.

"No, Jane Austen is really here. It's not like Santa Claus," she said, just a little sarcastically. "If there's an avatar—and they wear some kind of AV pin—then the dead person … uh disembodied … then they're standing right next to them."

"If it really is Jane Austen, that is. How do they know?" a middle-aged woman with long brown hair half streaked with grey asked.

"They have to … I don't know … it's some kind of test or something," Goth girl said, looking peeved that she now failed to be all knowing.

"It's a committee, an AfterNet committee, that vets the disembodied," Stephen offered.

"Sure, my uncle had to go through that when he died. It was pretty straightforward," another man, in his thirties and wearing a Life is Good T-shirt, said.

By now the orderly line that the store employees had arranged had devolved into a clump and Stephen found himself in the middle of it.

"No, that's different," Stephen said. "Your uncle, did he register with the AfterNet before he died?"

"Yeah, in the hospice," Life is Good guy confirmed.

"So it was easy for him because he'd had his field recorded," Stephen said.

"That's right, his field fingerprint."

"But somebody who died before the AfterNet, especially a long time ago, has to prove to a committee that they are who they say they were. And if they're famous, like Jane Austen, then they have to prove that to a committee made up of experts."

Thinning white hair lady said, "So it's like a court, you have to convince a jury."

"Yeah, usually," Stephen replied. "But in this case ... uh, Miss Austen ... she could answer a question or she knew something only she could know and so the committee decided that she had to really be Jane Austen."

"What was it? What was the question?" tweedy guy asked.

"Uh ... well, nobody knows. I mean the committee knows and she knows, but they can't reveal it."

"Huh," T-shirt guy replied. "So that's it. That's what makes her Jane Austen."

"That and what she's written," Goth girl said, happy to be able to enter the conversation again. "The excerpt's pretty good. Sounds just like Jane."

"What do you think?" asked a store employee who'd joined the group, absent mindedly handing out bottles of water from a basket she carried.

"And why do you know so much?" tweedy guy asked.

"I know a couple people on that committee," he lied. He was certain he probably knew someone on the committee. "I'm not convinced yet she's Austen, but I want to keep an open mind," he added, regretting it instantly because he was immediately bombarded by questions. He honestly hadn't intended to brag about his knowledge—well maybe just a little—but he also almost always answered a direct question without thought of the consequences, a trait that often gave him grief.

After a few minutes, however, he'd answered what questions he could and as usual with any group of Janeites, the conversation had turned into impromptu discussions about the books and Austen arcana. A few minutes before 1 pm, however, the discussions were interrupted when someone said, "Hey, I think they're getting started." Everyone turned to look into the store and they saw that many of the customers had clustered to one side of the store and then they heard a round of applause.

At the same time, the store employees allowed the first group of ten people to enter, although by now the crowd had doubled. Stephen hoped he would be in the next group to be let in but it was a full forty-five minutes before his turn came, along with Goth girl and T-shirt guy, who preceded him. They were led to the signing table and found a large group there, including most of the people who presumably had already had their books signed.

At the table were two women—one older woman wearing a business suit and the other presumably Jane Austen, wearing Regency costume. The avatar was pretty with brown hair correctly done up, wearing a cap. Her dress, with a proper empire waist, was a pale cream colour. It was a walking dress, with a fichu to conceal her décolleté. A spencer jacket was lying on the table beside her.

Damn, no wonder women think I'm gay. No man should know those words.

He couldn't quite decide whether wearing the costume was stupid or not, but he had to admit if you're going to go to the trouble of hiring someone to play the part of Jane Austen, you'd have to put her in costume for anyone to recognize her. After all, who really knew what Jane Austen looked like. Thankfully the avatar looked nothing like Cassandra's portrait. Instead she was young, probably in her mid twenties, with high cheekbones and a bright complexion. He was still too far away to see her eye colour.

"She looks very pretty," the woman behind him said.

"She looks pretty young," another woman replied to the first.

"You want her young, don't you," yet another woman, who had a British accent, said. "I always imagine her young, before she was published."

The line moved forward and now Stephen was fourth in line. A store employee—the woman who'd been handing out the water—asked him how many books he'd like to buy.

He told her two and she produced a handheld register that scanned his credit card and printed a receipt. She handed him his two books and proceeded down the line to the next person.

The line moved forward again. He could hear her voice now. She sounded British.

"To whom should I address it?" she asked.

"To Sardonyx," Goth girl replied, but then amended in a quiet voice, "Actually, make it out to Julia."

The avatar took the book, signed it and returned it. "Thank you, Julia. I very much hope you enjoy it."

Goth girl took the book from her and almost curtseyed, laughed and then turned away, wearing a big smile accentuated by her many piercings.

The line moved forward and now Stephen could see her eyes, which were hazel. Life is Good guy was talking to her and produced four copies with very specific instructions for the inscriptions. The avatar seemed not at all nonplussed and cheerfully spoke with him. Stephen was suddenly conscious of his own attire: baggy shorts and an untucked colourful print shirt.

The line moved forward again and now the woman before him blocked Stephen's view, so he paid attention to the other woman at the table. She looked familiar and he tried to place her, then recognized her as one of the local JASNA members. She caught him looking at her and recognition also appeared on her face.

Phyllis, that's her name, Stephen remembered. *Talked my ear off a year ago about the latest Wuthering Heights movie before I finally admitted I'd never seen it or read it. Hopefully she's forgotten that.*

The line moved forward and he found himself facing Jane Austen.

"Hello, Miss Austen. It's a pleasure," he said, handing her his two copies. Suddenly he had to fight the almost overwhelming urge to do a stiff Darcy bow.

She took the book and said, "Thank you very much, sir," and inclined her head.

It was too much and he couldn't help bowing his head ever so slightly.

"Two books, is it? And whose names should I write?"

"If you could address one to Stephen Abrams ... with a PH. And the other to Alice Davis."

"You're getting a copy for Alice?" the JASNA member asked. "You're

Stephen, one of her graduate students, aren't you. The one who doesn't like Emily Brontë?"

"Would that be Dr Alice Davis?" the avatar asked.

"What, oh, yes," he said to the JASNA woman, and then to Austen. "Uh … she couldn't be here and she asked me to …"

"If you're one of her students, then you are studying …" She looked at Stephen very directly and she seemed to be leaning her head slightly to the right, as if listening to something.

"Uh … yes … I'm a doctoral candidate and … uh … yes." He could feel his face flush.

Phyllis leaned over to whisper in the avatar's ear.

"Oh, something about the Enclosure Movement? That is your thesis?" the avatar asked.

"The Enclosure Movement and the changing demographics of the Regency world as revealed in the novels of Jane Austen," he said, rushing through the words from long practice, attempting to get it all said before a glassy-eyed look would possess the listener.

"I hope it will see publication someday. I have been informed that my novels contain all manner of deeper meanings when truly all I was doing was writing my little stories." She smiled and then returned her attention to his copies, signed them and returned them to him.

"Thank you," he said, "thank you very much, Miss Austen." As he said her name, it felt right and proper.

"You are welcome," she said, with a gravity that belied her youth. For a second he looked directly into her eyes. *Contacts, she's wearing contacts,* he thought, and the spell was broken. She turned her attention to the next person in line.

Stephen left the table slowly, looking back at her often. Each person she greeted seemed delighted to speak with her and each person received her smile. It was a Mona Lisa smile, a reserved smile, but warm nonetheless.

· Meet cute ·
Stephen and Mary spend the day

"**E**xcuse me, Miss Austen?"

Mary turned around, ready to acknowledge the greeting, a pleasant smile fixed upon her face, before she remembered she was off the clock, wearing jeans and two miles from the hotel and that she did not have Jane's voice in her ear.

"I'm sorry, you must have me confused with someone else," she said to the handsome man who had addressed her. But she still had the smile on her face and her arm already outstretched to accept his greeting, which she now uncomfortably retracted.

"Oh, I'm very sorry. I thought you were … but of course, you're not working." He looked down to conceal his embarrassment and stepped back, colliding with the table behind him in the small coffee shop. The collision prompted him to drop the bundle of pamphlets he carried in his left arm.

He bent down to pick them up and as he did so spilled some of the coffee he carried in his right hand.

"Oh crap," he said. He hurriedly put down the paper coffee cup and pulled the pamphlets away from the spreading spill.

Mary looked round quickly and saw a stack of napkins not far away. She snatched a handful and dropped them on the spill, preventing the coffee from staining any further papers.

"Thank you," the man said, still not looking at her while he retrieved his pamphlets. They were now both crouched down upon the floor and Mary also began retrieving his pamphlets, which appeared to be college blue books. Some of them had been graded with remarks on the covers.

With the blue books now recovered both stood up. Mary handed her stack back to him. He glanced at her, thanked her, lowered his gaze again and then looked at her again, venturing a smile.

"I … sorry for the …"

"Absent minded professor routine?" Mary supplied.

"Well, absent minded TA[1] routine," he said, his smile no longer timid. "You are her, aren't you. You're Jane Austen's avatar."

"Don't say it so loud, I don't want to be mobbed," she said, looking around at the disinterested customers, most of them probably unaware of her employer's fame or existence.

"Excuse me, are you going to order or what?" the barista behind the counter said to Mary. She turned back to the barista and gave her order and then asked her new acquaintance, "Can I buy you a coffee? To replace the one …"

"Yes," he said with a vigorous nod. "Thank you, just a medium plain coffee."

"We just ran out of 'plain coffee' so it'll have to be an americano," the barista said, after a consultation with her coworkers to confirm that there was no regular coffee.

Obviously that was a sore point with the man who grumbled, "OK, an americano."

Mary paid for their coffees while the man dumped the handful of soggy napkins, and his empty cup, in a trash bin.

"Shall we sit?" Mary asked. He nodded and she led them to a table.

"Thank you very much," he said after sitting down. "And I'm sorry to have accosted you."

"That's a bit of an exaggeration. I'm sorry I didn't know what to do. Wait, didn't I sign your copy? I mean didn't Jane sign it."

"Yes you did, or rather she did. Or the two of you did. This is kind of confusing."

"Tell me about it. It's Stephen, right?" she asked, amazed and, considering he was reasonably cute, happy that she'd remembered his name.

---

1 Teaching assistant

He nodded. "Yes, I'm honoured you remember. So, what you are doing here, so far from the hotel?"

"Well, I thought I was far enough away that I could remain incognito," she said.

His face reflected his discomfort. "I'm sorry that I ..."

"No, no, it's OK," she hastened to say. "You don't look like one of the more rabid Janeites. What are you, a professor?"

"Just a grad student and ... well, my thesis is about ... well Jane."

"Oh, so you *are* a rabid Janeite. And here I thought I could talk about something other than Austen."

Again he looked uncomfortable and Mary realized she'd again said something that could be misconstrued. Of course, truth was that as much as she was enjoying her job, she did want to talk about things non-Austen every once in a while.

"Well, thank you for the coffee," he said, and began to push back in his chair. To stop him, she reached out and put her hand on his arm.

"I'm sorry," she said. "That came out wrong. Look, I'm here in Chicago and Jane's given me the day off and I don't know what to do. Maybe you could suggest something?"

He sat back down and smiled. "Sure, there're a million things to do here. Do you like museums? Ever been to the Field Museum?"

Mary had nothing against a good museum and were she to spend a week in Chicago would undoubtedly visit it, but she didn't want to waste her one day on one.

"That sounds great. Where is it?"

So Mary spent the day at the Field Museum with Stephen and afterward walked along the shorefront, which gave her more exercise than she'd had in weeks. The book tour involved sitting in aeroplanes and at signing tables and she'd worried that she'd put on weight, but evidently the nervousness of her role had kept her thin, although her muscle tone was awful.

So she tried not to complain about all the walking for she was having a very good day with Stephen. She realized that she was having just the sort of day she'd have had in New York and recognized in Stephen a fellow starving student. He'd gained admission to the museum with a student pass and walking along the shorefront cost nothing and buying a hotdog from a pushcart cost little.

But finally her wobbly legs gave out and so by El² they headed back to where she'd left her car. Stephen felt happy that he'd spent the day with Mary, even though it meant that he'd have to work all day Sunday to finish grading papers. He always loved showing off Chicago to out-of-towners and the fact that he'd spent the day with Jane Austen's avatar made it extra enjoyable.

By agreement, however, he'd refrained from asking her any questions about Jane Austen. So he'd learned Mary was a struggling acting student who was now making more money than she'd ever dreamed of making, but in a role destined to go uncredited. He learned of her family and her childhood and her hopes and fears and he'd done his best to find her fascinating, which was an easy task, but all during their tour he'd been dying to know one thing.

"What's she like?" he finally blurted out on the El, unable to contain himself any longer.

"Wow, you held out a lot longer than I ever thought you would," she said.

"You don't mind?"

"How can I mind? I was more fascinating than Jane Austen for all of two hours," Mary said with a smile.

Stephen looked at her in the dying sunlight that flashed upon her face whenever the train moved between buildings. She looked like a film star in a silent movie and he stared at her, forgetting he'd asked her a question.

"So, do you want to know what she's like?" Mary prompted him.

The question broke the spell and he nodded his head.

"Well, she's like the best older sister there ever was, although I admit that since I'm not close to my older sister, I'm just guessing. She's really funny and … you know the person in the meeting who sits there quietly and you don't think they're paying attention? And then they say something that completely skewers the pompous ass that's talking—that's Jane.

"And she can be so prim and proper because she still talks like the books, you know, but then you realize she's seen it all. You Janeites worship her as the spinster from Hampshire with her little studies of people, but you just can't know the woman from that."

2 The "L" or "El" refers to the trains operated by the Chicago Transit Authority. Much of the train system is above street level.

"Little travelled, never married," Stephen said.

"What?"

"Sorry, it's a dismissive description of Jane Austen boiled down from Henry Austen's little biography of her. The family, after her death, really emphasized her Godliness and frugality and even temper. Henry called hers a life of little event, and maybe it was up until the time she died."

"Yeah, I guess so, but that's the thing about the afterlife, isn't it. You just keep adding to your knowledge and experience of life, for the rest of eternity. Oh, isn't this our stop?"

However Stephen was already rising, confirming it was their stop and the conversation was interrupted as they exited the train and the station and walked down to ground level.

"Well, I'm happy to hear Austen isn't the simple spinster, but that's just confirming what I'd thought all along. It's always galled me when critics say, 'She just wrote what she knew,' as if that isn't a great compliment. She knew people and their emotions and made them real, like no one before her."

"I wish you could know her like I do," Mary said, "not that I know that much about her life when alive. She keeps that to herself, but she certainly shares her observations and opinions about the here and now. And she knows a lot about everything, which I suppose is a consequence of being around for so long. She follows the news obsessively. Actually, she can be a bit of a bore about the news and is always giving me grief that I don't know anything about politics—and I'm talking US politics here. She has a lot of opinions about our peace keeping mission in India."

They had reached Mary's rental car in the parking lot and Mary looked back at Stephen, who had a faraway look in his eyes. She recognized that look.

"Oh, you haven't heard a word I've said. You've got that look."

"Huh? What look?"

"That 'I'd love to ask Jane Austen about … ' look. You've been dreaming up a million questions to ask her, haven't you?"

They were back in the car and Stephen's expression confirmed his guilt. "OK, busted. I'm sorry, it's just … yeah, I have so many questions. I'm sorry, I should have been thinking how much I enjoyed the afternoon … with you."

She hadn't started the car yet and was looking at him and thinking his guilty look was very cute.

"I'm leaving Chicago tomorrow morning and continuing the book tour and attending several Austen events. Are you going to any?"

"Uh, yeah, there's a small writer's conference in Colorado Springs in July."

"That's near Denver, right?"

"Near enough. It's about the middle of the month. But it's not an Austen event, it's a conference for ..." and now Stephen looked embarrassed. "It's a conference for romance writers."

Oh that's so cute, Mary thought and wished she had Jane with her to witness this man's charming discomfort. She did her best not to convey how cute she thought his admission. She started the car and exited the car park to cover her smile. Once in traffic, she said, "Wow, I wonder why we're not sneaking down for that. Maybe Melody doesn't want to cross into the romance genre, but you'd think Jane would be a fit. So you're a romance writer?" She asked the last as nonchalantly as she could, without any accusation in her tone.

However his reply made it clear he was touchy about the subject despite her effort to keep any judgment from her tone.

"I'm a liberal arts graduate student obsessed with Jane Austen and medieval literature so I thought I should try to find an outside source of income. And I started writing ... well a historical romance ... it just started out as fun and ..."

"Hey, you don't need to justify what you need to do to make money. I'm selling my body to support my acting school classes, which I've pretty much abandoned for an uncredited role as a Regency spinster. And I don't know how long this gig will last, but I'm having a great time and making great money. But when it comes down to saying what I'm doing ... I'm basically a ..."

She couldn't bring herself to say it. She was stopped at a red light, three cars back from the intersection, worried about her admission and its effect on him and shamed even more by the admission to herself.

Play-acting as Jane Austen's avatar sounded so high-minded and she had been doing it so long that she had almost forgotten the misgivings she had when she signed up at the avatar agency.

She could have just as easily been an avatar for a far more unsavoury character and asked to do unsavoury things. Of course she was making enough that she could go back to school for another semester, but eventually she'd either have to make it as an actress or be someone else's avatar.

Then she felt Stephen's hand on hers, and he said, "Don't say that, you're ..."

But his words were interrupted by the car horn that sounded behind them. She realized then that the light had turned green and there were no cars in front of her. She moved her hand from where it rested on the emergency brake to the wheel, breaking contact with Stephen's hand. She hoped he wouldn't perceive it as her taking her hand from him and shot him a smile, which he returned.

The revelations of their mutual desperation, however, kept their conversation to a minimum until she brought him to a bus station where he said he could catch a bus straight to his home. As he was preparing to leave the car, she said, "Maybe we could get together then, when you're in Colorado Springs?"

"I'd like that."

"And maybe you can meet Jane. I mean you did meet Jane at the signing, but ..."

"I know what you mean, I'd like that, but ... I'd like to see you again even more."

She saw the sincerity on his face and said, "Liar. But it's a very nice lie. I'll expect an email from you."

"You can expect a call. Would tomorrow be OK?"

"Oh God, now I'm sounding pushy."

"No, no, tomorrow night? After 8 pm? It's just if you call earlier ... well Jane would be there and ..."

"After 8 pm, then. I can talk to Jane Austen another time."

· How considerate ·
Stephen tells Dr Davis he's met Mary

S tephen kept trying to keep the grin off his face, but being a man with little ability to dissemble and being naturally outgoing, he knew he was failing miserably. Normally by this point of a faculty meeting he'd be getting sleepy or would be staring vacantly out the window, but his slight smile apparently made him appear, if not interested in the proceedings, at least cognizant of the topic.

"You have something to add, Mr Abrams?" asked the department head, who had been unnerved by the smile upon Stephen's face.

The smile melted from the unexpected question. He had no idea what the topic had been.

"No, it sounds like a good idea," he ventured to say, only then noticing the amused glances in the room.

"We are all gratified you approve of reducing your expense reimbursements. No doubt you are aware of the serious nature of the budget shortfalls affecting our department. I am sure your fellow graduate students will share their opinions with you. And with that, let's call it a day."

Naturally Stephen had to face a good deal of friendly abuse from the others because of his inattention, including a dope slap[1] that caught

---

1 A light, upward slap to the back of the head

him off guard and that hurt slightly more than the giver had intended. He waited in the room until his advisor stood next to him.

"Is there something you wish to tell me, Stephen?" Dr Davis said, with a wry smile.

They left the room together and walked down the hallway to her office.

"You were preoccupied this morning and I see that hasn't changed. And from that stupid smile you're wearing ... I assume you've met someone." They arrived at her office and she opened the door and entered. Stephen followed, feeling foolish for allowing his emotions to so openly show. But he could hardly deny his feelings.

"Uh, yeah. Sorry for being so ..."

"Smitten?" she suggested with a laugh. "God, you don't get to say that word often enough. So out with it, who is she? Not someone I know, I hope. I would hate to see you making googly-eyes at someone I know."

He grinned sheepishly. "You know her; you definitely know her."

For a second, he couldn't think how he could relay to her the enormity of his revelation or even if he should, and then he remembered the task his advisor had given him. He reached into his bag and retrieved the signed copy and handed it to her.

"Oh, thank you, I was afraid you'd forgot ..." but she stopped because he didn't quite relinquish his hold on the book as he handed it to her.

She looked at him quizzically, and then he nodded at the book and released it. The exchange left her puzzled. She looked at him and he again looked at the book and back to her. She opened her mouth, shut it, and then asked, "What are you trying to say, Stephen? I had previously thought you a gifted young man, but you are seriously testing my patience."

But Stephen couldn't quite say the words, "I think I might be dating Jane Austen's avatar." It sounded so preposterous in his head, but finally, haltingly said something to that effect.

"I sent you out to get a book signed. I didn't mean for you to fall in love. Well, well, Jane Austen's avatar. Tell me about her."

The invitation prompted Stephen to tell her the entire story of waiting in line, getting the book signed, later meeting her at the coffee shop and spending the day with her. He also snuck in an apology for not getting around to some of the other tasks she'd set him.

It would be unfair to say that Dr Davis wasn't pleased for Stephen, for she truly did like him and appreciate him. But her immediate reaction was that his news could prove immensely useful to her. And as he continued in his praise of the woman, she thought of a way that she might control the situation to her advantage.

"I'm very happy for you, Stephen, but you do realize some of the ethical considerations that arise from this?"

Stephen, who had just expressed his hope of meeting the avatar in Colorado, looked puzzled. "What? What ethical consideration?" But he realized the implications of her question as he responded. "Oh, I hadn't thought about that."

"Your objectivity will be called into question if you're romantically involved with the avatar of the subject you're ... dating."

His serious expression, however, warned her not to overplay her hand. His seriousness and integrity were the reasons she valued him and she didn't want him doing anything noble.

"I wouldn't say we're ... so you're saying I should ..."

"Wait, wait, I didn't say anything, just that you should be cautious. If I may be allowed a little self-aggrandizement, that is precisely why you have me as an advisor. I can tell you if you're allowing your feeling for ... what is her name again?"

"Mary, Mary Crawford," he said, and then hastily added when he saw the look on his advisor's face. "I know, that's kind of weird, but at least it's not Elizabeth Bennet."

"You are certain this person is Jane Austen's avatar?" she asked, suddenly worried that the poor boy had deluded himself.

"No, of course it's her. I mean she's on the dust jacket," he said.

Dr Davis looked at the book and on the back cover saw the picture of the author, or rather a painting/computer illustration. It was well done and she recognized it from its earlier release, but it was obviously not a photograph.

"No, on the inside front flap," he said, a little testily.

She opened the cover and looked at the flap and recognized the photo of the woman who had been hired to be Miss Austen's avatar.

"And this is the woman you met?" She gave Stephen a quick smile. "You didn't get hit on the head and all this was a dream?"

"No, I ... wait a minute." He reached into a pocket and produced his phone and after pressing a few buttons, he turned the screen around to show her. Standing below the fossil of Sue the T-rex,[2] she could recognize the woman who seemed identical to the picture in the book. Or as close alike as she could tell from the small image of the woman in contrast to the large image of the dinosaur.

"Very well, Stephen, I will assume you are not suffering from a mental disorder. Perhaps you'd better keep me informed of what you learn … of your relationship with this Mary Crawford, so that I can advise you if it might affect the objectivity of your thesis."

---

2   Sue, at The Field Museum, is the largest and most complete Tyrannosaurus rex fossil ever found

· Boston ·
The obligations of being civil

Courtney fidgeted nervously behind the desk as he listened to the woman. "I'm not sure if I agree with you, but I suppose I must read this," she said. "Everyone does seem to be talking about it."

He looked at the several pins and buttons the matronly woman sported, including the "I Believe in Jane" button that showed the new portrait of Austen. There was a JASNA pin and a very nice cameo with the famous Austen silhouette as well.

He offered her his most ingratiating wry smile, which tried to suggest he was embarrassed but pleased at his own success, but his charm failed to impress her.

So he took the book from her and after asking her name signed it: "To Caroline, whose skepticism and loyalty does her justice, Courtney Blake."

He returned it to her and she looked at the inscription and then at him and her stern look softened.

"Oh, thank you. I do hold great faith in Jane that she would never . . ."

"I understand, Caroline, truly I do. And I think if you read the book, I believe you'll understand I have great faith in Miss Austen as well and that I only followed where my research led me."

The stern look returned and he realized he'd overplayed his hand.

He smiled again but she merely said, "Thank you" and left. *Still, a sale's a sale,* he thought.

It looked as if Caroline might be the last customer for a while. It had been a long two hours with his constant looks towards Jane Austen's table and the long line that kept her avatar busy. Courtney had been often idle during the two hours and had seen surly looks from the people in Austen's line.

He began to doubt the wisdom of his agent suggesting joint appearances. He had two more occasions when he would appear with Austen. The Harvard Book Store was the first store to agree to the plan with a little trepidation, no doubt worried that Courtney would be burned in effigy or tarred and feathered. Fortunately none of that had happened and civility ruled the day.

He looked at the store clock and realized it was precisely two pm and stood, relieved that he could quit the store and travel to his next book signing in the evening. The group of women at Austen's table was still considerable, but he realized no one was actually waiting in line and he thought he could at least play a grand gesture and get a few props. He bent down to find his messenger bag under the table and saw that it had moved off to the side with his incessant squirming during the afternoon and so he had to squat down on the floor. He opened the bag to retrieve his copy of *Sanditon* but as he pulled it out, his iPad fell to the floor along with some loose change he'd thrown in and he had to gather those. Finally he stood, resigned that now was as good a time as any to ask Austen's avatar to sign his copy, but as his head cleared the edge of his table he saw the woman in question standing in front of him.

"Mr Blake? I was hoping you might sign my copy of your book." And she handed him a copy of *The Real Jane Austen*. He stood there with his mouth open, uncertain what to do.

"Oh, is that *Sanditon?* Perhaps I might return the favour?" And she put out her hand.

Her offer saved him from continuing to look foolish. He handed her *Sanditon* and she took it and bent to the task of signing it. He took the advantage of his chair, which was not a very gentleman-like thing to do. He opened his book and found that Austen had several Post-it notes peeking out from pages and the dust jacket was torn and repaired with Sellotap.

"To the REAL Jane Austen," he signed. "With the hope that my esteem of your works is the primary impression I leave behind, Courtney Blake."

He looked up from signing and saw that Austen's avatar had finished and he quickly stood. They exchanged books simultaneously and both quickly looked at the inscriptions.

Austen's avatar had written, in a good imitation of the original's signature, "To Courtney Blake, Thank you for making me so much more interesting than I really was. Jane Austen."

Fortunately his mind resumed its normal operation and he thought to capitalize on the moment. He said loudly, for he realized that Austen's admirers stood behind the author, "Thank you Miss Austen, that is a gracious sentiment."

She nodded regally and said, "And yours as well, Mr Blake. I hope this will put to rest any thought of ill-feelings between us."

She extended her hand, palm down and Courtney took it delicately in his and bowed. As he straightened, he saw that many of her admirers were taking pictures with their smart phones and cameras.

She has that advantage, he thought. *I have no admirers.*

Austen's avatar retreated after a gracious nod to him. The store manager came out to greet her and thank her for coming and several more pictures were taken. Courtney reached back down for his messenger bag and made for another exit so that he did not have to pass by Austen and her admirers. *One book signing down and two more to go. Maybe I can be sick both days.*

~

"He is positively grey," Jane said to Mary back at their hotel room.

"He's understandably nervous," Mary admitted while stretched out on the bed, trying to find something to watch on the telly. Jane was logged into the AfterNet, which meant Mary had to entertain herself by either tackling *Emma* again or going old school and actually watching television. But a Saturday afternoon offered little to watch. She considered taking a shower, but knew she was obliged to say "uh huh" and "sure" to Jane's continued belittlement of her bugbear.

"You're not even looking," Jane complained.

She turned her head to look at the picture displayed on the laptop that had already been posted on the facebook pages of many Janeites.

It showed them offering her hand to Blake who stood looking uncertain what to do.

"Jane, I've seen enough. He looks confused. You completely trumped him by going to him first. We were all graciousness. But I thought he handled it well and it was a nice inscription."

"He wrote REAL in capital letters. He clearly meant it sarcastically."

"No it doesn't, Jane. I mean yeah, maybe it is, but take the high road. You're Jane Austen for God's sake. You're supposed to be better than this."

She'd listened to Jane whinge ever since leaving the bookstore and was getting tired of it. She needed to take a shower before they went out again to attend a performance of a *Sense and Sensibility* musical. She just needed to shut Jane out and …

She realized Jane had not responded. "Jane?"

"You are, of course, correct, Mary. I have allowed myself to wallow in petty vindictiveness."

"Well, wallow might be too strong a word," Mary said, although she actually thought it the *mot juste*. "You just needed to get it out of your system."

"Sigh," Jane said. "You do begin to know me, Mary. I do tend to fly off the handle, but you have shown me that I must control myself."

"Oh, right. Well if you're done then, I'm going to take a shower. Are you going to be all right for a while or would you like to get out?"

"No, I shall remain here. Have a nice shower."

Mary collected her things and entered the bathroom. *She doesn't want to go walkabout*, she thought. *That means she's going to go online and kvetch about this to her peeps. Yup, I do begin to know you, Jane.*

~

Jane waited for the bathroom door to close before she went back online. She contemplated the wisdom of using one of her many accounts to comment about Courtney Blake, but she had spent—or mostly spent—her ire by complaining to Mary. She suddenly realized the debt she owed Mary. It reminded her of the times when she was separated from Cassandra and did not have her sister's moderating influence.

Instead she opened an email to Albert:

Dear Albert,

Please forgive me my recent silence for I have been monstrously busy. I did not know—really know—what work meant until this job. In my day, work meant doing one task until completion but now I must run from pillar to post leaving one task uncompleted before tackling yet another.

And so that is my excuse for not writing lately and for not arranging to set a date for our next chat. It has only now occurred to me and I hope you will agree to Sunday as usual.

Now as to my real reason for writing you today—other than my primary reason of offering my apologies: have you read that book about Jane Austen by that Courtney Blake? He apparently thinks Jane was some daughter of Sappho and has reinterpreted everything she's written as some manifesto.

People like him do not understand the world was very different for us. They want to take the values of the twenty-first century and apply it to our lives. Why even your time on earth was vastly different to mine! What a world of opportunity did not exist for a woman of my time? Of course that would colour my outlook and how I would express myself. How could a young man of today even hope to make sense of it?

That I shared a bed with my sister

But Jane stopped writing, realizing that she was about to reveal her identity to Albert, a step she was reluctant to take. She had begun to enjoy the fiction of herself as some poor drudge at Random House and thought it gave her an empathy with Albert's employment. She thought of some of the books she had read of successful people long married who fondly remembered their first home and longed for that simpler time. At present, she was reluctant to give up her simpler time with Albert.

She erased what she'd written and instead asked Albert of his family and of the baseball game she had watched with Mary two nights previous. This recollection required some editing as she recalled that she had earlier told Albert that some ill-feeling existed between herself and Mary, the new girl in the office. She began to invent a rapprochement that quickly spiralled out of control.

Why cannot I be this inventive when I am trying to write something new?

She ended the email when she started to speak of her oft-remarked mention of baseball in *Northanger Abbey*,[1] again almost falling into the trap of betraying herself.

In short, dear Albert, I shall endeavour to communicate more faithfully with you and I look forward to Sunday night.

Your very good friend,
Jane

~

Albert looked fondly on his sleeping great-great-great grandchild Julia. He was just enough of a romantic to believe he could see a resemblance to his wife Catherine and enough of a realist to know an eight-month-old might look like anyone with enough imagination. Julia was sound asleep in the arms of her father, who was sound asleep on the sofa, oblivious to the sound of the baseball game on the television. On the recliner beside him was Joe's brother, Ricardo, also asleep.

Albert marvelled at the complexities of his family in America. His granddaughter Maria had moved to the United States and to Florida, where Albert's brother had moved after the Second World War. Maria had married a man from Cuba and now Albert looked at his family that included AnnaMaria his great-great granddaughter, her husband Joe, his brother Ricardo, and the sleeping baby Julia. And that was simply the family in the house, not to mention Joe's children from another marriage and the family of his great-grandson in Muncie, Indiana.

Conversation having grown quiet in the living room, Albert went to the kitchen where AnnaMaria was making spaghetti.

"Everyone's asleep," Albert said as he entered the kitchen. His words

---

1   In *Northanger Abbey*, Austen wrote of her heroine, Catherine Morland: "It was not very wonderful that Catherine, who had nothing heroic about her, should prefer cricket, baseball, riding on horseback, and running about the country at the age of 14, to books." This early mention gives lie to the belief that baseball was invented in America, according to author Julian Norridge's book *Can we Have our Balls Back, Please?*

were communicated through the portable terminal that sat in its re-charging stand in the kitchen.

"You told them too many stories, Pop-pop," she said while putting the noodles into the boiling pot.

"No I didn't. I just told them about another baseball game I saw."

"From when?"

"Oh, sometime in the 1980s, it was just after I came to the United States. I remember ..."

"Stop! I get enough baseball from them in the living room without having to hear it from you."

He said nothing to this, a little hurt that she should stop him from talking. He was feeling a little lonely.

"What about your girlfriend. Tell me about her."

"What? Jane? Well she's not my girlfriend. And I just got an email from her."

"Did she apologize for missing your sex chat?"

"We do not have sex chats, you incurable romantic. We usually talk about ... well we usually talk about you ... and the family. She knows all about you. I don't think she's made a connection with her family, but then she died so long ago."

"You died a long time ago, but we still love you," she said over her shoulder as she lifted the lid off the bubbling pot. Albert could see the steam rise from the pot and wished he could smell his great- great grandchild's cooking.

"Yes, well this is an unusual family," he said. "Not everyone is as close to their great-great grandfather."

"She should come visit us, and for that matter, you should live here, not in that home." She started taking plates from the shelves and to the kitchen table.

"I like it there," he lied, "and I don't know if Ricardo is really that comfortable sharing the house with a dead man."

"He's lucky to have a spare bedroom here as it is," she said.

"You don't need me looking over your shoulder all the time. It's enough that I can visit you."

"OK, Pop-pop. Now tell me more about this woman of yours. You say she's a writer?"

~

"More interesting than I really was," Courtney said quietly to himself that night while lying on the bed in his hotel room. Then he turned off the light and tried to go to sleep.

· The Graham Norton Show ·
Indelicate questions

"So, is there anyone special in your life?"

Mary waited for Jane to say something in response to the silly question. The talk show host's famous leer was hanging in the air like the Cheshire cat and he kept nodding his head and winking.

"No one at the moment, thank you for asking," Mary answered, when Jane failed to say anything.

"Still the most beloved spinster in England, then."

"As you are the most beloved old molly[1] on the BBC," Jane finally said.

"As you are the most beloved ... talk show host on the BBC," Mary said, instinctively editing Jane's remark. She wasn't sure what a molly was, but could guess. Fortunately the answer and Mary's odd look satisfied the host enough to move on to the next guest.

Mary found that she had to answer on her own most of the questions addressed to Jane, and generally had to adopt the attitude of the disapproving aunt. She was baffled why Melody had insisted they appear on the show with its constant dreadful double entendres. There were certainly some aspects of British humour she didn't understand.

The show finally ended and after shaking hands with the now sub-

---

1   Regency slang for a homosexual

dued host, she joined Melody who'd watched from the studio audience.

"Well that could have gone better. You looked like you were hearing a Who again," Melody said. She turned on her terminal so she could hear Jane.

"It's not my fault. Jane froze," Mary said in a whisper. "And then … I'm not sure, but I think she called the host an old queen."

"I did not freeze," Jane answered, ignoring the more serious accusation. "And I apologize for the remark. I just suddenly saw the stupidity of it all," Jane said. "Why did you insist we appear on this show, Melody?"

"Look, let's take this somewhere else. There's got to be a pub nearby. If you're going to have a meltdown I need a drink."

Melody asked one of the production assistants they'd met earlier and learned of a wine bar actually in the broadcast centre and she offered to take them there in her car. Her presence made it difficult to talk and it took fifteen minutes before they had the anonymity of a booth and freedom to speak.

"What's this all about, Jane?" Melody asked after she finally had a glass of wine in front of her.

"I am sorry. Please forgive me my irritableness. It was unconscionable for me to use such a term."

"I only managed to get you a spot on the number two rated talk show."

"She said she's sorry," Mary said on Jane's behalf.

"And I am," Jane confirmed. "This schedule must be tiring to you both, but think what it must be like for a bicentenarian."

"You're trying to make me sorry for booking you?"

"Actually, I'm also getting a little tired," Mary said, in defence of Jane, and because she wondered if Jane was trying to obscure something from Melody. She took a large sip of her wine and felt the warmth go through her. Despite Melody's usual taste in plonk,[2] she found Chateau Television Centre quite agreeable. She normally didn't drink much, but the truth of it was their schedule was demanding. They had just returned to London after visits to Glasgow, Dublin, Paris and Barcelona, and were preparing for their visit to Chawton next week.

---

2 Cheap, but endearing wine, familiar to fans of *Rumpole of the Bailey*

"Well, I'm a little tired too," Melody said. "But you don't hear me complaining."

"We know you're a machine, Mel, but would it kill you to schedule some down time? I only ask for Jane, because she's so tired. Why she's a mere shadow of herself."

"Oh very witty, Mr Wilde," Jane replied. Mary recognized the remark as a reference to the *Monty Python* episode Jane had insisted they watch the previous night, another example of British humour lost on her.

"Who? Oh, Oscar Wilde. Is she still watching all those *Monty Python* episodes? That's why she's getting so cranky; she's staying up late watching TV."

The wine did its bit to relax Mary and Melody and Jane did her best to brighten their spirits, despite her distraction. She knew the schedule was gruelling for her friends and felt concern for them, but her real pre-occupation was the question the silly talk show host had asked her.

"Is there anyone special in your life," he'd asked, and she desperately wanted to say, "Yes, there is."

She thought of Albert and found that she missed him desperately. They had spoken, albeit briefly, just a few days ago, but the chat made her keenly aware of the distance between them, which made no sense at all. Before her fame, when they chatted online, they were on separate continents, but it felt like they might be sitting together on a bench on a summer day. But now when they chatted, she could feel the distance between them, either here in London or whatever city they were visiting in America.

I cannot continue to lie to him. That is the reason I no longer feel close to him.

But could she actually tell the world that "Yes, I, Jane Austen, the most famous spinster in literature, have found someone special."

"We should do something tomorrow," Melody suddenly said. "I can delay going back another day."

Mary looked at Melody with a little alarm. She tried to imagine how much money would be involved in abandoning her reservation and booking the flight for another day.

"Wouldn't that be terribly expensive?" Jane asked.

"I can invent an excuse for you to skip a book signing. Mary can develop some tummy trouble, and we can go sightseeing or something," she said, ignoring the question asked.

"I think you're getting drunk," Mary said.

"No, I definitely am drunk, but you two want a break. Why don't we go for a river cruise, up—or is it down—the Thames? I've always wanted to do that. Oh, we can go to Hampton Court. Wouldn't that be great to approach it by river?"

Mary had to confess her ignorance of Hampton Court and when it was explained to her, she privately thought the idea of traipsing through a big museum unappealing, but she was so amused by Melody's enthusiasm that she agreed to it.

Jane also agreed to the excursion and made a reference to *Three Men in a Boat*,[3] which had to be explained to her friends and led to a discussion of whether they could rent a skiff and a caution to bring a tin opener for the pineapples.

---

3 A comedic travelogue penned by Jerome K. Jerome, published in 1889. The full title is *Three Men in a Boat (To Say Nothing of the Dog)*.

· Chawton ·
Civility must be our guide

Mary nervously peeked through an opening in the marquee to see hundreds of seated Janeites waiting to see her—or rather Jane.

"Let me see, Mary," Jane commanded. Mary pulled her head back and allowed her employer to view the crowd, although it then occurred to her why Jane hadn't observed the crowd surreptitiously on her own, which question she posed.

"I hadn't thought about that. I suppose I am nervous."

"Oh great if you're nervous, where does that leave me?" Mary asked.

"Oh you'll do fine. I have the utmost faith in you. I think by this point you 'do' me in your sleep."

"I do hope you're not planning on going anywhere. That crowd looks …" She stuck her head back through the flap. "They look kind of grumpy to me."

"They're English; they always look kind of grumpy," Jane said as a joke, knowing it not to be true. Several hundred Janeites meeting on a pleasant summer day should be in festive mood. She also peeked through the opening again and had to admit they did look unsettled. She began to doubt her choice of excerpt, but it was too late to pick another.

Mary closed the opening and stepped back just as Melody joined them.

"Are you two excited? This is a great turnout! Well, of course it would be with you here and it's not like they ever not have a capacity crowd, but still, it's great!" Melody said.

Although Mary's terminal stripped Melody's tone of its false bravado, it was still clear to Jane her agent was doing her best to buck their spirits.

"It is very exciting indeed, Melody. And it is thanks to your efforts that I am here. I have never been so conscious of the thanks I owe you," Jane said.

That praise took Melody aback slightly, which effect Jane had intended, for she hoped to dampen her friend's enthusiasm so that it might not increase Mary's concern.

"Oh, well thank you Jane," she said, turning her head away, and saying, "But I owe you more for all the pleasure I've had from reading you."

Because she had turned her head away and the fact that emotion choked her voice, the terminal was unable to translate her words, but Jane did not need the translation. The look on Melody's face when she turned back made it obvious what she'd said.

Melody rubbed at her eyes and quickly became businesslike.

"Let's get away from the tent a little bit. I don't want anyone spotting you just yet."

Melody led them to a nearby tree, the shade of which offered Mary some relief from the sun. She still wore a raincoat to conceal her identity; something she thought would stand out on such a nice July day. But several people either actually wore light raincoats or had them about their person or carried umbrellas in anticipation of a downpour, and so her imposture was effective. The raincoat concealed her summer dress, which, while not a true Regency muslin, certainly was evocative of the period with its Empire waist. It would not stand out at most summer parties, although hopefully it would help identify her as Jane's avatar.

Their difficulty lay in the fact that unlike the North American Jane Austen society, few of the attendees wore Regency costume and so Mary must attempt to blend in.

Shortly another lady, a Mrs Enderby, joined them.

"Ms Kramer please, you must keep Miss Austen from the tent. Several people have seen her looking into the marquee. She will ruin the effect. And there's a delay while we try to find a way to increase the seating."

"Tell her I'm standing right here," Jane said, annoyed at the woman's reluctance to address her—or Mary—directly.

"A thousand apologies, Mrs Enderby. I confess I'm nervous and wanted to assess the mood of the crowd. I have never addressed such an august gathering before."

Mrs Enderby turned to look at Mary, although she couldn't quite meet her eyes. The organizer's peremptory attitude melted and Mary recognized her awe of meeting Jane.

"Oh, of course, I hadn't thought ... yes, it must be ... but you will do well ..." The elderly woman had almost addressed Jane Austen as "my dear," reacting to the avatar's age, until she remembered to whom she was talking. It was all rather confusing.

"You will do well, Miss Austen," Mrs Enderby concluded.

"Thank you. I am sure of it, for you and the other members have already shown me such kindness that I feel quite at home." She said the last with such a knowing smile that Mrs Enderby suddenly knew she was addressing the woman she had long admired. Jane Austen was home, at home among the grounds she had known two hundred years previous, and that knowing smile reminded Mrs Enderby that it was *they* who had come to her home.

Melody thanked Mrs Enderby, who returned to her task of finding more chairs.

"That was very well done, Mary," Jane told her avatar. "I only hope the others can be swayed by your charms."

"Great job, Mary," Melody also said independently.

After a further five minutes, Mrs Enderby returned and asked that they return to the tent flap and wait for their cue as the afternoon's presentation would shortly begin, and then she left them to enter the marquee.

From the tent, they could hear the volume of the crowd increase and then settle down.

"Thank you everyone for your patience while we skirted the health and safety laws and brought in more chairs. There does seem to be an unusually heavy turnout ..." the emcee said. He waited for the polite laughter to run its course.

"Although some of our overflow crowd may be attributable to the more than usual press coverage today ... they also seem to know that we have a special guest.

"But before we begin, we have a few announcements. As you know,

Professor Janet Todd was originally scheduled to give her talk, *The Real Mr Darcy*, and has graciously agreed to reschedule that talk for 3 pm tomorrow in this same marquee. We are sorry for the change, but if you've remembered to give us your email addresses, you should have known of this weeks ago.

"Oh, and there is a red Fiat parked on the lawn beside the house. Please move it to the meadow immediately."

Melody and Mary heard some laughter as apparently a member rushed to move his car. Mary took the laughter as a cue to remove her coat and handed it to Melody.

"Finally, I know that some of you may have misgivings about our 'surprise' guest and that you may be uncertain how to address her as you may have never met an 'avatar' before. All I can say is that civility must be our guide, something I am sure we have learned from the writings of Miss Jane Austen, whom I now have the pleasure of introducing. Miss Austen?"

Mary took a quick deep breath, let it out and then opened the flap and stepped through into a marquee filled with several hundred almost silent people. She remembered the advice she had once gotten from a teacher: "Eventually someone will clap."

She paused after entering, thinking eventually was a very long time until she heard that first tentative clap, then joined by another and another until most of the audience, remembering that civility would be their guide, were applauding.

She offered a little bow to the audience before proceeding to the emcee and took his proffered hand, to which he responded with a little bow as well, and relinquished the lectern to her, still amid the audience's applause. She stood there a few seconds, waiting for the applause to die down, and then spoke:

"Thank you Mr Carlisle and members of the Jane Austen Society. It is a privilege, an honour and any number of other good and wonderful things to be here today, addressing you on the day of your annual general meeting.

"I should say this is not my first AGM; my most recent was in 2007, although it's understandable you might have overlooked me." Mary waited a beat and was rewarded by tepid and confused laughter. "Happily I can now stand before you and thank you for your continued interest in my writing.

"I know many of you are still in shock that the AfterNet has recognized my identity. You have been free to speculate about me for a long time, but now you may be uncomfortable about those speculations … and that I am also free to speculate about you!

"If that is your concern, please know that my long perspective has left me philosophic about criticism, although I can understand that my unkind remarks in the letters Cassandra did not burn might leave you wary of my unvarnished opinion. But again, fear not. I have learned a measure of discipline, especially when I know one's tweets and postings may potentially be archived for eternity.

"Now let us move to the proximate reason for my visit today: *Sanditon*. I am, after all, an author on a book tour. I thought I might share with you the circumstances of when and how *Sanditon* was completed, some details of which may be news to you.

Mary thought she was finally winning over the audience. Jane too thought the attendees had relaxed in their seats. She began to search the faces, wondering if she might recognize anyone from her previous visits or from online conversation, when she noticed Courtney Blake in the audience, four rows back.

"As I'm sure you … oh, that phrase will become so tiresome. I will assume you know more about me than I do. You can imagine how upsetting it was to die. Whatever was the cause of it, I suffered increasingly and by my final days in Winchester I had lost my grasp of the world around me. And then suddenly I found myself free of pain but confused by that range of vision afforded the disembodied and the sight of my dear sister holding me in her arms."

Jane had now lost track of Mary's words, her attention on Courtney, who she thought affected a look of boredom. She was tempted to leave Mary's side but remembered her duty. She was supposedly ready to "feed" Mary lines if required, although that would require knowing where they were in the speech. She forced herself to pay attention.

Mary, meanwhile, thought the reference to Jane's death had definitely won the audience's sympathies.

"My first thought was that I had entered a madness brought on by illness, but sober reflection told me that I had passed from life to death. You will realize that I had not the knowledge of the afterlife we now enjoy. In fact my uppermost thought in the days following my death was that I had been found wanting … that I was not worthy of the kingdom of Heaven and that I was doomed to exist neither of this world nor the next.

"You can imagine how slowly the days progressed and how over time I began to lose my reason. But having lost my reason once before as I lay dying, I resolved that I should not succumb again and in my desperation I turned to the one solace that had comforted me all my life, my writing.

"Some people have wondered at my dedication to the craft. I wrote only six novels and had many fallow years and because I did not seek notoriety, some thought I did not seek fame. But Janeites—and my apologies to those who disown that term—certainly know of my keen interest in sales ... and reviews. To hear people talk of my stories was the greatest delight, and the greatest agony if they should be so dull as to not like them.

"I also have a reputation as a private writer, with the charming tale of hiding my work in progress at the sound of a squeaking door, not wanting to answer the question, 'Oh, what are you writing? May I see? How is it going? Where do you get your ideas?'"

Mary paused and Jane wondered if she might have lost her way. She was about to prompt her when Mary cleared her throat, took a sip of water and continued.

"Excuse me. Now my friends and relations would have laughed at this reputation for privacy, for they were my early critics. Some even learned to change the conversation for fear I might ask them to read my latest work.

"After death, however, privacy was not a choice. I must become my harshest critic and my most ardent admirer. Fortunately I had always written for my own enjoyment.

"But your first thought now must be, how could I write without a body or any means of recording my words? This was certainly a challenge but I had a few advantages that you in the modern world do not. First, I was already accustomed to 'writing in my head.' Paper was too precious to write heedlessly and so I usually had a very good notion of what I would write beforehand. Second, the time in which I lived still relied on oral traditions. It was a commonplace skill to recite poetry from memory not to mention whole scenes from theatrical entertainments.

"Thus I wrote in my head ... well, in my mind ... committing to memory what I thought good. And as you can imagine, removing from my memory proved more difficult. As to what I was writing ...

well it was natural to return to the book I was writing before my death, which you know as *Sanditon*.

"I had essentially finished the broad outline of the story before my death and with the concentration I could now bring to the task, I was able to complete my writing in a few months time, but I found that my memory of what I'd written was faulty. With each attempt at recitation the story would subtly shift. After the course of a decade, however, I had fully committed the book to memory.

Jane saw that most in the audience responded to the story Mary related. Even Courtney Blake seemed interested.

"I had returned to Chawton with my sister and mother and little moved from that happy home. I gained some measure of enjoyment observing the Austen and Knight families, but after my dear mother and then sister died, my connections to Chawton withered and I eventually left to travel the world.

"During this time, I would occasionally recite *Sanditon*, to ensure that it remainded intact, but my newfound knowledge of the world suggested changes. So again *Sanditon* changed in many subtle ways.

"After the discovery of the afterlife and the arrival of the AfterNet, I was finally able to commit my words to a permanent form. You can imagine my surprise, once I had the benefit of spell check, at the amazing discovery that friend is spelled 'F-R-I-E-N-D.'"[1]

There was hearty laughter at Jane's well-known idiosyncratic misspellings.

"So again, *Sanditon* changed. Then came my decision to finally see it published and you will realize this was long before the AfterNet certified my identity. So in my search for an agent, I was told again and again that what I'd written didn't seem to be the authentic voice of Jane Austen, that is until my work reached the desk ... or rather the battered MacBook of Melody Kramer, who understood that I was not the Jane Austen of Regency England. I was a Jane Austen who walked Flanders Field and stood on the brink of the Grand Canyon and who cheered when England first brought home the Ashes.

"That she chose to represent me then was, outside my family, the greatest gift I have ever received and the greatest debt I will ever owe

---

1 Austen titled one epistolary novel (part of her Juvenilia) *Love and Freindship*. There have been arguments as to how much credit should be given to Austen's editors.

to any person. Unfortunately, finding a publisher also proved difficult, which is when my agent proposed we find some way of proving my identity. And because of her efforts and the cooperation of both the Chawton House Library and the Jane Austen's House Museum, you find me here before you, rather uncomfortably wearing the mantle of my own legacy. It is a garment that no longer quite fits, but I still wear it proudly."

· Excerpt II ·
Physical comedy

"I know what you are about, Miss Heywood."

Charlotte looked up in surprise at this and found herself being observed by Mr Sidney Parker.

"I am sure that I do not know what you mean, Mr Parker," she said, and returned her eyes to the book upon her lap. She meant to dissuade him from any further observations by increasing the intensity of her study of the words that had ceased to interest her half an hour earlier, but he failed to note her scrutiny.

"I know very well of your machinations. And I heartily approve for I think Sir Edward totally unsuited for Miss Brereton."

At this she was very surprised. "I do not think I like being accused of machinations."

"Very well, spoils and stratagems then. You see I have observed you as closely as you observe those around you. At first I thought you non judgmental, but then I see you make your opinions of the little community my brother and the august Lady Denham have created." He chose then to sit—unasked—beside her on the low, stone wall looking out to shore.

"And how do you know that I make these opinions?" she asked, interested in his observation of her despite her desire that he be elsewhere.

"Oh but your face charmingly betrays you. When you witness some behaviour of which you disapprove, you look away and it is like a cloud briefly passing before the sun, and when you look back the cloud has passed and it is sunny again. Your disapproval is like that; hard to detect unless you look for it."

"And what of my approval? How is that displayed? Can it be so picturesquely described?"

"Of course. It is like the sun glinting off a piece of glass. But it too is gone in an instant."

Charlotte, still pretending to look at her book, laughed and then with a sigh closed her book. She then looked at Mr Parker and said, "How poetic you are. And from such fleeting expressions you deduce that I have conspired to … what exactly have I done Mr Parker?"

"That note, Miss Heywood. The fortuitousness of its discovery could not have been better timed. Miss Brereton is now free. And for Sir Edward too the match would have been unwise. He has no money; she has no money. Unless Lady Denham should grant either of them her estate in which case neither would need the other."

"You are as your brother described. You feel free to say anything."

"And you have managed to avoid denying that you saved that note and produced it when it might do the most … no, I cannot say damage for I think it was a sound decision."

"Mr Parker, I do not appreciate being accused of looking in dustbins for discarded notes."

"Oh ho, so that is how it was done! Very well, don't deny it. I like a bit of mystery. Now, what do you propose to do about Arthur?" At this he stood and walked in front of her so that he eclipsed her view of the shore.

"Excuse me?" she asked.

"Please, do not pretend that my brother does not give you pause. Were it not for my natural indolence I should have addressed his many shortcomings long ago. But with your energy of action I am sure we can have him sorted out."

"Again, Mr Parker, you labour under the misapprehension that my intent is to interfere in the lives of others." As she said this she looked up at him and the wind caught her bonnet, which not being properly secured, blew away, causing her to cry out.

That cry was enough to goad him into pursuit of the bonnet that danced and skipped along the stone wall to lead him a merry chase. She looked in wonderment at him; his tall angular figure denying him

Jane, Actually

the proper dignity of a man in pursuit of a lady's garment. At the last he stumbled forward and with outstretched hands caught the bonnet before it could hop the wall and continue down the road. Unfortunately he secured the bonnet only at the cost of his upright attitude. Miss Heywood knew it would be better to look away from his discomfiture, but she could not help but be intrigued at this little drama. She did, however, return her gaze to the shore once Mr Parker began his long walk back to her. Presently she was aware of him standing beside her.

"Your bonnet, I believe," he said, quite gravely. She turned her head to him, prepared to laugh again, until she saw that his fall had proven more serious than comic. She gasped to see his trouser leg torn and ...

"Your knee! It is bleeding!"

"Is it? Hadn't noticed," he said with that peculiar male attitude of denying that which was blatantly obvious. He again offered her the bonnet, which she took, whereupon he sat next to her on the stone wall again. He winced as he took his seat.

"Mr Parker, I think you're quite injured!"

"No, no, just a scratch. One can't get injured chasing a bonnet. It just won't do."

She looked at him as if he had lost his senses but in fact he was simply loathe to display his pain and admit his embarrassment of how poorly he had acquitted himself. Later Charlotte would realize this was the moment when her estimation of him changed, when he revealed himself as more than just a man with an ironic sense of the world and instead simply as a man willing to endanger himself for something as silly as an errant bonnet. This self-realization, however, was for the future. In the present, she only viewed him as a man who foolishly seemed to be denying that he was in great pain and bleeding—and that this injury had occurred while in her service.

She took the bonnet he had handed her and quickly bound his knee with it, a duty for which it proved to be well suited.

"I've gone to a lot of trouble to retrieve that for you and now you've gone and ruined it," he said.

"You are a very silly man, Mr Parker, but I thank you. And now we must get you back to your brother's house for I fear my bonnet is inadequate to the task of staunching your wound. Can you stand?"

"Of course I can stand," he said, although at this point inspiration struck when it occurred to him that Miss Heywood really was quite pretty.

‹ 228 ›

"Actually, it does hurt a little. If I might have your hand to assist me?"

She ruefully offered her hand, annoyed that she now was destined to spend so much time with the one man she most wished to avoid. She helped him to his feet and together they walked back to Trafalgar House, he perhaps limping more than was warranted—or perhaps it was sufficient for his purposes.

· Denver ·
The Tattered Cover

Mary clicked the send button with regret. She told her friend not to suggest her for the play because she was certain she'd still be working with Jane in October—after all, that was the date for the JASNA AGM in Fort Worth.

But sending the email forced her to think of the future, which hadn't been discussed. She had no idea what might happen after October. She had signed a one-year exclusive contract with the avatar agency and had notified her school she would be leaving after Jane had picked her to be her avatar. She actually couldn't work as an actress during that time in exchange for a steady pay packet. She couldn't go back to school until the new year.

But will Jane need me after the AGM? The thought filled her with sadness; she truly enjoyed playing Jane Austen.

She never thought she would become an actor trapped in a role, not at the age of 23. Of course, playing Jane was a role like no other. The script was being written in real time, she had no time to learn her lines and she had to deliver them without thinking. It was all rather daunting, especially with the playwright and director standing next to her the whole time.

And yet she thought they pulled it off beautifully. She could now finish Jane's words for her almost as fast as Jane could think them and over time, she was losing herself so much in the role that she didn't know where Jane stopped and she began.

I've got to ask Jane how long a gig this is, she thought. *Because if it does end after October ... I've got to make plans to continue my life after this.*

The loud wail of the baby in the next booth broke her thoughts. She checked her phone for the time and realized she should get back to the hotel. She quickly finished her sandwich and tried to ignore a slight twinge in her mouth. She dumped the paper wrapper into the waste bin by the door and walked back to the hotel.

The traffic was loud on the downtown Denver street and the sun was particularly hot as she made her way to her Lower Downtown hotel. It had been suggested to her by the bookstore as being convenient, historic and charming. By now on the book tour, however, all Mary required was clean and quiet with good Internet access. But a mention of the Tattered Cover when booking the room gave her a slight discount and the Oxford Hotel was certainly convenient.

She went to her room, opened the door and called out to her roommate.

"There you are. I thought you'd forgotten," Jane's digitized voice said from their laptop.

"Sheesh, I'm a minute late," Mary said, which was not literally true. By the clock on their shared laptop, Mary was nine minutes late and Jane had been watching the clock with her usual preoccupation.

By now, Jane had lost much of her anxiety when finding herself alone behind a closed door. She knew Mary would eventually return or that a maid would enter, but still she chafed, especially when expecting Mary to return at a specific time. The misery of the two months she had spent trapped in a room still haunted her.

But Mary had seemed to want to eat her lunch alone and Jane had taken the time to compose a long email to Albert. Every second past Mary's expected return, however, added to Jane's discomfort.

Mary knew the source of Jane's upset and reassured her employer. "I'm sorry I made you worry, Jane." She decided not to throw back at her the times she'd worried about Jane's late-night forays.

Mary was speaking from the bathroom where she was brushing her teeth. It wouldn't do for Jane Austen to smell of an Italian special with onions and extra peppers. Then she stripped off her jeans and T-shirt and took her costume from the closet.

"I wasn't worried," Jane replied, "just anxious that we shouldn't be late for our appearance."

"Uh huh," Mary said, certain that Jane had envisioned her crushed under a bus. It was the writer in her employer, she knew, that made her think of tragic ends for her avatar. She knew Jane wasn't obsessively planning her demise; it was more an idle exercise in plotting, but it still sometimes unnerved her.

"I don't plan on needing my own avatar anytime soon, you know."

"Of course not Mary. I don't know what you're thinking."

"So you're pretty excited about this book signing. What's so special about Denver? Have you ever been here before?"

"Not recently, but I have been in contact with many JASNA members in Colorado and hope to meet them here. And the Tattered Cover is one of the biggest book stores in the region and Melody has said I should … we should be extra nice."

"When are we not?" Mary asked, rather pleased at her phrasing, which was lost on Jane, of course. She thought she sounded like Maggie Smith playing Lady Catherine de Bourgh, and then wondered if Maggie Smith had ever played Lady Catherine, or was she thinking of Judi Dench?

"You seem to be taking extra care in your appearance," Jane said.

Mary only distantly heard Jane's comment while she was attending to her makeup.

"I only notice that you are applying makeup. I thought you did not apply makeup when representing me."

"What? Don't be ridiculous. I always put on some foundation to try to match your flawless complexion."

"Yes, but I am referring to your lipstick."

Mary looked in the mirror and realized she had in fact applied lipstick.

"Oh, sorry, I guess I was preoccupied," she said, and quickly removed it.

"Are you expecting someone, Mary?"

Mary debated lying but considering how close they were and that she never knew when Jane was about, it would be impossible to keep a relationship secret from her. And so she decided to come clean.

"Maybe. Well, yes. There's a guy I met in Chicago. We signed a book for him." She added the last comment as if to make Jane somehow complicit.

"We have signed any number of books, Mary. How am I to be expected to remember one person in particular?"

"He's Dr Alice Davis's graduate student."

Jane thought back and did remember the man in question.

"Oh, he was a rather nice young man. And how did you come to be acquainted? I don't remember meeting him subsequently."

Mary was now brushing her hair back and pinning it up before putting on her cap.

"We ran into one another in a coffee shop later that day."

"How serendipitous," Jane said, wishing she might have eyes to roll. *Not the running into a young lady at the park ploy*, she thought. Still it pleased her to know that things never changed and young men still dreamed up methods for "running into" young girls.

Mary emerged from the bathroom, properly attired, and unplugged the portable terminal from the computer, and placed it in her reticule.[1] She also inserted the earbuds and turned them on. She gave a quick glance about the room, wondering if there was anything she required. She decided against taking the spencer.

She walked to the front door and took a quick glance in the mirror, adjusting her "AV" pin right side up and left the room, giving Jane plenty of time to exit.

"We spent the day together," Mary continued, once they were in the hallway.

"Oh yes, I remember you did seem very happy the next day. What is his name?"

"Stephen Abrams, and he's in town ... actually he's in Colorado Springs attending a writer's conference, but he said he would stop by the book signing and ... well if you won't need me the rest of the day ..."

Jane was tempted to make a joke and pretend to be hurt at being abandoned, but she could tell if she did make such a joke Mary might take it seriously. The truth was that Jane had grown a little too reliant on Mary to keep her company and she should go out with her young man.

"Of course you may spend the rest of the day together, but only after we've been properly introduced."

They'd left the hotel and as usual Mary's costume elicited some

---

1   A small purse closed with a drawstring

notices and even a car horn, which caused her to jump. She almost responded as a New Yorker, but thought the sight of Jane Austen flipping someone the bird might cause her employer some embarrassment.

"Well, he definitely would like that. Maybe we could sit with him for a cup of tea and you could chat."

They walked down Wazee Street and turned right at the 16th Street Mall and could see the bookstore ahead of them.

Once inside, Jane felt the comforting presence of a very strong AfterNet field.

"OMG!" Jane said. "Mary, you will not believe the AfterNet field in this store. I have never experienced its like."

Mary grinned at Jane's enthusiasm and then pointed to a prominent sign in the store that explained the entire store was an AfterNet hotspot and also the process for joining the local store chat rooms.

"Mary could you … would you excuse me for a moment?"

"I will carry on without you," Mary said silently, for a store employee was approaching her with an already outstretched hand.

"Miss … Austen," the woman said, after quickly glancing at the AV pin. "I'm Laurie Smith. We're so honoured to have you here."

Mary returned the appropriate pleasantry, remarked on the charm of the store, the fineness of the day and the large banner welcoming her. She enjoyed employing the full Austen charm offensive and yet again marvelled at the effect an English accent, a Regency costume and the aura of Jane could have. More than once Jane had told her to turn it down. "I was not that charming!"

"Yes, perhaps we should go to the room where you will give your talk," Ms Smith finally said, and then led the way through the store.

"Is Miss Austen actually with you?" Ms Smith suddenly asked in a whisper. Mary was surprised at this, for she had seemed to understand the etiquette of addressing an avatar.

However, Mary replied, "No, I don't think so. I think she was surprised by your store's field."

The woman sighed. "I thought so. The disembodied always get a little lost their first time in the store." She was leading Mary down a corridor that seemed to take her to an adjacent building. "I'll broadcast a message to the chat rooms and see if I can find her." They approached the meeting room. "Can I get you anything? Water, tea?"

"Water would be appreciated. I am not used to this dry climate."

"Oh believe me, compared to winter it's positively damp. And here's where you will give your talk and sign. We think it will be a very large turnout but we can limit the signing."

"That shouldn't be necessary. I ..." But Mary's reply was interrupted by her phone ringing and she knew from the ring that it was Melody.

"Excuse me, that's my ... our ... Jane's agent."

Ms Smith left Mary, who answered her phone.

"Hi Melody."

"Mary? Is Jane there?"

"No, Jane's exploring the store. I guess it has an awesome AfterNet field."

"Good ... I wanted to talk alone. Everything's a go for tomorrow. I heard back from the Denver chapter and they have reservations for ten so Jane ..."

"I'm back," Mary heard Jane's voice say in her earbuds.

"Hold on Melody, Jane's back. Let me tie you in."

Mary took her terminal from her reticule and synced it with her phone.

"OK, we're both here," Mary said.

"Yes, Mama, we are fine. We called you from the airport." Jane said. She assumed Melody was worried that she hadn't heard from them.

"I was just a little worried that you hadn't called from the hotel," Melody said.

"Would you have been awake had we called?" Jane asked. She knew that Melody had only just returned to New York. Her agent, after leaving England, had added a quick Los Angeles trip.

"Tamara would have picked up."

"Hah!" Jane said. "You prove my point. You both needed a full night's rest. And now Mary will look properly rested for her young man."

Mary's eyes widened. She had hoped to keep her date with Stephen from Melody.

"What young man? Do you have a date Mary?"

"She does," Jane said. "One of Dr Davis's graduate students. They met in Chicago."

Mary winced at Jane betraying all the information about Stephen. Melody no longer held Dr Davis in much regard. Davis had written a review of *Sanditon* that praised the writing and the story but some of the remarks seemed to question Jane's authenticity. Jane had not been bothered by the review, as she was happy with Davis's commendations on the modernity of the style, but those same commendations Melody viewed as an accusation.

Mary was also worried that Melody would object to her seeing Stephen because of the morals clause she had signed.

"When is this date, Jane?" Melody asked.

But Mary quickly spoke. "After the reading. We don't have anything scheduled the rest of the day."

Mary waited for Melody, who eventually said, "Well if it's OK with Jane."

She breathed a sigh of relief, with just a little irritation that she must now seek approval if she wanted to go on a date. And yet that was the agreement she had signed. During her conversation, customers began to arrive and Mary smiled pleasantly at them. She avoided the temptation to turn away. In the early days of her representation of Jane, Melody had wanted to avoid photographs of Mary, as Jane, speaking on her cell phone. But after the first photo of Jane Austen on her cell phone had become an Internet meme, Melody had not only stopped her injunction, she practically encouraged it.

"It is all the same to me," Jane said, "but I want pictures of your young man."

"A little discretion also might be a good thing," Melody advised.

Mary must now endure some good-natured teasing from Melody and Jane but the return of Ms Smith ended the call. Ms Smith returned to her interrupted discussion of the agenda and then asked again if Mary needed anything.

"That water would be lovely."

Their hostess suddenly remembered her earlier promise. "I'm so sorry I forgot. I'll get you a bottle ... no, we can't have Jane Austen drinking from a bottle."

She dispatched someone on the task of finding a glass of ice water and then returned to say it was time to get started. Mary took a seat in the front row while Ms Smith went to the lectern. The audience had been steadily arriving and now all the seats were filled with several people standing in the back.

"Thank you everyone for coming," Ms Smith said. "It's a little early to start, but we've already filled the room and the fire department would frown if we tried to squeeze in anyone else. And if we start early, that allows more time for questions and answers.

"As you all know, our guest today is Jane Austen who has just published her completed *Sanditon*, the book she was writing before her death in 1817."

A store employee arriving with a glass of ice water distracted Mary's attention. He first tried to deliver the glass to the lectern but Ms Smith discreetly instructed him to give the class to Mary.

"So please join me in welcoming Jane Austen," Ms Smith concluded, while the man was still putting the glass in Mary's hands.

Mary had been so distracted by the delivery of the water that she missed her cue until she heard applause. She quickly took a sip of the water and felt a repeat of the sharp twinge in her mouth and wondered what it could be about, but she did her best to cover her discomfort as she shook Ms Smith's hand.

"Thank you. It is such a pleasure to visit Colorado again. I was last here in 1947 and I have such wonderful memories of my first view of the Rocky Mountains. I am embarrassed that I have waited so long to return, but I return finding the state of Colorado and the city of Denver more lovely than ever."

At that moment Mary realized that Stephen was standing in the back row of the room and made eye contact with him. Jane observed this and asked, "Is that him?"

"Yes, now hush," Mary said silently in reply and to disguise their conversation she took another sip of water, carefully this time, not allowing it to reach the side of her mouth that twinged.

"I had forgotten, however, how dry the air is," Mary said, as she put down the glass.

"I do remember him. He is quite handsome, and look, he waves at you."

While Mary talked, Jane continued in this chatty fashion until Mary was forced to mute her earbuds.

~

"Have you any idea how difficult it is to talk while you're giggling in my ear?" Mary asked after the last question had been answered. "What are you, twelve?"

She had just finished shaking the hand of an enraptured woman in her sixties who for five minutes had been relating her entire association with Jane Austen since reading *Pride and Prejudice* in high school. She was finally alone and wanted to use the time to chide Jane.

"Do not be cross, Mary. I am merely enjoying the prospect of a budding romance."

"We talked about going for a drive in the mountains. I don't think that counts as a budding romance."

"I agree. A romantic dinner would be a better choice."

"And hardly discreet. Melody would have a fit if there's a picture of Jane Austen out on a romantic date. My only worry is it leaves you on your own in the hotel room for a long time."

"Pish. I am easily kept amused with a good Internet connection. You rarely have time to be yourself; I insist you do this. After all, even Melody had no serious objection."

That had not escaped Mary's notice. "Yeah, that was strange. Does it seem to you she's been distracted lately?"

"I think she allows no time for herself, which is precisely the danger you are in if you do not … ah, finally he approaches."

Stephen had hung back during the farewells, but as the last of the people left the room he came forward.

"Hi, Stephen," Mary said. "I'm glad you made it in time for the reading."

He hesitated, unsure how to address Mary. "Miss Austen, a pleasure to meet you again," he finally said.

"We're alone, well except for Jane. You can call me Mary." The moment she said this, however, they could hear the sounds of people approaching the room and Ms Smith and another woman entered.

"Oh, here you are, Miss Austen," Ms Smith said, "I want you to meet … oh, hello." She pulled up short at seeing Stephen and must have read Mary and Stephen's body language and realized she had interrupted an intimacy.

"Ms Smith …"

"Laurie, please," she said.

"Laurie, may I introduce Stephen Abrams. He is a graduate student who is studying … me. Stephen, this is Ms Smith, who works here, at the Tattered Cover."

"Nice to meet you," he said, putting out his hand.

"And you. Were you here for the reading?"

"I was one of the last to squeeze in. I just drove up from Colorado Springs," he added.

"Oh, are you at UCCS?"[2]

"Uh, no, University of Chicago. I'm attending a … conference … and I wanted to … interview Miss Austen … about the paper I'm writing."

"He's charming, but not very elegant," Jane said in Mary's ear.

"And who is your friend?" Mary asked Ms Smith, to rescue Stephen.

"Oh, pardon me. This is my friend Jeanette. She's a fan but she couldn't make it in time. She works at our Colfax store."

The next thirty minutes were spent with pleasantries and Mary must sign Jeanette's copy of *Sanditon* and inquiries as to what were their plans for the rest of the day. Stephen tried to avoid looking at his watch and Mary tried to avoid noticing his glances, even though she also chafed at sacrificing their time together.

Finally they were able to part with Ms Smith, her friend, and two other store employees who arrived to meet Miss Austen.

"OK, if we hurry, we can get to the mountains while it's still daylight," Mary said once she was alone with Stephen. It was an exaggeration, of course, for in July they had many hours of daylight left.

"Pardon me, but do I not have an opportunity to speak to your young man?" Jane asked.

"What?"

"I would like to speak with him directly … before you abandon me in our hotel room."

"Argh! OK, Stephen, Jane wants to talk to you before we …" She stopped because the smile on his face made it obvious he had no objection to speaking with Jane. "Oh right, the girl of your dreams. How about we go back to the hotel, I can get changed, and then we can meet you in the coffee shop and you and Jane can chat?"

This plan was agreed to and Mary hurried back to the hotel while Stephen remained behind at the bookstore a few minutes—to avoid to be seen leaving together. Mary quickly changed clothes, all the while ignoring Jane's speculations, and hurried down to the coffee shop where Stephen was waiting.

Stephen had already ordered Mary a coffee, apparently remembering her order from their meeting in Chicago, which pleased her, although she would have preferred plain water. She thanked him and then put the terminal on the table so that Stephen and Jane could talk directly.

2　The University of Colorado at Colorado Springs

"So you are the young man who had Mary so excited after Chicago," were Jane's first words, to Mary's embarrassment.

"Thank you Dolly Levi,"[3] Mary said. "Ignore her, Stephen."

"Uh, OK. I mean, it really is nice to see you … to talk to you again, Miss Austen."

"To be precise, this is our first direct communication—without Mary as interlocutor. And I do apologize for teasing you both. Making young people blush is one of the few pleasures I have left."

"Oh this is typical Jane," Mary said. "She says something outrageous and then she puts on the charm."

"I guess that's what I've always hoped you'd be like," Stephen said.

Stephen's obvious worship made Mary roll her eyes, which Jane chose to ignore.

"Now, I believe your thesis had something to do with the Enclosure Movement?"

And so Stephen began to ply Jane with questions relevant to his thesis. To Mary, most of the questions were incomprehensible, despite her study of Jane's life and times. She heard Stephen and Jane refer to the Reform Act, open field farming, famine, climate change, riots and Karl Marx. She kept looking at her phone to check the time, which was approaching four.

"So did Knightley enclose the commons?"[4]

"Mr Knightley? No, of course not."

"But then what was all that about digging drains and moving rights of way? And the gypsies attacking Harriet? It sounds like the underpinnings of …"

Mary had had enough and said so. "Fascinating as this is …"

Jane got the hint. "Quite right, Mary. You and Stephen had hoped to travel to the mountains. Mary shall give you my personal email address, Stephen, and you may ask any question you like. Your thesis sounds fascinating and again I wonder at how very clever I was to put all these observations into a simple love story."

---

3 The titular character of the musical *Hello, Dolly!* about a matchmaker in turn-of-the-century (the Twentieth Century) New York City

4 George Knightley is the hero of *Emma*. His brother, John, is married to Emma's sister, Isabella. Unlike John Dashwood in *Sense and Sensibility*, Mr Knightley did not enclose the commons (see the footnote in the chapter titled *Ripples*)

Mary rose when she saw Stephen about to voice another question.

"OK, we better get going," she said. "Oh, wait, I have to get you back to the room. I'll be right back." She said this last to Stephen.

As Mary was retrieving her terminal from the table, Jane said, "Well goodbye, Stephen, and I hope we meet again soon. And I shall be disappointed if Mary does not tell me you have rescued her from a grizzly bear."

· Rocky Mountains ·
Awkward

"I don't know, Jane usually navigates," Mary said.

"We can just use the GPS," Stephen suggested.

"No, I should be able to read a map as well as a dead Regency author. OK, here it is, we take the Interstate 70 exit west … it's just a mile or two more … and then Evergreen Parkway."

Mary was providing Stephen directions to a nearby mountain drive that had been suggested to her by the hotel concierge.

"See, we should have plenty of time," Stephen said, and pointed to the dashboard clock that indicated it had just gone past five.

"I don't know, they still look far away," she said.

"It should go pretty quick once we're on the interstate. Look, there's the exit."

He negotiated the wide, curving exit and then they were climbing a steady grade through a cut in the foothills. Soon Stephen was forced to pass lorries labouring up the slope.

"How far to Evergreen Parkway?"

"Maybe ten miles. Jane would know precisely."

"You're talking about her a lot. I thought you were looking forward to a little time apart."

"I was, but now I'm worried about leaving her alone, which is stupid considering she's usually out on her own at night."

"What do you mean?"

"Oh right, you don't know. Well Jane likes to go walkabout at night, at least that's what Melody calls it. She doesn't like being cooped up in the room after I go to sleep, so I have to let her out and then she turns up in the morning. It's like having a cat. Oh, I shouldn't have said that. Melody would have a cow if she heard me telling anyone this."

"Why?"

Mary, however, was busy marvelling at all the traffic climbing up the foothills and the realization that the foothills were impressive on their own.

"Huh? Oh, she doesn't like anything that makes Jane sound weird. She's pretty protective of Jane."

"Well it doesn't sound weird to me. Anyone would be strange after being dead all that time."

"And she's not strange, not at all," Mary said in defence of her friend. "It's not like she's wandering around like a ghost or something."

Of course, Mary often did wonder exactly what Jane did on her nightly excursions, and she wondered whether Jane, before the discovery of the afterlife, was a full-time voyeur. Jane had a knowledge of human—peculiarities—that no self-respecting daughter of a clergyman should possess, and yet she viewed most of those peculiarities without judgment.

"I don't suppose you ... oh wait, is that Evergreen Parkway?" he asked.

Mary looked at the map on Stephen's tablet and said, "Yes, and we stay on it until we turn right onto County Road 66, which is Squaw Pass Road. So what were you about to say?"

"It's nothing, I just wondered if ... if Jane ever did anything that made you think ... no, forget it."

Mary looked at Stephen, who tried to pretend he was intent on looking for the road that would take them to Echo Lake, but he guiltily looked at her when he noticed her scrutiny.

"Don't be all mysterious. If you have something to ask, ask."

"OK, has Jane ever done anything to make you wonder if she really is Jane Austen?"

"No, of course not. Why do you ... do you doubt she's Jane? Didn't you get the answers you wanted from her?"

"Yeah, sure, that was incredibly helpful. I admit it's a little counter to my argument that she intentionally inserted those elements, so I have to attribute her remarks properly."

"What does that mean?" she asked, misunderstanding him.

Stephen started panicking, realizing his trait of not editing his remarks was again getting him in trouble.

"It doesn't mean anything. It's just you started talking about Jane doing strange stuff."

"No I didn't," she said, alarmed at his question and also worried that she'd divulged more about Jane than she should have. "I just said she takes walks at night. You're the one who said it was strange."

"And it's not. I'm sorry I asked. I mean … can you forget I asked? I really don't have any reason to doubt she's Jane. I don't know why I asked."

"Turn here."

"What?"

"This is the road to Echo Lake[1]."

Stephen turned sharply into the right hand lane without a chance to signal. Luckily he'd already slowed for the traffic light and there were no cars behind them.

"It's forgotten," she said.

"Thanks. I really don't know why I asked," he said, feeling guilty because he knew precisely why he'd asked. Dr Davis's suspicions had influenced him and he didn't want to admit that to her. "Maybe I just figured …"

"You know I really can't forget it if you keep talking about it. And now the light's changed."

Stephen looked up and saw that the light had indeed changed. He turned onto the road and hoped he would soon find that grizzly bear.

---

1 Echo Lake is about 40 miles west of Denver and is part of the Denver Mountain Parks system. The lake and nearby Echo Lake Lodge are at 10,600 feet. The Mount Evans Scenic Byway, America's highest paved road, begins at the lodge and ends at the summit at 14,264 feet.

· Toothache ·
All too mortal flesh

Jane peeked into the bedroom again and saw Mary sprawled out on the bed, her feet tangled in the sheets and most alarmingly, not visibly breathing. When she looked at Mary in infrared, however, she could see that Mary's heart was beating and it also seemed to her that Mary's body temperature was elevated.

She went back into the seating area of the hotel room and continued typing her message and sent it and then waited anxiously. Possibly ten minutes elapsed until she noticed the hotel door open, but stopped by the door limiter. A minute later, she was rewarded by movement from the bedroom and finally saw Mary, looking frightful and wearing nothing but an oversized Colorado Rockies[1] T-shirt and exercise shorts, dragging her body to the door.

Mary looked through the peephole and then opened the door, held a brief conversation with a hotel employee and then ruefully looked over to the computer where Jane sat. After a few more words exchanged with the man, Mary closed the door and walked over to the computer. She looked confused for a moment but then woke the computer from sleep.

"Finally," Jane said after the computer awoke. "Mary, I was so worried. It's ten o'clock. We will miss the signing."

---

1 The Colorado Rockies professional baseball team

"Oh God, Jane, I feel awful," Mary said, and then dropped into the couch and nearly onto Jane.

"You are ill?" Jane asked.

"It's my teeth. I couldn't get to sleep until 4 a.m. What time did you say it was?"

"It's just gone ten, but if you are unwell ... you have a toothache?"

"I guess so, but I've never had problems with my teeth, only now my jaw hurts and I have this awful headache." Mary cupped her right hand behind her jaw and the look of pain on her face brought back a memory to Jane.

"It is a wisdom tooth, I fear. I remember Fanny holding her jaw in just that way. You must see a dentist."

Mary was confused and asked. "Fanny Price had ... what do you call it, an impacted wisdom tooth?"

"No, my niece Fanny. We had to take her to Mr Spence, the dentist and he ... well perhaps the science of dentistry has advanced. But you must make an appointment immediately."

Mary, who had a positive fear of dentists, was uncertain what to do.

"When we get back to New York ..."

"Which will be in three weeks time. No, you must make an appointment immediately. I fear you may have an infection. Certainly you look to me as if you have a fever. On this I insist."

"But ... but how do I find a dentist ... I mean here in Denver."

"I believe there are websites that offer advice on finding a doctor or dentist. Or even better, ask the concierge."

Mary numbly nodded and used the phone.

"Concierge. How may I help?"

"Hi, this is Mary Crawford in room 431. I don't know if you can help me, but I've got a toothache and ..."

"Of course, Miss Crawford. I know of a very good dentist nearby. Would you like me to connect you?"

Mary said yes and she was soon talking to a receptionist who said there was a cancellation that morning and she could come at 11:30. This information she relayed to Jane who promptly ordered her to get ready and that she order a taxi.

To Jane's satisfaction, Mary readily agreed to everything. Jane enjoyed taking care of Mary and realized that being of use to others was something she greatly missed.

"You may wish to see to your appearance, dear," Jane suggested. "You look a fright."

"I guess I can take a quick shower."

"Do so while I investigate what modern dentistry can do for your condition."

"OK Mom," Mary said.

Jane used the time to find reviews of the recommended dentist and found he was generally awarded high marks although apparently he did not rate highly for bedside manner. She also learned that removing an impacted wisdom tooth was considered routine although she doubted Mary would endure that procedure today.

~

In which surmise she was proved correct.

"It's a missing filling, that's all," said Dr. Aubrey, who was looking at Mary's X-rays. He was holding the strips of film to the light. Behind him Jane was fascinated at the images of Mary's teeth, mostly unblemished by the white spots that indicated fillings.

Jane was able to hear the conversation because Mary kept her terminal in a pocket, which at Jane's request was left on. Mary was not wearing her earbuds, however.

"Why do you want to hear me talk to the dentist, Jane?" Mary had asked on the taxi ride to the dentist's office.

"Your health is of the greatest concern to me, Mary. First, because you are my friend and second because you represent me to the world," Jane said. In fact, her actual interest was that it was simply a very long time since she had a personal interest in the health of an individual. And she was always sympathetic to the thought of anyone requiring a visit to a dentist.

"I never suffered the supposed English curse of poor dental health, although my poor mother and sister did, and I will not have your teeth appear in anything other than good order."

Jane had had a tooth pulled and her father had gone to the considerable expense of a gold filling for her, but overall she had escaped her sister's torment and that of her nieces.

"I can see why you thought it was a wisdom tooth; however, you've got nothing to worry about," Dr. Aubrey said.

"Why's that?" Mary asked.

"You're lucky, you don't have any. Not everyone develops wisdom teeth. You're just further along the evolutionary ladder. Nope, you just lost a filling. Eat anything sticky or chewy recently?"

Mary thought back and recalled the caramels that she'd scooped up from a hotel front desk.

"That probably did it, but we can fix you right up because my root canal cancelled."

"You're going to do it now?" Mary asked.

"Unless you want to go around with a perpetual toothache. Your nerve is exposed. The pain must be awful."

Mary had to admit it was, but as she had always a fear of needles and especially dental injections, she weighed for a second the pain in her tooth against her fear. Fortunately reason won her over.

"OK, let's get it over with."

"Oh I always love an enthusiastic patient," the dentist said.

"Sorry, I just don't like injections."

"Nobody does, but don't worry, I'll give you a topical anaesthetic spray before I give you the injection. You won't feel a thing."

"Promise?"

He merely grunted an affirmation, however.

Jane observed this exchange and wondered how far to trust the dentist. She was familiar with the lies of doctors, including the promises made by her own doctors and the treatments she now knew were ineffective.

At this point, the dentist was called away by his receptionist and Mary used the opportunity to insert an earbud.

"I hope you're still here Jane," she said, as she lay back in the chair, her eyes closed.

"I am with you Mary. I am glad you don't have an impacted wisdom tooth."

"At least you don't have to put up … oh, that was stupid of me," Mary said. "I'm sorry … I don't know what made me …"

"Do not concern yourself, Mary. I was thinking the same thing. I despised doctors and dentists, or at least in retrospect I did, and I am sorry you are suffering."

"Are you on the phone?" the dentist asked as he returned from taking a phone call himself. "I'm afraid we have a cell phone's off policy in the office."

"No, I was talking to …" Mary realized it was more trouble than it was worth to explain to him that her friend was Jane Austen. She removed the earbud and put it back in her pocket.

He "harumphed," which the terminal did not translate for Jane, but she could understand his judgmental look—the look of a high priest who has found a supplicant noisily sucking a sweet during his service. He then lowered Mary's chair and took a device that looked like a small metal gun, attached to a hose, and quickly applied it to the inside of Mary's mouth. Jane saw Mary jump in the chair.

"Oh you're such a big baby," he said to her. "That didn't hurt."

Mary had to admit it didn't, but the sound of the topical anaesthetic sprayed onto her gums had surprised her. *If he'd simply told me there would be a hissing sound, I wouldn't have been surprised,* she thought.

"It will just take a few seconds for it to numb up," he said, and he glanced vacantly about the room while waiting. The dentist's assistant/receptionist then appeared with a tray, which she handed him. He silently took the tray and put it to one side and then took from it a syringe.

Jane thought it a rather alarming looking device, far more intimidating than the disposable syringes the medical profession had adopted. It was very large and the overhead light glistened off its shiny metal surface.

"Open," he told Mary, who seeing the device approaching her, shut her eyes tightly. "Just relax …"—he glanced over to his assistant who showed him the patient's chart—"… Mary. You won't feel a thing."

Jane observed Mary try to relax, but as she was in a chair with her feet above her head and awaiting the needle, she failed.

Jane watched the needle enter Mary's open mouth and then the doctor's hands blocked her view, but when she saw the little jerk of Mary's body …

And then Jane realized she was on the floor and for the first time since she had died she realized that to all intents and purposes she had fainted. For one brief glorious instant her mind had shut down and now she was back. She slowly rose to her normal level and heard the dentist ask, "Now that didn't hurt, did it?"

"Yes it did," Mary answered back with some vehemence, but she quickly added, "but not a lot."

Jane knew from this exchange that her … well, she had to call it unconsciousness … must have lasted only a second, but the experience unnerved her and she left the examination room and retreated to the hallway.

She had been aware of every second of every minute of every day for almost two centuries and this was the first time a second, perhaps two, had elapsed without her consciousness. It was both glorious and so very frightening. She had heard the stories about the disembodied who had essentially forgot themselves, to have gone beyond the madness caused by their depravation and given up their being. They were anecdotal stories, of course, for like the world before the discovery of the afterlife, such an abandonment of self was a one-way trip.

She wondered if her loss of consciousness was a taste of that abandonment and what was the cause of it. Was she so concerned for Mary that the sight of the needle caused her to panic? Was this a panic attack or what in her day would have been called hysteria?

That thought revived her. *I do not suffer from hysteria,* she thought, even though that was arguably what happened. *I ridicule women who do,* she added, and she conjured the image of those characters she had created who loudly indulged in hysterics.

To soothe herself, she imagined standing and smoothing her dress and feeling the cool muslin beneath her fingers, every wrinkle disappearing with each stroke. Finally she re-entered the examination room, and saw the dentist applying his drill to Mary's tooth and the fine spray of water and tooth enamel that issued from her friend's mouth.

She quickly retreated to the hallway and remained there until Mary emerged a half hour later. Mary looked to her left and right, obviously trying to make contact with Jane, who connected to the AfterNet field.

"I'm here Mary. Are you all right?"

"Yes, Jane," Mary said quietly. "Let's get out of here."

Mary quickly paid and practically ran outside. Once free of the building, she called the taxi company and asked to be taken back to the hotel. Then she sat down at a bench to wait.

The dentist's office was in a small shopping area not too far from downtown in a residential neighbourhood. Most of the buildings were small and old and included restaurants, a flower shop, a bicycle repair shop and a comic book store. The dentist's office was in the largest building, but it still looked like it was built in the 1930s with some Art Deco styling. It was a very pleasant block but all Mary wished was to see the back of it.

"Was it very painful?" Jane asked.

"Not bad, but now I've got whale tongue. Is it OK if we don't talk?"

Jane had no idea what Mary meant by whale tongue, as she'd never experienced the numbness of a local anaesthetic, but she assured Mary they need not talk. They waited about ten minutes for the taxi to arrive and Mary largely remained motionless during that time except to periodically probe her numb cheek with her hand.

Mary quickly got in the taxi, barely allowing Jane enough time to enter, and not sliding over to give Jane room, who had to clamber over Mary's body.

Jane observed the dull look on Mary's face and thought perhaps she was overindulging in self pity.

"It couldn't have been that bad, Mary. You had the advantage of anaesthetics, which I never had."

Mary looked to Jane, said a silent obscenity, slumped against the door and then closed her eyes for the ride back to the hotel.

· The Fort ·
Jane wears the buffalo hat

"You're sure you'll be OK? Melody will kill me if she finds out I let you go," Mary asked Jane, and then to the ladies who'd just arrived, "It's really important to always, always make sure she's made it through the doorway. Believe me, it's easy to forget. And if you get in a crowd …"

"Mary, you are frightening Ms Hornung and Ms Reineke," Jane said. "I am sorry, she's quite the solicitous mother."

"And don't let her go wandering off on her own," Mary continued, trying to distil for them in a few minutes the tricks of caring for a disembodied author.

"Please, Mary, I will be perfectly fine, won't I?" She addressed her question to Susan Hornung and Barbara Reineke, the two women from the Denver-Boulder region of JASNA, but they were too surprised to reply. They had come to Jane and Mary's hotel room, thinking they were to collect Jane Austen and her avatar and take them to the Fort restaurant, where they would meet eight other JASNA members. Now they'd been informed that Jane's avatar was recovering from a dental procedure and could not accompany them, but Jane herself could.

Ignoring their non-response, Jane continued: "I do not see why these ladies should suffer the loss of my company. And I am very desirous of seeing this frontier fort."

"It's just a replica of Bent's Old Fort[1]," Ms Hornung replied, while tentatively leaning toward the terminal Mary held in her hand. She didn't think she was ignorant about the disembodied—she had disembodied facebook friends—but this wasn't the image she had in mind when she suggested they take Jane Austen out for dinner. She had envisioned chatting with her avatar and not talking to a small box.

"But there will be Indians?"

"Well no, I mean I don't think so," Ms Reineke said. "Actually, I've never been there. I mean maybe there are … re-enactors."

Ms Hornung shook her head no. "Perhaps we should reschedule this?" She didn't much like the idea of being responsible for the famous author.

Arguing with Jane, however, was proving to be more than Mary could handle at the moment. Her tooth was throbbing and she desperately wanted to get in bed with an ice pack. She also knew how important it was for Jane to be distracted on this day.

"I'm sure it will be OK. The terminal's fully charged and you have my cell number. OK, have fun Jane."

The women attempted further protestations but soon they found themselves in the hallway outside the hotel room.

"Oh this should be fun!" Jane's voice exclaimed from the portable terminal. Both ladies jumped in surprise at the sound of her voice.

~

Susan Hornung couldn't stop looking at the empty passenger seat. Sitting in her car but invisible to her was Jane Austen, her favourite author. She'd read the six novels so many times—*OK, Mansfield Park not so often*—she could recite passages from memory and often did to the annoyance of others. She had seen countless adaptations of the novels and of course read a good deal of the fan fiction, but mostly eschewing the ones with zombies or vampires. She had been to England twice and

---

1   Bent's Old Fort was a trading post along the Sante Fe Trail in southeastern Colorado. The building that stands there now is a recreation. The Fort Restaurant in Morrison, Colorado, is a replica of the re-creation, and famously serves game meats and other oddities, such as rattlesnake, alligator and Rocky Mountain Oysters.

visited Winchester and Bath and Lyme Regis and had been a JASNA member for fifteen years.

But this was not what she expected meeting Jane Austen would be like.

In the back seat, Barbara was having similar thoughts. This Jane sounded more like Mrs Bennet or Miss Bates than Elizabeth Bennet.

"What a delightful city this is. Did you know I first visited Denver in 1895? It was very different then ... well naturally it would be, more than a hundred years ago, and yet I remember it very well. Some of the streets of your downtown retain the same names I knew but otherwise ... it is hard to reconcile. The mountains, however, retain their majesty. They are the purple mountains majesties, are they not? but why purple? They are in no way purple, but surely it is a matter of the light."

"It's from the dark firs and other trees, I think," Barbara offered. "Maybe when the forests were thicker, it was more purple."

"They're more purple at dawn, I think," Susan conjectured.

The conversation lapsed for a while. Jane was enjoying the novelty of being in the care of relative strangers, although her joy was tinged with some guilt that she had left Mary alone in the hotel room.

Guilt was not her only emotion, for she also carried a barely acknowledged resentment of Mary. She was actually happy to be away from her for just a bit. Her avatar was the best of companions and a very competent representative, but sometimes she envied the life Mary was enjoying, which was in fact her life. As she gazed out the window, these complex thoughts and emotions silenced her stream of observations.

Susan and Barbara, however, were alarmed by Jane's sudden silence and yet reluctant to restart the conversation. Eventually, Barbara said, "I want to tell you Miss Austen how much I enjoyed *Sanditon*."

"Thank you, and please call me Jane, and I hope I can claim the honour of calling you Barbara."

"Thank you," Barbara said.

"And if I may also ask the favour of calling you Susan?"

"Please do ... Jane," Susan answered.

"I apologize if I am not quite the Jane Austen you were expecting," Jane said. The second she said it she gave thanks the terminal could not really convey the self-pity behind her words.

"No, we're quite happy to ... it's you we came to ..." Barbara said.

"Please forgive me, I phrased that badly," Jane said, embarrassed at her words. "I only meant that … it was presumptuous to ask that you be responsible for me. I am quite prepared to take care of myself and have done so for a very, very long time. But it is kind of you to take me to the restaurant … especially today."

"You're welcome," Susan said. "We thought you shouldn't be alone on July 18th."

"You were already aware of the significance of today?" Jane asked.

"Well duh, we're Janeites," Barbara answered, and then was mortified she'd just said "duh" to Jane. "I mean we saw what day you'd be in Denver and we called your agent and she thought it was a great idea. We had it all planned out, but when your avatar …"

"Her name is Mary."

"When Mary got her toothache, we assumed it was off."

"I'm afraid we kind of forgot that she's not really you," Susan added.

"That is understandable," Jane said. "There are times when I forget. But today I especially feel separate and alone and I appreciate your being so kind as to take charge of me."

"It's our very great pleasure," Susan said warmly, any misgivings now vanished.

"You should be with family and friends on such a day," Barbara added.

~

Jane was happy. Her new friends were the very best sort of company and not just because they were Janeites. They were relaxed and happy, fuelled partly by the mint juleps that seemed *de rigueur* at the restaurant, and no longer awed by the famous author. They sat on a patio table with a beautiful view, not of the Rocky Mountains but of the city of Denver and the plains that stretched out to infinity. The lights of the city outshone the stars in the sky, which made Jane realize how long it had been since she had seen a truly dark night. But the heavens were still illuminated by the aircraft that congregated by the airport, far to the east of the city.

Of course their early conversation was stilted and involved many of the *pro forma* questions Jane had come to expect: *How are you finding the book tour? Where is the next stop? Have you ever been to an AGM before? What actress do you think should play Charlotte Heywood?* Once the drinks and the appetizers arrived, however, the questions were of a higher calibre: *What did you mean when you thought Emma a heroine only you might like? Were you aware Fanny would be thought of as so unlikable? How different is Sanditon from the book you would have written while still alive?*

Jane enjoyed answering these questions, and remarked that she was always happy to critically discuss these matters with fellow Janeites. Her remark prompted the question what did she mean "fellow Janeites," which allowed Jane to say that she was a member of JASNA, JAS, JASE and JASA.[2]

"I confess I now view my six novels as the work of a different person altogether. I know many novelists late in life look back in wonder and puzzlement at the passions that fuelled their early work and I am no different. I am continually amazed at the insight my fellow Janeites offer into the person I was."

"I'm more worried about people ... UNINTELLIGIBLE ...who try to make you into something you're ... that book ..." said a woman who sat at the other end of the table from Jane. The terminal apparently had difficulty recognizing her words, either because she was too far away or speaking too quietly. Jane thought a second to remember the woman's name before asking, "I'm sorry, Rita, I'm afraid I didn't hear that."

"Oh, I shouldn't ... no ... UNINTELLIGIBLE ... east forget it," Rita said, even quieter this time, obviously embarrassed by what she'd said.

"Do you refer to Mr Blake's book?" Jane asked, guessing the topic.

"None of us believe that book, Jane," one woman said.

"And none of us think it's anyone's business," said another.

"What happens in the Regency, stays in the Regency," Barbara said. Everyone laughed at this last comment, although its significance was lost on Jane.[3] Her confusion didn't matter; the joke managed to steer the conversation from the topic, for which she was grateful.

Shortly after this, the food arrived and the conversation took on a

---

2 The Jane Austen Society of North America, the Jane Austen Society of the United Kingdom, the Jane Austen Society of Europe and the Jane Austen Society of Australia.

3 A reference to an advertising campaign urging people to visit Las Vegas, Nevada: "What happens in Vegas, stays in Vegas."

personal tone, as each person talked to her neighbour. Jane feared she might be left out of the conversation somewhat, so she did her best to ask questions about the food.

"Excuse me, Betty, that is elk?" she asked the woman across from her as the waiter set down a plate.

"Yes ... Jane. I'm sorry that you ..."

"Please don't concern yourself and I am sorry to ask you questions while you're eating. I don't believe I ever ate elk when alive."

"It's quite wonderful. I had elk the last time I was here," another woman said.

"I don't think elk is common to the British Isles," Betty said.

"Of course it is," someone else objected. "Didn't the queen shoot one ... I mean not shoot one in that movie?"

"That was a red deer."

Soon the women were producing smartphones and tablets and Googling information about elk—"the American Indian name is wapiti"—and the Queen—"she's a lovely lady; why would anyone want to get rid of the monarchy"—and visiting the website of the very same restaurant they were sitting in to view the menu they had just ordered from.

Jane was very amused at the activity caused by her casual remark. She thought of her Darcy and how he would disapprove of the commotion and the inappropriateness of consulting smartphones while engaged in the very serious business of dining.

Would Darcy be one of those men who checks sports scores at the table? Jane wondered. *People think I created Darcy with impossibly high standards, but he simply exhibited the correct manners of the day. A modern-day Darcy might very well be tempted to check on his stock portfolio or the results of a test match, or would he prefer football?*

The dinner continued merrily. Jane wondered whether Melody might arrange more intimate gatherings of this sort, rather than the large bookstore signings.

Finally the meal was finished and their waiters were clearing the table and offering the dessert menu. But Susan stood up and gathered the attention of the women by clinking her water glass with a knife.

"I think we would all like to thank Jane for joining us tonight and especially for all the joy she has brought us over the years." The women applauded and Jane felt quite moved. "And I'm sure we're all hoping the next book won't take two hundred years." The laughter, Jane judged by the looks of the other diners, must have been quite loud.

"Now we all know what a ... significant day this is for Jane. It's a day that many of us mourn, but I'm told by Melody Kramer, she's Jane's agent, that last year they actually celebrated today as a kind of second or half birthday. Now Jane, they celebrate birthdays at this restaurant with a certain tradition."

Suddenly several of the wait staff appeared, one of whom was holding some sort of furry object with horns, and to Jane they appeared to be singing. The terminal couldn't translate the words. The waitress holding the furry object came behind Jane's chair and put it on the table, next to the terminal. She now realized the furry thing was meant to be a hat.

"We had hoped we could put the birthday buffalo hat on your avatar, Jane."

Jane was at first appalled at the idea of poor Mary being forced to wear the ridiculous hat. She shared with Mary a reluctance to appear ridiculous and knew her friend would have blushed at the prospect. The other women were all looking at the hat and several were taking photographs and Jane realized that to refuse to wear the hat would be tactless.

"I'm sure Mary—my avatar—is bitterly regretting her opportunity to wear the ... buffalo hat on this special occasion. Might I suggest that each of you wear it in turn?"

This met with general approbation and in turn, each woman wore the hat and many pictures were taken and then a cake was produced with the words "Happy Birthday, Jane!" written in icing.

Everyone then sang "Happy Birthday!" and many other diners joined in the singing and especially in the applause as the Janeites used her full name.

"Thank you, thank you everyone. I shall always remember the day I wore the buffalo hat," she said. "And I shall insist on photos being sent to me."

～

"And then they all wore the buffalo hat and they all looked very silly," Jane said.

"That's nice," Mary said in a sleepy voice and with half-closed eyes. She yawned while answering: "I hope there're pictures."

Mary's reply was slightly garbled by the terminal, but Jane guessed what Mary had said. "Oh yes, I insisted, but you are tired and I should let you rest."

For the last fifteen minutes, Mary had been trying to convey to Jane how much she desired rest. She had managed a few hours sleep while Jane was gone, but had awakened at ten o'clock with Jane still not returned.

She had become accustomed to Jane's walkabouts and was not too worried and occupied her time by watching a movie. She was enjoying the experience of watching it alone, without needing to explain to Jane every cultural reference. And for once she felt free to watch something stupid. Not that Jane ever commented or criticized Mary's taste, but sharing a hotel room with the very model of English literature precluded one from suggesting they watch a Jim Carrey movie.

As midnight approached, Mary was beginning to grow anxious. Just a little after midnight, however, she got a call that Jane had returned and she walked down to the lobby and met Ms Hornung and Ms Reineke, who had very obviously been making merry. At first Mary was alarmed that they had been driving, but it was explained that Ms Hornung's husband had driven them back from the restaurant, allowing for some of the delay.

Mary thanked them for showing Jane a good time and they left still in good spirits, spirits Jane was still enjoying. She nattered away at Mary, telling her how much she would have liked the restaurant and describing each of the diners and their habits and peculiarities in detail.

Mary listened to this with a smile, happy that her friend had such a good time and disappointed she had been unable to attend, although she was happy to have escaped wearing the buffalo hat. She did not enjoy looking stupid.

But a full half-hour of this left her desperately wanting sleep and her final "That's nice" was her last word of the evening.

Jane saw her friend fall asleep and was tempted to make one last observation about the unfortunate choice of spectacles of one of the JASNA ladies.

Oh, I had best let her sleep. I can tell her in the morning. She does look all knocked up.[4]

She realized how much she wanted to tell Mary about the evening and suddenly knew that was the thing that was missing from her relationship with Mary.

After all, in many ways Mary was as close to her as her own sister. Since the start of the book tour, they had been together constantly. She and Cassandra, however, were often parted, sometimes for months on end and during those separations they would write long letters about what they had seen, who they had met, what people were wearing and who had danced with whom. Even dear sisters benefited from time apart, if only for the opportunity to tell stories from the perspective of having witnessed events alone.

The very small irritation she had earlier felt, that very small resentment that Mary was living her life, was now gone. She would have been delighted to see Mary wearing the buffalo hat and would have traded on that story for a good long while. She could just imagine Mary's look of annoyance and knew it would have mirrored her own in the same situation. And she knew that Cassandra would have counselled her to accept the wearing of the hat with good grace and dignity.

Looking at Mary, she knew that she could never want another to represent her. She decided to email Melody to see if they could make their partnership permanent.

---

4 Exhausted

- Homecoming -
Excess baggage

Melody shoved the door closed with her butt and announced, "I'm home." She dropped her purse and computer bag to the floor and let the carry-on bag tip over with a loud thud, but there was no response to her announcement.

"Where is she? It's almost nine," she said. The flat maintained its silence until the sound of a jingling collar signalled the arrival of their cat Sally, who stopped short once she caught sight of Melody. Sally was really Tamara's cat, but still Melody didn't think she deserved the suspicious look she was getting.

"Stupid cat," she said, before crouching down and offering her hand. After a little hesitation, Sally approached and allowed Melody to scratch her before running to the kitchen in hopes of food.

Melody stood up, her back stiff from the flight from Los Angeles, and followed Sally. Walking past the dining table, Melody saw that Tamara had made a neat pile of the letters addressed to her. She stopped to look through them quickly while ignoring Sally's pleading. Once Sally was wrapped around her leg, however, she tossed the letters back onto the table.

"OK, food, I know." In the kitchen, she opened the refrigerator, looking for an already opened can. As usual it was buried in the back. She had to move a takeout box aside to retrieve it.

"Provenza's," she said, reading the name of their favourite Italian restaurant. She'd promised Tamara they would go to Provenza's before she'd left for the two-week trip.

She fed the cat a tiny spoonful, even though she'd undoubtedly already been fed, as a peace offering. It was gone instantly and the cat, perhaps knowing that she'd been given an illicit meal, quickly disappeared.

Melody exchanged the cat food for a bottle of pale ale and took it back to the living room where she collapsed onto the couch. Despite the still long late summer day, it was dark, a consequence of their being on the east side of the high-rise. She found the TV remote as usual buried in the couch cushion and reached up for the reading lamp. After a few seconds of unsuccessful fumbling she turned to look and saw that the floor lamp was gone, replaced by a new Japanese-looking lamp made of rice paper shades and wood.

She looked around the living room with no sight of the floor lamp that she'd bought from a thrift shop for her first apartment. It had three battered aluminium cones that were originally adjustable. One of the switches had never worked and the two remaining cones tended to flicker. It was always a source of contention, Tamara always arguing it needed to be binned.

After a little searching, Melody found a dial on the new lamp that incrementally controlled the brightness. The paper shades sent out a soft glow, in comparison to the spotlights from the old lamp.

The sound of keys in the front door attracted Melody's attention, as well as that of Sally, who burst out of the bedroom. The door opened and bumped into Melody's carry-on bag.

"Mel? Are you home?" Tamara called out as she pushed aside the luggage. The scraping sound alarmed Sally who jumped straight up.

Melody rose from the couch and answered, "I just got in." She hurried to the door, picked up her purse and luggage and gave Tamara a quick peck on the cheek.

"I thought you wouldn't be home until tomorrow," Tamara said. "Stop it Sally, it's not dinner time," she told the cat, who was circling her leg. "You're fat enough already."

"We finished early so I booked an earlier flight," Melody answered as she returned from putting her purse and luggage in the bedroom.

"You ate the ticket?" Tamara asked, surprised that her penny-pinching lover would ever willingly pay full fare.

"I wanted to come home and see you," she said. "It was worth it."

She didn't add that she no longer booked no cancellation tickets, one of the benefits of being Jane Austen's agent.

Tamara took Melody's hand and they embraced and Melody drank in the smell of Tamara's hair.

"I'm really glad you're home, too. We've missed you. Stop it Sally!" she said to the cat, who'd stood up and lightly sunk her claws into her slacks.

Their intimate mood spoiled, Tamara asked, "Did you eat?"

"I brought a sandwich on the plane," she said. "How 'bout you?"

"Pizza at the office. Hizzoner bought."

"Ooh, pizza with the mayor."

"And five others from the planning department … and the rest of the mayor's staff. We have the big announcement next week, remember?"

Melody nodded as if she had some idea to what Tamara referred.

"Liar. You have … OK, Sally, I'll get you something."

She scooped up the cat and took it into the kitchen. Melody considered saying something, but thought better of it. The incredibly small morsel of food she fed Sally could hardly make much difference anyway.

That task done, they retired to the couch, Tamara taking a glass of wine with her. They snuggled, their bodies naturally settling into their matching curves.

"New lamp," Melody observed.

"It finally died," Tamara said. "Honestly, there were sparks when I tried to turn it on. Look at the outlet; there are scorch marks."

"I believe you," she replied, although she tried to see the outlet from where she sat.

"Things happen around here if you're gone for two weeks."

"Like going to Provenza's."

"Among other things. I'm really glad you're back. How long before you leave again."

"It's not that bad," Melody said, knowing full well she was only home for the night.

"Yes it is. I hate having to look at a calendar to find out if you're home. Aren't you going to England again?"

Melody sighed. "Not for another two weeks."

"It would be nice if you could spend some time at home."

"Wouldn't you just be at the office if I was?" Melody asked, and regretted it immediately. Her tiredness and the beer had dropped her guard.

Fortunately Tamara only said, "Probably," and then was silent.

Melody was congratulating herself that her stupid remark hadn't sparked an argument when Tamara said, "I have something to tell you."

· Back to Bath ·
Albert imagines the worst

BertieFromHants says:

Where are you Jane?

JaneAusten3 says:

Still in NYC, Albert.

BertieFromHants says:

And what are you editing now?

JaneAusten3 says:

Another young adult novel. Apparently being bitten by a vampire is the source for most teen angst.

Jane wrote this while looking at the square before Bath Cathedral and the Pump Room and the hundreds of people dressed in Regency costume. The festival, as ever, was a surreal event for Jane. She had been in Bath during the festival twice before and each time she promised herself she would not return, for the effect was disturbing.

She quite appreciated the obvious enjoyment of the participants and their desire to recreate the past, specifically her past, but naturally no one had ever given thought to how it might appear to the person whose name was lent to the festival. At a quick, first glance the crowd looked like a Regency gathering. From her vantage point with Mary beside her, all she could see were the re-enactors assembling for the promenade, which in itself was such a strange concept, looking like a civil insurrection of the ton.[1]

What most assaulted her eye, however, was the confusion of dress, with styles ranging from the time of several different kings named George and through to the Victorian. And there were some costumes that would never pass muster in any age with a strange artificiality of fabric and colour impossible during her time. She also saw stitching, fit and design unworthy even of her own poor skills as a seamstress and not a few garments that seemed held together with Velcro and pins.

There were, of course, those participants whose costume and manner were meticulously appropriate to Jane's time in Bath, but they bothered her even more. They made her realize that when she imagined her corporeal existence, her image was not of her productive and mostly happy years in Chawton, but of their removal to Bath and the first betrayal by her father (the second being his death). *Why should my mental image of myself be from that time?*

BertieFromHants says:

Hello, Jane? Is there something wrong?

Albert's question awakened Jane from her reverie.

JaneAusten3 says:

I am sorry, I was answering a question from a co-worker. It is unforgivably rude of me.

BertieFromHants says:

Then I should allow you to return to work. I don't want you to get fired for talking to a friend.

They ended their chat, a much shorter one than usual, with promises to talk again soon, but they did not set a date, which was their custom. Jane was too preoccupied to realize this, especially as the time was approaching for the promenade to begin.

"We're about to begin. Are you done updating your blog?" Mary asked.

"Just finishing."

---

1   The ton, or haut ton (also haute ton), is borrowed from the French and during Jane's lifetime referred to high society, the fashionable

"Ladies and gentleman, if I might have your attention!" boomed Martin, the emcee of the promenade. "We are about to begin and I would like to re-introduce our guest of honour, Miss Jane Austen, who …"

A polite round of applause interrupted his introduction.

"… who would like to say a few words."

Mary walked to the microphone, offered her hand to the emcee, thanked him, and turned to the crowd.

"Thank you, Martin, and thank you everyone for celebrating Bath and the Regency and my own contribution to that tempestuous age. I am fair brought back to those days by the sight of you, young and old and from so many parts of the world. I confess, however, that my presence here may be somewhat controversial, even though this festival bears my name. You may know that my opinions of Bath were … somewhat decided …"

The crowd laughed at this.

"… and possibly might be described as uncharitable. This city seems to take a positive delight in reminding people of my harsh judgments. But I tell you now that Bath and Jane Austen are inextricably linked and I am honoured that I have been asked to officially open the festival. Please forgive me any of my ill-chosen remarks. I can only say that Bath is now as much my home as is Hampshire and I would like to again thank the Right Worshipful Mayor of Bath for bestowing on me the Long Service Award, for which they needed to create a two hundred years category."

Mary again waited for the applause, which was much louder this time.

"And now I declare, 'Let the promenade begin.'"

Mary then put her hand on the emcee's proffered arm and they left the square and strolled toward York Street.

All that Mary said, however, was lost on Jane, who continued to brood.

All lies, Jane thought. *When did I learn to lie to so easily? I have gone so far as to pretend that I am editing a young adult vampire novel, although I rather liked the idea of it. Stupid woman! Do not distract yourself. I must tell Albert the truth before the AGM,* she resolved, and hurried to stay with Mary and the promenade.

~

Albert ended the chat with great misgivings. They had failed to set a date for their next chat in their rushed goodbyes. Jane had seemed reluctant to talk and eager to quit. It was all the more unusual for she had initiated the chat. At first he thought she had some news for him, but then she talked of inconsequentials. *And why would a co-worker be asking her a question at six in the morning. True, she might be working unusually early at her office, but why would a co-worker be that early.*

The co-worker might also be disembodied, he thought. Soon he was constructing an elaborate scenario for why she might be at her office so early and the identity of the mysterious co-worker who demanded her attention.

You're a fool, Bertie. How can I be jealous of this person I've just dreamed up. How can a dead man be jealous of another dead man claiming the affections of a dead woman? It's ridiculous and you're just a ridiculous old fool.

But why does she now conceal her location? he asked. *Her AfterNet profile no longer lists her location as New York City and in fact the location heading was missing.*

I should never have suggested we attend the AGM. My offer to pay her registration was too forward. She obviously retains the proprieties of her time when alive and was offended. But then why did she call me?

But unvoiced in his thoughts was the worry that perhaps Jane *had* shed those proprieties. After all, what loyalty did a disembodied woman owe a disembodied man?

Instead he consoled himself that she had never said she wouldn't attend the AGM, although that immediately invited the thought that she could always attend it but without his company ... or in the company of another.

I could send her an email asking whether my invitation was ill-advised. But he gave up that idea, fearing an answer.

I will simply send her an email saying that I forgot to ask when we would next chat. That way I put the blame on me.

· The Men's Club ·
Stephen chats with his roommates

Stephen was a little startled when his computer quacked to warn him of the upcoming chat. It should have been no surprise, for he'd been looking forward to it all day, but he was again lost in the inventory from Chawton. The mind-numbing depth of the project had sucked him in and he had found himself following fake leads and clicking on tantalizing links that revealed mundane objects, rather like Catherine Morland finding the laundry list when she had hoped to find evidence of some Gothic intrigue.[1]

And so the multiple alarms he had set to remind him of the chat proved providential, and he quit Virtual Chawton and turned to his web browser. He clicked the bookmark he'd saved for the chat and logged into the AfterNet. A look at the clock in the menu bar of his laptop assured him he was still four minutes early but a glance at the number of people in the chat room showed him he was the last to arrive.

Apparently he was not the only one looking forward to the chat. Almost immediately his future roommates greeted him, their onscreen avatars waving their hands or brandishing their swords or firing signal flares or doffing their hats or whatever they were using to signal their

---

1 You can find this in Chapter 21 of *Northanger Abbey*

greeting. His avatar, a proper Regency dandy, jauntily twirled his cane in response.

The background of the chat room resembled a Regency ballroom, and the assembled avatars looked incongruous against the parquet floor, the chandeliers and the plaster reliefs on the walls. All the men chose a military theme, redcoats from the Napoleonic War, one man in the green jacket of a rifleman and another wearing the infamous armour of Henry VIII with the giant codpiece. And a Tommy from the Great War.

Might we be over compensating here? he thought. *Do even literate disembodied men feel a little emasculated for enjoying chick lit?*

The visual was more than a little distracting so he maximized the chat transcript, reducing the animated characters to a thin strip at the top of the browser window.

BeauAbrams has entered the room
BeauAbrams says:
Greetings gentlemen. Glad you could make it.

He got effusive replies from the men in the room and again the avatars, relegated to the top of the window, signalled their greetings. Stephen felt a little embarrassed that his simple offer to be a roommate to the disembodied men prompted such gratitude. In fact he hadn't given his offer much thought; he'd been asked by one of the AGM organizers and readily agreed once he learned his registration would be reduced $50.

Of course he hadn't expected to become such friends with the men and if time were money, he'd probably lost the $50 savings and more in the time he spent in his weekly chats with the men and the separate conversations he held with them via email, twitter and facebook. It was almost like getting five uncles who wanted to tell you about their lives and families, but he didn't mind. His was a small family, so he found a great deal of enjoyment in becoming a favourite nephew.

All the men except Albert were aged between 50 and 70 when they'd died, and he imagined them all with a twinkle in their eye. They were all white males with a taste for literature and all had been married.

The oldest among them, based on when he died, was Albert, who was also the youngest when he died at 27 and the man Stephen felt closest too. His avatar was the Tommy.

BertieFromHants says:

Ah, the hour produces the man.

BeauAbrams says:

I see the party's in fulls wing. But before we get too far along, I just want to remind everyone to send in your field fingerprint. We're still missing a few.

AlanJTimison says:

Guilty. I'll send it tomorrow, first thing.

WalkLikeADuck says:

Me three. Sorry, I meant to last week. Slipped my mind.

BeauAbrams says:

Yes, well you know my terminal will be preset with your fingerprints so …

AlanJTimison says:

Yes maam.

WalkLikeADuck says:

He's worse than my wife

BeauAbrams says:

And I'm afraid I got bumped off the list for the Regency tea at the woman's club. I guess they overbooked and they asked if I'd mind skipping it.

The men—except for Albert—expressed themselves on the subject of tea.

mikechapman says:

I was never much of a tea drinker when I was alive.

WalkLikeADuck says:

Those little sandwiches couldn't satisfy me.

AlanJTimison says:

Real men don't trink dea.

Stephen wondered how genuine was their lack of remorse. Men who'd willingly go to a Jane Austen AGM probably would enjoy tea, but for some reason his past chats with the men had devolved into a bizarre Victorian men's club with Benny Hill overtones.

He watched ruefully as the men traded suggestions about substitutes for the tea involving strip clubs, dog racing and a cigar bar. He got a private chat message.

BertieFromHants has requested a private chat

BertieFromHants says:

Sorry Stephen. They seem determined to embarrass you.

BeauAbrams says:

That's OK, Albert. I know they're just high spirited.

BertieFromHants says:

Yes, boys will be boys. I shall try to convince them that you are not a ... Jell-O shots sort of person, whatever that is.

BeauAbrams says:

That would be appreciated. I know they would have liked to go to the tea. It was my fault for not registering sooner.

They quit their private chat and Stephen and Albert did their best to sway the men from indulging in fraternity shenanigans. "I will not ride a mechanical bull," he warned.

Eventually Stephen promised that he would put his name on the cancellation list for the tea and suddenly their attitude toward the manliness of tea changed.

mikechapman says:

well to be sociable I would go

lastchance says:

To borrow from Willy Sutton,[2] that's where all the women are. So sure, I guess tea wouldn't be so bad.

After this was resolved, the men started swapping stories of their youthful escapades, each story being more outrageous than the previous. After a particularly salacious recount by Alan, Stephen claimed he needed sleep and wished the men good night. He lurked for a time though, trying to follow the various threads of reminiscences.

They were not the typical image of men interested in Jane Austen. He recalled a former girlfriend who'd been baffled by his love of Jane—"real men don't read Jane Austen"—but these were fully realized men who liked Jane Austen. They might pretend to a bluff, hearty masculinity, but they were as in love with Jane as he.

When the topic moved to Jane's presence at the AGM, it was clear their opinion ran toward a belief that she was the true Jane, and their

---

2   Willie Sutton, a prolific American bank robber, supposedly said, "Because that's where the money is," when asked, "Why do you rob banks?"

attitude became worshipful. Their double entendres disappeared to be replaced with speculations of what she might be like and whether she would appear in any of the chat rooms during the AGM.

He had to admit it was really cute how the men quickly shed their rakish behaviour once they talked about Jane. And then he laughed at how embarrassed the men would be if they'd known he'd called them cute.

I really need to watch a Bruce Willis film, he thought as he put his computer to sleep and then himself.

· Seattle ·
The other shoe

"What do you know about this?" Melody asked as she pushed her laptop toward Mary, who was scooping cream cheese from a little plastic package to schmear onto her toasted bagel. It was a bagel in name only, but habits die hard. They were sitting in the free breakfast room of their hotel, which was almost empty. Jane and Melody had come down earlier and Mary found them conspiring. Mary had had a difficult night's sleep and was still dragging. Before answering, she took a careful sip of her coffee, but the contents of the pump pot had grown cold.

"What do I know about what?" She looked at the laptop and saw an article at *The Daily Beast:* "Jane Austen scholar questions identity of Regency author."

"I don't understand, what is this?" She was confused and still groggy and not quite sure why they seemed unduly concerned. It was unfortunate, of course, but they knew there were some who still didn't believe Jane was Jane.

"That's what we're asking you," Melody said.

"Melody, don't accuse her. Mary, dear, we just wondered if your Stephen might have given you any idea that Dr Davis felt this way about me."

"What? Dr Davis?" She looked more closely at the screen and realized the article was about Stephen's graduate advisor. "It's asking a lot to just accept this is the real Jane Austen," the article quoted her as saying. "There's no reason to doubt her, of course, but the opaqueness of how the AfterNet certifies identities just leaves one wondering what criteria were used to vet her identity."

Mary read the rest of the article and saw that Davis actually gave several reasons why Jane might not be Jane, without coming out and denouncing her.

"Why would she say this?" Mary asked. "And no, I had no idea she felt this way."

She looked up at Melody who was still glaring. "Honestly, I don't know and I …"

Her phone stopped her and the ring tone—the latest catchy summer song—indicated the caller was Stephen.

"Hello," she said, "Yes, I just saw it. How could … yes, she's right here, and Melody too. Uh huh … OK." She activated the phone's speaker. "Go ahead."

"I'm so sorry, Miss Austen. I don't know why she said those things, but I know she's been … well she was annoyed by your open letter." Melody directed an "I told you so" look to Jane. "Somehow she's gotten it into her head you were talking about her."

Unfortunately Jane didn't quite catch all that Stephen had said; Melody's terminal having had difficulty recognizing the voice on the phone's speaker.

"What did he say?" Jane asked.

Mary realized the problem and told Jane to switch to her terminal after syncing with her phone, and then she repeated Stephen's remarks.

"But my letter was not directed to her, Stephen. I have nothing but respect for her."

"Did you know she was going to confront Jane?" Melody asked bluntly.

"No … well, no. Maybe I should have seen it coming. I think a lot of it is resentment. For some reason everyone thinks she was on the AfterNet committee and everyone thinks the decision was unanimous, so she keeps getting interviewed."

"Maybe if Jane could meet with Dr Davis and explain …"

"No Mary, I don't think that would be wise," Jane said. "At least not at present. Much of this problem is of my own making. I should have consulted with Melody before I wrote my open letter. Fortunately we now have a publicist who can repair what damage there might be, but perhaps we are flying off the handle. Graciousness should be our tone, don't you think, Melody?"

Melody, still glaring at Stephen, as represented by Mary's phone, was caught off guard. "What? Oh, if you say so Jane."

"And Stephen, thank you for your call." Jane said. "It was kind of you."

"You're welcome," he replied. Recognizing a dismissal, he apologized again and spoke a further few words to Mary privately, and then rang off.

"I don't think we can trust him," Melody said.

"How can you say that? It was pretty decent of him to call and apologize!" Mary said.

"It was a very gentleman-like thing to do, I agree," Jane said soothingly. "But perhaps we should simply exercise prudence. After all, if we say something indiscreet in front of Stephen, then we can hardly blame him if he accidentally divulges it to Dr Davis."

Jane was pleased to see Melody and Mary nod. She had said something to which they could both agree and it recalled to her all the times Cassandra had settled or prevented arguments.

In truth, Dr Davis's remarks did not overly upset Jane and she was not disposed toward action to remedy them. After having met so many Janeites, signed so many copies and addressed so many groups, she had come to believe that most accepted her as the real Jane Austen. According to their surveys, Melody's publicity campaign had swung the majority of readers into the "I believe in Jane" camp.

Mary, of course, was still reeling from the news. By extension, she felt complicit in this attack against Jane, but she also knew that Stephen had no hand in it. He was undoubtedly a Jane supporter. *Everything he's ever said …*

But that thought stopped her. Naturally they'd often speak of Jane and she had confided to him some of her frustrations and anxieties and challenges of representing the author. She'd told him numerous funny stories about Jane's personality. *What if he told them to Dr Davis? Did something I say make her doubt Jane?*

Then Mary remembered some questions Stephen had asked on their drive to the mountains in Colorado. She couldn't remember the exact words, but she thought he'd asked her if she ever had any doubts of Jane. She felt a stab of panic that fortunately went unnoticed.

Mary's guilt, however, was nothing in comparison to Melody's. *How did I miss this? I thought Davis was on board.*

She had kept up a regular correspondence with the eminent Janeite, although it had been largely one way. Melody had often tried to arrange a meeting between Jane and Davis, but their schedules had never meshed—not even when Jane and Mary were in Chicago. And Davis had demurred when asked for a book plug, although that was in response to a request from Random House. *Oh God, I should have asked directly.*

But that was one of the tasks that had gone undone, first because she had taken on too much on her own and then because of her retrenchment after Tamara's revelation.

Their thoughts explained their silence while Mary distractedly chewed the cardboard bagel. Seattle no longer seemed like the victory lap before the AGM they had anticipated.

· Beauty is truth ·
A whole new perspective on life

"Can I just say how exciting it is to meet you, Miss Austen, and how amazing *Sanditon* is?"

"Why I think you just have, my dear," Mary said with a forced laugh she hoped wasn't too dismissive. She added the laugh because Jane had surrounded her remarks with the [laugh] code. The result was an improvement on Jane's earlier efforts; at least now the laughter was in the upgraded Elizabeth digitized voice, but it still sounded like someone playing a Beatles song backward.

"Oh, yes, so I have," the unmistakable graduate student said, with a laugh and a little shake of her head left and right, reminding Mary of the blonde joke involving shoulder pads.

"However I am uncertain how you can know that *Sanditon* is amazing as you have only just purchased it."

"Oh, I've already read it on my Kindle. But I had to come here to buy a real book so you could sign it."

"Then I must think of something very special to write for someone who has bought two copies. May I have your name?"

"It's Alethea ... with a TH ... and an EA ... and another E."[1]

---

1 Alethea and Catherine Bigg were sisters of Harris Bigg-Wither, Jane's fiancé for a day. His different last name came about because his father had decided to honour the cousins whose property he'd inherited, Manydown Park.

"Yes, I think I know how to spell it. Let me think."

Then Mary heard in her ear, "Mary, sign it …

'Beauty is truth, truth beauty —
and Jane is her friend. That is all
Alethea need know for now.'"

Mary signed it slowly, Jane repeating the words. She added the signature far faster from long practice and handed the book back to the bubbly woman.

"Oh thank you, Miss Austen, thank you."

"What was that quote?" Mary shot back to Jane.

"It was me doing rubbish to Keats.[2] I hope I won't be meeting him online. Was she the last of them?"

The bookseller approached them. "Well, I think we're finally done, Miss Austen," she said. She still had a frozen smile on her face, borne of her awe of meeting Austen and the novelty of speaking to an avatar.

"Ms Fentriss, how can I express my gratitude for this turnout?"

"Oh, please, I'm only sorry your … that you had to sit here two hours. Isn't your, aren't you …"

"I admit I am tired and should enjoy the tea you had spoken of earlier. I wanted to discuss your post about visiting Bath and your delightful visit to Sydney Gardens and thought you might enjoy a story or two about my recollections."

The bookseller's eyes lit up, any reserve now lost. "I would be … ecstatic, Miss Austen."

"Please Miss Fentriss, call me Jane, that is if I might call you Laura."

"There's a teashop just a few blocks from here … Jane. And if it's all right with you, perhaps a few friends …"

"Of course, I would be delighted," Mary responded with a smile that masked her true feelings. Ms Fentriss left them momentarily to call her friends.

"Oh great, I thought tea would be in the store. Now it's high tea with a bunch of Janeites," Mary said. "And we already have dinner tonight with those movie executives Melody arranged."

Harris's father changed his son's name to reflect that, but not his daughters. Jane and the sisters were good friends, even after Jane broke the engagement. Alethea and another sister, Elizabeth, visited Jane frequently during the author's final days.

2 John Keat's *Ode on a Grecian Urn*

"I am sorry Mary, but Miss Fentriss has been very supportive and her blog is influential."

"I'm sure she's a lovely woman, Jane, but I had wanted to talk to you about ... I wanted to explain ... to apologize about Stephen."

"Oh don't be tedious, Mary. You have no need ... oh, that was quick."

"They were just waiting for my call," Ms Fentriss explained as she returned. "Shall we go?"

The teashop was just a few blocks away and was charming. Ms Fentriss had only invited two friends to join them and they arrived in short order. All three were passionate Janeites and Mary told them several stories about Godmersham Park, the other home of Jane's brother Edward. One story led to another and another and soon the other patrons realized Jane Austen was in their midst.

After an hour of captivating her audience, Ms Fentriss had to remind Mary, "Oh my goodness, the time. I had promised to return you to your hotel by four."

There were general cries of disappointment at this and even Mary would remain, but Jane reminded her, "Melody was very insistent we be on time."

Mary made her goodbyes to the other women and patrons and then she and Ms Fentriss went back to the bookstore to obtain the bookseller's car.

"Thank you so much for meeting my friends, Jane," she said as they drove back to the hotel.

"It was my pleasure," Mary said, and genuinely meant it.

"I just want you to know ... I don't agree with Alice Davis ... with what she said in that *Daily Beast* article."

"That is very kind of you to say, but she only expressed understandable doubt," Mary said, at Jane's request.

"Has she even met you?"

"No, we haven't met."

"Then that explains it. If she were to meet you, she'd know."

The store was only a short distance to Jane's hotel and she was delivered in good time. After a heartfelt parting with Ms Fentriss, Mary and Jane returned to their empty suite.

"She's not even here yet," Mary complained.

"We are a few minutes early. Doubtless Melody is busy planning her campaign against Dr Davis."

"You know you're taking her attack against you pretty calmly," Mary said as she removed her costume and prepared to take a shower.

"Did you know that after *Emma*, I kept a sort of journal where I recorded everyone's opinion of my books? In fact it was the only journal as such that I ever kept. I tried to pretend I treated each comment equally, that I valued the negative opinions as well as the positive, but truthfully I despised every slur and slander against my children. That is what I called my novels. Isn't that silly?"

Mary did, of course, know this, as she knew almost everything about Jane, but she only answered, "No, I don't think that's silly at all."

"Being dead does offer a whole new perspective on life, Mary, depend on it. I have had the most amazing months of my life. Just think of that, of this world for more than two hundred years and the last several months have been the most amazing.

"I will not pretend that Dr Davis's comments are unwelcome, but what of it? She is entitled to her opinion."

· Regret ·
"Oh God, I went too far"

Stephen walked with ever slowing steps to his advisor's office, his resolve fading with each step. It's not that he was scared of Dr Davis, although he was; as his advisor, she could make his life hell. It was more that once he confronted her, he couldn't make allowances for her anymore. He'd put up with her obsession that Jane wasn't Jane, because at least it was … academic. At first it was fun rummaging through Virtual Chawton and he'd even found information for his own thesis, but lately Dr Davis seemed consumed by the topic.

He stopped just outside the door, reluctant to enter and confront her. He was about to leave when he heard: "For Christ's sake come in already."

So he took off his backpack and tried to enter as nonchalantly as he could.

"Hey, Doc," he said, while trying to casually toss his bag onto a chair, and missed. He grimaced at the sound of his iPad inside the bag hitting the floor. He took a seat, picked up his bag and put it primly on his lap.

Dr Davis looked up from the website she was visiting, peering at Stephen over the top of her reading glasses.

"You came because of that story," she said matter of factly.

"Well, yes, and because we have a standing appointment," he said, just as casually.

Neither said anything for about half a minute. Stephen fingered the zipper on his backpack while she pretended to resume reading the website.

"Do you want to talk about it?" he asked.

"No, not particularly."

"It's just that it made me look rather stupid in front of Mary and Jane."

Finally she looked up from her laptop and asked, "Oh, I am sorry, but did it ever occur to you that maybe she's not Jane Austen?"

"No, it never occurred to me. The AfterNet vetted her and that's good enough for me. I've read *Sanditon* and it's good, maybe it's not *Pride and Prejudice* but it's funny and it's warm and it's different and pretty much everyone loves it but you." *Everyone but you, you miserable old cow*, he thought.

The look she gave him left him with the uncomfortable feeling she had intuited his "miserable old cow" thought. "You don't see how it's completely different from everything she's written?" she asked.

"Sure, but that's how I feel about all her books. And this book is the product of someone who's been dead two hundred years so of course it's going to be different." He said this with his first note of anger. It wasn't as if he'd expected her to apologize for making him look bad with Austen, but he had hoped she might acknowledge she'd gone too far in the interview.

"Well, I am sorry I made you look bad in front of your girlfriend," she finally said.

"Look, Dr Davis, forget about that. The fact is, there's an official Jane Austen now, and nothing you can do is going to alter that fact. You don't want to be on the wrong side of this. They're going to crown her at the AGM, you know it. And if you start bad mouthing Jane ..."

"Thank you very much for your advice, Stephen. I shall take it under advisement. And now that I know your opinion, I think it would be wise to not speak of the matter. I would not want to jeopardize your standing with the Austen camp." She returned her attention to her laptop.

"Fine. I already sent you what I found this week. Then we're done."

"For now. I am actually rather busy, so perhaps we can give it a miss today."

He nodded, rose from his chair, collected his bag and left her office, thinking he'd just thrown away the last two years of his life.

She looked up after he left. She'd actually been looking over the email he'd sent with his latest findings. As usual his work was impeccable and his email filled with little jokes and asides, obviously created before he'd learned about the article.

Stupid woman! You've gone too far, and now you've antagonized a good student … and you've lost your spy.

Her last thought made her feel a little guilty and more than a little sad. She hadn't known when she'd crossed the line from being annoyed at the idea of an Austen claimant to being an obsessive crank. She still had enough presence of mind to know that's what she'd become. Literary scholarship was full of obsessive cranks and she cringed at the idea she was now akin to those who questioned the identity of Shakespeare.

But I can prove it if the letter and journal are authentic. And if I'm wrong, then Stephen's right and I've alienated everyone who's bought into this stupid I Believe in Jane nonsense. Oh God, I went too far.

VOLUME III

Titbits III
Heard outside a JASNA AGM during the street promenade

PASSERBY: "What's going on? Why's everyone dressed up?"
JANEITE: "It's the annual Jane Austen convention. This is the promenade where we walk around in period costume."
PASSERBY: "Who's Jane Austen?"
JANEITE: "She was a Regency author. She wrote *Pride and Prejudice*? You know, Colin Firth, wet shirt."
PASSERBY: "Oh yeah. Sure, sure. Is she here?"

· A large spanner ·
Davis's accusation causes anxiety

indy walked back into her living room, still in a state of panic over the conversation she'd just finished with Dr Davis, one of the scholars who would be presenting a breakout session. She had called Davis because of what she thought must be baseless rumours of bad feelings between her and Jane Austen.

Unfortunately the rumours weren't baseless, which she would have known if she'd bothered to pay attention to the Internet, but she'd been too busy with organizing. She and the other North Texas members had been working nonstop to prepare for the AGM, and she hadn't been following the news of Austen's book tour.

Then yesterday she started getting calls from Ajala Johnsson and Joan Ray and even Davis's former colleague Elisabeth Lenckos,[1] warning her there could be trouble at the AGM.

And so she didn't know until yesterday that Davis had publicly challenged Austen's identity. She quickly looked up the articles and even saw a BBC video of Davis doing so. She was obviously uncomfortable at being questioned directly on the matter and tried to pull back from directly calling Austen a fraud, but clearly she was challenging the author's identity.

---

1   Elisabeth Lenckos is a lecturer at the University of Chicago's Graham School and a Chawton House Library Research Fellow

"Cindy, do you have the address for the streaming site? JASNA New York wants it," Beth Ann asked.

Megan also took advantage of Cindy's return: "Caroline can't pick up Austen at the airport. Should I call Barbara?"

Cindy realized all eyes were on her as she stood there, unable to make any sort of response.

"Hon, what's wrong?" her husband asked. He stood and walked to her and took her hand.

"Somebody died," Megan said, her automatic reaction whenever someone looked shocked.

"No, nobody died," Cindy said. She looked around her home, at the three people in the dining room using her table to finish stuffing the goodie bags and at her kitchen where her two sons were making sandwiches. From the open door to the garage she heard the sounds of people making up the information packets.

"Megan, Beth Ann, let's go in the backyard." She didn't mention her husband but kept a grip on his hand and they all left through the sliding glass doors and onto the deck. It was still pleasant outdoors, with just a hint of coolness from the shadow the late afternoon sun cast onto the wooden deck. She took a seat at the table that was weighted down with the placards and banners that would direct participants to the AGM.

"Are you sure nobody's dead?" Megan asked again.

"Nobody who wasn't dead already," Cindy said. She just had the sudden thought that if she died she'd still be able to attend the AGM, and then remembered the uncomfortable talk she'd had with her husband about what they would do if either did die.

She gave a slight shudder that alarmed her husband. "What is it, hon?"

She explained the situation to her two coordinators and to her husband, who in these final days was at her beck and call.

"So we've gone from *Two Hundred Years of Sense and Sensibility* to *I Believe in Jane* and now it's what, *I Don't Believe in Jane*?" Beth Ann asked.

"What exactly did she say, hon? Did she really say she would denounce Austen?"

"She said ... something like ... she said she has a document and if Austen would identify it, it would satisfy her. I don't know what's gotten into her. I tried to explain the AGM's not the place to make an accusation like this."

Her husband disagreed: "I don't know, maximum exposure and all that. I'm just saying." Cindy gave him an irritable look. He was a defence attorney and always looked at things from the wrong side.

"Is there anything we can do?" Beth Ann asked. "Well, not us ... the larger us. Can somebody try and talk her out of it."

"I don't know. She said she wouldn't publicly challenge Austen at the AGM, although she's practically done that online. I'm going to call everyone I can think of; maybe somebody can convince Davis this is not a good idea. The other possibility, I guess, is if we can get Austen and Davis to meet before the breakout sessions."

"How does that help?"

"Well, it only helps if Jane can convince Davis she's wrong ... I mean convince her she's really Austen. Oh God, this is just awful." She took a deep breath and continued. "OK, no sense in crying about it. Beth Ann, we need to get everyone in a room together, away from everyone else. Can you find out if there's a conference room at the hotel we can use?"

Beth Ann replied, "We've already booked every room at the hotel, but I'll see. When do we need it?"

"Well, Austen doesn't arrive until tomorrow, and Davis doesn't arrive until Wednesday, so let's see if we can get a room Wednesday or Thursday."

"That'll be cutting it close."

"What else is new? And Megan, can we find another speaker to take the place of Davis if ... or another activity? Maybe we talk to one of the workshop people."

"We already have a contingency for this," Megan said. "We just combine two of the breakout rooms into one. You don't get the breakout session you signed up for, but ..."

"Right, I forgot, but if we can find ... oh, this is awfully bad form, but we can ask Paula. Considering we bumped her because of Jane, it's awkward, but I'd still rather have a presenter, plus the time it would take to re-configure the room. OK, off you go, start making calls."

Beth Ann and Megan looked at each other, aware they'd just been dismissed. They left and as the sliding door closed behind them, Cindy took the opportunity to slump and lean against her husband.

"Why did this have to happen on my ... I mean our AGM? Next

year would be New York City. They know how to handle warring celebrities. Criminy."

"When's the last time you ate?" her husband asked. When she didn't
answer, he said, "Thought so. I'll get the boys to make you a sandwich.
I've got to drop off the check with the caterers. Got to leave now." He
stood up and kissed her on the top of her head. She put out her hand,
hoping he'd squeeze it one last time, but he was already going back
into the house. She dropped her hand back to her lap and sat a moment
before retrieving her phone from her back pocket. She looked up Ajala
Johnsson's number and prepared to have to explain the whole sorry
business again.

~

Alice looked at the caller ID of the newest person to call and scold her.
It was Dr Ray in Colorado Springs, a woman she admired a great deal.
She turned off her cell phone instead of answering it.

I know I'm making the biggest mistake of my career ... unless I'm right.

Her computer beeped to tell her she had an email and saw it came
from Deirdre. She put the computer to sleep to keep it from reminding
her, from prodding her, from forcing her hand.

She'd always been a person who would mulishly push back against
anyone telling her what a mistake she was making. Her father had
learned the best way to control his daughter was with reverse psychology, which worked throughout her adolescence, but as she got older, she
learned to disguise her bloody-mindedness. But still each phone call,
each email, just kept pushing her toward a confrontation with Austen.

Then her desk phone rang and in a contrary mood snatched it up,
hoping to pick a fight with whomever was calling.

"Alice, it's Court. I got the report and I'm heading back in a couple
of hours," he said quickly. He'd already tried several times to call and
took no chance of her hanging up.

"Oh, Court, I'm glad you called. I would look pretty stupid if I
exposed Austen without that report."

"I already forwarded you a copy of it. Check your email."

She awakened her computer and found Court's email and its attachments.

"Thanks," she said.

"I've been trying to call for hours. I've left voice mails."

"I'm sorry, I've been getting a lot of calls. The cat's out of the bag, it seems. Everyone seems to know what we're up to."

"It wasn't me," he said, the worry in his voice very evident.

"No, I know that. It was me. I practically said I would call her out. I don't know what I was thinking."

"Yeah, that's not going over too well. Everyone over here loves Jane. They're all wearing these buttons."

"It's the same here. Even my students wear them."

"Have you ever thought … well, we might be very unpopular."

"I'm not doing this to be popular, Court."

"Well, maybe you're not, but … damn, I can't even remember why I'm doing this. I thought we had a common enemy …"

"If we expose an impostor, people will thank us, Court. You're not thinking of withholding this information, are you?"

"No, of course not. The journal and the letter will go public one way or another. Mrs Westerby clearly needs the money. I just don't know if releasing it at the AGM is the best way to go. I don't particularly want to be attacked by pitchfork-wielding Janeites."

Alice bleakly laughed at this thought, the image of bonnet clad women carrying pitchforks and torches. It was the first time she'd found anything funny that day.

"Point taken, Court. It has been spiralling out of control, and I'm afraid I'm the one who's been the cause of a lot of it. But perhaps we can turn this to our advantage. They want us to meet with this fake Austen before I give my talk, and I think we'll take them up on that offer. Then we can accuse her in front of witnesses. We'll record the whole thing on video."

· The Great State of Texas ·
Contemplations at 30,000 feet

"We've just entered the Lone Star State, ladies and gentlemen," the voice of the pilot said over the cabin speakers. Mary looked up from her copy of *Emma*, her attention drawn to the proclamation.

"He always does that," the male flight attendant told her, as he stopped to pick up the empty coffee cup on Mary's seat back tray. "He's an Aggie.[1] At least he doesn't say 'Yee haw!' anymore."

Mary smiled at the flight attendant and went back to the book, disappointed that she was still reading a Miss Bates paragraph. She'd now read the other five novels, seen movie and television adaptations of them all and of course knew *Sanditon* like she'd written it herself. She'd seen the Gwyneth Paltrow and Kate Beckinsale[2] adaptations of *Emma* and thought them delightful. But she had yet to actually finish reading *Emma*.

She'd heard that everyone had an Austen novel they least cared for, usually *Mansfield Park*. But for Mary, *Emma* was the dud that just sat there daring her to finish it. Reading it was like the experience she had

---

1 A person who attended Texas A&M (Agricultural and Mechanical) University in College Station, Texas

2 Before she battled vampires, Kate Beckinsale played Emma in a 1996 ITV television adaptation

when a child and her mother forced her to finish the meatloaf she'd made, chock-a-block with onions and green peppers. She shared her distaste for onions and green peppers with her father and her mother usually kept those vegetables to a minimum, but her father was out of town on a business trip and her mother decided to make meatloaf the way she liked it. Mary sat at the table for three hours, forced to finish the cold meatloaf with appropriate adolescent histrionics.

She never understood why her mother destroyed something perfectly good—hamburger slathered with ketchup—with something so fundamentally awful.

Miss Bates was like onions and green peppers. Mary detested the woman. She reminded Mary of Mrs Henley, a neighbour, who would corral Mary's mother on the porch for long conversations. They'd be on their way to the store and Mrs Henley would want to tell them stories about her son who was in a private school. She told them about his grades and his athletic activities until Mary would start tugging at her mother's hand, eager to get away. But her mother would nod agreeably and ask questions that would prolong the agony.

After they finally escaped, Mary would ask her mother why she stayed to listen to Mrs Henley, and her mother would say it never hurts to be polite.

She contemplated just skipping the entire page-long paragraph but she sighed and read it anyway, not with any great attention admittedly. She decided her mother was right. It never hurts to be polite, even if you do force your daughter to eat onions and green peppers.

Mary looked to the empty seat beside her, hoping Jane hadn't noticed the sigh and deduced the cause. She didn't fear Jane's disapprobation. She just didn't want to be drawn into another long discussion about the book and why she didn't like it.

But Jane said nothing and Mary assumed she was either trying to write or in a chat with the other disembodied passengers. Mary eventually gave up trying to read and instead closed her eyes, but without the distraction of the book her mind wandered to the topic she couldn't escape.

Jane and Melody had finally addressed the question of what would happen after the AGM: they'd offered to buy Mary's remaining contract with the agency if Mary would agree to be Jane's avatar for a further five years.

"I can't imagine anyone else who could be Jane's avatar," Melody had told her. "Everybody, including me, thinks you're great and you and Jane obviously get along. Even I forget who I'm talking to sometimes."

Which was not necessarily the right thing for Melody to say. More than ever, Mary was determined that she didn't want to be trapped into playing Jane forever. And yet, she could not imagine her feelings if she saw another avatar take on the role.

True, Jane and Melody had said they had no plans to seek another avatar, but Mary wondered if their resolve would hold once the promotion for the *Sanditon* movie began or Jane finally finished her "something new."

This must be what it's like to play James Bond, she realized, but she had the further complication that she had become best friends with the director, screenwriter and producer.

"Ladies and gentlemen, we've just begun our descent to DFW," the flight attendant who'd talked to Mary said over the intercom. He then put on a Texas drawl that mimicked the voice of the pilot. "Please move your seats back to the upright position, replace your trays to the locked position and give your seat belts an extra tug. Yee haw!"

The plane's descent angle steepened, the controls on the wings made their usual alarming sound and Mary willed away her thoughts and worries. Whatever happened later, she had one final performance of the book tour coming up and she was going to make it her best yet.

· Fort Worth I ·
Albert arrives

lbert realized his difficulty once he arrived at the ground transportation pickup area. Although he felt justifiably proud of his planning, he realized he'd not researched how he would get to the hotel. Back home, he knew his bus routes by heart or could easily text a taxi to deliver him wherever needed. But confronted with the confusion of the Dallas-Fort Worth airport, he realized he would need to find a public terminal and determine what bus to take or go to the expense of arranging a taxi or airport shuttle.

But then he saw the four women standing together near the Super-Shuttle pickup stand and thought he might be in luck. Three of the women were of that certain age and from their clothing and deportment he thought they might be Janeites also just arrived and awaiting transport for the hotel. The fourth woman, by contrast, was much younger, with multicoloured hair and wearing low slung jeans and a midriff revealing T-shirt that would normally make her an unlikely candidate to be a Janeite, but the words "Dead leaves!" on her T-shirt proved her to be part of the group.[1]

He decided to join them and jumped inside before the doors closed.

---

1   In *Sense and Sensibility*, Elinor and Marianne Dashwood ask Edward Ferrars of news of Norland (the home the Dashwood sisters vacated upon the death of their father):

Once the driver was on his way the thought occurred to him that the women might not be staying at the Renaissance Worthington, but a glance at the itinerary being referred to by one of the ladies listed the hotel. He settled into the back of the van, perched atop the luggage, and observed the women. They were all happily chatting, almost certainly about the AGM or Jane or both in that spontaneous communion common to Janeites. He wished he might join them but reasoned he'd soon have the opportunity to talk about Jane once he reached the hotel.

Unfortunately that opportunity was delayed because their van never left the airport on their first or second attempt. The driver kept returning to the airport, visiting two of the five terminals, and picking up additional passengers. It was not until their third time returning to the airport that the van, now laden with six women and one man, left the airport for the interstate and the drive to Fort Worth.

Despite the ridiculous cowboy hat worn by the man, he also appeared to be a Janeite judging by his instant rapport with most of the women. The last woman to have entered the van was by the same measure very obviously not a Janeite. Albert thought he detected the common explanation, "We're here for a Jane Austen convention. She was a writer in the English Regency. No, she's not appearing at the convention, she's been dead two hundred years."

But then he realized that explanation would now need to be amended to include Jane's presence. The anticipation of her presence might also explain the very animated appearance of his fellow attendees. Again he wished that he might join them.

The van arrived at the Worthington without incident and deposited Albert, three of the original group of four women (the younger

---

"Dear, dear Norland," said Elinor, "probably looks much as it always does at this time of the year. The woods and walks thickly covered with dead leaves."

"Oh," cried Marianne, "with what transporting sensation have I formerly seen them fall! How have I delighted, as I walked, to see them driven in showers about me by the wind! What feelings have they, the season, the air altogether inspired! Now there is no one to regard them. They are seen only as a nuisance, swept hastily off, and driven as much as possible from the sight."

"It is not every one," said Elinor, "who has your passion for dead leaves."

one would presumably stay at another hotel) and the man wearing the cowboy hat. The women did not proceed to the registration desk but the man did, and Albert followed. As he approached the desk, he felt an AfterNet field and was welcomed.

"Good morning, how may I help you?" an anonymous someone asked.

"Uh, I'm Albert Ridings and I'm checking in for the Jane Austen convention."

"Very good sir, but registration for the disembodied is being handled by your group. If you'll return to the escalators next to the main entrance and go up one floor and across the bridge to the convention centre, you'll find the registration desk."

"Oh, thank you," Albert replied, a little disconcerted about not needing to register with the hotel. He really didn't know what to expect, this being the first time he'd ever actually officially stayed at a hotel.

He retraced his way back to the escalator and stared at it with misgivings. He preferred stairs to the rather tricky process of moving his insubstantial self in time with the steps. But he didn't want to hunt for the stairs and find himself wandering aimlessly. He stepped forward and willed himself to remain in place against the steps. He was halfway up when someone running up dislodged him and he found himself sliding down the metal divider between the up and down escalators. He was unceremoniously dumped at the bottom and understandably cursed.

He looked around and saw the stairs that led up to what appeared to be a restaurant that perched over the hotel lobby. He took the stairs, a much easier proposition than the constantly changing purchase of the escalator steps, and emerged onto what was probably a breakfast/lunch serving area. But another short flight of stairs led up to the same level the escalator serviced and after a few simple turns he found himself facing the walkway that joined the hotel side to the convention centre. He quickly found the registration desk and felt another AfterNet field.

"And who do we have here? Welcome to the AGM. I'm Stephanie. And your name is …"

He realized the field was attached to a full AfterNet terminal and could see that Stephanie was disembodied and that her username was pemberleydreamz. On the registration desk he located the terminal, probably unnoticed by the living.

"Uh, Albert Ridings."

"Very nice to meet you Albert. Are you registered?"

"Yes."

"OK, you can either log on to the AfterNet and I can look you up that way, or if you can remember your confirmation number, I can register you that way. I'd recommend logging into the AfterNet."

"Of course," he said, and quickly logged in.

"OK, Albert, you're good to go. I've sent you an email with the password you'll need to access all the hotspots in the main ballroom and all the breakout sessions. And it includes the virtual goody bag and also an invitation to the first timer's chat tonight and tomorrow night."

"I'm not a first timer," he objected.

"What? Oh, no, we're all first timers now. This is the first time the disembodied have been able to register separately so they decided we all get to be considered first timers. Have you been coming to the AGMs for a while?"

"This is my third time."

"Oh well, in that case … hold on … OK, would you like to maybe help out some of the real first timers?"

"I'd be delighted."

"What a gentleman you are, Albert. I'm sending your name to Patrick … whose last name I can't remember. He's the coordinator for the disembodied and he'll probably email you or text you or something … and I checked, we've got all your contact info. I hope you have a nice time."

"Thank you. Oh, I have a roommate?"

"Sure, sure. Hold on, what do I do if you have a roommate? Let me look it up … oh, this is simple, your roommate is Stephen Abrams and it says here he's already checked in and let me email you his contact information and let me forward you his picture so you can recognize him and the password for his portable terminal and you're all set."

Albert thanked Stephanie for her help, although he was a bit overwhelmed by it, and then immediately used the terminal to access all the information she'd just provided. He didn't need Stephen's information, but he did use the terminal to send him a text saying he'd arrived at the hotel. Then he sent Jane an email saying he'd arrived.

He also looked at the schedule included in his virtual goodie bag—really just a lot of attachments to his confirmation email. There wasn't much going on yet. Although he had much in common with the women at the AGM—and it was mostly women—he had no interest in the first group activity that afternoon, a visit to a doll museum. He hoped that he might meet Stephen or even better Jane soon, although he supposed it was possible Jane might be interested in a doll museum.

He decided to spend some time in the dealers' rooms. There were three rooms and from the listing, he thought one room mostly sold books; one sold clothing, posters and knickknacks; and the last said it sold Texas curiosities.

Naturally he went to the book room first. He remembered his first time to an AGM in 1992 and before the discovery of the afterlife. He was just a lonely ghost then and all he could do was look at the book covers and try to get a sense of the content and hope he could find someone reading a copy. Of course at that time, much of the Jane Austen fan fiction was very casual and some of it was just Xeroxed copies. Looking at the wealth of fan fiction today was very different, as was the young lady holding a portable terminal who stood beside a table heavily laden with books. He caught the field and realized her terminal was set to anonymous access.

Beryl says:
> No, I haven't read that one yet. Who did you say wrote it?

Albert looked at the ID badge the woman wore that identified her as a vendor. It said Beryl and he realized she was in conversation with someone, and since no one living was around, surmised it was another disembodied person.

susannovick says:
> Karen Amon-something. She's English. It's from the viewpoint of Charlotte Lucas and how she's dealing with being married to Mr Collins. I wish I could remember her last name.
> BertieFromHants has joined.

BertieFromHants says:
> It's Aminadra, I think. Karen Aminadra. I read it, it's very good. I got a little uncomfortable with where I thought it was going, but it never went there.

Beryl says:
> Well thank you, sir? I'll look into that Susan, it might be an author we want to pick up.

susannovick says:

OK, ta Beryl.

susannovick has left.

Beryl says:

Bye Susan. So, thank you, Bertie?

BertieFromHants says:

Yes, Albert Ridings. You're welcome. This is your table?

Beryl says:

Yes, the Longbourn Circulating Library. Everything is 10 percent off.

BertieFromHants says:

Oh, good, it's just I don't buy many physical books. Sometimes for my grandchildren.

Beryl says:

Oh, we've got several good books for children.

She walked to the other end of the table and opened a book with brightly coloured drawings.

Beryl says:

It's a Cinderella/Mansfield Park mashup, with Fanny Price as Cinderella. Well it's a natural isn't it?

Albert had to admit Beryl was a good saleswoman, for he bought two books for his great-great-granddaughter and learned of another that he would buy as an e-book from Beryl's website. The books would be mailed, of course.

He spent almost thirty minutes talking to Beryl and was joined by another woman asking if Beryl had an audiobook available. Albert thought he should excuse himself while Beryl helped a living customer, but Beryl introduced the woman to Albert and they held a strange conversation with Beryl as their intermediary.

Albert left the room thirty-five dollars poorer but with a warm glow. It was the first time since his death that he'd actually bought something from a person in a real-time exchange, rather than over the Internet. If he did not have Jane's and Stephen's company to look forward to, he would be happy to deem the AGM a success already.

Once outside, he made for the terminal he'd earlier used to register and found that he'd received an email from Stephen.

Albert,
Glad you made it here safely. I'm in the hotel bar with your roommates.
Come on down and meet the crew.
Stephen

Albert walked back from the convention centre and toward the lobby and from there found the way to the hotel restaurant. He entered and looked around for Stephen and found him by virtue of his being a man sitting alone at a round table set for six. He appeared to be talking and Albert guessed the portable terminal before him was capturing his words.

BertieFromHants has joined.
BeauAbrams says:
Albert! Another of our merry band has arrived.

Stephen stood from his chair and offered a little bow, which Albert found charming, although the effect was a little spoiled by the bow not being remotely bent in his direction. Albert also saw that each of the empty place settings bore a little tent-folded placard with a name scrawled in marker pen. He found his name and took his seat.

BertieFromHants says:
Good to meet you, Stephen. And the name cards are a smart idea. Who else is here?
AlanJTimison says:
Hi Albert, Alan here.
WalkLikeADuck says:
Hello Bertie. Rob Perkins. Nice to meet you in person, so to speak.
mikechapman says:
Good to meet you too, Albert.
orribleiggins says:
pip, pip, Albert old boy
BeauAbrams says:
Ted Alexander gets here tomorrow
WalkLikeADuck says:
Bertie, you just missed Stephen's admission. He's been dating Jane's avatar.

That statement made look Albert look at Stephen, who was clearly embarrassed. He also realized that Stephen's behaviour, sitting alone at a table for six and talking to himself, had attracted the attention of several people in the restaurant.

BertieFromHants says:
> This is a surprise, Stephen. You might have mentioned something ... wait, is this the woman you met on your ... conference.

AlanJTimison says:
> Oh, at the romance writer's conference.

BeauAbram says:
> Why did I ever make the mistake of befriending you lot? And Rob, I never said I was dating her, just that I'd met her a few times.

mikechapman says:
> Oh, now it's a few times. So have you met her employer?

orribleiggins says:
> she's definitely easy on the eyses

BeauAbrams says:
> At the book signing in Chicago, yes, obviously through Mary.

BertieFromHants says:
> I forgot her name is Mary Crawford. And very lovely I recall from seeing pictures of her. So you've known her since Austen was in Chicago.

The men continued this way for some time, enjoying the sight of Stephen's embarrassment. They eventually extracted from Stephen a promise of a personal introduction to Jane's avatar. Then they moved to the more practical matter of how Stephen would share his room with them.

WalkLikeADuck says:
> Remember, hang a tie around the door knob if you want to be alone.

BeauAbrams says:
> Thanks, Rob, I'll do that. OK, so tonight we're all going to the rodeo bar, but as I said, no bull. And no, Miss Crawford will not be in attendance. Maybe I'll dance with her at the Regency ball.

AlanJTimison says:
> If it's all the same, I will miss the rodeo bar. I had hoped to meet someone while here in Fort Worth.

mikechapman says:

Why you sly dog, Alan. But say no more, I will respect your privacy. But how will you get back in the hotel room when you return late at night?

AlanJTimison says:

Ahem, I might not get back till morning.

BeauAbrams says:

And with that, I call this meeting to a close. I'm going up to the room to take a shower. If anyone wants to come up, follow me, otherwise I'll be back down here in half an hour.

· Fort Worth II ·
Jane arrives

Jane followed Mary through the airport slowly and at a considerable distance. Anxiety, guilt and fatigue dogged her steps, making her feel as if she were moving in a dream. She knew full well the reasons for her apprehension and had been weighing them since the plane landed: depression that even after a successful book tour, she still must fight to defend her identity; worry that Mary still had not come to a decision about remaining her avatar; anxiety that she remained uninspired; and most of all, guilt that she had yet to confess to Albert.

She had chatted with him two nights previous, in penance for all her missed or abbreviated chats with him. He was excited about the AGM and wanted to know which breakout sessions she would be attending. She knew her reply was tepid, but truly, could topics such as—"Talk silly like Mrs Jennings"[1] or "The Secret Agenda of Austen's Card Games"—excite her? She needed no lessons to talk like Mrs Jennings and she didn't think she had a secret agenda depending on whether her characters played *vingt-et-un* or whist or lottery tickets. *Well, maybe lottery tickets.*[2] She could understand why Janeites might

---

1 This was actually an enjoyable breakout session at the AGM
2 In *Pride and Prejudice*, Lydia Bennet was fond of playing lottery tickets, a card game of no skill and well suited to the silly, youngest Bennet sister

find such topics entertaining, but that did not mean she could gin up much enthusiasm.

She knew she was being excessively tetchy, but once in her funk, it was hard to escape her mood. And then she realized that she could no longer see Mary ahead of her. She rose a little above the crowd but still could see no sign of her. She was not overly concerned, however, as she assumed Mary would proceed to the baggage claim area. But in the process of looking around for Mary, Jane had disoriented herself.

She tried to recall anything about the airport but other than remembering that DFW was one of America's busiest airports, she knew nothing. Ordinarily while travelling by herself, Jane would plan ahead, committing to memory the layout of the airports and cities she would visit, but she had failed to do so this time, an indication of the extent to which she depended upon Mary. She soon reached the end of the semi-circular terminal and then went back in the other direction and saw a sign indicating in which direction the baggage claim area lay. After a few minutes, she saw Mary.

In her imagination, Jane had supposed she would find Mary anxiously looking in the crowd for her invisible employer, but instead she found Mary standing behind the luggage carrousel, waiting with a frown on her face, her arms crossed and her suitcase already retrieved. Jane realized Mary's expression almost mirrored her own as captured by Cassandra's watercolour.

Jane captured the field of Mary's terminal and was prepared to offer her apology for getting lost but Mary's remark interrupted her: "Honestly Jane, I told you to stay by me. What would Melody do to me if I lost you just before the AGM?"

Her words wiped any thought Jane had of apologizing and instead she started to say, "She would say it's your fault for losing me." But the kindness of fate intervened when someone reaching for his luggage brushed her aside and disconnected her from Mary's terminal.

Jane wasn't sure quite how much of her remark was transmitted so as soon as she reconnected to Mary's terminal, she said, "She would accuse us both of not paying attention, with some justification. I'm sorry Mary, I'm afraid I am not looking forward to the AGM."

"Why? What's worrying you? I mean beyond the obvious." She extended the handle on her suitcase and started walking away from the luggage carrousel. "Let's exit here and I can look for a taxi," she added, pointing in the direction of the exit. Originally they were supposed to be picked up by a JASNA volunteer but their delayed flight had made that impossible.

Jane followed and said, "It is the end of the tour and my best hope for convincing Janeites that I really am Jane and ... and you still haven't said whether you will continue as my avatar and ..."

"We still have time to talk about that," Mary said. She avoided looking toward where Jane should be.

"Please don't put it off much longer. I realize the airport is hardly an appropriate time or place, but you asked what concerned me, and this is one of my worries."

They now stood outside the terminal and Mary looked for a sign indicating where she would find a taxi stand. She had looked up the airport terminal layout the previous night and guessed it would be to her left and soon saw a sign indicating she had remembered correctly. A taxi was pulling up just as she arrived and soon they were on their way to the hotel.

Inside the cab, rather than employ the ruse of talking on her phone, Mary communicated with Jane directly through her terminal. Fortunately the driver seemed more interested in his country-western music than conversation.

"OK, you have a lot on your plate, but didn't you fail to mention your argument with your boyfriend?"

Mary regretted her words immediately. She wasn't quite sure why she'd thought it, but that was an increasing danger as she'd become so proficient with the terminal.

"I'm sorry, that's none of my business."

"How did you know ..." Jane asked, and realized that her words now made it impossible to refute.

Mary turned to look at Jane, smiled and said, "Well we share the same computer. You might want to clear your browsing history, or at least remember to close the window after you chat."

"Oh, yes. I suppose I did forget to do that."

"But that wasn't my only clue. You're a lot different after you talk to him, assuming Bertie is a him."

"Yes, Albert is a gentleman. And what do you mean I'm different? Do I have a glow about me?"

"You make a lot more jokes and are generally sillier. And today you're grouchy, so I guessed you had an argument."

Jane said nothing in reply, surprised that her friend had observed so much of her.

"So what was the argument about?"

"There was no argument, only a little ... there is some awkwardness ... oh Mary, I have not told him I am Jane Austen."

"What?" Mary said out loud. Her exclamation caught the attention of the driver who turned down his radio.

"Is there something wrong, ma'am?" he asked.

"Just wondering how much farther to the hotel," Mary responded.

He assured her it was only another ten minutes and returned the radio to its previous volume.

"What? You haven't told him?" Mary asked silently. "Who is this guy anyway?"

Jane gave Mary a quick explanation of her relationship with Albert and Mary had to make sure she did not vocalize any "oohs" and "ahs" at how cute she thought their friendship.

"So you haven't told him you're *the* Jane Austen. He still thinks you're some crazed Austen fangirl."

"I don't think that is his impression of me."

"So more to the point, why haven't you told him?"

"It's ... complicated."

"Oh my God, that's got to be the most modern-sounding thing I've ever heard you say. Jane Austen says, 'It's complicated.'"

"Well it is. And it is further complicated by the fact that I have ... recast my success as a consequence of my employment."

"Come again?"

"I have explained my many absences by saying that the pressures of my new job ..."

"You've lied to him? Where are you supposed to be working?"

Jane explained the fiction of her job as an editor at Random House. The more she explained, the deeper was her shame. She almost could feel her cheeks burning.

Mary was more than a little amazed. Even though she knew the real Jane Austen could be irreverent, dark, acerbic and even occasionally profane, she always thought of Jane as someone who steered a narrow course. To discover a Jane who made up whoppers was a revelation.

"You do know the phrase 'the best laid plans,' don't you?"

"Yes, I am familiar with Burns, and it's schemes, not plans."

"You don't love him, do you Jane?"

The question shook Jane, but she answered quickly, "What an absurd question."

"It's just that usually people do the stupidest things when they love someone. And if you don't mind me saying, that's like *I Love Lucy* crazy."

Jane had no idea who the Lucy Mary referenced might be, but she denied any similarity.

~

Melody tapped on the door and waited anxiously for Mary to open it. She smiled weakly at two women who walked down the hallway, their JASNA badges hanging prominently from their necks. Both were wearing I Believe in Jane buttons. They returned Melody's smile as they passed.

Mary opened the door and Melody quickly stepped inside.

"Hi Mel," Mary said, but Melody stopped her from saying anything further.

"Put Jane on speaker," she told Mary.

"Uh, OK." Mary went back to the suite's desk where her terminal was plugged into her laptop. She sent the output of the terminal to play through the computer's speakers.

"Everything's arranged for tomorrow," Melody said without preamble. "Davis has agreed to meet ... even without a representative from the AfterNet."

"Excuse me?" Mary exclaimed. "She wanted someone from the AfterNet!"

"I did not know this," Jane said.

"I didn't want to worry you any more than was necessary. Thank God for bureaucracy. There's a lot involved to overrule an AfterNet certification so despite Davis's theatrics ... so it's just the JASNA president and what's her name ... the regional coordinator."

"Cindy Wallace," Jane supplied. "No one else?"

"That's all."

"Oh, that's good, right?" Mary asked.

Melody laughed and said, "How do I know? I mean she's banking everything on convincing two people Jane's not Jane. Does that mean she's desperate or does it mean she's so sure ... I just know that the Fort

Worth organizers are happy to have it decided quietly. They don't want a cat fight in front of the members."

"They could just refuse to let her talk," Mary said.

"That would raise a stink too. No, we have to defuse this now. I'm afraid I let this get out of hand. I should have been on top of it."

"It is not your fault," Jane said. "Dr Davis has made up her mind that I am an impostor. Past a certain point, it is impossible to change a person's belief."

"But what kind of proof does she have to make an accusation like this?" Mary asked.

"It doesn't matter. I can only assume that being a scholar, Dr Davis believes she has credible reason to discredit me. Melody, has the nature ... the format of this meeting been decided?"

"Yes, Davis wants to make her accusations in front of witnesses—I've asked Alan if he can be here as well—and she wants it recorded. And when she ends up humiliated, she agrees not to say anything during her break out session."

"And what if I'm humiliated?" asked Jane. "And by that, I am not confessing that I am an impostor. I merely posit the possibility that she has evidence I cannot refute."

Mary and Melody looked at where they imagined Jane to be.

"We stand by you, Jane," Melody said. "My faith in you remains, since that first query letter you sent me. I got a shiver down my back that day and I've never lost that feeling."

Mary said, "And I've shared a room with you and been your voice for nine months. You're a decent and honourable person and I believe in you and ... and being you is a privilege I hope I have for a long time to come."

"Thank you both. You make me realize that Jane Austen is more than just one person. It requires the work of three."

· Showdown ·
Jane confronts her accuser

Melody walked back and forth within the confines of the small conference room the hotel had provided for their confrontation with Dr Davis.

"She's making me nervous," Mary said to Jane, silently.

"Allow her her pacing." Jane replied. "It is preferable to her tapping her teeth."

"Ugh. I hate that. How about you? Are you OK?"

Jane decided to put a brave face on it. "Please do not worry about me. Being dead makes one philosophic. What's the worst that could happen? But I admit I do worry about the reputation of ... and do not be alarmed if I slip into the third person ... I worry about the reputation of Jane. I would rather relinquish my claim if I could avoid the ignominy of an argument before the members here assembled."

"You're not giving up are you? I meant what I said before. I can't imagine not representing you, for as long as you'll let me."

"I will do what is necessary ..."

The door opened, stopping Melody's pacing and interrupting Jane. Ajala Johnsson and Cindy Wallace entered, both looking troubled. They were about to close the door behind them when Alan Pembroke entered.

"Alan!" Melody cried. "You made it."

"Of course. I couldn't let you deal with this on your own. You need moral support. Mary, how are you? And Jane?"

Mary quickly put Jane on speaker.

"Thank you for coming, Alan," Jane's voice said. "It is a terrible imposition on your time."

"You're really my only author, Jane. I couldn't possibly stay away. But who are these ladies?" he asked. He beamed at them in his Uncle Gardiner way and they cast aside their dour looks.

"Alan Pembroke, with Random House. I know you, Ms Johnsson, from my JASNA newsletter. And you must be …"

"Cindy Wallace, the regional coordinator for North Texas."

"Good to meet you. Sorry it must be under contentious circumstances, but we'll soon sort this out."

The women nodded in agreement, a little flustered by his attention and his seeming implication they would sort things in Jane's favour.

"Er, perhaps you should remove those buttons," he observed, and vaguely pointed. "It might unnecessarily antagonize Dr Davis." They both looked down at their "I Believe in Jane" buttons in surprise, and then hurriedly removed them.

The door opened again and admitted Stephen Abrams.

"What are *you* doing here?" Mary demanded. He paused in the doorway, uncertain what to do.

"I asked him to attend," Jane explained. "I believe him to be blameless in all this, as he has tried to explain to you. He had the good sense to contact me and may truly be a third party. After all, he has fallen out of favour with Dr Davis and you certainly do not care for him."

Ms Johnsson and Ms Wallace understandably were confused by this exchange and also unnerved by Jane's digitized voice. To date, all their transactions with the famous author had been with Mary or with Jane via email. To hear her flat, digitized voice was disturbing.

Mr Pembroke approached Stephen and offered his hand. "Alan Pembroke. I have no idea who you are, but Jane seems to vouch for you."

"Uh, nice to meet you. Stephen Abrams. Dr Davis is my graduate advisor."

"Oh. That puts you between a rock and a hard place, doesn't it?"

"Yeah, I guess it does." He turned to address Mary. "Look, I really knew nothing about this. You've got to believe me."

"Time for that later, young man," Mr Pembroke observed. Stephen had left the door open and standing in the doorway were Alice Davis and Courtney Blake. As in a Western movie trope, all conversation in the room had stopped and everyone was staring at the new arrivals.

"Dr Davis, please come in," Ms Johnsson said with a hesitant smile. Her words broke the impasse and Alice and Courtney entered.

"Dr Davis, I think you know Cindy Wallace, the North Texas regional coordinator."

"We've talked," Alice said, and curtly nodded to Ms Wallace.

"And you are ..." Ms Johnsson said to Courtney, unsure who the man was.

"Courtney Blake," he supplied. "You may have read my book, *The Real Jane Austen*."

"I haven't had the ... pleasure yet," Ms Johnsson said, frostily. She then introduced them to Mr Pembroke.

"So glad you could come," he said, as if he'd invited them to dinner. He shook hands with Alice and tried to hide his wince occasioned by her firm grip. Then he turned to Courtney. "I'm afraid I'm unaware of your involvement in this, Mr Blake."

"He's with me," Alice said, as if that explained it all.

Courtney coughed and said, "Actually I'm the one who found the documents."

"What documents?" Mr Pembroke asked.

He was about to offer further information but was stopped by a cold look and a question from Alice: "And where is Miss Austen?"

Mary almost spoke up but remembered Jane wanted to be on her own for this.

"I am directly before you, Dr Davis. I appreciate your coming and allowing us to resolve this privately," Jane said.

Alice was unfazed at Austen's "voice," but Courtney took a half step back.

"I make no promise to keep this private. In fact, events outside my control will make it very public."

"Well, that's as may be. Now may I introduce my avatar, Mary Crawford."

Mary stepped forward and extended her arm. They shook hands quickly. "You should be taller," Alice said, and her eyes dismissed Mary.

"Is that video camera working?" Alice suddenly asked, and pointed to a camera on a tripod in a corner of the room.

Ms Johnsson responded, "Not yet, I'll turn it on, if you insist."

"Perhaps ... Stephen, would you mind filming what will transpire here?"

Stephen was taken aback by the request from his mentor. He felt like she was trying to make him a party to her accusations.

"That's an excellent suggestion," Jane said. "Would you be so kind, Mr Abrams?"

Stephen nodded his agreement after some hesitation. Ms Johnsson then took the camera from the tripod and gave him some quick instructions.

Once the camera was recording, Alice continued. "We can resolve this in a matter of minutes, if Miss Austen can simply identify a certain document and give a brief description—just an outline—of what the document is about. "

"You've found an Austen manuscript?" Cindy Wallace asked.

"I found it," Blake answered. He put his messenger bag on the conference table and took out an accordion file. From the file, he extracted a photograph of a piece of yellowed paper. A ruler in the photograph showed that the paper was small, about four by five inches. The two JASNA woman stood and gasped.

"Journal of Jane Bigg-Wither," Stephen read softly.

"Please point the camera at the document, Stephen," Alice instructed him.

"What the hell is this?" Melody demanded.

"That's for Miss Austen to tell us," Alice said.

"I have never seen this before, Dr Davis."

"And yet it's in your own hand."

"Prove that," Melody said.

"It's already proven," Alice said. "Court, show them the Sotheby's report."

He produced another item from the accordion file. Everyone could see it was written on letterhead bearing the name of the London auctioneers and appraisers. Stephen grabbed the report and began studying it.

"According to Sotheby's it's written in Austen's hand," he said, "and they should be familiar with it, as they just sold *The Watsons*. It's also written on paper and with ink authentic to the period."

While he was saying this, the camera was untrained and Alice quietly reached out to point the camera back toward the document.

"That is as may be, but I am still unfamiliar with this," Jane said.

"I admit that appears to be my handwriting, but I most certainly did not write it."

"I think I've proved my point," Alice said.

Stephen objected: "Excuse me, but you haven't proven anything." He trained the camera on his mentor. "Miss Austen says she didn't write it and this report only says they can't prove it isn't genuine."

"How is that different from the proof this woman provided the AfterNet? How do any of us know what she told them? Presumably she told them something only Jane Austen can know. Well I say only Jane Austen would know what was in this journal and if this woman will just offer a brief outline, then you will have my apology."

"Well where's the rest of it?" Mary asked.

"Safe at Sotheby's. Did you think I would bring it with me?"

"This is insane," Melody said. "Are you seriously trying to defame Jane with this?"

Ms Wallace said, "I have to agree. Dr Davis, you can't make these accusations against Miss Austen in your presentation."

"I never said that I would."

"Where did you get this anyway?" Stephen asked.

Courtney cleared his throat and said, "From an old woman in Leicestershire, England. Her mother left it to her … and not much else. Here, I have photos of the despatch boxes I found them in. It's about three hundred pages in all."

He produced the photos from his bag and handed them to Stephen, who eagerly took them.

Ms Johnsson tried to return to Alice's denial: "Are you saying you didn't tell Cindy you were planning to 'expose' Miss Austen?"

Now Alice looked momentarily confused and said, "I may have … misspoken. I realize that making such an accusation at the AGM would cause a commotion."

"Oh, so you've brought us here for nothing," Melody said.

Melody's sharp words roused Alice. She said, "On the contrary, I've accomplished my purpose of putting you on notice, in front of witnesses, that I do object to this woman being proclaimed as Jane Austen."

"Stop calling me … her … 'this woman,'" Mary protested.

"Ms Johnsson, please put a stop to this. If this woman"—and here Melody pointed to Alice—"has no other proof …"

Now Alice smiled broadly. "I never said I had no other proof. I would be happy to give Miss Austen another opportunity to prove her identity." She said "Miss Austen" very deliberately.

"Court, show them the letter."

Courtney produced yet another photo from his bag, this time of what appeared to be a letter. The letter, which had been folded, was laid flat. The recipient was plainly visible, but the rest of the writing had been intentionally blurred. He also produced another photo of the letter in a small battered frame. The letter was folded so that only the recipient was visible.

"And before you ask, the original is now at the British Library in London. So, Miss Austen, do you recognize this?"

Jane had difficulty seeing because the others were passing the photos back and forth or were hunched over them.

"If you might put them in the middle of the table?" she asked.

Ms Johnsson placed them as directed and Jane looked at them closely.

"How did you get this? I thought Cassandra ... yes, I do recognize it."

"You do?" Alice asked, the look of surprise on her face evident to everyone in the room. She took several seconds before she said anything further. "Then prove it. What does it say?"

"I would rather not ..."—her accuser saying "Ha!" interrupted her—"... but as you put me on the spot. You must realize I never intended to send it. Once I began, I knew it would be too cruel to Mr Bigg-Wither and would drive a wedge between our families. I am ashamed I ever wrote it, but I kept it as a reminder that the sharpest wits should remained sheathed. I assumed Cassandra had burned it."

"Oh Jane, everyone's done something they're ashamed of," Mary said.

"Precisely," Melody said. "I hope this satisfies you, Dr Davis."

Although she was obviously surprised by the turn of events, Alice rallied.

"No, I'm not satisfied, not unless she can remember specifically what she said in the letter."

"It's a little much to ask that she remember what she wrote two hundred years ago," Mr Pembroke objected.

"She famously recalled *Sanditon* from memory," Alice countered.

And then Jane said: "'Were I to marry you, Mr Bigg-Wither, it would be an abdication of those principles by which I have apparently chosen to live my life. Without consciously intending it, I have decided that marriage without love is a betrayal, and I can assure you our marriage would bring neither of us love. That I might have affection for you is entirely possible and that you might return that affection is also possible, but love is out of the question.'

"Is that sufficient to convince you that I am the author of that letter? Or must I betray the portions of the letter that … is it sufficient?"

As Jane had spoken, it was obvious that her accuser recognized those words.

Alice now stood, slowly.

"Where are you, Miss Austen? Where are you now?"

"I stand to the left of my friend, Ms Kramer."

Alice turned to the empty spot so indicated, and said, "It is sufficient. I am … I think those are the exact words …"

"Near enough," Jane said.

Alice swallowed, trying to understand the enormity of what she'd just accomplished.

"I was wrong," she said quietly.

"But what about the journals?" Courtney asked in a small voice, and then louder, "She still hasn't explained that."

An exclamation from Stephen drew everyone's attention. He'd been recording his mentor's admission and now lowered the camera. "Ha! I knew the name sounded familiar. He's in the missing and returned inventory from Virtual Chawton."

Stephen put down the camera and picked up his tablet. "Give me a second. Thank God I synced it." He was furiously tapping the screen of the device. "Got it!"

He put the tablet on the table.

"Dr Davis had me looking through the inventory, to see what Miss Austen might have used to prove her identity." His remark elicited an angry look from Mary.

"It was before we met," he said in reply to the look. "Anyway, I remembered the name Gorrell-Barmes, the name on the despatch box." He pointed to one of the photos that displayed the name painted on the lid of one of the boxes.

"It's here in the inventory, look."

He enlarged the image of the ledger sheet that was displayed on his tablet. A blurry handwritten entry showed: "Returned to Major Gorrell-Barmes, SOE, the 'journal': Good riddance to bad rubbish."

"The Jane Austen Society in the UK must have owned it at one time. They were formed to save Chawton Cottage and must have found it."

"Excuse me, what's Virtual Chawton?" Mr Pembroke asked. Stephen explained about the project to put everything Chawton related online.

"Presumably then if they returned the thing to this major ..." Mr Pembroke said thoughtfully.

"You mean it's a fake?" Cindy Wallace asked.

Melody answered, "Absolutely. If they didn't want an 'original' Austen manuscript and called it bad rubbish then it's a sure bet they knew it was a fake." She turned to Alice. "My God, if you'd just asked your graduate student to look it up ... what a monumental waste of time."

Alice didn't reply. She took a seat at the table.

Melody was not finished, however. She leaned in close to the woman and asked, "Do you know how much damage ..."

"Enough, Melody," Jane said. "Enough."

Mary put a hand on Melody's shoulder and gently moved her away from the woman.

"No, I don't think we're quite done," Stephen said. "What did you mean earlier, that events beyond your control would make it public?"

But Alice said nothing and Stephen asked again, "Dr Davis? What did you mean?"

"Uh, she meant the sale of the journal," Courtney said. "Sotheby's was going to announce tomorrow ... its discovery ... a teaser before they announce it's for sale."

"Then maybe you ought to tell them it's a fake," Stephen said. "What about the letter?"

"Like she said, with the British Library. Mrs Westerby ... the old lady who owns it ... she was going to give it to the library and sell the journal. I guess now she'll just sell ..."

"If you would be so kind, Mr Blake, please tell her I will buy it," Jane said. "If she is a descendant of the Gorrell family ..."

"Yes, of course. Right." He gathered up the photos and put them back in his messenger bag. "Well then, best we are off, Dr Davis."

He helped her to stand and then turned to address the others. "I'll notify Sotheby's. I'm sorry ... about the trouble. I thought ..."

"I thought it was genuine," Alice said, "because it served my purpose. Yes Court, we should go."

· Falling on his sword ·
Stephen begs forgiveness

"Please Mary, I had no idea what she was up to, you've got to believe me."

Mary tried to ignore him as she collected the terminal from the middle of the table and disconnected the speakers. The only people left in the room were herself, Stephen and presumably Jane.

"I haven't talked to her for two weeks. Hell, I didn't even know about this ... showdown until I got a phone call from Austen telling me to come to this meeting."

"Jane called you?" she asked, not looking at Stephen while she searched for her earbuds.

"Yes ... which is pretty weird. There's something about talking to a dead person over the phone that's unsettling."

Mary finally found the earbuds in her bag and inserted them.

"They prefer to be called disembodied," Mary said, but not very loudly.

"Do not be tiresome, Mary," Jane told her. "And let the poor man explain himself."

"We have that BBC film crew coming up to the room in thirty minutes and I have to get ready," Mary silently said to Jane.

"That's not as important as you talking to Stephen now. Hear him out."

"Very well," Mary said out loud. "So you're telling me you had no idea Dr Davis wanted to accuse Jane during her breakout session?"

She shoved back one of the chairs around the conference table.

"No. I mean yes, I had no idea."

"And you had no idea she had it in for Jane?" She shoved back another chair while Stephen followed her.

"OK, that I knew. I mean that's why I called you, when you were in Seattle."

"And before that, you didn't know? You didn't know when we met in Chicago, for instance?" She moved another chair but Stephen stopped following her.

"Uh … well, yes I knew that … she asked me to look into … um …"

Mary turned back to face him. "Spit it out," she said, and shoved another chair against the table. He jumped back at the sound.

"Well like I said earlier, she wanted me to find out how Austen claimed her identity. That's why I started looking through the Chawton inventory, to see if there was some letter or memento that'd been overlooked. It was a long shot, but once I got started, well it was fun. And that's how I knew about the missing inventory list … you know, the thing that cast doubt on the journal." He wanted to add, "The thing that made my advisor look stupid and put a fork in my academic career."

She looked back at him as he said the last, the pleading in his voice unmistakable.

"Oh, yes, although I'm not really sure I understand. Why 'good riddance to bad rubbish?'"

"It's a mystery to me as well, but it might have something to do with that SOE."

"What's that mean?"

"I think it means Special Operations Executive. During the war, it was a top-secret department that played tricks against the Nazis. They did all sorts of propaganda and assassinations and blew things up, and they also had to be really good at making fake documents."

"How exciting," Jane said. "That certainly adds a level of intrigue."

"So you think …"

"We might never know. A lot of what they did is still secret so it might be difficult to find out anything about this Gorrell-Barmes, but I guess the Austen society must have known there was something hinky about the journal."

"Hinky?" Jane asked.

"How do you know all this?" Mary asked, impressed despite her anger.

"One of the romance thrillers I wrote is set in World War II."

"Oh, that's ... that's very clever."

"He's a writer, Mary? You never mentioned this."

"So am I forgiven?"

"I don't know. You still should have said something to me."

He looked down at the floor as she made this accusation.

"Yeah, well I should have. It's just ... well I didn't think you'd exactly warm to me if I told you I was working to expose your boss."

"That is a very valid point, Mary."

"And I didn't find anything. Everything Dr Davis did, she did on her own. I never even knew she had ... an accomplice."

"Oh, I suppose ... how do you think things stand with you and her?"

He pushed another one of the chairs against the conference table. "I don't know. I don't know if I want her as my advisor anymore. It's funny, you know, because she really taught me how to be an academic, how to not take anything at face value, and then she goes and falls for this journal."

"I guess people believe in what they want to believe," Mary said. "And I guess I believe in Jane."

◦ Not just a river in Egypt ◦
Albert suspects his Jane is <u>the</u> Jane

A lbert watched as the woman who seemed to be the target of everyone's anger left the room, followed by a man whose part in the
silent drama he couldn't fathom. They had taken with them the
extraordinary documents, or pictures of documents, that they
had earlier produced.

Austen's avatar, his roommate Stephen, the elderly man, the woman
he recognized as the current JASNA president, a tall woman he didn't
recognize and a short woman he thought must be Austen's agent remained behind. They appeared to be mutually congratulating each
other, but for what he was uncertain.

The whole thing was a mystery, from the time earlier in the day
when Stephen received the phone call that made him seem so queer.
He'd been talking with Stephen when his friend got the call and Stephen pretended it wasn't anything important. Later when Stephen excused himself from the country-dance workshop, Albert followed him
to the conference room.

The mystery of the meeting, however, was nothing in comparison
to the documents the large woman and her friend had produced. The
title of the one was so shocking that he was surprised no one heard
his gasp. And when the large woman and her friend had left with the
documents, there was visible relief among those remaining.

Journal of Jane Bigg-Wither? What could it mean? I must have read it incorrectly.

He wished for another look and then saw that Austen's agent had taken photographs of the documents with her phone. He moved closer to get a better look, but then the woman sent the photos as attachments to an email. He watched as the woman quickly addressed the email to JaneAusten3@theAfterNet.net.

The surprise of seeing that address eclipsed every thing else he'd witnessed. *Why would she forward an email to my Jane?*

Soon the meeting appeared to end. There were some handshakes and smiles and people began to leave. He followed Austen's agent out the door when he realized that Austen's avatar and his roommate remained behind. He briefly considered remaining, but then thought he'd already intruded enough.

He left the conference room and slowly made his way toward the lobby area. Judging by the bustle, the breakout sessions must have just let out and the lobby was filled. He needed a place to sit and thought of the walkway to the hotel one floor up and the chairs along the windows. He looked at the escalators and decided he had no desire to negotiate them and resigned himself to riding in a lift.

He found six women waiting for the lift and entered with them when it arrived. Fortunately the women were all engaged in a conversation and stood closer than usual, affording him enough room in the lift that he wasn't buffeted. The lift quickly travelled the one floor and he tried to exit but was confronted by the crowd of women awaiting it. He only just made it through the closing doors. Then he had to dodge and weave until he could find an unoccupied chair in the hallway and sat, hoping he could puzzle out the mystery.

Perhaps my Jane is a friend of this woman, he thought, but without conviction. It seemed unlikely that his Jane would know *the* Jane's agent.

Try as he might, he could find no reason why the woman might send an email to his Jane, except one. Albert had learned the lesson of Occam's razor during his time in the trenches, which many of the generals never had. He knew that the simplest explanation of a thing was probably the best, and in this case, the simplest explanation for why the friend and agent of Jane Austen would be forwarding an email to his Jane was …

Still he shied away from voicing the thought. If it were true, then it would mean that his Jane had lied to him.

But he just as quickly shied away from that thought as well. Jane has never claimed to be ... Jane. *Not once has she ever ...* Then he thought of her AfterNet profile, which mirrored the biography of the Jane Austen.

Of course he hadn't believed the profile when he first saw it, no more than he believed the profiles of the many Napoleon Bonapartes and Winston Churchills and Lord Nelsons and Genghis Khans he'd heard of or met. Most were either clearly insane or poseurs, but a few were quite rational and enjoyable companions. He had just assumed some people wanted a more compelling biography for their afterlife. Even he had amended the details of his death, preferring to tell Jane he died on the battlefield rather than the dull reality of dying of influenza on a hospital cot.

So I can't say that Jane has ever directly lied to me ...

But that thought brought back all the doubts he'd experienced the past several months and his suspicion that Jane had been less than truthful.

What a complete and utter prat I've been! She's been lying to me about everything. All that stuff and nonsense about her job. She just didn't want to talk to me anymore.

He thought of all the missed chats and her fictions about arguments with co-workers and her humorous anecdotes. *Was any of that true! What was I to her?*

He got up from the chair, full of a rage that his incorporeal status could not dissipate. In his knockabout days he would have been spoiling for a fight, or a drink, or a drink and a fight. But in his disembodied state, his only release was movement and so he fought the crowd and went outside and wrapped in his own anger and misery, stalked the streets of downtown Fort Worth.

· The Seinfeld of literature ·
Jane savours her victory

J ane and Mary returned to their suite only five minutes before the BBC crew was to arrive. Melody was already waiting for them but gave them the good news the film crew was running late and they had another fifteen minutes. They quickly prepared Mary, changing her out of her semi-disguise that she used to move throughout the hotel and into her costume.

Jane wasn't needed for this part, of course, and instead took the time to savour her victory. Although she'd professed a philosophic attitude toward the outcome, she was still pleased to have put the odious Courtney Blake in his place. She was less happy to find herself at odds with Dr Davis.

She was also upset that her victory was accomplished by confirming the existence of the letter. The high-minded paragraph she had recited gave no idea how much bile and vitriol she had put into it.

And now everyone may see it at the British Library, where it will join my desk.[1] *Ah well, who visits a library these days?*

All things considered, she decided to consider the day a success and

---

1   The British Library has Austen's portable writing desk, a sloped wooden box with a hinged top, which opened to reveal paper and writing supplies. It sat on a desk that remains at the Jane Austen House and Museum (Chawton Cottage).

her one desire was to share that success with Albert. Watching Mary and Stephen untangle their relationship because of his very understandable failure to inform her of something that would put him in a bad light made it obvious that she should confess all to Albert.

Her behaviour, however, was far less honourable than Stephen's. *I have actively dissembled ... no, call it what it is ... I have actively lied to him.*

She had planned to confess after the AGM, but now she realized, in being unable to share her success with Albert, the consequences of her deception. She determined then that she must tell him the truth. She searched for him online but he was nowhere to be found.

It is my own fault. I have heartlessly neglected him since arriving. She wallowed in these thoughts for a time before the possibility that he might have left the AGM occurred to her.

She looked over the recent emails he'd sent her, to see if he'd said anything about leaving, but found nothing other than his obvious upset that they'd been unable to meet.

She briefly considered confessing to him in an email, but she thought it improper. Even if she couldn't see him and he her, she felt she owed him an explanation in a private real-time conversation. Toward that end, she sent him an email explaining that her schedule had opened up and she could meet him that night to chat.

The film crew arrived while Jane was writing. They quickly found a suitable spot for filming in the suite, settling Mary into a comfortable chair beside a large poster of *Sanditon*. The presenter, Amanda Vickery, introduced herself and was punctilious to address Mary as Jane.

Jane was familiar with Vickery's books, having enjoyed *The Gentleman's Daughter*, which she thought helped dispel somewhat the impression that Georgian marriages were loveless unions based on money and status.

Vickery was currently filming a documentary that had originally been titled *The Many Lovers of Jane Austen*, but in light of Courtney Blake's book and Jane's identification, it was now to be called *Jane Austen Today*.

After fifteen minutes of setting the lighting and audio levels, they were ready to begin.

AMANDA VICKERY: Thank you, Miss Austen, for giving me this opportunity. I am an unabashed fan.

JANE AUSTEN: You're very welcome, Ms Vickery. And I've enjoyed your books as well.

VICKERY: Always nice to hear, thank you. And still for me a little unreal, that I should actually be talking to Jane Austen. Since the discovery of the afterlife, I've hoped that of all the great authors, you could find a way to reclaim your identity. So many of your admirers identify with you and claim you as a friend. Why do you think that is?

AUSTEN: I assure you it was not grand design on my part. I wrote my novels primarily for the enjoyment of my family and friends. I imagined what joy my sister or father would experience when reading this or that, and perhaps because that was my goal, my stories seem personal and the voice of the author seems like that of an intimate.

VICKERY: But you don't pretend that you wrote only for family. *Mansfield Park* and *Emma* you wrote after the success of *Sense and Sensibility* and *Pride and Prejudice*. There seems to have been a calculation and experimentation there, resulting in very different novels.

AUSTEN: You are correct, perhaps with the consequence that those novels are not as popular, but I do not regret my decision to try something different or to appeal to a larger public or to write something that pleased me more than it might please others.

VICKERY: I mentioned before that I had hoped you could reclaim your identity, but I wonder why it was so important to you, a woman who never sought recognition for her work.

AUSTEN: Now here, Miss Vickery, you ask a question that I know you know to be a lie. I always sought recognition as a writer. I revelled at the sight of the title page of *Pride and Prejudice*, proclaiming it as being written by the author of *Sense and Sensibility*. What I did not want is notoriety.

VICKERY: What you've also done is fail to answer the question. Because I can't help but think you've achieved both recognition and notoriety with your reclaimed identity.

AUSTEN: Oh, pardon me. Yes, I am afraid I now have some small notoriety, which I had hoped to avoid. Now as to why I went to the trouble, and it was considerable, to reclaim my identity. I am afraid it all comes down to pettiness. Despite the efforts of many scholars, such as you, to represent me as more than just a literary spinster, I am afraid that is precisely what I have become. I have become known for writing books with little plot and no sex. Someone called me the Seinfeld of literature[2]—I had to look up the reference—meaning I wrote books about nothing. Others have belittled my novels as being only about relationships and marriage, as if that isn't the biggest challenge, hope and desire of most of the people in the world. While at the same time a dedicated cadre rank me just below Shakespeare, which while flattering, is arrant nonsense. I thought if I could regain my identity, I could argue for a middling sort of reputation.

VICKERY: So you couldn't be content with simply seeking a publisher for *Sanditon* as ... as ...

AUSTEN: Precisely, you see the difficulty. What name would I use? In today's publishing world, I could not be anonymous. And yet I had no desire to use a *nom de plume*. I wanted to write again as the author of *Emma* and *Persuasion*, but no publisher or agent would have me as such, until I met Melody Kramer, my agent and now my business manager. She recognized that establishing my identity was paramount.

VICKERY: You could have self-published. You could decide to publish as Jane Austen even without reclaiming your identity.

AUSTEN: I was prepared to do just that, but fortunately it was not necessary. As you know, *Sense and Sensibility* was essentially self-published; I am no stranger to taking matters into my own hands.

VICKERY: Moving on to *Sanditon*, is this another novel about nothing ... or nothing more than relationships and marriage?

AUSTEN: I very much fear most people will view it as such, although I think it quite different. In fact, Janeites have long remarked that the little of it I wrote before death seemed very different from the other novels. And my death and experiences have undoubtedly combined to produce something markedly different, even though many will undoubtedly complain it is just a book about the gentry hoping to make a suitable marriage.

VICKERY: If I might ask a difficult question, is it hard to write of such things now that you're ...

AUSTEN: Now that I'm dead?

VICKERY: Yes, I mean obviously you've been dead some time, but ... how can you ... can you still feel ... is it still as personal to you, the

---

2 A situation comedy, starring comedian Jerry Seinfeld, that ran on American television from 1989 to 1998. The show has been described as being about nothing.

silly dramas, the misunderstood intentions, the little lies that make up romance?

AUSTEN: Oh yes. Still very real to me.

· Timing is everything ·
Albert's letter arrives

Jane paced the hotel room as she composed her thoughts. She was alone, Mary having left after the film crew to eat lunch while Melody was busy trying to arrange a flight for Tamara. That information was a surprise, for Jane had assumed the flight had already been booked.

She was glad of her isolation. She had even forgone using the computer while trying to compose her explanation and apology to Albert. Unfortunately, she could not quite find the right words—or rather she could not avoid the temptation to excuse her conduct rather than simply and honestly accept her guilt.

She said to her imaginary Albert: "Without my wanting it—in fact despite my efforts to the contrary—my life and reputation is more than just that of good daughter and faithful sister. But with you, I am just Jane and that is how I wanted to represent myself, without the baggage of ..."

No, I did not say baggage before. Why can I not recall what I just said moments earlier? Am I such a slave now to Google Docs that I cannot write without a crutch?

Or is the problem that I am writing and not ... feeling. Is this how people actually speak? Certainly it's how Elizabeth and Darcy spoke, but did I ever speak in such a fashion? Do people really speak in such complete thoughts? Do I now doubt the very essence of everything I have ever written?

I must focus. I must say this to Albert as soon as I possibly can. Why does he not respond?

That last thought made her hurry back to the computer and check her messages and email to see whether Albert had responded. He had not replied to her earlier emails and texts, but this gave her more opportunity to rehearse ... *craft* ... her apology. It had now been several hours since she sent her message that she wished to chat, however, and it was not like Albert to ignore her.

This time, however, she was rewarded by seeing Albert's email address in her in box, but the subject line—Leaving AGM—confused her. She opened the email and the salutation alerted her that she had delayed her apology too long.

Dear Miss Austen,

You are no longer my Jane, it would seem, for now I know the truth of it. I saw your agent address an email to JaneAusten3@theAfterNet.net, an address familiar to me as belonging to my friend. I confess I further observed what your agent wrote and by this I know for a certainty that the woman I have known for three years as Jane really is that Jane Austen, a woman I have known for nearly a hundred years.

To say that I am embarrassed and hurt by this revelation would be an understatement. In fact I am so shaken that I must resort to explaining this to you in a letter, rather than confront you in a chat. You see, even my choice of verb–confront—indicates what tone I would take were we to chat. I would confront you; I would accuse you of hiding the truth from me; I would demand an explanation.

And so I must take refuge in an email, so that I can choose my words carefully and examine exactly how you have represented yourself to me, to see whether I have just cause to censure you.

You have never claimed to be Jane Austen, except by your choice of username and you have never claimed not to be Jane Austen, except by your choice to refer to your corporeal existence in the third person. That, however, is a common enough custom among the disembodied, so I cannot judge it intentionally disingenuous. And you have always been a harsher critic of your work than I, an unabashed admirer, but that may be a trait common to any author. Upon our first meeting, in that now defunct chat room, you certainly had no obligation to purport to be Jane, and had you actually claimed to be Jane Austen, I almost certainly would have dismissed you.

Taken separately then, you are guilty of no overt act; nevertheless I am hurt and ashamed and saddened by what I cannot help but perceive as a pattern of deception. It has been ten months since the news that you have reclaimed your identity and in all that time, you failed to tell me of your good fortune. Friends share their good fortune, Jane; that you failed to do so makes me wonder as to our friendship.

You also misrepresented the nature of your "employment," which I almost thought you had invented as an excuse to reject my offer of paying for your admission to the AGM. And now with some embarrassment, I think how ridiculous was my offer to a woman who is probably wealthy beyond my poor ability to imagine. I must also re-evaluate all the times that you failed to meet me for a chat or failed to suggest we schedule a meeting.

I do not wish to lose your friendship, Jane, but I fear I already have. I can only conclude you no longer desire the friendship of a simple wuzzer.[1] And if that is the case, then perhaps I must re-examine my good opinion of the one bright star of my lonely existence. That this revelation has robbed me of the friendship of a good woman from Hampshire is a tragedy that I can endure, but to be robbed of my esteem and admiration for that Jane Austen who sustained me in my darkest days is a tragedy from which I may never recover.

Albert Ridings

PS I will be leaving Fort Worth presently. I can't remain at the AGM; everything here reminds me of you.

Despite her incorporeal state, it still felt to Jane as if her stomach turned and although she did not faint as she had done in the dentist's office, she moved quickly to the bed and allowed herself to fall. She lost the AfterNet field as she moved away and the image of Albert's letter dissipated, but the words still lingered in her thoughts.

At first, the shame that suffused her eclipsed the hurt caused by the

---

1   In Hampshire, a wuzzer is a local, a word not much used anymore

letter, which was considerable. The hurt was intensified by the fact that Albert's accusations were all true and justified, but for the moment her shame was more intense. She even made it worse for thinking for one second: "If only I had confessed to Albert sooner," but she knew that would not make her crime any the less.

Oh what have I done? she asked, and then felt a little foolish for both asking the obvious and for the drama of it. *You know very well what you did and even had you apologized before Albert discovered the truth, it still would have lowered you in his estimation*

But my deception was not unkindly meant, she argued, *even if it was self-serving. He himself said we would not have formed our friendship if I had represented myself as Jane Austen.* And so, like any person confronted with a hurt largely self-created, Jane did her best to deny herself some of the blame.

In all her thoughts, however, she did not address the question of why she should feel so devastated. She did not ask herself if she feared the loss of a friend or that of a person for whom she felt an even stronger emotion.

· A terrible mistake ·
Albert tells Stephen what he's done

Stephen arrived a few minutes late at the hotel restaurant for his lunchtime meeting with his roommates. He sat alone at a small table in a corner. He wished they could try another meeting place, but his friends said the hotel's AfterNet hotspot gave them great access to the Internet. A side benefit of meeting in the same place was that the waitress now knew him and his invisible friends.

"Ice tea with lime, right?" she asked.

He confirmed this and then she asked, "Do you want the big table again?"

"No," he said, glancing at his terminal. "I don't know how many of them will turn up, and I think I saw your manager wondering why I had the whole table to myself."

"It's no big deal if you want it," she said.

"No, I'm wondering if I'm being stood up. I might as well order. Could I get the tuna fish sandwich and fries?"

She nodded and left to get his iced tea.

He sat patiently, wondering how many of his roommates would appear and whether he could insist on a different restaurant. He was chuffed[1] by his hope of a rapprochement with Mary and that led to a

---

1 Well pleased, for our American cousins

profound feeling of happiness, which was odd considering how he had grovelled at her feet for forgiveness.

When Albert arrived, he found Stephen sitting with a contented smile on his face. Despite his own anguish, Albert couldn't help but comment. "You look happy, Stephen."

"Who's that?" Stephen looked at his terminal to find out who had arrived and smiled at the information. It figured that the only one he could rely on to meet him for lunch would be Albert.

"Oh, Albert. Hi. Yeah, I guess I'm pretty happy."

"Does this have something to do with Miss Austen's avatar?"

"Mary, yes. I think she's forgiven me."

"What did you do that required forgiveness?"

"Well, I guess it's debatable what exactly I did wrong, but you know with women, it's best to accept blame and … I can't really go into it."

"Perhaps I should also beg forgiveness, Stephen. I'm afraid I followed you into that meeting this morning."

He told Stephen what he'd observed and his conjectures as to what had transpired.

"Yes, that's the gist of it. I guess I should be mad at you for following me around, but now I'm relieved I've got someone to talk to about this. Mary's pretty devoted to Jane, so I can't say anything critical about her."

"Do you still doubt her identity?"

"No, I never really did. It's just Dr Davis … I think I have to start looking for another graduate advisor."

"Has it occurred to you that being a friend of Jane Austen might be a boon toward that goal? You may find other professors would be eager to be your advisor."

"Oh, I guess I hadn't thought of that. But I'm still bummed about me and Dr Davis."

"Don't give up on that relationship, Stephen. You obviously have great respect for her and she may yet come to her senses. And I think I have some sympathy about her complex attitudes toward Jane."

"What do you mean?"

Albert debated how much to tell Stephen, but like his roommate, he appreciated having someone to talk to. And although Stephen's sandwich had arrived, none of their other roommates had, so Albert decided to take advantage of the opportunity to tell of his revelation.

"And then I saw her agent forward those photos to janeausten3@ theAfterNet.net."

"Wait, that's Jane's address. I mean Jane Austen's real address."

Albert was surprised to have this confirmation. "You know her address?"

"Yes, she gave it to me, so I could ask questions about my thesis." The statement surprised him. "I guess I do move in high circles. But more to the point, you're dating Jane Austen!"

"You might speak more quietly," Albert suggested. He guessed from Stephen's animated expression that he'd spoken loudly.

Stephen also noticed another diner look his way, so he continued more quietly. "Sorry. It's just hard to believe."

"Well, you're dating her avatar."

"Point taken, but we're not really dating. We've gone sightseeing and exchanged a lot of emails and texts. Wait, so you had no idea she was really Jane?" Stephen asked this while chewing, but Albert was able to comprehend.

"No ... not really. Jane, my Jane, always made so much fun of *the* Jane. And ... she would encourage me to do the same. Oh Lord, some of the things she got me to say."

"Wow, I don't know what to say ... except congratulations? Must have come as something of a shock, though."

"You have no idea. About that, I actually came here to tell you I was leaving."

"Leaving what? You mean the AGM."

"Yes. I'm ..." But as he struggled to explain, he realized it sounded rather petty. "I am upset with Jane, for not being honest with me."

Stephen briefly considered this. "Well, yeah, but you have to see it from her side. It would be a lot to expect ... I mean it would be pretty hard to convince someone that you're the Jane Austen."

"That's not what upsets me. I mean it is, but there's more to it."

Stephen looked down at his food, hardly touched. It was getting hard to concentrate. "OK, what else is there?"

Albert then explained to Stephen about Jane's fake job.

"That's kind of cute. Jane Austen—working girl."

"I think you miss the point. She made up this story because ... she's no longer interested in me."

"That's the stupidest thing I ever heard."

Albert was about to object to this characterization of Jane when he realized what Stephen meant.

"No one's going to make up a story like that if they don't ... you know ... have feelings for you."

"You really think so?" Albert asked.

"You're upset for another reason," Stephen prompted.

Albert took a moment to reply. He suddenly realized that Jane's confession at least negated his original worry. "I thought ... that maybe ... she might be seeing someone else."

"You're a glass half full kind of guy, aren't you?"

"What?"

"What I said before. Jane got in over her head and for some stupid reason made up this elaborate story ..."

"But she kept missing chats ... or she cut them short ... or we never set a date."

"And how long did this go on?"

"Months."

"Look, Albert, you're making me reassess my evaluation of you as a smart guy. When a woman needs to shoot a guy down, she does it. Anyway, what explanation did she give?"

Albert's conviction that he'd made a horrible mistake increased. "I don't know. We haven't talked. I sent her an email."

"That's a little harsh. It's like breaking up by text."

"I didn't want to say something stupid in a chat."

"OK, so what did you say?"

As Albert related the contents of his letter to Jane, the growing look of horror on Stephen's face left him no doubt.

"I think perhaps I have made a terrible mistake."

"No shit, Sherlock. Did you even tell her you love her?" Stephen surprised himself with the question. Up to now, he'd been reluctant to ask Albert if he loved Jane. Albert pretended to be surprised by the question as well.

"What? No, of course not. What a ridiculous suggestion? How can there be love between such as us?"

"Wow, love is blind, isn't it? OK, we've got to find a way to fix ..."

"Hey, sorry I'm late, Stephen," a new voice said in Stephen's ear. Stephen looked at his terminal and realized another of his roommates had arrived.

"What have I missed?" asked WalkLikeADuck.

· So the drama ·
"What poor love can two ghosts have?"

"Well of course you should have told him, but he should have understood why you didn't," Mary told Jane. "And it was pretty inconsiderate to send you this letter just before your keynote," she added.

Jane looked at her friend and saw that Mary's eyes were bright with anger, and she thought how close they had grown.

"I think he was unaware of the consequences when he wrote it," Jane said in defence of Albert.

"Well that's just perfect, isn't it? It's your most important speech tomorrow and he dumps you ..."

Mary instantly regretted her words. It wasn't clear at all that Albert had "dumped" Jane. He had only made clear how hurt he was at his belief that Jane had betrayed him.

"I ... I don't think he ... I shouldn't have said that. Oh God, I've gone and made it worse." Now her anger was gone and was replaced by a mortified look.

"Don't worry, I had already contemplated that Albert's affections for me ..." But now Jane's attempt to comfort Mary only made her feel the hurt more keenly. Even without a body, she felt the sting of tears well up inside her.

And for just that brief second, Jane existed for Mary like she had never done before. She longed to reach out for her friend and squeeze her hand to let her know she comprehended the depth of their mutual despair. But all she could do was let loose the tears Jane was unable to summon.

For a few seconds then, Mary and Jane remained silent, Mary for the reason that she didn't know what she could say without making the situation worse and Jane because she thought she must harden herself or else she would be undone by grief. Finally Mary could not abide the silence.

"Jane, are you all right?"

"Yes, and thank you for being such a dear friend, but I cannot afford to indulge in sadness. As you remind me, and as I am sure Melody … oh, I do not relish telling her of this."

"Maybe we should keep this between us," Mary suggested. "Even with Prilosec, I don't know that her stomach could withstand … all of this."

Despite her sadness, Jane wanted to smile at the thought of Melody's high dudgeon at the discovery that not only did Jane Austen have a boyfriend, but also that he'd ended his suit just before the keynote. "I agree. I think we should keep Melody in the dark."

"So what do we do now?" Mary asked.

"Do?"

"Yes, to … uh, respond."

"I had hoped to explain to Albert about … everything, when I received his email."

"Oh, that's bad timing. But what do you do now?"

"I honestly don't know. Perhaps nothing."

"But you've got to make him understand you were going to tell him."

"I cannot 'make him' do anything. If he thinks that I care so little for him that I would not tell him such an important matter … then perhaps he is right."

"Oh please, don't be fatalistic about this," Mary said. "I know you love him."

"Do you? You hardly know anything about him."

"No, but I know you, and I know you wouldn't let someone be this close to you if you didn't care for him. Don't throw it away."

"I think you're too much of a romantic."

"I didn't use to be, at least not until I met you. And if anyone is a romantic … I mean why didn't you tell him about you."

"It doesn't matter now."

"Yes it does. Tell me."

Jane walked away from Mary, as far as the terminal would allow.

"I enjoyed being his Jane. Not that Jane from so long ago. With him, it felt new again. I cannot explain it."

"That sounds pretty romantic to me."

"Again, it doesn't matter. My only thought can be the keynote tomorrow. If I allow my worries to consume me ..."

"But if you love him ..."

"What poor love can two ghosts have? Love is for the living, for people like yourself and your young man."

That surprised Mary. "What, Stephen? I don't love Stephen."

"Perhaps not yet, but in the future."

Mary was about to further object but thought better of it. She didn't want to explain that while she enjoyed Stephen's company, she didn't expect anything more than a friend with benefits.

"Whatever, but back to you and Albert. Why are you so afraid to admit you love him?"

"Kindly refrain from presuming to know my feelings, Mary."

Say something, Mary thought. *Tell her what an incredibly stupid mistake she's making. Tell her it's thinking like this that made her into the world's most famous spinster.*

But then she thought of her larger responsibility to Jane, especially as she had agreed not to inform Melody of the affair. She decided, for the moment, not to antagonize Jane any further.

"OK, sorry for speaking out of turn. If you don't want to talk about it, fine. Anyway, we have to get ready for the autograph signing and then the portrait."

The shock of receiving Albert's letter had driven all thought of her duties from her.

"Oh, I had forgotten. Would you very much mind, Mary, attending to that alone? Only, I am ... I would like some time to compose myself. I'd rather not endure ... "

"Uh, sure, but what if I get a question I can't answer?"

"You can always send me a text with your terminal, although I suspect there is little you don't know."

After a few more protestations, Mary agreed to the scheme. She realized that preserving Jane's equanimity was paramount and resigned herself to the task.

~

Mary's smile faded after the last person in line left with *Sanditon* in her hands and Jane Austen's signature with personalized note. She was utterly tired, even though the organizers had limited by lottery the number of people who would get an autographed copy. She assumed it was because she didn't have Jane in her ear to entertain her, offering her little criticisms of each person or crafting personalized notes for each one. Instead, Mary had written the same personalized note fifty times.

Three more days of this, and then a break.

But that thought did not comfort her; it only increased her exhaustion. She did her best to hide it as she rose from the signing table and thanked the JASNA volunteers who waited with her as the room emptied and while she waited for Melody to arrive with the photographer.

The task of making small talk, unfortunately, did not prevent her mind from churning.

What am I going to do? Did I promise Jane I would sign a contract? It was the heat of the moment. Surely they'll understand. And what did I say?

She tried to recall her exact words: Something like 'I hope I'll always have the privilege of being your avatar.'

She had earlier hoped she could explain to Jane that she'd said those words unguardedly, but then Jane told her about Albert's letter and again she felt the need to support her friend.

She'd been surprised by her instant defence of Jane, even though she thought Jane was stupid to have deceived Albert. It made her realize that Jane was no longer just her employer, but a friend to whom she had made a sort of promise.

And, of course, Albert's letter only increased Mary's desire to remain by Jane's side. It would be like leaving a movie before the lovers unite—*before Elizabeth realizes Darcy paid off Wickham*, she thought with a smile. *Oh God, she's gotten into my head and can I ever get her out? Nine months ago I hardly even knew who she was.*

Further contemplation was interrupted by Melody's arrival. Mary thought Jane's agent seemed strangely subdued, but perhaps Melody was still recovering from the drama of the morning showdown.

"Hi Mary," Melody said quietly. "How'd the signing go?"

"No problem," she replied, quickly reminding herself of the lie she and Jane had concocted.

"Is Jane with you? I have to ask her a question and she hasn't been answering any of my emails."

"No, she left right after the signing. I'm surprised you didn't bump into her on her way out," Mary said without hesitation. "She's going on one of her walks, I'm afraid." She decided not to elaborate on her deception.

"Oh, well tell her to answer her damn emails," Melody said, although she did not make her remark with any vehemence.

"Is everything OK, Melody? You look a little down."

"No, everything's OK."

"You'll feel better once Tamara arrives. Was she able to get a flight for tomorrow?" Mary knew that there had been some difficulty about Tamara's flight because they'd put off booking it until the last minute.

Melody grimaced, stood and then answered, "Yes, she gets in very early." She walked away from Mary and toward the backdrops the photographer had earlier set up.

"Now I know what's wrong. You forgot to take your heartburn pill this morning."

Melody nodded without looking at Mary. "Yes, that's it. Where is that photographer? We've only got this room until three. Damn, Jane should be here."

She's gone from depressed to cranky, Mary thought. "I don't think it really matters, Mel."

"Still she ... no you're right. I guess you can handle this on your own. You know it's a load off my mind that we won't have to find another ... oh, finally. You're late," Melody told the photographer.

Mary, with a sinking heart, prepared once more to pose as Jane Austen.

~

Mary fumbled for her phone, worried for a brief irrational second that Jane, still on walkabout, had been in a car accident. She looked at the display and saw it had just gone twelve and that her caller was Stephen. She had just fallen asleep despite her troubled thoughts.

"Mary, is Jane with you?" Stephen asked without a hello.

"What? No, she's gone for her walk. Why are you calling so late?"

"I'm sorry, I just didn't know what else to do. Do you know that Jane has a boyfriend?"

His question erased any lingering sleepiness. She turned onto her back and raised herself up, adding an extra pillow for support.

"How do you know about that?" she asked, rather confused.

"Because her boyfriend is my roommate."

That comment required several minutes of explanation from Stephen before their conversation could continue.

"And then he sent her an email telling her that he was leaving the AGM."

"I know, she told me about it," she said, her voice betraying her anger.

"Well he now realizes how stupid he was and he wants to apologize."

"Does he know how much he hurt Jane? And what was he thinking, telling her off the day before the keynote?"

"OK, we know it was stupid, but what about her? Did she have to lead him on? Couldn't she trust him enough to tell him?"

"It's more … complicated than that," she said in rebuttal, and then related Jane's explanation of her actions.

"I think this is the first time she's ever really been in love. I mean think of it: she had to wait two centuries before she experienced the kind of love that makes you do monumentally stupid stuff."

Stephen considered this a moment. "It's pretty romantic," he said finally.

"Right, that's what I said."

"So what do we do now? Albert wants to apologize, but she won't respond to any of his emails or chat requests."

"I don't think she's been online all day. She went all fatalistic after she got his email. She actually said, 'What poor love can two ghosts share.' So the drama."

With a catch in his voice, Stephen said, "We've got to do something." He cleared his voice before continuing, affected by Jane's words. "I've gotten to know Albert and I think he's a decent guy, and I don't want to be responsible for ruining Jane Austen's chance at happiness."

Many months later, Mary would consider that comment as the moment when her regard for Stephen changed.

"Well it won't be easy. She almost tore my head off when I said the same thing. And we can't upset her until she delivers the keynote."

"But we can't let her go through the keynote thinking Albert wasn't there for her," he countered.

"I'm not going to aggravate her any further by mentioning it. We've got to find some way of her knowing he didn't skip on her without making her so upset that she gives a bad keynote."

"Uh, you're giving the keynote, aren't you? I mean technically speaking."

His question confused her for just a second. "Oh, yes, technically I'm the one up there speaking the words, but Jane is in my ear, and it won't help if she's sulking. And half the keynote is the question and answer so I need … oh wait, that's perfect. I think I know how to do this."

"This sounds like a cunning plan."

"Oh it is. She's still going to rip my head off, but it will be after she gives her speech."

· Keynote ·
Do you believe in second chances?

"**S**top fussing with me, Melody," Mary finally said, her frustration overcoming her natural caution with Jane's agent. They were waiting outside the main ballroom for Jane to be introduced.

"Your AV pin is upside down," Melody said.

Mary looked down at the pin and was about to say that it looked all right to her, but caught herself at the last moment.

"Oh, thanks," she said as Melody righted the pin.

"She has been fussing," Tamara said and smiled, while absently brushing back a tendril of Mary's hair. She was a little bleary eyed for she had arrived early that morning. Mary returned the smile, thankful that Tamara's arrival diverted some of Melody's attention.

"But it's worth it. You look very pretty," Tamara said. "In fact you both do."

Melody looked away, a little embarrassed at Tamara's praise and at being called pretty. Tamara had convinced her that as Jane Austen's agent, she should look a little more upmarket. Melody wore a tailored suit that had been ordered before she left for the AGM and that Tamara had brought that morning.

"I still look like a troll," Melody said.

"You look stunning, Mel," Mary said. The gold, embroidered fabric and the suit's sculpting accentuated the short woman's abundant curves.

"No one has complimented me," Jane said, and then worried her comment might be interpreted as a whine, which in truth it was. Tamara did correctly interpret Jane's comment, transmitted via the small speaker on the terminal Mary wore on her arm, as a peevish complaint.

"Your aura has never looked lovelier," Tamara said. The comment surprised Jane, who didn't think Tamara was the sort who pretended to see the auras of the disembodied. Then she saw the playful grin on Tamara's face.

"Thank you, I think the green suits me," Jane said.

"Very calming, very serene," Tamara agreed. "In fact, I need a picture of the three of you."

"Of the four of us," Melody said. She turned to the young woman who was waiting to open the door for them. "Excuse me, could you take a picture of us?"

The woman, whose attention was bent on hearing the cue to open the door, was startled.

"You're going to go on soon," she objected.

Melody gave her a cold look and said, "It's still the introduction of the person who's going to introduce Jane."

"OK, whatever," the young woman said, a little unnerved by Melody's look. Melody took the camera from Tamara, handed it to the woman and gave the requisite instructions. Then Tamara, Melody and Mary quickly arranged themselves, with a space left for Jane between Melody and Mary.

"If you could just squeeze in a little ... oh right." The young woman suddenly realized who was in the gap. She took the picture and looked at the LCD on the back of the camera, almost expecting to see Jane in the picture.

"I think that looks good," she said, and handed the camera back to Tamara, who looked at the picture and saw that it was acceptable.

"Perfect," she said, but Melody took the camera from her and without looking handed it back to the young woman.

"Take another, just to be sure," she instructed. The woman took the camera but also opened the door to the ballroom and glanced inside to make sure there was still time. Satisfied, she closed the door, and the foursome reassembled. This time Jane actually stood in the gap left for her and the picture was taken.

Tamara took back the camera, pronounced the photo even better than the previous, and made a show of putting the camera into her purse.

"OK, I'm going to go inside and find a seat," Tamara said. "Break a leg, Mary ... and you too, Jane."

She touched the back of the woman waiting to open the door and asked, "Can you let me in?"

She was about to object but caught Melody's glare and opened the door. Tamara slipped inside.

As soon as she left, Melody started bouncing on her feet, then winced at the pain from her fashionable shoes.

"Don't worry, Melody, everything will be fine. This is not our first rodeo," Jane said, and was delighted at the look on Melody's face.

"Oh please, don't say things like that, Jane," Melody said with a groan, but smiled regardless.

Mary tried to smile as well, but suddenly worried at the subterfuge she and Stephen had arranged. She might soon face the wrath of both Jane and Melody.

"And don't you let her say something like that, Mary."

"I'm just her mouthpiece," Mary said and shrugged her shoulders.

"Oh great, the two of you will be the death of me." Melody then took the terminal from Mary's arm and clipped it to the back of her dress.

"Get ready," their attendant at the door informed them. She put her hand on the door handle and a few second later a knock from the other side alerted her. She turned back to Melody and Mary, nodded, and opened the door for them. Mary entered first and after a pause, Melody entered and turned sharply to find her seat.

As soon as Mary emerged from the cluster of people who had been waiting at the entrance, the audience began applauding and the camera flashes lit up the room. Mary had enough experience by now to be looking down, rather than risk being blinded, but she was still caught by surprise. The front row was now standing to take pictures and in a slow wave, the rest of the people in the ballroom stood.

Mary carefully walked to the stage, careful to lift her dress as she climbed the steps. The regional coordinator Cindy Wallace was applauding from behind the lectern and then walked to meet Mary. She stretched out her hand, but then had the idea to offer a curtsey, which Mary returned. Then they clasped hands, to applause. Ms Wallace retreated from the stage and Mary stood there to receive Jane's applause.

She noticed that not everyone stood and that some did not applaud as enthusiastically as others. She also looked to her left and saw a young man wearing headphones who nodded to her and pointed, indicating the wireless microphone she wore was now live.

Mary nodded her head several times to accept the applause but after a count of ten, she motioned to the audience to sit.

"Thank you, thank you very much for your warm welcome. It is hard to believe that I now stand before the members of the Jane Austen Society of North America at your Annual General Meeting. Less than a year ago, I was just one of the many billions of disembodied who could not claim their own name, and now I am proclaimed Jane Austen. It is a humbling thought that one's identity hangs from such a slender thread."

Mary's image, which had been displayed on the large screen behind the stage and the two smaller ones flanking it, was now replaced by a series of articles about Jane's identity being recognized by the After-Net. The headline of the last article read: Jane Austen's identity now 'a truth universally acknowledged.'[1]

"And I do stand before you with a measure of humility and gratitude and embarrassment and with a very real sense that I have to show myself worthy of my own legacy. My six novels seem so small in comparison to the movies, television series and documentaries about them. They seem so small in comparison to the societies such as this one and the society in my own homeland and in Europe ... and South America and Australia and Japan. They seem so small, so infinitesimally small, in comparison to the universe of Jane Austen fan fiction, where my characters are endlessly falling in and out of love or have been re-imagined as vampires and werewolves or detectives, and where even I have been re-imagined as such."

The audience laughed as a series of book titles were projected on the various screens in the ballroom, the last showing a ghostly pale Jane as a vampire with a trickle of blood upon her chin. Mary turned to look at the last image and then faced the audience.

"I look like Miss Havisham[2] ... eating a jam tart," she remarked,

---

1 The first sentence of *Pride and Prejudice*: It is a truth universally acknowledged, that a single man in possession of a good fortune, must be in want of a wife.

2 A character from *Great Expectations* by Charles Dickens

which elicited more laughter. She had to wait until the audience quieted.

"Please understand that I fully appreciate the importance of this community. After my death, I saw my popularity fade away and I faced the contemplation of my literary death. But wondrously, I did not completely fade away and I saw successive generations rediscover me."

The audience laughed again as a portrait of Mark Twain appeared with his quote: "Every time I read *Pride and Prejudice* I want to dig her up and beat her over the skull with her own shin-bone."

"Every adaptation, every continuation, every movie, keeps me alive for the next generation. Yes, there have been some liberties taken that have irked me, but let me be honest, I should be little more than a wikipedia article were it not for the people in this room and countless others before you. I should be nothing more than the province of graduate students studying obscure Regency female authors. I should be a dusty book on a dusty shelf in a dusty library, but you have found and continue to find something of value in my words and in the very boring life of a woman who travelled little and never married. You have found something that is worthy of assembling from every corner of North America once a year in a different city.

"And from the bottom of my heart, which still beats though I have no body, I thank you, utterly and completely."

Mary had to stop for the entire audience stood and applauded and there were no half-hearted meeting of hands this time.

"I told you this would happen Jane," Mary said to Jane.

"Only because of the eloquence you bring to my words, my dear."

Mary nodded and smiled at the applause; happy for the joy it must bring her friend. And she found herself with tears in her eyes and for the first time, she truly felt the power within her, to move people, to excite them, but it was a power she exercised not for her gratification, gratifying as it was. She was moved to do this for her art and for the body of work of another. She took those words Jane had supplied and together they made something so powerful that she feared the applause would never stop.

"Please, please," she said with a voice made rough from tears. "I'm supposed to give a thirty minute talk."

There was laughter at this, which broke the spell. Mary motioned the audience to sit and as they sat she took the opportunity to dry her eyes with a tissue.

"Now to return to the challenge of my own legacy, which is not a new problem for me. In fact every author faces the challenge of meeting expectations and, it is hoped, exceeding them. However, I am perfectly aware there are people in this audience who don't care for one or more of my novels or who have never even read some of them. It's understandable that people have favourites; I certainly do."

Behind Mary some quotes appeared: "I want to tell you that I have got my own darling child [*Pride and Prejudice*] from London." And another quote: "I can no more forget it [*Sense and Sensibility*], than a mother can forget her suckling child."

She turned to look at the quotes. "Yes, those are a little embarrassing two centuries later," she said with a cock of her head after turning back to the audience. "I cannot express how mortifying it is have to every single silly thing you've ever said immortalized in print. But I digress. Any author—at least any author of integrity—always has to attempt something new. And many have thought I was attempting something new with *Sanditon*, or *The Brothers*, as I thought of it. And yes, I was trying something new, just as I tried something new with *Emma* and *Mansfield Park*. And yes, I am well aware that *Mansfield Park* is the novel that many have never finished or even attempted.

"But after so long a gestation, can I call *Sanditon* my new novel? Can it be still be something to compete with all the continuations and adaptations? That, of course, is for you to decide, but I think it rather good, precisely because I have laboured on it for so long. It has evolved with the decades and the centuries and I blush to call it timeless, even though it remains a product of my life and times."

The screens showed a succession of Regency images, including a Cruikshank[3] caricature of the bloated Prince Regent, a cartoon of women wearing wetted muslin gowns, another of John Bull[4] begging for food and the David painting of Napoleon on his horse.[5]

---

3   George Cruikshank (1792–1878) was a noted caricaturist and book illustrator

4   A national personification of Great Britain in general, and England in particular

5   Jacques-Louis David's *Napoleon Bonaparte, First Consul, crossing the Alps at Great St. Bernard Pass, 20 May 1800*

"Even though the world has rushed by me while I was silent, I find that things, the important things like love and honour and decency, remain the same. And yet I can't deny that some of the innocence I once had is gone. Like Mrs Bennet's complaint about the Longbourn entail, I have realized that many of the strictures and inequalities of the Regency are inherently unfair and grate on modern sensibilities, and yet I know that those same inequalities remain quintessential elements of a Jane Austen novel.

"So long-time Janeites, please forgive me if *Sanditon* offers a knowing nod to modern-day readers, while at the same time those of you—and there must be a few—who expected a Jane Austen for the twenty-first century, must be patient.

"Because I can assure you I have fully embraced the modern world. I tweet, text, post, email and chat with a facility to rival that of any teenaged girl. My friends know I am addicted to social media and electronic devices."

A well-known photo appeared on the screens showing a woman in Regency dress lounging by a pool with a cordless phone in her hands.

"This photo is so last century," Mary said with a sigh. "Look at the size of that cordless phone. I really must have a new picture taken. But I digress again, a symptom I fear of my dwindling attention span. Now where was I? Oh yes, in keeping with this modern world of instant communication and texted marriage proposals and rejections, I promise that my next novel will be something new, but I assure you it will be recognizably in my hand.

"However that next novel still waits to be born and to borrow from my father, it will consist of 'effusions of fancy by a *very* mature lady and consisting of tales in a style entirely new.'[6] Thank you again for your kind acceptance and recognition, and I humbly remain your servant, Jane Austen."

The audience stood and applauded even louder than before, although to Jane, of course, it was silent.

"Of all the blithest sounds ... I would trade everything to be able to hear again," she said to Mary, but the noise was so much that Mary

---

6 The Reverend George Austen is thought to have written, on the cover of a hand-bound notebook containing Austen's *Evelyn* and *Catharine, or the Bower*, this inscription: "Effusions of Fancy | by a very Young Lady | Consisting of Tales | in a Style entirely new"

could not understand her friend's words. She was grateful when the emcee came onto the stage.

"Thank you Miss Austen," she said into her microphone. "Thank you," she repeated in a louder voice, and then she added, "Really, if you want to ask Miss Austen your questions, you will have to stop."

The applause diminished and eventually stopped.

"Thank you," the emcee said again. Now we have two microphones set up so please form lines. And our disembodied members can use the AfterNet hotspots to ask questions as well. And please give your first name only."

Lines quickly formed behind the microphones and the emcee said, "OK, let's start with the microphone on my left. Please ask your question."

A young woman of not much height wearing a "Dead Leaves!" T-shirt stood on tiptoes to ask her question. "It's such an honour to address you Miss Austen. I've adored your books all my life and ..." She was interrupted by the young man with headphones who adjusted the height of the microphone. The emcee used the opportunity to give some guidance.

"I'm sure we all want to thank Miss Austen, but if we all do, we won't have enough time, so please just state your name and question," she said, in a pleasant tone but one familiar to schoolteachers everywhere.

"Yes, ma'am," Dead Leaves girl said. "Uh, my name's Ashlyn and uh ... I want to know, oh, I loved *Sanditon*, uh ... how different is *Sanditon* from what you originally meant to write ... before you ... died?"

"Thank you, Ashlyn," Mary replied. "And I'm happy you enjoyed *Sanditon*." She waited just a second for Jane's comment before she continued.

"I think it is essentially the same story I meant to write," Mary continued. "But it may be more comic and physical than my other novels, possibly in compensation for my ... situation."

"It is also perhaps more calculating than if I had completed it while still living. I have to credit Mr Dickens for that. My stories have always been ... well some laud them and some criticise them for the value my characters put on money and wealth. But Lady Denham ... I am afraid her portrayal suffered as I had greater awareness of the suffering of others. I was far crueller to her than I was to even Fanny Dashwood.

"But at the same time, I could not give way to the despair and hopelessness of Mr Dickens, which may also explain the somewhat broader comedy of *Sanditon*. I needed to balance the damage Lady Denham inflicted with the essential good humour of Charlotte and the Parkers. I hope that answers your question," Mary concluded.

Dead Leaves girl nodded happily, and the emcee now called for a question from the other line. An elderly man, stooped but with bright eyes and evident delight, asked, "Thank you, Miss Austen. My name is Edward and I wanted to know whether you've had success connecting with your family. Although I enjoy good health now, with each year, I'm afraid I contemplate my own ... well, you know." He nodded and quickly withdrew from the microphone.

"I think I understand your question, Edward. Of course since my identity was confirmed, I have been in contact with many of the living descendants of the Austen, Leigh, Knight and Perrot families. But I think your unspoken question is whether I have communicated with my dear sister, Cassandra, and I am sad to say I have not. I am, however, happy to say that no one has ever attempted to falsely represent any members of my family.

"I would dearly love to talk to Cassandra, or Henry or my father or mother, but I fear the long span of years ... I wish you well, Edward."

Mary noted Jane's abrupt conclusion and with little difficulty conveyed the sadness she had detected.

The next question asked was whether Jane ever planned to try her hand at other genres.

"Oh, it would be tempting. I look with envy at the skill and success of JK Rowling or the allure of writing a murder mystery, but my narrator from *Mansfield Park* said it best, I let other pens dwell on such stuff. But as I alluded to earlier, I do embrace the twenty-first century and my next book will be set in the here and now, and do not be surprised by my heroine texting and tweeting. I can't let Helen Fielding[7] have all the fun."

Mary was surprised to be relaying Jane's words, not thinking Jane had made any decision about her next novel; and then she wondered at Melody's reaction, for she did not think a modern-day novel was what Jane's agent had anticipated.

Mary's musings prevented her from judging the crowd's reaction,

---

7 The author of *Bridget Jones's Diary*, which borrows many elements from *Pride and Prejudice*

but Jane, more adept at reading body language, hastened to reassure the audience.

"Do not for one second think I turn my back on the Regency, however," said Jane, who was also contemplating Melody's ire. "I simply want a chance to explore modern sensibilities and make some sense of it." Mary relayed those words.

The emcee waited until the audience quieted before saying: "OK, now I think it's time we took some questions from our disemembered … uh, disembodied members. We have two volunteers who'll be asking the questions, Julie Henshaw for the women and Stephen Abrams for the men. Why don't you ask the first question, Stephen?"

Stephen's name surprised Jane, who had not known her avatar's friend would act as a voice for disembodied questioners.

Stephen stepped up to the microphone and made a show of adjusting his earbud. He didn't know why; it just seemed appropriately theatrical even though he doubted anyone would notice. He coughed once, and said, "Thank you Miss Austen. The first question is from Albert, and his question is, 'Do you believe in second chances?'"

"Hello, Albert," Mary said for Jane. "That's an intriguing question. Could you elaborate?"

Stephen grinned at the sight of Mary's puzzled look, thinking she might be overacting.

"Uh, this is Albert speaking: 'In your novels, many characters make terrible mistakes, and yet those mistakes are forgiven. Elizabeth forgives Darcy for trying to separate Bingley and Jane; Henry Tilney forgives Catherine Morland for suggesting his father is a murderer; and Captain Wentworth forgives Anne Elliot for refusing him. So in your life, did you give people second chances? Did anyone wrong you that you eventually forgave?'"

For several seconds, Mary said nothing while waiting for Jane to respond. "Of course I did, Albert. It is Christian charity to forgive," Mary finally said, when Jane continued her silence.

"That is good to hear," Stephen said uncertainly, not sure who had replied. However he did not step away from the microphone and the audience's attention was split between him and Mary.

At first, Melody was unaware of the drama, her thoughts still on Jane's earlier revelation that her next book would be set in modern day. It slowly dawned on her, however, that the mood of the room was oddly expectant. She turned her attention to Mary, who once again had the appearance of someone hearing a Who.

She whispered to the woman sitting next to her, "What's going on?"

"I don't know. Someone asked if Jane believed in giving people second chances."

The emcee was also confused at Mary's distracted attitude, and wondered if she were contemplating saying something else or was purposely avoiding saying anything further.

Of course these few seconds of silence actually represented a spirited debate between Mary and Jane.

"What is this, Mary?"

"You wouldn't answer any of his emails," Mary said silently. "He tried to apologize."

"This is my Albert asking the question? I thought … he is here?"

"Yes, he's right here in the ball room. Look, you need to say something to him. People are wondering why I'm standing here with a frozen smile on my face."

"Tell him: 'But some mistakes are harder to forgive,'" Jane said to Mary.

"I'm not going to say that."

"If you wish to remain my avatar, you will."

Finally Mary said it out loud, with very evident displeasure. The emcee, who was about to suggest another question be asked, wondered at the sudden change of tone in Mary's voice.

"Uh, thank you, Albert," the emcee said nervously. "Julie, who's our next …"

"Maybe those are the ones most deserving of forgiveness," Stephen said loudly.

"We should give others a chance to talk," the emcee said.

"Even still, some mistakes can be forgiven, but the damage can't be undone," Mary said, regretting what she was being forced to say.

Now the audience sensed that the exchange between Stephen and Mary seemed unrelated to just a typical question and answer between Jane Austen and a fan. Stephen could hear whispering around him. He looked apologetically at the people staring at him and made a gesture toward his earbud and then toward the terminal he wore on his arm. He added a shrug as if to say it wasn't his fault.

"We really should let someone else ask a question," the emcee said again with desperation.

"Albert says thank you for your consideration," Stephen finally said, and then stepped back from the microphone.

"You see, he didn't leave," Mary said silently to Jane. "He was here for your speech. If you just would have responded to any of his emails, you'd know he was sorry for overreacting."

"Mary, this is not the time nor place to discuss this. I will thank you to pay attention to the person who now asks her question."

"Hi, Miss Austen, my name's Edith," the next questioner began, "Would you ever consider writing a sequel to *Pride and Prejudice*?"

· Yadda, yadda yadda ·
Jane learns of Melody's anguish

"I don't understand, when did you get a boyfriend?" Melody asked for the third time.

"That hardly matters, Melody," Jane said, trying to make her agent understand her displeasure. "Mary had no right to interfere in my ..."

"In your affairs, that's what you were going to say. For God's sake, why didn't you tell me?"

"Perhaps I feared an overreaction." Jane said this regretting again that there was no way her computer-generated voice could convey sarcasm.

"Well I'm sorry if it's my job to worry about how people will react to the news that Jane Austen has a boyfriend, and has had ... how long has this been going on?"

"There is no this, Melody. Two people of very mature age have entered into a friendship ..."

"How old is he? How do you know anything about him? Who else knows about this?"

Jane paused before answering, a little alarmed at how flushed her friend had become.

"You're becoming overexcited, Melody. Please sit down. I think you're supposed to breathe into a paper bag before you faint."

Melody realized that she was indeed feeling faint, but she thought she had good reason. *What if Albert's some poseur twenty something? What if he's really a woman? What if he's not even dead?*

That last thought, at least, restored some sanity. Surely, she reasoned, Jane would be able to know whether the man were dead. His AfterNet profile would confirm that.

"What's his name again?"

"Albert, Albert Ridings, and I can assure you that Albert is a gentleman and that he died during the Great War."

"Does he have a verified identity?"

"No, he does not, but we can hardly hold that against him, can we? And we have been friends these past four years. And no one knows of us apart from you, Mary ... and apparently Stephen."

"Who's Stephen?"

"That is Mary's boyfriend ... the young man who asked the question for Albert. You have met him—Dr Davis's graduate student."

That information hardly reassured Melody. Instead it reminded her that she had only navigated one crisis to be met with another.

"Wait, why do you want to fire Mary? Which is completely ridiculous, by the way."

"And why is that?" Jane asked.

"Well first, she's your best friend and ..."

"No, you're my best friend. Mary is an employee."

"An employee to whom we have offered a five-year contract and who the public has come to accept as you. We can hardly fire her and besides, you'll regret it."

Melody finally sat on the edge of the bed in Mary's hotel room. Mary was in Melody's bedroom to escape Jane's wrath, while Jane vented her anger to Melody.

"You do look unwell," Jane commented, her anger blunted. "Is it your heartburn?" She suddenly feared it might be more serious as she watched her friend sink in on herself. But suddenly, Melody exclaimed, "No, it's your stupidity, Jane. If you have a chance at happiness, why won't you take it?"

This reaction surprised Jane. "But just a moment ago, I thought ..."

"Then I was thinking like your agent—and you caught me by surprise—but now I'm thinking like your friend. If you actually love this man ..."

"Love? Who said anything of love?"

"Oh be real. You just had a lover's quarrel in front of a thousand people."

"So like Mary you presume to tell me what to do."

"Yes, and I'm telling you you're an idiot if you don't hold on to love." As she said this, she looked down and Jane realized it was to hide her tears. This alarmed Jane much more than any health fears she might have for Melody.

"Melody, what's wrong?" Melody tried to turn her head away, but not knowing Jane's location, failed.

"It's nothing, I'm just tired."

"You're tired? Now I am truly worried. Should I call someone? Tamara?"

Now Melody groaned and said, "If you must know, things have been difficult between me and Tamara."

"Oh, I am so sorry. I had no idea."

"No, and neither did I. That's the problem. Don't worry; we're sorting it out. Nothing irrevocable happened, it's just a misunderstanding that wouldn't ... shouldn't have happened ..."

"Oh Melody, what ... do you want to ... how can I help?"

Melody left the bed to get some tissues from the bedside table. She blew her nose and came back to sit on the edge of the bed again.

"She told me after I finally got home from our Chawton trip. Someone at her office made a move on her."

"Pardon? What does that mean?"

"Another woman ... uh, took a liberty with her, when they were working late at night. Nothing happened, of course, but Tamara told me ... she said the woman thought ... she's new in the office ... she thought Tamara wasn't with anyone. They'd already had a lot of late nights and because of the time difference, she never heard Tamara talking to me on the phone. So she thought Tamara was available."

"I see. But you said that Tamara ... that nothing happened."

"I've become so ... tangential to Tamara's life that a co-worker had no idea that I existed."

"That is an exaggeration, Melody. It was just an innocent mistake."

"It gets worse. Tamara told me ... she thought maybe she sent signals." And before Jane could ask what signals meant, Melody amended: "That she invited this person's attentions." She looked away from where she thought Jane might be.

"Yes, I understand the concept well enough," Jane said. "But you said that nothing happened."

"That's not the point. I've neglected my relationship so much that …"

"No, it is the point. Tamara's love for you is strong enough to weather any temptation."

Suddenly Melody smiled and said, "She said I pierce her soul. I didn't think she'd ever read you."

Jane scrambled for what to say. "Oh … and I am sure she knows the reverse."

"It's just … ever since …"—and here Melody was about to say "you"—"… ever since I became successful, things have been awkward. She doesn't begrudge the success, but now she thinks … it feels one-sided to her."

"Adjustments have to be made is all," Jane said. "You have taken on too much."

"I used to be the one who complained that she was always at work … and it was really just guilt … or envy … that she made a lot more money than me. Now it's the other way round." A spasm of guilt swept Melody's face. "And when I did cut back, this fiasco with Dr Davis happened." She lapsed into silence then, a little exhausted by emotion but also relieved to have confided to Jane. Finally she remembered that Jane was also suffering.

She composed herself and said, "And then I find out you've got a boyfriend … and you kept that information … from your best friend."

Jane had also been silent, wondering what other comfort she could offer her friend. The worry caused by Melody's revelation had driven from Jane all thoughts of her own problems.

"Well you've been so busy," Jane replied without pause … or thinking.

The look of shock on Melody's face and then laughter reassured Jane that her friend was not offended. "Oh you little … I'll get you for that someday. Right, back to you. Has my tale of woe made you appreciate how precious love is … yadda, yadda, yadda?"[1]

Jane wondered at the terminal's translation but thought she understood the gist.

"I may accept Albert's apology. And Mary's."

---

1 An expression meaning and so on and on, etcetera or und so weiter

"Actually, I think *you* owe them an apology. You really told him you were a junior editor at Random House?"

"Yes, I'm afraid I did."

"That could make for an interesting story ... which I guess we'll have to talk about another time. But right now, you and Mary need to get ready. The two of you have a ball to attend."

· Three words ·
'Oh for God's sake, just tell him you love him'

Stephen looked at himself in the mirror and brushed back his hair, which was getting long, far longer than he actually enjoyed wearing it. He could pretend it was work and school that was to blame, but he had to admit he'd actually encouraged his last hairstylist to leave his top looking kind of floppy. When the hairstylist asked if he meant "sort of a Hugh Grant look," he had not contradicted her.

He didn't know what he'd been thinking. He was good looking enough, in an awkward, tall, slightly stoop shouldered sort of way. He had light blue eyes and dark brown hair with a square chin, all of which were good, but his thick eyebrows and thin frame detracted from his appearance. He did not have the impeccably crafted shy look of Hugh Grant, but more of a "where did I leave my car keys" quizzicality. Maybe dating Jane Austen's avatar—or entertaining the thought of it—had been subtly encouraging him to adopt a more stylish persona.

He now realized that he'd been staring in the mirror for quite some time and remembered that he did have an audience in the five men with whom he shared his room. He straightened and reached for his toothbrush and toothpaste, only remembering as he was bringing the brush to his mouth that he'd brushed his teeth before taking his shower.

Suddenly the men in the room seemed very real to him. Previous to this he'd thought of the men as existing in some sort of void or dimension only tangentially congruent with his own reality, but now he thought of the men as all behind him, looking over his shoulder at his reflection in the mirror.

He gave a quick involuntary shiver that was only witnessed by Albert. The other men were online and hanging out near Stephen's terminal and two of the men weren't even in the room, having remained behind in the main ballroom after the last presentation.

Albert wondered at Stephen's shiver and hoped his friend wasn't getting a cold. He seemed fine, however, brushing his teeth very enthusiastically. The act made Albert reflect on all the little matters of personal hygiene he'd dispensed with and all those that he'd never had the need to experience, like the fascination with making one's mouth a foamy cauldron with toothpaste, an experience Stephen enjoyed so much he'd brushed his teeth twice in the last half hour.

As Albert watched, Stephen looked aside and then quickly rinsed his mouth, looking as if he'd heard a noise, and then Albert saw Stephen talking over his shoulder. Albert went back to the terminal and saw that one of his roommates—Mr Higgins—had addressed Stephen, advising him it was time they proceed to the ballroom.

The men had returned to the room after the keynote and dinner to allow Stephen to change his shirt. One of his table companions had spilled coffee.

BeauAbrams says:
OK, I'm hurrying
orribleiggins says:
You look gorgeous, Stephen. I'm glad you're representing us.
AlanJTimison says:
But if you don't hurry up, you may not be able to claim a dance with Miss Henshaw
BeauAbrams says:
I'm sure she'll save a dance for us

But Stephen was ready to go. He put his conference badge around his neck and was about to disconnect the portable terminal from his laptop before he thought to make sure he left no one behind. He looked at the window representing the chat room and realized only three names were listed. He spoke aloud and watched his words appear online.

BeauAbrams says:
Wait a minute, we've only got three people connected
orribleiggins says:
Clarence and what's his name stayed behind in the ballroom.
BertieFromHants says:
That would be Mr Chapman and Mr Perkins.

Stephen felt stupid for not having done a head count when he got back to their hotel room, but he was hardly their nanny. If the men wanted to do other things, that was their business, but he still felt irked that the men hadn't said anything.

BertieFromHants says:
They said they'd sent you a message.
BeauAbrams says:
OK, well they're on their own. As for the rest of you, it's time to go.

He quickly unplugged the terminal from his computer, put the terminal in his inside front jacket pocket and inserted the earbud. He then took a quick glance around the room, turned off the light and opened the front door. He counted to ten to make sure everyone had exited and then closed the door behind him. He walked down the hallway a short distance and then removed the terminal from his pocket. It showed three connected users and thus assured he walked to the lifts.

Where he found three women, two of whom were in Regency costume. He nodded to them politely and the younger of the costumed women replied with a curtsey. It was a gesture whose charm was wearing thin. Before he could press the call button, he heard a bing and seconds later the lift doors opened.

He motioned to the three women to enter, avoiding saying "Ladies first." They joined the already crowded lift and he was about to enter when he thought he heard a sound from his earbud.

He realized the problem immediately and stepped back and told the people in the car "Forgot something in my room" and waved at them to continue. He made a show of returning to his room but as soon as he heard the lift doors close he returned and pressed the call button again.

"Thanks Stephen," he heard someone say in his earbud.

"No problem," he said out loud.

A minute later, the doors opened again and this time the lift held only two people, so he entered.

They continued to the lobby and the door opened to a knot of attendees talking animatedly. Stephen side stepped them and tried to make sure there was enough room for his roommates to follow. He was starting to feel like a mother goose making sure his goslings were following.

He worked his way down the edge of the hallway, now filling up with people going to the various night-time events. Not everyone intended to go to the ball; some elected to play cards (mostly poker but a few played whist or bridge); and some people eschewed the dance in favour of watching Austen movies in one of the small ballrooms. But most people were headed for the main ballroom and the dance.

Here he found more congestion as people lingered outside the doors of the ballroom, exchanging greetings rather than entering. Fortunately he noticed there were other double doors flanking the entrance and saw someone exiting through those doors, alerting him to an easier way for his friends to enter.

"Follow me," Stephen said, and took his goslings through the side entrance. One he opened the door, however, he understood the real reason there was a delay entering. Those people not dancing and just watching were arrayed around the outside of the ballroom, making it difficult to enter. Stephen knew it would be difficult to continue to shepherd his group.

"OK guys, I think you're on your own now," he said.

In his earbud, he heard the men trying to respond, the digitized voices of the terminal relaying their remarks one after another.

"I have no idea what you just said, Stephen, but I think I'll mingle," someone he thought might be Alan Timison said. Albert's digitized voice was the only one he easily recognized.

Another person said, "I think we're on our own, Stephen. The terminal can't translate over all the noise."

And another: "You might have to speak more loudly, Stephen."

And still another: "Thanks, Stephen. Don't forget you promised to dance with Miss Henshaw."

Stephen listened as the terminal informed him that all the men had left the chat room and immediately afterward that BertieFromHants had requested a private chat. He accepted and heard Albert's digitized voice in his earbud.

"I don't see her yet, or at least her avatar."

"Mary," Stephen said, absent-mindedly, not liking her being called an avatar. He was trying to find an inconspicuous place to hold his conversation.

"Pardon me," Albert amended. "I do not see your Mary. They undoubtedly hope to make an entrance later. Has Mary said whether Jane ... is Jane very upset?"

"All I know is I got a text from her saying that she's in hot water with Jane because of it. But let's look on the bright side, at least Jane knows you didn't leave."

"I'm sorry to hear I've landed Mary in the soup. I hope I haven't cost her her job."

"I doubt it. Mary's already the public face of Austen and except for this ... I know she gets along with Jane." Actually Mary's text message had Stephen considerably worried.

"... if only Jane would return my texts." Albert said.

"You haven't sent any more since the keynote?" Stephen asked, thinking it might be good to let Jane ponder without further prompting.

"No I haven't. There's no sense in making her further upset." Albert looked around the ballroom. "Everyone seems to be having a good time," he observed, hoping to change the subject, but the observation made him remember how much he had been looking forward to dancing with Jane.

Stephen recognized the wistfulness in Albert's observation. He wanted to reassure his friend but was interrupted before he could say anything.

"Stephen, you're either waiting for Miss Austen or Miss Crawford. Or is it both?"

He turned and saw Dr Davis appraising him.

"Oh, hi!" he said with enthusiasm at seeing his advisor, before remembering that their relationship had probably changed for the worse. "Uh, you're right, I'm waiting for them both."

"That was ... an interesting keynote," she said. "Especially the question and answer session."

"You stayed for it?" he asked.

"I did. The temptation to run away and lick my wounds was strong, but ... Stephen, I am very sorry for the situation I put you in. You must have had a difficult time explaining it all to ... Mary and Jane."

She now looked away, and Stephen thought that he'd never seen her so vulnerable.

"It got a little tense," he confirmed, and would have left it there, but his concern about Jane and Albert and Mary caused him to add, "but another drama is brewing and ... I shouldn't ..."

"Oh, I see," she said, but not really understanding. She was a little nonplussed that her confrontation with Austen had faded in importance.

Stephen wanted to explain, but of course he couldn't without revealing confidences. He desperately, however, wanted to mend fences.

"I'm very sorry that ... in the meeting, I couldn't ... I just couldn't ..."

"Please don't think you have to explain anything, Stephen. I was in the wrong." As she said the last, she met his eyes.

"Does this mean you accept Jane as ... Jane?"

"Lord, no," she said with her harsh laugh. "I reserve judgment, but I am forced to admit I have no proof against her and I ... I will not seek proof against her. After her keynote today, it's obvious to me how popular she is and it would be foolish to fight a losing battle.

"I do hope my stupidity has not cost me a graduate student, someone I've come to depend on and someone who gave me good advice that I chose to ignore."

Stephen smiled and said, "See you Wednesday?"

"Yes, at our regular time," she answered. Just then, the dance that had been underway when he arrived ended.

"Uh, would you like to try country dancing?" he asked.

"And I just said you gave good advice. You know my opinion that all this nonsense gets in the way of the serious study of Austen, and besides, I should look like a bull in a china shop. Wait for your girlfriend."

She left him abruptly and he realized that the only reason she had been in the ballroom was to talk to him.

"That was the woman from the meeting yesterday, the one who was questioning Jane's identity," Albert said.

"Yes, my graduate advisor. I thought for sure I'd be looking for another, but maybe not."

"I'm afraid I still don't know all that transpired in that meeting."

"Well, since you weren't exactly invited ... I'm sorry, said that without thinking."

"No, you're quite right. I wouldn't be … Jane wouldn't be mad at me if I'd just kept my nose out of things that don't concern me. And now Mary suffers from my stupidity as well."

"Don't beat yourself up over it. There's been enough stupid to go around the past couple of days."

Albert was about to reply when simultaneously his roommates and Ms Henshaw arrived.

"Stephen, there you are. Have you forgotten your promise to dance?" she asked in a loud voice. "There are several ladies who are looking forward to this."

"Stephen, Ms Henshaw is here," someone said in Stephen's earbud.

"Quick, before the next dance starts," another said, his comment overlaid on the previous. Stephen had no idea who said what.

"Introduce us."

"No, of course not, Ms Henshaw. I've been looking forward to this, and so have my roommates. Uh, may I introduce: Mr Albert Ridings, Mr Alan Timison, Mr Michael Chapman … um, Mr Rob Perkins and Mr Clarence Higgins. Is that everyone?" Stephen asked, after looking at the display of his AfterNet terminal.

"Susan, please call me Susan. And accompanying me, I have Ms Agnes Hutchins, Mrs Catherine Stone … I mean Stein, Miss Mary Ellen Meyers, Mrs Nora Latham, Ms Roberta Hoskins … I mean Miss Roberta Hoskins, I am sorry, and Ms Shawonda Dobie. Well, let's find a line to join," she said, and took Stephen's arm in a surprisingly strong grip and led him to the shortest of the three lines that had formed in the ballroom. She was dressed in Regency costume and seemed to be very familiar with country dancing.

When she heard the name of the next dance, she clapped her hands together and pronounced it fun. Stephen, however, was too intent on listening to his fellow roommates.

"How is this supposed to work, exactly?" a voice he thought might be Alan's asked. "Don't we just use the hotspots in the room?"

"No, the idea is we use Ms Henshaw's terminal to talk to the ladies and we follow Stephen and when he gets separated from Ms Henshaw we stop talking," someone said.

"Why, what's the range on her terminal?"

"No, that's the idea, so it's more like a real dance."

"Well whose stupid idea was that?"

"That was decided at the meeting for the first-time AGM attendees. It's not my fault you didn't go to the orientation."

"Then we better set up private chats with the ladies."

"That's what I've been trying to tell you."

Stephen gave up trying to follow. The most important thing he'd learned was that all he had to do was dance with Ms Henshaw—Susan. So he turned his attention to understanding the directions the dance caller was issuing, but that proved impossible. His partner had decided that *she* should instruct Stephen, but her incomprehensible volley of dance terms left him hopelessly confused.

"No, no, the odd numbered couples are 'active' couples and progress down the line. The even numbered couples are 'inactive' and progress up the line," she said to him as if he were a simpleton.

The dance, which Stephen learned was called "Hole in the Wall," finally started. Susan assured him it was a simple dance, but her instructions soon had him confused. When he heard her say—"Join hands and go clockwise ... now turn to your left ... your other left"—he collided with her rather violently.

Albert returned immediately after this and began to give Stephen advice. He told Stephen when to turn and in which direction.

"You've done this before," he said to Albert, but his partner interpreted the comment as directed to her.

"More than once. It's a popular dance for beginners," she said.

He and Ms Henshaw progressed through the line until they found themselves at the other end, which event coincided with the end of the dance. He had just made the last set without any mishap and was disappointed.

"But I was ... I was just getting the hang of it," Stephen said. "Can we dance again?" he asked her.

Still feeling sore from their collision, she answered, "I ... uh, I did promise the next dance to someone else. And the next dance ... oh, hello." Her guilty look turned into a surprised look and Stephen turned to follow her gaze.

"Mr Abrams, I believe you had promised the next dance to me," Mary said.

Stephen was stuck for a moment what to say until Albert said, "Introduce her to Ms Henshaw."

"Oh, right. Um, Ms Henshaw, may I introduce you to Mary ... I mean, Miss Austen, may I introduce you to Ms Henshaw. She probably knows who you are," he said ungallantly.

"Christ, that's Jane Austen," one of his roommate's exclaimed.

"Stephen's going to dance with Jane," someone else said.

"QUIET EVERYONE!" Albert said. "Give him a moment."

"Thanks, Albert," Stephen said, although so quietly he wasn't sure the terminal had detected him.

Both ladies, however, heard his remark and viewed him quizzically.

"I'm sorry," he said, pointing to his earbud, "too many voices in my head."

"I understand," Ms Henshaw said. "I have several women in my ear who want to say how happy they are to meet you, Miss Austen, and ... they all believe in you."

"That is very kind of them, and I am sure I'll have a chance to thank them all privately in a chat room. Now, I hope you won't mind me claiming this next dance?"

"I am happy to release ... relinquish him to you. Perhaps we can dance again later this evening?" Stephen suddenly realized that despite his poor performance his desirability had increased.

"Thanks, that'd be great," he said, and took her hand in his and bowed over it.

"You're supposed to kiss it," Alan told him, which Stephen ignored.

Ms Henshaw then left and Mary began to speak, but he interrupted her.

"Could you give me just a second?" he asked. Mary consented with a smile and Stephen walked a short distance away.

"OK guys, I'm going to take a little alone time here. I'm going to turn off my earbud and the speech recognition, but leave the terminal on."

"We'll be OK," Albert said.

"Yeah, just remember to turn it back on," someone he thought might be Mike Chapman said.

The dance caller, however, announced they would take a little break before the next dance to allow people to take refreshment.

~

As soon as Mary arrived, Albert searched for Jane in the locally hosted chat rooms. He soon found the username JaneActually listed in the appropriately titled Meet Jane Austen chat room. He saw that JaneActually was a verified AfterNet account belonging to Jane Austen.

> BertieFromHants has entered the room

JaneActually(VID) says:

> I'm sorry I was delayed in joining you, but I had a series of interviews to do before I could enter the ballroom.

ILoveJaneAusten says:

> With who, I mean whom?

JaneActually (VID) says:

> The BBC, NBC and the Minneapolis newspaper—I'm so sorry, I forget the name.

Helen.Carnahan says:

> I'm glad the media recnogizes youre speaking her was a big deal.

JaneActually (VID) says:

> Yes, it's very gratifying, but my greater pleasure is in meeting everyone here

AlanJTimison says:

> Everyone here believes in you, Jane.

KarenKares says:

> We heard rumors that someone was trying to say you're not really Jane, but I don't have any doubts.

JaneActually (VID) says:

> You're very kind, Karen. You're all, very kind.

Shawonda.Dobie says:

> I adore Sanditon Mis Austen it sso funny

WalkLikeADuck says:

> I definitely think you should write mysteries … with a disembodied sleuth.

poppethoskins says:

> ooh, like Miss Marple form beyond the grawe

JaneActually (VID) says:

> That's a delightful suggestion Mr Duck, Miss Hoskins, but I wouldn't want to pre-empt Dame Agatha.

orribleiggins says:

That's right, we disembodied have to stick together, Miss Austen. Your work proves we still have worth and that we can still contribute.

JaneActually (VID) says:

Thank you, orribleiggins. Now if you'll excuse me, I think the next dance is to begin and I have already promised it. I shall return to this chat room periodically, however, and look forward to future conversation.

JaneActually (VID) has left the room.

BertieFromHants has left the room.

To whom has she promised a dance? Albert wondered, just as he received the message: JaneAusten3 has requested a private chat. He accepted.

"Jane, you must know how sorry I am for causing you such pain. I let my anger blind me and I acted rashly." He sent his words out into the void as quickly as he could, not sure how long Jane would allow him to speak. But as quickly as he sent his message, he received from Jane: "Shall we dance? You promised me long ago that we should."

Albert's quick contrition surprised Jane and Jane's offer surprised him.

"Yes, I would love to dance," Albert said happily, although he now felt as if his apology had been ignored.

"Shall we use the young man who asked the questions at the keynote and my Mary as surrogates?"

"His name is Stephen, and he's my roommate," Albert replied. He unconsciously positioned himself next to Stephen.

"Is he? It is a small world indeed. I know him as well. Then may I assume it was your question he asked and that he and Mary colluded with you to ask it?"

"Your avatar, Mary, had no part in it."

"That's very gallant of you, Albert, but as she and Stephen are dating … well, no matter, she has already admitted to it."

"I'm very sorry to have caused trouble between you and Mary."

"Somehow I doubt that … charade … was your idea."

"Well no, it wasn't, but after I sent you that letter … I desperately needed to speak to you. When they suggested their plan … I readily agreed."

The mention of the letter occasioned a flash of anger in Jane, which she fought to suppress. Fortunately Albert still had more to say.

"I did not realize that the meeting that I … overheard … that it was … that there was such danger for you."

His comment brought home to her that Albert had seen things that must have him confused. She debated explaining to him the fictitious journal, but then she would have to explain the very real letter. Her confusion did, at least, have the effect of defusing her anger.

"Albert, you should know that not everything …" She did not know how to continue.

"Stephen explained most of what happened. It's sufficient that I know that your identity was threatened, but now that has passed. I should not have been there but …"

Now it was his turn to stop, for he did not want to say that the reason for his being there was his suspicion that he had lost Jane's affection.

"I know full well why you there, Albert. I had been distant with you, primarily because I was busy with … no, I lie again. I was distant for I had been deceiving you for years and did not know how to explain away my deception. And before you say another word in apology, I now own up to my sin being the greater."

Her comment made him look for her, an action he knew to be stupid and nonsensical, but he sought her out nevertheless. Finally he consoled himself to look upon her avatar.

Mary and Stephen had walked to the refreshments table and were drinking punch. He had unconsciously followed them. They seemed to be happy—he saw Stephen laugh at a joke from Mary—and was reassured that any unpleasantness with Jane had been resolved.

Jane had also followed the couple and observed Stephen more closely. She also noticed that many of the guests observed Mary and Stephen as well and that their easy rapport caused some comment.

She thought she should say something to Mary, but then was reminded of her own pleasure when she had been the object of speculation at assemblies. She was about to remark on this to Albert when she realized that the next dance was to begin.

"I think the dance is to begin," Albert asked. "Shall we join Stephen and Mary and follow the convention of using their terminals?"

"What convention?" Jane asked, and Albert explained the convention that had been suggested at the orientation meeting. He felt a little silly as he did so.

"What a charming idea," Jane said. "We truly will be dancing."

~

"How do you think they're getting on?" Stephen asked as Mary sipped the too sweet punch. She'd only just arrived at the ball and really didn't require refreshment but Stephen had fetched it and so she felt obliged.

"Something wrong with the punch?" he asked, quickly drinking the remainder of his cup. The dance had left him surprisingly thirsty.

"No it's fine," she answered, and fought to suppress her distaste of it. Then remembering his previous question, she replied, "I have no idea how they're getting on. Jane was ready to rip my head off right after the Q&A, but later back in the room ... she and Mel talked and something happened. At least Jane's no longer talking about firing me. So she's calmed down. I don't know how she feels about Albert, though."

She said the last in a whisper, although the general noise made it unnecessary. Occasionally they'd been interrupted by introductions, but it was obvious that a certain awe kept many from approaching Austen's avatar uninvited. She wondered for a moment if people were worried that they couldn't approach her without someone to make an introduction. And that thought led her to the image of Mr Collins, the obsequious clergyman from *Pride and Prejudice*, who'd presumed to introduce himself to Darcy. She couldn't help but smile at the image.

Stephen was feeling very guilty, forgetting that she was actually author of the scheme, and was about to apologize again when he saw her slight smile.

"What's funny?" he asked.

"Huh? Oh, I just I've become a Janeite."

Her response was so unexpected that he laughed and she looked at him with an even wider smile.

"It's not funny. You don't have any idea how complicated this has become."

"But I should have. I know how much Austen guarded her privacy."

"Hey, it was my plan, not yours. I just hope it worked in the long run. Better she should be mad at me than Albert."

He wanted to remark how her comment did her credit, but saw she was distracted.

"They're getting ready for the next dance." She put her punch glass on the table behind them and then took his as well. "It's *Mr Beveridge's Maggot*, thank God. I know this one by heart."

She unmuted her terminal to inform Jane.

~

Jane saw Mary's remark, although the terminal translated it as "It's Mr UNINTELLIGIBLE Maggot."

"Oh no, I've never actually danced that," she said with some alarm. She was familiar with the dance from the various filmed adaptations of her novels and from watching Mary practice it, but she had never bothered to learn it.[1]

"You realize that your avatar does the actual dancing," Albert said.

"But if I am to follow her ... you think I'm being silly, don't you?"

"Just a little, but I did promise to dance with you. I just never realized it would take this form."

Jane and Albert followed Stephen and Mary as they joined a line, and at the insistence of the caller, they were moved to the front.

"Ladies and gentlemen," the caller announced, "we have the pleasure of dancing *Mr Beveridge's Maggot* with Miss Jane Austen herself." She bowed to Mary, who returned a nod of suitable condescension.

"Oh great, everyone's watching and I don't have a clue how to dance this," Stephen muttered.

"Don't worry," Mary whispered to him. "Every savage can dance."[2]

He smiled at the reference and said, "Thanks, that actually helps."

Fortunately the caller, perhaps recalling Stephen's previous performance, led them through two practice rounds.

Albert did his best to follow Stephen's inexpert steps. Jane followed Mary's practiced steps with little difficulty. Not much conversation passed between any of the four during the practice, although Mary silently asked Jane if she and Albert were dancing with them.

She was a little reluctant to ask because they'd said hardly anything to each other on the way down to the ball. So her anxiety was understandable as she waited several seconds for Jane to reply, "Yes," and then after a few more seconds, "thank you."

---

1   *Mr. Beveridge's Maggot* and *Hole in the Wall* are English country dances that should be familiar if you've watched a few Austen movie adaptations. *Mr. Beveridge's Maggot* was featured in the 1995 BBC adaptation of *Pride and Prejudice*. (In this context, maggot means a whimsical fancy.) By Jane Austen's day, *Mr. Beveridge's Maggot* was considered ancient. Jane Austen and Tom Lefroy (and Harris Bigg-Wither) can be seen dancing *Hole in the Wall* in the movie *Becoming Jane*.

2   Uttered by Fitzwilliam Darcy in *Pride and Prejudice*, Volume I, Chapter 6

Mary was still trying to decide how to respond to that when Jane said, "The choice of dance is fortunate. You know it so well."

"Too bad Stephen doesn't."

"Oh, he does not do so badly." Mary thought Jane's comment encouraging, but little more could be said because the dance was about to begin.

~

Stephen bowed deeply at the beginning of the dance—perhaps, because of his height, a little too deeply. Mary curtseyed perfectly and then stepped forward to offer her hand, prompting him to take it. They rotated around in one direction and then the other and then again until he was little unsure if he should have been in his starting place.

Then he realized that Mary was prompting him to go around the next couple in line. Somehow that motion reminded him of Darcy and Elizabeth, or rather Colin Firth and Jennifer Ehle in the adaptation he knew best. He now acquired some confidence for the next set of exchanges, although he failed on his first attempt of exchanging back to back with Mary.

Where it all suddenly clicked into place was the back and forth with two couples abreast that was so emblematic of the dance. Slowly a smile formed on his face and he stopped looking down at his feet.

"Thank God he's lost that look of deadly earnest," Albert remarked.

"Excuse me?" Jane asked after a few seconds. Albert realized Jane was playing the game and that he'd spoken out of turn. He waited until Stephen and Mary were reunited.

"I said that Stephen has improved."

"Yes, he shows promise. It's a pity Mary has no more regard for him than friend, for I think he wishes for more than friendship."

"It's a little complicated ..." he had to pause while Stephen and Mary separated. He was about to explain further when they rejoined but Jane spoke first.

"Love is always complicated," she said, perhaps wilfully misunderstanding him. "Or rather, people make it complicated, with layers of misunderstanding and ... deception. It is a novelist's stock in trade. Albert you must know how deeply I am ashamed of my deception and I beg your forgiveness."

But Albert had obeyed the rules of the dance and had "lost" connection with Mary's terminal.

"What did you say?" he asked as Stephen and Mary rejoined.

"I said I am sorry to have deceived you," Jane replied quickly. "Please forgive me."

"Only if you'll ..." He paused until Stephen and Mary reunited. Fortunately they had just reached the end of the line and Stephen and Mary must wait a turn.

"... forgive me my insensitive behaviour. I don't know why I acted so stupidly toward someone I ... care for."

Jane paused to consider her next words. "'Care for?' How timid that sounds. I doubt I would have been so upset with someone I just care for?"

"It's true we have never spoken of any deeper affections Jane. Perhaps we're too sensible to entertain thoughts of love."

It was time for Stephen and Mary to progress through the line and Albert and Jane effortlessly followed them.

"But love requires hands to hold and lips to kiss," Jane said.

"'Let me not to the marriage of true minds admit impediments,'³ as the man said," Albert said in response.

Stephen and Mary again separated and when they returned, Jane replied: "What does love even mean for us? What form does it take? How do we show it or profess it?"

And suddenly Albert realized he must be the hero of his own story—of their story. With an eloquence he never knew he possessed, he said, "All I require from you is three words, uttered once. I require no minister, no ceremony, no announcement. All I require is the sure and certain knowledge that you love me, for if you, whose opinion I hold more dear than any one I have ever known, say those words, I know that it is writ in stone. You would not say those words simply to comfort me or on a whim. You would only say them if you meant them."

How well he knows me, she thought. *But then in the space of a few short years, I have spent more words with him than with any man I have ever known.*

"But I have never let you truly know me," she said with an attack of guilt. "How can that be a basis for love?"

"You have leaked your soul to me drop by drop. Despite your decep-

3 From William Shakespeare's Sonnet 116

tion, and despite my overreaction to it, I think I know your heart and soul and I think you love me."

"But what does that matter when …"

"Oh for God's sake, just tell him you love him!" Mary silently screamed into her terminal. She had stopped in mid step while Stephen and the other dancers continued, causing a small collision.

Jane saw the confusion. Her avatar remained motionless and now the crowd was beginning to notice the commotion and that Mary was the cause of it.

"YOU WERE LISTENING!" she said to Mary, angered that her avatar would again presume.

"Tell him you love him or I swear I'll scream," Mary said, still silently, but Jane could see Mary's face and throat colour from emotion.

"You had no right to listen," objected Jane.

"Tell him!" And for just a second, Jane fancied that Mary could see her and she wilted before the determined look of her friend.

"I will, I will, just continue dancing," she said.

"Say it now," Mary demanded.

"Yes, I love you, Albert." Jane said it as quickly as she could and with her words came a tremendous relief and a disbelief that it should have been so hard to say.

Albert, surprised by the exchange between Jane and Mary, was taken aback.

"What? You do?"

"Yes, I love you."

"Jane! If I could only kiss you …"

And Mary, still listening, loudly whispered to Stephen. "Quick, kiss me."

"What?"

"Just kiss me. Now!"

And Stephen did.

· Antigone...with zombies ·
Six months later

"Defy our father! It would be the death of us all," Mary cried out. She took a step toward Zoe, the actress playing the part of Antigone.

"No! No! Mary—Ismene is timid—don't get all in her face," the director said. "Dial it down a notch and try again."

She bit back the remark she was about to make.

It's just not worth it, they'll just cut me and hire somebody else if I tell him how wrong he is.

"OK, David," she said instead. He smiled and she read through the lines again straight to the end of the scene.

"Good read through, everybody. Let's take five, and by the way, I heard at least two ringtones while we were reading, so please turn off your damn phones."

He dismissed them and caught Mary as she left the room, "Thanks for taking direction, Mary. I know Ismene is written as standing up to her sister, but I wanted to do something different."

"Oh, sure," she said, happy to know she hadn't misread the character. She was going to say more but he'd already turned away, apparently eager to have another little talk with somebody else.

He's wrong about Ismene, of course, but it was nice of him to say something.

It wasn't a great play—Antigone set against a modern-day zombie apocalypse and faux Greek tragedy dialogue—but she tried to treat it as seriously as she could. After all, the playwright was in the room as they rehearsed the read-through.

Admittedly it was a bit of a cheat, rehearsing actors for what was supposed to be a cold read, but she understood what was riding on their performance. If they were successful, the producers might get a backer to stage a production.

Well it's not my worry. If the playwright isn't going to fight for what he wrote ...

She went down the hallway, looking for a vending machine, but was interrupted by the gentle vibration of the phone in her purse. She fumbled for her phone, took it out and frowned at the unfamiliar caller ID.

"Hello."

"Ms Cranford?"

"Who is this?"

"I'm Jessica Hanson, the casting director for *Sanditon*. It's a movie based on Jane ..."

"I'm familiar with it," Mary replied, sure her voice conveyed confusion and more than a little suspicion.

"OK. I got to tell you, it was hard finding you. Actor's Equity didn't have a Mary Cranford on record."

"It's a new stage name. I only just changed it."

"Well I finally found you, that's what's important."

Mary decided to avoid holding the conversation in the hallway and found a door leading outside. She'd thought the door led to the street, but instead found it opened onto an alley. It was late afternoon on the early spring day and the alley was already shrouded in darkness. She wished she'd brought her jacket.

"How can I help you, Ms ..."

"Hanson. Look Ms Cranford, forgive me for asking, but who is it that you know?"

"Excuse me?"

"No, it's none of my business. Well you probably know why I'm calling."

"No, I really don't."

"You don't? Well we've got a part for you. It's just a walk on, or maybe it's a cameo ... that can't be right ... I'm not sure. Anyway, we're shooting next week, so I hope you can make it. You are a SAG[1] member, aren't you?"

"Look, can I call you right back? Well in … in an hour? I'm actually in a read-through right now."

"Uh, sure, but it's really urgent. Call me back in an hour."

Mary made sure she had the woman's number before disconnecting. Once off the phone, she looked for someplace to sit and saw in the middle of the alley a white plastic lawn table and a few plastic chairs. She walked toward the table and deduced from the fag ends on the ground that she'd found the smoking area.

She sat on one of the chairs after sweeping away a food wrapper and then called another number.

"Mary! How delightful! We were just wondering how you're getting on."

"Hi Jane. What, are you with Melody?"

"Yes, she's here. Do you want to call back to the office? Then I can put you on conference call."

Mary had to smile at her image of Jane sitting at an old-fashioned telephone switchboard.

"No, it's you I wanted to talk to."

"Have you seen the trailer yet?"

Mary was confused by the *non sequitur*, then realized that Jane was talking about a movie trailer for *Sanditon*.

"How can they have a trailer for a movie they haven't even filmed yet?"

"It's apparently quite common. It's called a teaser trailer and uses clips from earlier movies."

"Oh, no I haven't. I'll look for it. Actually, that's the reason … I got a call from the casting director for *Sanditon* … they want me to do a walk on."

"What is that?"

"And I thought you were an old movie hand. It's just a small part in a movie without lines."

"Oh, I had hoped for something more … substantial."

"What? You knew about this?"

---

1   The Screen Actors Guild is an American labour union representing professional film and television actors in the United States. Actor's Equity represents stage actors.

"Of course. I asked Melody to arrange it."

That news pushed her back and made her realize the back of the brittle plastic chair had separated from its arms. She switched to a different chair.

"Uh, I thought my contract didn't allow me to ..."

"Do you want to appear in *Sanditon* or not?"

"Well yes, of course," Mary said.

"It's a welcome back present, a last fillip to your vacation ... before you return to work."

"I still don't know how it will work. If anyone recognizes ..."

"There is no danger. You are to play the fortune teller."

"Jane, there is no fortune teller in *Sanditon*."

"Apparently there is as of the last rewrite ... something about 'a device to propel the script forward.' I have to warn you the role likely won't survive and you may only appear as a DVD extra and Melody has made my objection known ..."

"Gee, great job selling it. I'm kidding. I'd be happy to have any part in a movie."

Thus assured that the movie offer wasn't a mistake that she would have to refuse, she and Jane were free to talk of other things.

"And how did the Florida trip go?"

"A little overwhelming, I must confess. Albert's family is ... quite extensive."

"And did they all love you? Like I said they would."

"I believe they did. And it was fun to just be Albert's 'lady friend.'"

"And did you go to Disneyland?"

"Disney World ... and I'm sure Albert has already related to you my embarrassing incident."

"I know, it was so cute. How long did you have to wait in lost and found?"

"It was no more than three quarters of an hour. They are very efficient. Florida has a very large disembodied population."

"And how's Mel doing?"

"Sigh. Still at a loss, I'm afraid. She's thrown herself into work, as usual. But I'm meeting Tamara for lunch tomorrow. Maybe I can talk some sense into them separately."

"I'm sorry I haven't been there for you."

"Nonsense. You needed to pursue your own dreams for a while. I did get a call from Stephen the other day. He asked about you."

"Oh poor Jane. You're stuck in the middle of everyone's love life. I'll call him. I promise"

"You are both in Chicago. Surely you can meet him."

Mary then heard her name being called from the other end of the alley—"Cranford! Get your ass back in here. Cranford!"—and then the sound of a slamming door.

"Got to go, Jane. They're calling for me."

She made her goodbye and hurried back inside. As the door closed behind her she heard the rumble of an elevated train. The sound, combined with Jane's mention of him, reminded her of the first day she'd spent with Stephen.

Titbits IV

Reports of Mark Twain's afterlife no exaggeration; literary world reacts

NEW YORK (AP)—The rumors of his death may have been greatly exaggerated, but it's definitely no exaggeration to say that Mark Twain is arguably America's most important author and undoubtedly one of the greatest humorists of any age or nation. His identification by the AfterNet, therefore, has the American literary scene awhirl.

A spate of new biographies have presaged the return of Samuel Langhorne Clemens to the modern day. Author Courtney Blake, author of the latest, and perhaps most controversial biography—"Mark Twain, a Lust for Life"—responded to speculation that Clemens (who used the *nom de plume* Mark

read more

About the author

Jane, Actually is Jennifer Petkus's third book. Previously she wrote *Good Cop, Dead Cop* (the first book about the AfterNet) and *My Particular Friend* (a Sherlock Holmes/Jane Austen mashup). Once she stops writing in the third person and publishes this book, she'll return to the task of writing *The Background Noise of Souls* (the sequel to her first book) and *Our Mutual Friends* (the sequel to her second book).

Ms Petkus is a member of JASNA, Doctor Watson's Neglected Patients, The Wodehouse Society and Rocky Mountain Ki Society (she has a first-degree black belt in aikido but refuses to test for second degree because she's old). She has been a reporter and a web designer but can now be best described as an unsuccessful author. Her friends derisively call her a kept woman. She is happily married. She watched Neil Armstrong walk on the moon live. She likes to make furniture and scale models, but is not very good at either.